Circled

Anne McAneny

Farrington Press

This book is a work of fiction. The names, characters, places, and events either are drawn from the author's imagination or are used fictitiously. Any resemblance to actual persons, living or dead, or events or locales, is entirely coincidental.

ISBN 978-09888469-9-9

Cover design by Tyler Anderson

For Big D and the Boise Idahos

They made her a grave, too cold and damp
For a soul so warm and true;
And she's gone to the Lake of the Dismal Swamp,
Where, all night long, by a fire-fly lamp,
She paddles her white canoe.

~From The Lake of the Dismal Swamp by Thomas Moore

Circled

Part of the *Crime After Time* Collection

Chapter 1

The Thump

Macy LeGrange never saw the back of her own head. If she had, she'd have noticed long strands of honey-colored hair with an unexpected wave in the middle and a mild curl at the ends. A hat maker would have deemed it a wide head while a modeling agency would regard it as round, but none of that mattered to the driver about to hit her.

His eyes were not on Macy's head, nor were they on her rusty blue bike with the new horn and the old chain, and they most definitely were not on the road. The driver saw the fourteen-year-old softball star from neither the back nor the front. If he had, he'd have spied a smiling face that lit up Beulah, South Carolina, wherever it went. He'd have noticed the sneaky glint in the wide-set eyes that broadcasted a future in better places than a sleepy town on a murky swamp sourced by a raging river. He would have swerved his four thousand pounds of metal and parts because he'd have appreciated how others rose up in the morning with the sole intention of making Macy LeGrange smile and, if lucky, laugh. For hers was not a reticent childhood laugh, bashful in its insecurity. No, this girl with the heart-shaped lips and ever-pink cheeks possessed a laugh worthy of a jolly, self-assured woman, one with the confidence to decide what she found funny and what she did not. And she backed that laugh up with bright, jovial eyes that danced like blue fairies against the darkness of the swamp's hungry waters.

One thing the driver would have known for sure: Macy was bound for beauty, inside and out, because this—her innocent, hopeful stage of life—was her awkward stage, leaving others unable to fathom what adulthood might hold.

They'd never find out, of course.

There were those who, after the thump, nodded knowingly at the way Macy moved on to the next dimension. She flew gracefully, almost contemplatively, through the air—the tap of the car's front bumper sending her from seated-and-coasting to airborne-and-feathery in the course of a millisecond—but in her final moment, her eyes alighted upon love. And she knew it would never leave her alone. She let it cradle her like a cocoon, and she sensed that it would follow her wherever she traveled next. As she reached the descendant portion of her trajectory toward death, she knew that it would never let her down.

Chapter 2

Twelve Years Later

My tattoo burned. I'd swear a ghost was dragging a snuffed match along the underside of my forearm. Not as bad as the days it scorched me, but still annoying. I scratched at it after shifting my reluctant Subaru into third, but the sensation of fiery phosphorous on skin only multiplied. Maybe it was something besides my usual tattoo premonitions. I glanced down to make sure a family of fleas hadn't taken residence on my flesh. Nope, nothing but the design I'd sketched for the Inks & Kinks manager years ago. I'd slapped down a fake ID and a folded hundred-dollar bill with only one request: *no questions.* Five minutes later, the biker with the shabby beard and wonky eye had pierced and tinted my skin, elbow to wrist—a series of 8-shaped links in the pattern of a long, thin oval. A strand of DNA? A tribute to infinity? Who knew? It meant different things on different days. But if I stared at it long enough, it began to move. Which is usually when I put the vodka away.

I glanced up and nearly clipped a Ford parked on the side of the road. Jerking my wheel to the left in response, I almost swiped Chad Ryker's Blazer as it whizzed by me doing seventy. High times on desolate Old Pleasant Road today.

Despite the forty mile-per-hour difference in our speeds, Chad managed to wave as he passed, proving once again what a genial ex-boyfriend he was. Chad and I had ended on good terms because in Beulah, South Carolina, home of Black Swamp and its assorted wetlands, you either ended on good terms or you moved. Plus, he was the deputy sheriff; I'd no doubt need him as a source for future stories. We'd broken up eleven months ago, but I still missed the sex. Best of my life.

Honest, raw, and pissed off. What could I say? We both had issues. But there was something about a guy who never believed he could be the best at anything that made him try that much harder—and he'd tried us both into ecstasy more times than I could count.

Chad flew past the stand of cabbage palmettos that fronted Boyd's General Store, and then banged a hard right, skidding into the dusty parking lot. That was when I noticed thick strands of smoke performing a slow hula dance above the treetops.

I followed his car into Boyd's lot. I'd have followed him simply because I got paid to be nosy, but I was headed there anyway for my morning caffeine fix. I had a long day ahead at The Herald as I prepped for my big retrospective article: *The Week*. With its ups and downs, and emotions ranging from mad grief to ecstasy to uncompromising sorrow, *The Week* was the cruel scalpel that had redefined my childhood—the way tragedies always realigned the landscape of youth.

Whoa. Unless I liked my coffee served at 450 degrees, I wouldn't be sipping an extra-large-with-cream-and-sugar any time soon. Random SUV's, along with Beulah's two fire trucks and Sheriff Ryker's black-and-white, occupied all eight parking spaces of Boyd's General in a haphazard manner. Flames, now extinguished, had left the smoking remnants of the store ugly and plain—much like the owner.

Dang! Boyd could be dead in there, as crisp and lifeless as the brisket he served on Sundays, and I'd just gone and lost today's round of *Dammit, Be Nice, Chloe*. Wasn't even 8:00 a.m. yet.

But being nice would prove difficult without my morning cup of joe. Boyd Sexton, Jr., despite being an all-around sleazeball, brewed the best coffee in town. My morning had just grown worse, which was hard to believe given how it had started . . .

#

A little over an hour ago, I'd returned from my regular run, sprinting the last hundred yards along the river's edge as I envisioned a wild pig pursuing me for motivation. Sucking wind, I'd rounded the final turn on the dirt path that served as my driveway and spotted a parked pickup truck. *Carver Brothers Foundations and Roofs* was painted on the side in a girly, yellow font. Might seem odd that I needed help with my foundation since I lived in a house on stilts, but those tall piles held up everything I owned, along with my view of Black Swamp, and lately, they'd grown worse for wear.

My house sat where the Nuckatawny River met Black Swamp. Came complete with gators, the aforementioned wild pigs, beavers, turtles, otters, bald eagles, and countless bugs, plants, and trees. The stilts kept my house at the height I liked, with plenty of distance from critters.

Not fond of strangers, I sidled up to the truck. No Carver brothers in sight. I climbed the fourteen steps to my back deck and found the door wide open. I sure hadn't left it that way. Through the window, I spotted a guy in a brown cap leaning against my kitchen counter. He was smoking a cigarette and staring at my fridge. Apparently inspired by the promotional magnets dotting my freezer door, he reached into his pocket, pulled out a bright red one of his own, and stuck it on there. I could just make out the words: *Carver Brothers. We Do Foundations.*

Guess they also did breaking and entering, but maybe that wouldn't fit on the magnet.

I slinked in through the open door and heard my toilet flush. A second man, taller than the first, exited the bathroom, not even pretending to leave enough time to wash his hands. A bare memory of a hand-rolled cigarette dangled from his chapped lips. His hunched shoulders extended no wider than his hips, and his gangly arms were all sorts of apish. He

5

looked about 40, but if he was the Carver brother I'd heard about, his skin was prematurely puckered from copious drug use.

"No smoking in my place," I said by way of introduction.

Instead of being startled or apologetic, Carver-Brother-the-shorter slowly craned his head in my direction, flicked his ashes into my open trash can, and cocked a brow. "Why not?"

"Stop me if you've heard this one before. Because I said so."

He grinned. "Yeah, I heard that one before." He glanced at the tall one. "Never worked for Mom, did it, Zeke?"

Zeke sucked on the last bits of his ciggy, then pinched it between thumb and forefinger as he popped it out of his mouth and exhaled. The smoke spewed through my kitchen via a mouth gap where one would normally expect a tooth. "It sure didn't, Levi. Not even once."

I stepped toward them. "Do I look like your mom?"

Levi ran his eyes up and down the length of my five-foot-nine-inch body, clad as it was in a bright, clingy shirt and black running shorts. The shorts boasted an enhanced waistband that I'd jiggered six months earlier with limited sewing skills. Levi took his time, and I let him. I wasn't much in the boob department, but I didn't sport a lot of jiggle, either, and I'd been told by some that my face wasn't half-bad—not bad at all if I put on make-up or curled my poker-straight brown hair. Though I rarely did.

"Nope," Levi said with a grotesque glint in his eye. "You definitely do not look like dear ol' Mom."

Zeke guffawed on cue.

"Johnny sent us over to work on your foundation," Levi continued, "and Zeke here needed to use the bathroom. Figgered you wouldn't mind."

"Door was open," Zeke added by way of explanation for stinking up my entire kitchen.

"Foundation work is usually performed outside," I said. "And I told Johnny not to send smokers."

"Why?" Levi asked.

"I find them gross and dirty, and they invariably litter."

Levi blew a plume of smoke toward my ceiling. "That so?"

"You guys armed?" I said, taking two more steps in their direction.

The geniuses exchanged a look of surprise. "Armed? No." Levi smirked. "Should we be?"

I reached around to my waistband and pulled out a pea shooter—hadn't dragged that sewing machine out for nothing. I grabbed a rag from the kitchen table and rubbed it up and down the abbreviated shaft of the cute .22, drying it off after a sweat-inducing run. "No," I said. "Just thought you might want to know that I am." I held my piece casually, with confidence, as if I could shoot the stink off a skunk, which in this case might prove useful. And then their eyes saw something, in my expression or stance, and they knew: it would be nothing for me to remove those cigarettes from their cold-sore-infected mouths with a nice set of matching bullets.

Zeke's mouth fell open and I was surprised a family of flies didn't make an escape. He snuffed out his cigarette in my trash can, but Levi didn't prove quite as cooperative. "What are you planning to do with that, little lady?"

"Nothing, yet. But just so you know, I'm more than capable of disarming you."

"Told you, we ain't armed."

"Wrong arms. Ever try holding a cigarette with your foot? Need real flexible toes, not to mention hips. And lighting the match is a bitch."

Levi's eyes narrowed. I'd made an enemy for life, but he'd hardly be the first. He jammed his cigarette back into his mouth and raised both hands. "All right, all right. We're going." He gestured for Zeke to follow, and the two of them skittered past. I moved back just enough to let them by and could hear Zeke mumbling some vague threat about a *wench* and *gator chowder*, but he kept moving.

Levi, on the other hand, turned back after passing through the door. "I heard about you," he said, tossing his cigarette butt onto my deck. "You're that reporter chick. Chloe something. The one who keeps a ten-foot gator for a pet."

Never one to dispel a good rumor, I glanced at my kitchen clock, then back at Levi. "Feeding time, as a matter of fact. Now you tell Johnny to send over a new crew or he's going to find himself on the front page of The Herald with a none-too-flattering headline."

Levi's body tightened as he realized I was indeed the Chloe he'd heard about. I kept polishing and glanced at his discarded cigarette butt. "I told you, Levi. I don't like litterbugs."

He bent down and scooped up the butt. "All right, now, let's stay calm."

As he scraped the ashes with his fingernail, desperate to erase all traces of himself from the premises, I stepped onto the deck. "Do me a favor, would you?"

He swallowed hard and stood up. "What's that, ma'am?"

"Tell your brother to wash his hands after using the facilities. Nobody likes a pig."

"I sure will. You can count on that." He scampered across the deck, his bottom tucked forward as if anticipating a bullet. Then he dashed down the stairs, joined Zeke in the truck, and the two of them peeled out. Their back tires spit up mud before finding traction and they left a divot in my driveway, but Johnny would fix that. In fact, Johnny would be fixing my foundation for free.

\#

I parked my Subaru behind Chad's Blazer, blocking him

in, and then I glanced at Boyd's General Store. If it hadn't been for the five minutes I'd spent cleaning my bathroom after Zeke's malodorous visit, I might well have been inside Boyd's when the fire started. Maybe I owed those Carver Brothers a debt of gratitude.

Nah.

I gazed at the remnants of the store and felt a jolt of emptiness. While Boyd's had never enjoyed a heyday, it had stood as a Beulah landmark—a wooden, one-story building with a grey, wood-slat porch and a rickety wheelchair ramp added for Boyd Senior before he died. Multiple, slipshod additions—made of whatever material was on sale at the time—had added to its questionable character over the years. Allegedly, a substantial basement existed below, but Boyd Junior never let anyone down there. The place had always struck me as an ugly, misshapen box that had blown off a garbage truck and landed in the middle of a field. Alone and isolated, it sat against the backdrop of a cleared patch of forest—one of Richie Quail's abandoned development projects. But the clearing had served as the perfect field for baseball and soccer games for every kid who'd come up in Beulah. Scored more than a few home runs there myself.

Now, the bare metal frame of Boyd's waved at me from behind a curtain of rising steam, the beams surely mimicking the dance of the earlier flames as they flagellated like charmed snakes. I grabbed my camera, stepped out of the car, and snapped some pictures. My editor would love me for it.

The metal sign reading BOYD'S GENERAL STORE & SUNDRIES lay on the ground, folded over on itself, half-melted. It was a wonder it hadn't shaken the whole town when it landed. Behind the sign, every fireman, deputy, and volunteer in Beulah milled about, fighting to be useful so they'd have a good story to tell tonight.

I crept up to where I wasn't allowed, but as the town's

crime and features reporter, I eschewed boundaries daily; no one seemed to notice anymore. Besides, I had a way of acting like I belonged. People usually fell for it.

Some firemen lumbered by, minus their heavy gear, meaning it must be safe to enter. I waved to a few of them, then ventured in through the former front door. I'd been in and out that door so many times, it felt strange not to pull its handle. I sniffed. Definitely no coffee, but the odors ran the gamut: charred wood, burnt chemicals, wet paper, and devastation. What remained of the endcap displays looked like the cypress knees that dotted the swamp, water dripping onto them from the few remaining beams that were still wet from the hoses' onslaught.

I stepped over the hot metal of the register that lay sideways on the floor. Oddly, it showed a balance of $0.33 due. I snapped a picture since I'd need it for my retrospective article, anyway. The article included profiles of the Lucky Four lottery winners who represented the *up* part of *The Week*. They'd purchased their winning Power Pot ticket right here at Boyd's, twelve long years ago. I glanced at the depressing image on my camera. Hardly the photo I'd been hoping for. I'd envisioned one where the four winners would reunite at the checkout counter, jointly holding a replica of the winning ticket: 03-08-10-28-31-41. I knew the sequence by heart because those six numbers had been my only note on the article for weeks. While I'd jumped at the chance to cover the story, I hadn't been nearly as eager to tackle the nitty-gritty. Too many wounds—still open.

I cruised down the *Staples* aisle that had confounded me as a kid: no staples, no staplers. My friend, Hoop, had explained what it really meant when we were about nine. Then he'd mocked me for it until the day he vanished, six years later.

Rory McShane, Beulah's bluest-eyed fireman, raced up

from the basement with an unexpected grin. He'd moved to Beulah from Ireland when he was seven. Poor guy had carried the reputation of the tough-guy-bad-student through early childhood, but as it turned out, he'd suffered from undiagnosed dyslexia. Through it all, he never lost his Irish brogue or his requisite twinkle, and people couldn't help but find him adorable.

"Hey, Rory," I said. "Everyone all right? Any word on Boyd?"

"Hey there, Chloe. There's a word, all right. Try *felon*."

I gasped. "Arson?"

"Not sure about that one yet, but quite a sight in the basement." He tilted his head and spoke softly in my ear. "Full-on drug operation. Marijuana—lots of it—and meth ingredients everywhere, along with a safe full of cash. Luckily, we got the flames out before they engulfed the lower level."

I looked toward the wooden steps leading to the basement. Now I understood why Boyd had restricted entry to employees only—he'd been the only one.

Rory's right eyebrow shot up when he saw me eyeing the stairs. "Better not go down, Chloe. Sheriff Ryker's in a foul mood, gathering evidence and whatnot."

I gave him a conspiratorial smirk. "Tell you what, Rory. You ever catch Strike Ryker in a good mood, you let me know. We'll put it on the front page—above the fold."

He winked and headed outside where a barrier was being erected to keep the gawkers at bay. I realized I was well inside the barrier; felt like carte blanche to me. With a quick glance in the fire chief's direction, I hurried down the stairs.

Hubbub abounded. A dozen people, most in uniforms or suits, crowded the small space. Sheriff Strike Ryker barked out orders while one underling took pictures and another dusted for fingerprints. Two young deputies-in-training scratched and sniffed the healthy-looking cannabis plants—

twice—before the sheriff stopped them with a glower. Not a surprise. Strike Ryker often substituted facial contortions for words.

Since it was only a matter of seconds before I got booted out, I used my smartphone to snap discreet pictures of the plants, bleach, battery acid, drain cleaner, and NyQuil. I reluctantly gave Boyd credit. A general store specializing in *sundries* was the perfect place to stock up on ingredients for Grandma's favorite meth recipe.

The sheriff consulted with his son, Chad—the one who doubled as my good-in-bed ex. Chad had been adopted by Strike and Jacqueline Ryker after the sheriff became one of the Lucky Four lottery winners. Despite being a thirteen-time loser in the foster care system, Chad had found a home one year before aging out of the system. He'd stayed with the Rykers for only a short time before heading to college, and then he'd returned to Beulah to work as Strike's second-in-command. Some said he looked like Superman, but only if Superman had near-transparent, glassy cobalt eyes, and lips that begged for a ChapStick sponsorship. Well, I guess he kind of did. But Chad's looks came with a personality engineered by Pessimists Anonymous—a group that never met because it just wasn't worth it. Still, he'd been the more optimistic one when we dated.

Both Ryker men, the sheriff and the deputy, stepped in my direction, so I pressed myself against a solid, thick door, hoping to disappear. A rotten, slightly metallic odor seeped out from whatever disgusting crawlspace lay behind the door. When a firefighter squeezed by me, I flattened my head against the door to give him room.

And that's when I heard it. Ticking. Constant. Threatening. Counting down?

I pressed my ear flush against the door, trying to block out the ambient noise.

"Chloe!" bellowed the sheriff, making me jump. "What are you doing down here?"

Strong, stout Strike Ryker rotated his head to me, his green eyes gleaming beneath bushy brows, his too-thick shoulders hunched forward in angry bulldog mode. Blessed with a handsome face, the sheriff had downplayed his good looks with a permanent frown, leaving furrows so deep that now, halfway through his fifties, weeds could sprout from them. "Don't you know this is an active—"

Something in my expression—or maybe the severity of my outstretched palm—cut him off. His gaze narrowed as I pointed to the door and whispered, "Bomb."

Chapter 3

The room blew up. Not literally. But it did explode with a panicked bustle. Apparently, even the subtle mention of a bomb in a room filled with flammable chemicals, sent otherwise professional adults into a frenzy.

Firefighters and officers rushed the stairway, looking cartoonish as they fought for space. Chad was the last to go, heading upstairs to manage the crowd, which left the sheriff and me alone with the tick-tock-tick of fate. The sheriff no doubt remained out of a stoic sense of responsibility, while I, the sharp-eared reporter, felt a warped ownership of the situation.

"Boom?" I said with a grin.

He scowled and pressed his cauliflower ear against the door—he'd been a state-champion wrestler before making it big on the amateur boxing circuit. He confirmed my suspicions with a nod and a sigh, and then we both jumped as the stairway burst to life beneath rapid footfalls. It was Rory, his blue eyes beaming against the pink flush of his pale Irish skin. "Sheriff," he said, "I hear we got a bomb."

"Could be, Rory," the sheriff whispered, as if the bomb might hear him. "It's possible some sicko drew us all down here to get blown up."

"Or maybe Boyd rigged something up," Rory suggested, not quite picking up on the whispering tone. "In case his little side business ever got discovered."

The sheriff grunted one of his fifty grunts, this time an agreeable one.

"If you don't object, Sheriff," Rory said, "I'd like to suggest that you and Chloe exit the room and leave it to the experts."

The sheriff huffed, his rounded shoulders swinging

toward Rory. "Who we got that knows anything about bombs?"

Rory's grin lit up the shadowy room. "You're looking at him, sir. My great uncle Danny in Derry County, Ireland, taught me all I needed to know—and then some."

After a bit of back-and-forth, during which Rory cited his family's long, scarred history in Northern Ireland, the sheriff stepped back and gestured toward the door with a flourish. "All yours then, Rory. Have at it."

Another firefighter rushed down the stairs, jittery as a jackhammer. "Found the key in the register," he said, thrusting the small piece of metal at Rory with a shaky hand. Then he raced back up and shouted over his shoulder, "Good luck, Rory!"

Sheriff Ryker and I wished Rory the best and made ourselves scarce. We waited outside with what seemed like the entire town. Word spread faster than flames in Beulah, as confirmed when another deputy edged up to me and mumbled, "Heard you gave those Carver brothers some trouble this morning, Chloe."

I fixed him with a sly side-eye. "Gave 'em what they deserved, Joey."

He nudged me, then stepped away as he responded to his ringing phone.

The sheriff busied himself calling in bomb experts from neighboring towns, but before any of them could fathom something exciting happening in Beulah, a delighted Rory McShane emerged from the remains of the building. A round of applause and cheers greeted him as he victoriously raised his palm, which held a five-inch tall, silver skull.

"Rory, what in tarnation is that?" shouted the sheriff.

"It's a skull, sir."

"I can see that. But why is it ticking?"

Rory grabbed the top half of the skull, above the brow

bone, and yanked it.

The crowd jumped back en masse, throwing arms in front of faces and pushing children from harm's way as they braced for the BOOM.

Instead, they heard Rory's peal of laughter as he showed them a clock's face. "No bomb, folks. It's just a pocket watch."

"A skull pocket watch?" the fire chief said, disgusted. "Of all the . . ."

Chad and I stepped forward with the sheriff to have a closer look. No one seemed to object to my privileged presence; I'd kept them safe, after all—from a watch.

"I'm familiar with these," Rory said, indicating the shiny skull. "My grandpap collected them. Quite valuable in some circles. It's called a Vanitas, like our word for vanity. Grandpap referred to it as a *memento mori*. Forget what that stands for, though."

Having studied my share of root words for spelling bees, I spoke up. "It's a reminder of mortality, of time always ticking toward the inevitable *mori* . . . death. With this one"—I gestured to the skull—"the designer merged two symbols that mark the passage of time."

The sheriff, never one for drama, interrupted the crowd's oohing reverence. "So it's nothing. Probably been down there for years."

"I don't think so," Rory said. "Needs to be wound, see?" He showed the sheriff the winding mechanism near the clock face's Roman numeral three. "I'd say someone put it there, or at least wound it, within the last few days. Plus, this Vanitas looks clean, not like the rest of the room."

The sheriff cocked his head. "What was behind that door, anyway? A crawl space?"

"Definitely not," Rory said, enjoying his moment in the spotlight. "Come see."

He led us through the building's skeletal remains and

back down the stairs with the palm-mounted skull leading the way. As I descended, my tattoo scorched me and a sudden rush of nausea filled my stomach. The dual sensation had happened only a few times before; it was my body's way of telling me to turn around, to not set another foot in Boyd's basement. But my feet kept finding the next step, one force pulling me down, another tugging me back. The conflict was dizzying.

I took the final staggering step into the basement.

"See?" Rory said, gesturing to the now-open door. "It's some sort of cold-hearted space, that's for sure." I took a deep breath and followed Chad over, smelling his peppery deodorant, wanting to lose myself in his tailored jacket or do anything but look inside the room where the Vanitas had been ticking. I did it anyway.

Rory was right. The small, ten-by-ten-foot room was chilling. A solitary-confinement sort of place, cinder-blocked in on all sides—a makeshift cell that had suffered no ill effects from the fire. Impenetrable, except for the door. For anyone trapped inside, a single lightbulb overhead would have been their only source of illumination or hope, but even that was shattered. Its scattered fragments dotted the hard, dirt floor. But the prisoner, had there been one, couldn't have reached the short string to turn on the light because he or she would have been attached to the pole in the center of the room—by the rusty handcuffs attached to it.

I switched my phone to flashlight mode, unable to speak, barely able to breathe. Claustrophobia pressed in on me, not from the walls that stood only a few yards from each other or from the corrosive smell coating my nostrils, but from a presence in the room that sheathed me like a deathly embrace.

I aimed my light toward the rear of the room where the cinder blocks had been painted a crusty gray. A hushed silence fell over the room when the flashlight's beam landed on a stain.

"Is that...?" I said as I fought hard not to be sick.

"Sure looks like it," the sheriff said. "Gonna have to get Sherilyn over here pronto."

Chapter 4

"It's blood, all right," said County Medical Examiner Sherilyn Lewis. Sherilyn sported pink hair today, along with tiny feather earrings that looked plucked from one of Black Swamp's prothonotary warblers. Her tee-shirt boasted: *Forty's the New Fourteen in Cougar Years.* The word *Years* was lost between her tiny waist and form-fitting pants, but I knew what it said because I'd given her the shirt last year. She crouched down to examine the back wall of Boyd's basement cell.

At that moment, I wouldn't have noticed if one of the female deputies jumped on the rusty pole and started performing a stripper routine; I was laser-focused on the dried stain Sherilyn was scraping into her evidence bag. It was as if Jackson Pollock's temper had gotten the better of him and he'd cast a palmful of red paint against the wall, where it smashed, blobbed, and then cried bloody tears—but why it cried out to me with such intensity remained a mystery.

"Doubt we'll get a match," Sherilyn said, "but it's worth a shot."

Sheriff Ryker huffed out his chest, reminding everyone why he'd held the amateur welterweight championship belt three years running. When he exhaled, his ribs returned to place beneath severely crossed arms. "Send me a full report on that, Sherilyn."

"The only kind I do, Strike," she said with a wink of false eyelashes. Sherilyn and the sheriff had always enjoyed a platonically flirty relationship—flirty on her side, platonic on his. This particular interaction, though, made me want to kick them both in the shins. I'd been rooted in this stifling, medieval chamber since spotting the blood, ignoring Chad's multiple pleas to leave it to the professionals. I needed answers now.

"Run it against the missing persons reports over the last ten years," the sheriff said.

"Make it twelve," I corrected, the bitterness in my voice grating against the sheriff's composure.

He glanced at me, and we exchanged a dozen years' worth of mutual frustration. He gave the slightest of nods. "Make it twelve, Sherilyn. Start with county, then work your way up to state and federal. Cover all the bases."

"Will do," Sherilyn said before sauntering to the corner, her steps noiseless against the dirt floor. "What's this?" she mumbled as she clasped tweezers around an eight-inch length of silver duct tape, folded and stuck to itself. It had been mostly buried, but to someone like Sherilyn, it'd been screaming for attention. She deposited it into an evidence bag and continued scanning the room.

As my eyes became fixated on the pole, my heart pounded until it felt like my ribs were buckling beneath my shirt. Scrapes along the pole's black paint allowed vertical scratches of silver to peek through, but the scuff marks ran only from inches above the floor to waist-high. Desperate handcuffs encircling desperate wrists, sitting down in exhaustion, standing up in hope—or defense. Again and again, until . . . what?

The blood and the duct tape did not bode well for whoever had traversed the metal post in this lonely chamber. A shiver crisscrossed my midsection as I fought the dire images flashing in my head. *No way, not Hoop. Swamp or circus. Swamp or circus.*

"Sherilyn," I said, my voice unsteady, "you got an approximate age for that tape or that blood?"

She tilted her head one way, her lips the other. "I sure don't, Chloe. Something tells me neither is recent, but let's let the lab do the talking."

Beulah boasted a top-rate forensics lab, thanks in large part to Sheriff Ryker, one of the Lucky Four lottery winners. After paying off his wife's substantial medical bills, he'd channeled most of his lottery winnings into a preschool for lower-income kids, a pet shelter, and upgraded forensics equipment for Beulah, not to mention the college tuition and other expenses involved in adopting Chad.

Chad returned to the room; he'd been helping search the larger basement area. Perhaps sensing my need for support, he stationed himself next to me, but I resented the intrusion. I couldn't put a finger on the dreadful feeling swallowing me whole, but I felt bound, body and soul, to some vibrating train track with an engine bearing down, the noise bombarding my head. The train's arrival promised a pain worse than anything the physical world could dream up.

And then the train picked up speed.

Sherilyn cocked her head, her eyes alighting on something new, her jaw clamped in a show of enthusiasm. Evidence was her drug, after all. I watched, resenting her zeal, as she took three long strides to the opposing wall.

A strange fullness thudded within my ears and I may or may not have heard Chad insist that we wait outside as he touched my arm.

Sherilyn bent down and reached out with her tweezers, grasping what looked like a single green thread. My head shook compulsively. I knew what would follow, yet in some sort of self-preservation mode, I convinced myself that the thread was nothing more than the violently removed leg of a long-dead spider. *Who cared about a spider leg? Couldn't they grow new ones?* I wanted to scream out in protest, to tell Sherilyn to let nature take its course, but the sentiment got crushed in my swelling throat. *Why was Sherilyn bothering with such a minor detail? How ridiculous!* But then she lowered her head within inches of the filthy floor and grasped the non-item—just a stupid spider leg—with her sharp retriever of things best left buried. She pulled slowly and kept pulling, like a magician revealing a never-ending handkerchief.

The train bore down on me, never even applying its brakes. It had been too long. I'd hoped too much.

From beneath the years of grime and rot that this dank cell had accumulated, came a strip of cotton cloth, held fast in Sherilyn's tweezers.

No! No! No! He'd made it to the circus! He'd trained the fiercest of creatures! My thoughts became whimpers, but I had to believe. *He'd struck out on his own, a grin on his face, life overflowing from his sunny, vivid eyes.*

Sherilyn continued her magic act, extricating the narrow strip of green and black-checkered plaid material. It was worn and shredded, as if removed from its wearer by force. Its colors were muted, its stitches filthy, its message haunting.

I doubled over, my heart drained of hope, my head drained of blood. Nightmarish thoughts flooded my mind. *No way Boyd Junior could have defeated a spirit that immense. No way that scrawny loser could have emerged the victor in such a mismatched battle.*

I pounded my thighs and saw nothing but pure, steely blackness as pain hit me with psychic fury. The train made impact and I never felt my head hit the ground. The last sensation I processed was Chad supporting me as I fainted.

Chapter 5

Awareness came roaring back before full consciousness. I'd never felt more stricken. The minuscule space my body occupied in the world felt empty and cold. I was a diver beneath a sheet of ice—arms flailing above my head as I pressed against the frosty glass, only to be pushed deeper, where the pressure crushed my skull. Yet I had to breathe. I needed to survive, at least for now, despite the certainty that life would be devastating.

Breathe . . .

Oxygen ripped through me, an ice water jolt to my veins. Life hurt like a bitch. Still dark, though.

Voices. Clanking glass. A floor being swept? Chad? Yes, Chad murmuring: "Like a boyfriend or something?" Sherilyn's voice now, tangy and sweet, like marmalade in summer, answering: "Disappeared . . . never talks about him much." Chad's voice again, and then another snippet from Sherilyn: "Not a good time for Beulah, that's for sure."

Opening my eyes was like wrenching two glued boards apart, but my lids succumbed. Dangling above my nose, of all things, was a tiny spider working frantic legs—spinning silk and getting nowhere fast. *Welcome to my life, little guy.*

No sooner had I thought it than I swatted angrily at the creature, missing by a mile while my head throbbed. Chad's face suddenly appeared above me, his look of concern unable to mar his astounding good looks. I'd seen his face from this angle before, but only when he was panting and horny, not sympathetic and pitiful. I didn't like this new expression at all.

"No," I said, trying but failing to sit up.

Suddenly, the cold, hard sensation of Boyd's cement floor rose through my back and thighs, and everything came rushing back. I was lying in the room where Boyd had cultivated a drug business to support his lame lifestyle as a chain-smoking loser who lived in a third-floor walk-up with stained sheets for curtains. And I was next to the room where he had—

"Chloe," Chad said gently. "You fainted in that room where the skull watch was. No biggie; the air in there was pretty stifling."

Ah, sweet, innocent Chad. *Get a clue.* "Whose blood was it?" I asked. "Who was the duct tape used on?"

He grinned. "Kind of hard to tell in ninety seconds."

"Is that all I've been out? Feels like a lifetime."

"Sorry. Same old life. I carried you out here so you wouldn't contaminate a crime scene." He cringed slightly after he said it.

Sherilyn, standing nearby, glanced over. "Welcome back, hon. Thank God you didn't throw up in there. Feeling better?"

I grabbed Chad's arm and hoisted myself up.

"You were mumbling *swamp or circus* when you passed out," he said, the question implied.

My heart became a clenched fist. "Was I?"

"Sherilyn told me how you thought that strip of cloth might have belonged to a friend of yours. Hoop Whitaker?" My fisted heart wanted to punch him, but he placed a warm hand on my arm. "I hope you don't mind my saying, but you've got to look at things objectively."

"Objectively?" I said. "This might be the first thing that makes sense in my life since I was fourteen."

For a flash, Chad looked hurt. He'd been a significant part of my adult life and, in his view, we'd made sense as a couple, at least for a while.

"Okay," he said, "but you've gotta take a step back."

"And how should I do that, Chad?"

"Well, I've got the fashion sense of a slug, but seems to me every kid and his brother wore checkered flannels like that ten or fifteen years ago. Still popular today. That green and black material Sherilyn found could have come from anywhere."

"No. That was Hoop's shirt, his second skin, and sometimes his pillow." I stepped closer to Chad to make sure he got the message. "Hoop was wearing that shirt the last time I saw him—the last time anyone saw him." I looked around. "I need to smell it."

Chad exchanged a concerned look with Sherilyn.

"You never know," I said defensively. "The sense of smell is the most evocative. It's rooted in our brains."

"That might be true, Sweetie," Sherilyn said, "but that piece of plaid is evidence now. Can't have you snotting it up, if you know what I mean." She gave me a supportive squeeze. "You hang tight, and no more jumping to conclusions, okay?" One of Sherilyn's new techs called her over to look at something.

I brushed myself off and caught a glimpse of the small room where I'd fainted. Emotion overwhelmed me, but I bucked up. "This is going to wreak havoc with my story."

"Your big piece?" Chad said. "I thought it was about the lottery."

"Not just the lottery. The article covers the whole week. That's why I'm calling it *The Week*."

"Before my time, I guess. What else happened? Something to do with this kid, Hoop?"

I swallowed away the lump in my throat and tried to keep emotion at bay. "It was seven days of dire contrasts, ultimate highs and lows," I said. "That's how my editor pitched it, anyway."

"It wasn't your idea?"

"No. Someone called up and suggested it, complete with a monetary donation if the article got published right after the twelfth anniversary. I need to turn it in next week." I refrained from mentioning how I'd lunged across the room to claim the article as my own the moment my editor had pitched it.

"It was our own Wizard of Oz," I continued. "Like Beulah got swept up in a horrible tornado and then plunked down in some strange land. First, Macy, a girl in my class, got hit and killed on her bike by Avis Whitaker, right here on Old Pleasant Road."

"Where it curves around near the swamp?" Chad said.

"Yeah. She was only fourteen, and Avis Whitaker was the town's loveable drunk. He'd gotten hooked on painkillers for a bad back and eventually turned to alcohol. After he hit Macy, he crashed into a big oak tree, went into a coma, and died five days later. Meanwhile, his son, Hoop—"

"Wait a minute. Your friend, Hoop, was Avis Whitaker's son?"

I nodded, the small gesture more challenging than it seemed. "He disappeared without a trace the same day Macy died." I swallowed back the growing lump, realizing that no time buffer would ever be enough. "Of course, none of us knew about"—I nodded toward Boyd's basement cell— "whatever this room is. We were all just in shock that Hoop missed Macy's funeral and never showed up to visit his dad in the hospital. Who could blame him, though? I mean, imagine the love of your life being catapulted from the world by the father you worshipped."

"Hold up. This is getting better, or worse, I guess. Hoop's dad accidentally killed the girl he was sweet on?"

I nodded. "We were all young, but Hoop made no secret of his feelings for Macy. They would have been an item soon enough. A lot of people thought he must have drowned in the swamp, or, you know . . . lots of ideas floated around. Your dad dredged what he could, set up search parties, but . . ." My shoulders shrugged of their own accord as my eyes stayed glued to the floor. It became a chore just to breathe as I realized how rarely I spoke of the events aloud. "They found his bike in the swamp a few weeks later but I've never believed that Black Swamp would take one of its own."

"What do you mean, *one of its own*?"

"Hoop was a swamp rat. Always hunting snakes or befriending alligators or getting birds to land on his shoulder. Claimed he could tame the beavers if he wanted to."

"A Dr. Dolittle-Huck Finn combination?"

"If you sprinkled in some crazy."

Chad took a moment to reflect. "Macy, Hoop, and Hoop's dad," he said. "The town lost three people in one week."

"And then we gained four winners." I sounded far from celebratory. "Fate pulled off quite the balancing act because the day after Macy's funeral, we had the biggest lottery win the state's ever seen—shared by a foursome as unlikely as the ones who traipsed down the yellow brick road. The ticket was sold right here at Boyd's."

Chad looked dubious as he glanced around. "Doesn't sound like your article's going to end with someone clicking their heels and saying, 'There's no place like home.'"

"Definitely not. But maybe we'll finally be able to pull back the curtain on some things."

"What in holy hell?" The voice was coarse and angry, and I realized how rarely I'd heard Boyd Junior speak. My adrenaline shot through the roof. I wanted to tackle him, throttle his skinny, greasy neck and kick his gaunt frame through the wall, but I remained in frozen shock. I grabbed the end of a table and held on. Chad's strong hands gripped my arms, either to keep me from fainting or to prevent me from committing murder.

The sheriff caught my reaction, too, so he grabbed Boyd—a claw gripping a straw—and dragged him up the stairs. Away from the evidence. Away from me.

My rage multiplied. How dare the sheriff deny me the

opportunity to see Boyd's reaction as his secrets were splayed open? To savor the moment when Boyd spotted the open door leading to his personal torture chamber?

I made for the stairs but Chad jerked me back. "Not a good idea, Chloe."

"This is none of your business, Chad, and I need to hear what that idiot has to say for himself."

"Let Strike handle it. Because right now, it's none of *your* business."

I wheeled on him, hotly aware of the seconds ticking by as Boyd concocted some lame-ass story to feed the sheriff. "Really, Chad? How good of a job has old Strike been doing exactly? For years, he's been up there buying bread and milk in the general store and—oh yeah—lottery tickets, while this drug operation thrived right under his nose. And people have always complained about the funky smells coming from this basement, but never once did your father investigate."

"You don't know that."

"Yeah? Well, don't even get me started on other crimes occurring down here that went unaddressed by the sheriff." I sliced my eyes toward the adjoining room.

"Come on, Chloe, that's not—"

I didn't hear the rest. I twisted my arm free, pain shooting from wrist to shoulder, and bounded up the stairs just in time to see Boyd being dragged toward the sheriff's car, his wrists cuffed. The crowd had multiplied to include a news crew, ten cars' worth of commuters, young moms with toddlers, and a group of skateboarders, all clustered in the parking lot to enjoy the excitement.

I bolted out, my feet flying, my body cutting through the throng like a razor, but as I got within five feet of my mark, the sheriff spotted me. He spun Boyd around and shoved him into the back seat of his black-and-white cruiser. The sheriff might have been fast, but I was on fire. I got a hand on the car door and slipped my leg in its path before the sheriff could seal Boyd inside.

"Chloe," the sheriff said, his eyes slitted, his lips bunched in an angry circle, "this is a police matter. You got no right interfering with an arrest. Back away."

"I got no right? What about Hoop's rights, Sheriff? What about him? No wonder you never found his body. No wonder he didn't turn up *anywhere* in the last twelve years. Because he was being held prisoner by this sick excuse for a human being." My voice began to crack. "He's probably buried in the field out back."

Boyd, whose head was sagging crookedly inside the car, angled his chin out and lifted a lazy eye in my direction. A scar sliced his scraggly eyebrow, creating a vertical slash above his pupil. It made that particular brow look like a bat in flight. Everything about him was cockeyed, including the stupid scowl on his face. "Hoop?" he said. "Hoop Whitaker?" He sounded like a slow three-year-old trying out the name for the first time.

I lunged at him for even daring to utter the name, not sure what I would do if I got hold of him but knowing it would hurt. The sheriff kept me from finding out as he planted his boulder of a body between us. I used my height advantage over the stocky lawman to poke my head around and address the mangy animal inside. "How dare you say his name! You shouldn't even be allowed to breathe the same air as Hoop Whitaker. And let me tell you something, Boyd Sexton, no matter what you did in your sleazy little dungeon, you never held a candle to him. Because he shined! So don't you sit there like some smug jerk when you're nothing but a drug-dealing, dropout loser who couldn't even hack high school."

Boyd moved his head around slowly as if awakening from a bad night's sleep. "Don't know what you're talking about, but seems to me . . . Hoop Whitaker didn't finish high school neither."

My adrenaline performed an encore. Straining against the sheriff and trying to deal with the shifting realities of the morning, my world spun out of control. Blood rushed through me in both directions. I didn't know whether to kick the car, head-butt Boyd, or scream for justice.

I settled for kicking the car—hard—and screaming. "He didn't graduate because you killed him! You killed him, you bastard! Don't deny it!"

I kicked the car again, brutally enough to dent it.

"Hey, hey, now." It was Chad's voice, insanely mellow in comparison to the situation. He'd come up behind me. I vaguely felt his hand on my upper back. No doubt he and the sheriff had been signaling to each other to extricate the crazy lady from the situation, but they also knew what I was capable of. They approached with caution.

I couldn't tear my eyes from the contemptible creature in the back seat. "Just give me five minutes with him, Sheriff." My voice went eerily quiet. "I'll just talk, I swear. I just want to talk." Between the dirt on my clothes, the hot, raging redness of my skin, and the hair falling randomly in front of my face, a passing stranger might well mistake me for the one resisting arrest, but I didn't care. This was my one chance for justice. The skanky, grotesque scarecrow in the back seat was my only chance to learn the truth.

The sheriff shook his head. *No.*

A skateboarder cruised by, laughing, holding his phone up as he video the confrontation. Fine with me. Let the world bear witness to the moment when I finally closed the circle that had ripped open my heart twelve years ago.

I breathed hard, surprised not to see fire erupting from my nostrils. "Dammit, Sheriff! Let me talk to him. He killed Hoop! Don't you understand?"

"Get her out of here, Sheriff," came Boyd's coarse voice.

"She's infringing on my rights or something." He sneered at me, his dark eyes dancing. "Got nothing to say to her anyway. She's crazy as a rabid dog."

I squirmed around the sheriff and got close to Boyd's face, although Chad's grip on my wrists cuffed me as surely as the suspect. "You think you're the one giving the orders now, you pathetic worm? You're going down for this. Murder one. You're gonna fry."

Chad hauled me back, whispered in my ear. "This isn't helping matters, Chloe. Anything he says now is inadmissible and we don't want him getting it out of his system."

But the culmination of a dozen years of anger had taken the wheel. I kicked the air as Chad pulled me back. "You'll pay, Boyd Sexton! Front page! *Sick pedophile deviant gets the chair!*"

The sheriff finally got his chance to close the door, but Boyd thrust his foot out this time, wedging it open. "Last I checked, a few pot plants don't make the news, bitch."

"I saw you looking at him, Boyd! I saw you! You always wanted him."

The sheriff kicked Boyd's leg so hard that a crack rang out, but Strike Ryker excelled at subtlety; no one saw any hint of police violence.

Boyd let out a grunt of pain and drew his leg back. The Sheriff slammed the door, huffed around to the driver's seat, and took off.

"We've got him, Chloe," Chad said. "He's not going anywhere for a long time."

I heard the words but took no comfort. The sheriff's car grew smaller as it drove away. *A long time*? A long time wasn't an eternity. It wasn't a lifetime lost.

Chapter 6

Five Days Before the Thump

"And I'm supposed to go where with my little girl, Richie?" Melanie LeGrange said into the phone. "You want us on the street?"

Macy LeGrange's gaunt but beautiful mom, Melanie, probably thought she was shouting with vigor and standing taller than her five-and-a-half feet, but in reality, her words entered the phone like a drowsy sigh, surely stirring no empathy in Richie Quail, their landlord.

The former high school cheerleader listened to Quail on the other end of the line, and then spoke in a murmur as she supported her head with her palm. "I know you need your money, Richie. Darrell's check should definitely arrive tomorrow."

Even Macy had to scrunch her face at that whopper. No way Richie Quail was buying it—again. All parties involved knew that fifteen years ago, Melanie LeGrange had fallen for the wrong high school jock: Darrell LeGrange, narcissistic bully. At the time, Darrell must have looked like security and sexiness all rolled into one, but that image had proven as false as his wedding vows. According to the old stories, Macy's touchdown-scoring, home run-hitting father would swagger out of the high school weight room, a sheen of sweat coating his oversized muscles and a dare-you-to grin aimed in Melanie's direction. The mutual attraction had taken them down the aisle and to a subpar honeymoon in Atlantic City, where they conceived Macy. Melanie wised up after that and got on the pill, but over the course of the next decade, the disagreements escalated from mild to riotous, and the words from unkind to spiteful. Darrell's career skipped from car salesman to construction worker, and ultimately, to bounty hunter, while his appearances at the dinner table grew almost nonexistent. The sheen of well-earned sweat had long since dulled, and finally, twenty-eight months ago, he'd swaggered out of Melanie and Macy's lives for good, taking their savings and his female assistant with him.

"Listen, Richie," Melanie said before getting cut off. "Yes, I've considered that . . . Yes, I've got applications in now for two jobs."

Macy cringed inside. The last application her mother had filled out was for Macy's reduced-price lunches, and even that had been denied due to Darrell's court-ordered child support payments. But those checks had proven as elusive as the criminals he tried to hunt.

Macy patted her mother on the back and indicated she'd be outside. She liked to give her mom privacy when Richie Quail delivered his lectures on *personal responsibility*. Supposedly, Quail had been so skinny in high school, he'd been nicknamed Quail the Rail, but Macy couldn't conjure such an image. To her, and to all the tenants of his ratty duplex development, he'd never be anything but Quail the Whale, 300-plus pounds of not-so-lean mean.

Macy stepped outside and the humidity almost flattened the waves in her hair. Even the weeds in the tiny front yard had wilted and matted themselves to the ground like pressed flowers in a frame of mud. But the oppressive heat seemed to lift when a familiar boy with shoulder-length blond hair, lean arms, and a crush as big as the moon, skidded up to Macy's yard on his 3-speed Schwinn. That bike held itself together with string, wire, and hope, but for Hoop Whitaker, that was more than enough.

"What a day!" Hoop shouted, showing off blinding white teeth, made brighter by his mud-caked skin.

"Every day's *what-a-day* to you, Hoop," Macy said, trying to resurrect a sunflower from its slumped posture.

"That's because every day, Macy, I'm closer to getting out of this place. And I got every intention of taking you with me, so be ready."

Macy smiled and waved away Hoop's fantasy. "I ain't going nowhere," she said, resigned but not discouraged. "Gotta stay around and help Momma."

Hoop dropped his bike to the ground, found a stick, and stabbed it in the ground next to Macy's sunflower. "Your Momma doing any better today?"

Macy took a long look at Hoop, her blue eyes huge and compassionate. "She got out of bed to answer the phone, so that's pretty good, but it ain't like it is for you and me, Hoop."

"Whaddya mean?" He pulled a piece of twine from his pocket—Hoop had an endless supply of everything in his pockets—and he tied Macy's sunflower to his improvised stake.

"You and me," she said, "we have good days and bad days—"

"Mostly good, I'd say."

"Sure. But for Momma, it's like the bad days got a hold of her and pulled her so low that she can't dig her way out, at least not yet. Maybe not ever. Some days, it's all she can do to get to the kitchen and eat a piece of toast."

"Clinical depression," Hoop said matter-of-factly while picking up a stone. "They got medicine for it." He skipped the stone along a huge puddle that had formed where a rusty playground once stood. It had included a chipped yellow see-saw where he and Macy had met at age five. Hoop's stone bounced twice, spurring Macy to grab a smooth, flat one shaped like a guitar pick.

"Clinical depression?" Macy repeated as her stone plunked into the water. "Where'd you hear a term like that?"

"My dad taught me. He might be half-drunk most days—and full-on drunk the others—but before he hurt his back, he taught math and statistics and such. Pretty smart guy." Hoop got a triple skip and smiled. "But numbers don't add up so good when you look at 'em through a bottle, so lately, the money going out and the money coming in, they don't have an equal sign between 'em anymore."

Macy grunted. "I know about that. We got another eviction notice yesterday, nastier than usual. Momma's in there now talking to Quail. You know, he treats her the way he does and they came up together. Doesn't seem right."

"Business ain't personal, Macy. It's just business, and rent is his business."

"Yeah, but Momma said even in high school, he was rotting as he was ripening."

Hoop laughed at the description. "I believe that, but Quail's got a weakness you can use."

"He does?"

"The 14-carat carrot."

Macy thought on that one for a second. "A gold carrot?"

"Yup. Gotta dangle it so it catches the light in his eye."

"I don't follow."

"You gotta make Quail think you're about to give him something better than what he's expecting. That man cannot resist the promise of a payout. Got a bit of a gambling streak in him, you ask me."

Macy harrumphed. "We got nothing to give him."

"Neither do we. But he thinks my dad is coming into a big disability payment as soon as the insurance company rules in his favor."

"Is he?"

"Not likely, but I dressed up the promise in some fancy language, threw in the name of a law firm, and made it sound all legitimate and such."

"And that got Quail off your back?"

"I promised him half the settlement if he'd see his way clear to reducing our rent for a year."

Macy shook her head. "Hoop Whitaker, I thought you never lied."

"Never to *you*, Macy. Never to you. And besides, I didn't really lie. My dad *is* due a big payout, but it'll never come through. Those companies keep the cases in court till they fizzle out. But in the meantime, we're paying seventy-three cents on the dollar of our usual rent."

"Seventy-three? That's real specific."

"With the numbers I tossed out to Quail, that's the percent it came to." He grinned. "Had it all figured ahead of time."

Macy gave up on skipping stones and dug around the weeds for a slingshot she'd made the month before. "Don't know how you know so much, Hoop."

"Spend your life with me, Macy. It'll be a forever of learning things."

"Ain't you gonna be off charming snakes in the circus?"

Hoop looked at her like she was nuts. "Only for three years after high school. Then I'm getting full-on rich. Don't tell my dad, but I can run circles around him when it comes to numbers, and I'm a damn sight smarter with money."

Macy smiled. "Remember in third grade, you figured how many minutes till we'd be married, and how many seconds we'd spend together in our lives?"

"Remember? I got the clock ticking in my head right now. Six and a third million minutes till we're married, then a smidge over 1.6 trillion seconds together, assuming we marry at twenty-seven like you want, and if I make it to average male life expectancy. Sound square to you?"

Macy grinned, never knowing how to react to Hoop's wild predictions but ever enamored of his mind. She'd been hearing his numbers for years now, and once in a while, lying on her lumpy mattress with its faded purple sheets, she'd try to figure them out, but they always ended in a jumble in her head. "Sounds good," she said, "except I'm planning to live to a hundred and ten. Gonna need a few more seconds than you."

"Widow Whitaker, they'll call you."

Macy chortled. "It does have a morbid ring to it."

"Gotta go," Hoop said, as if an alarm had gone off in his head. "Snakes'll be running soon."

"Now that'd be a first."

"What would?"

"Snakes running. Far as I know, they only got one way of getting around, and that's slithering."

"They swim like the dickens, too. But you wait." He mounted his bike. "Someday I'm gonna get me two of the finest hoop snakes there ever was, and I'm gonna train 'em to stay looped and use 'em as bicycle tires. Gonna give you the first ride."

Macy released a full-throttled laugh at that one. "Those snakes are only a legend, Hoop, and a crazy one at that!"

"No, ma'am," he said. "Seen 'em with my own eyes. They bite their own tails and turn into wheels to escape an enemy or attack."

"Thought you never lied to me." She cast a big stone with her slingshot and hit a spot on a hickory that had seen its fair share of pings.

"I ain't lyin'," Hoop shouted as he pedaled away, turning his head back to shout. "I'd'a caught one already, but they roll away when they see me coming. Every. Dang. Time."

His laugh echoed down the lane as he cycled away, his green and black shirt flying behind him like a triumphant flag.

It always seemed to be what-a-day for Hoop Whitaker.

Chapter 7

I'd decided to prep for my Richie Quail interview at home—immediately after my editor had ripped into me about how reporters should never *become* the story. Probably wouldn't keep her from running those pictures of me attacking Boyd, but who could blame her? Conflict sold papers, or at least got more clicks.

I'd been moping on my back deck for over an hour already, toying with sentences for my article, but the humidity had glued the laptop to my thighs, and my writing had grown bitter: *Boyd Sexton, Jr., the screaming asshole who sold the winning lottery ticket to the Lucky Four, hasn't been so lucky recently. The suspected pervert is currently under investigation for kidnapping, murder, drug-dealing, and lifelong douchery.* The sentences I'd already deleted had been far less charitable.

Giving up, I'd picked up the binoculars on the table next to me to search for the small alligator that usually hung out between two Bald Cypresses stuck in a permanent kiss. With no sign of my lazy friend, I scanned the area—and that was when I'd spotted the nose.

Thought it was a turtle head at first. They tended to do that, the turtles. Peek their heads out, on the lookout for food or predators. On good days, they'd mount a log, rest their innards, and sun their wrinkled skulls. On bad ones, they spent their time avoiding becoming the main ingredient in turtle soup. Used to feel sorry for turtles, confined to life in a stockade, but as I got older, I envied those shells—a place to curl into oneself whenever the world got too scary or realistic.

But no, it was not a turtle. Definitely a human nose.

I zoomed back in on the nostrils in the water. The lowering tide was now making a forehead visible. I knew who it belonged to. Had suspected it from the start. It was my neighbor, Mrs. Grace Elbee, one of the Lucky Four. Few would be surprised by this turn of events. Mrs. Elbee had struggled to stay afloat these last few years. Apparently, she'd lost. What a morbid day this was turning into. Now I'd have to venture into the water and protect the body until the troops arrived.

I gazed down one more time to verify her location. Her hand was now visible, lying across her chest. *But what was up with her fingernails?* Painted neon orange, they reeked of hedonism, like they should be topping the digits of a wild party gal—anyone but Mrs. Elbee. Had she decided that if she couldn't romp on the wild side, random body parts should? Because those nails were out for an evening of gigolos and lime daiquiris, while their owner had spent the last few years wandering around town, lamenting a life that had never lived up to its promise. In fact, no one could have been less neon in outlook than Grace Elbee.

I grabbed my cell and called Chad. We had to get Mrs. Elbee out of there before the tide lowered anymore. Bugs, birds and vultures would be on her like pluff on a duck soon enough.

"Hey, Chloe," said Chad's weary voice through the phone. "The answer is *no*. We still don't have results on the blood or the flannel."

I'd already called five times for updates; both Sherilyn and Chad had opted to ignore my last two attempts.

"I'm not calling about that," I said. "I found Mrs. Elbee."

"Aw, geez. Is it what we thought?"

"Sure looks that way."

Grace Elbee hadn't been seen for several days, though no one had noticed until yesterday.

"This is turning into some day," Chad said. "Where is she? Black Swamp?"

"Of course."

"Floater?"

"Looks like she settled on something. Alligator might've flipped her face-up."

"An alligator with no appetite for crazy?"

"Sounds about right."

"You with the body?"

"No, but I'll head out now."

He sighed heavily. "Okay if we park in your yard?"

"I'd be disappointed if it ever grew grass."

"Give me fifteen minutes. I'll be there with bells on."

"A bit jolly for you, Chad."

"Didn't say they'd be ringing."

Through my binocular lenses, I caught a flash of unexpected movement. I needed to react. Response to movement was a critical survival tactic for swampers. It helped us avoid the prick of fangs carrying turbo-charged venom, or the clutch of jaws that could snap an arm like a twig. But the movement turned out to be Yoga Guy, my across-the-river neighbor, transitioning from Downward Dog to Modified Cobra. Our back yards faced each other, his in the kitschy, expensive area known as New Beulah, mine in what the New Beulah folks called Back Beulah, which translated to *swamp*.

Eight months ago, Yoga Guy had built a three-story, mostly glass monstrosity that put my shack-on-stilts to shame. We'd never met, but lack of a formal introduction hadn't kept me from lusting after his muscular, lithe body the last few months when he exercised outside. Something about the way he held his Warrior Pose longer than expected, and the way his biceps and chest bulged out an extra inch. In truth, everything about him seemed just a tiny bit off proportionally, as if his parents had been poorly matched. But he came close enough to *seriously handsome*—and seriously mysterious—to stoke my voyeuristic tendencies.

Yoga Guy suddenly glanced in my direction. Although he couldn't possibly see me from half-a-mile away, I jerked my lenses back to Mrs. Elbee. Half her body was now above the water line. I really needed to get out there.

I tossed the binoculars on the table and stroked my tattoo reflexively. Mrs. Elbee had found the guts to go through with it. The least I could do was show her some respect.

Chapter 8

I loved the swamp, but it could be equal parts beautiful and cruel. Some outsiders viewed it as the river's garbage filter. Technically, they were right. The swamp sucked in pollutants from the river's water, held them tight in its sediment, and magically converted all that waste into eel grass, orchids, bald cypresses, water tupelo, and swamp white oaks. Even provided enough nourishment for a thousand different plants and animals, from otters to muskrats, waterfowl to warblers, and crayfish to mussels, not to mention a rainbow of flowers and whatever was needed for mosquitoes to multiply at a staggering rate. They weren't bad most of the year, but in the summer, look out.

We were part of a unique stretch of wetlands that included freshwater swamps, bottomland hardwoods, and marshes that formed where rice fields were once attempted. The history ran deep, with disputes over land use and aggressive logging operations, but in the end, Beulah had been blessed with a remarkable combination of features. Our area proved especially unique because Black Swamp merged with salty Crater Marsh not far from where I lived; I could enjoy the smell of pluff mud with its fusion of questionably delightful odors, along with the richness of the forested waters, all from the comfort of my deck.

I thought of Black Swamp as the original recycler, providing dignified death and bountiful life to so much, including me. Often, it seemed the only reason to stay around at all. And while it hadn't been quite so kind to Mrs. Elbee, it would have recycled her, too, given enough time.

I donned old black waders and pulled back my long, straight hair. Retrieving a corpse wasn't the best way to distract myself from the investigation at Boyd's, but it would have to do. With my first step in the water, I felt a slithering pressure along my leg. I shrugged it off. To the snakes below, I was nothing but a moving tree stump, maybe a cypress root. I pushed through the water as the soft, pliable bottom yielded to my weight. Thirty yards out, when the water reached my waist, I glanced around, hoping that Old Bastard and his ilk hadn't ventured out for an early lunch. Nope, no rows of dark gray scales surrounding me. No suspicious-looking rocks with jaws and lazy, marble eyes.

Five minutes later, I came upon Mrs. Elbee, plain as day, dead as dead, and more bloated than I'd realized. She looked relaxed, almost kind. Not at all like the real Grace Elbee. The real Mrs. Elbee had honed the edges of her personality to a weary bluntness—a chipped, dull blade that would press and irritate rather than slice and scar. Suspicious of all people and everything new, Mrs. Elbee would blurt out complaints and accusations to anyone within earshot.

Twelve years ago, at the lottery award ceremony—an event reeking of manufactured pomp and panache—a mustachioed official in a navy suit had handed each winner an oversized check for four million dollars. Mrs. Elbee had scowled, glancing from the man to the check, even reading hers upside down when forced to pose for photos. Then she rubbed her hand along the front of the cardboard until finally crying out, "Is this real? Doesn't look the least bit real to me." The official had winked at the audience like a cheesy game show host before informing her that the giant check was merely for show, and that the real one would have taxes taken out. She'd sneered knowingly before casting it to the stage floor and stomping away. Not until she and her husband had moved into their 5000-square-foot home and put serious miles on their new cars and boats, had she believed in the winnings. Even then, she'd snarled her way through the next decade, worried about her son's inability to cope, her husband's inability to stay sober, and her conviction that their good fortune could be wiped away at a moment's notice.

Now, she'd tossed it all away herself, with a helping hand from Black Swamp. Black Swamp was obliging like that.

I drifted the body to a pleasant rise of mud that offered enough space for two people, and eased her gently atop the aggressive bottlebrush grass, smoothing a patch for myself while awaiting Chad's arrival. The last few years had seen Mrs. Elbee walking around town, carrying random objects that spoke to her *from the beyond*. The recent candlestick had been particularly troubling but seemed to give her comfort. After her husband's death from drinking and boating, she'd poured her remaining winnings into her son's rehab stints. He, in turn, had poured them down his throat.

"This is an awkward way to meet," said a male voice with such a rich timbre that I was convinced God himself was welcoming Mrs. Elbee at the gates of heaven.

I whipped around, my hand flying to my chest. It was Yoga Guy. Hadn't even heard him approaching.

"I'm sorry," he said. "Didn't mean to startle you."

"Startle? How about frighten the living daylights out of me? You were quiet as a snake."

He climbed out of the water, naked from the waist up, and there, in the flesh, were those pecs and arms and that weird little muscle around the waist, just above the hip bone, that I thought only existed in airbrushed magazines.

"Not the first time I've been compared to a snake," he said with a grin. Those teeth might jut, but they worked wonders on his overall appearance. The smile made everything fit. And that nose, despite its wandering dominance, suggested a confidence and masculinity lacking in most Beulah men. Meanwhile, the bushy eyebrows . . . well, still disturbing, but at least they took after the lustrous mix of dark waves and curls crowning his head.

"Poor Mrs. Elbee," he said.

I stared at him in surprise. How did Reclusive Yoga Guy from New Beulah know Old Lady Elbee from Back Beulah?

"Very disappointing," he continued. "You called it in, too, I assume?"

"Yes, they should be here soon."

"I guess her demons got the better of her. She and I met at the Farmer's Market about a month ago, haggling over the same object." He sat down, facing the same direction as me, with Mrs. Elbee's body acting as a warped coffee table between us.

"You know, I don't recall asking a crazy man to join me."

"Crazy? How so?"

"Who enters the swamp barefoot? In yoga pants no less?"

He glanced at his pants as if seeing them for the first time, and then smiled at me, his dark eyes steady and entrancing. "Why do you call these *yoga* pants, particularly?"

I used a jumping fish as an excuse to turn my head and hide the blush of my cheeks. Had I just outed myself as a voyeur? I glanced back over, shrugged, and feigned confidence. "Anybody can see those are yoga pants. You're not the only one who works out."

He flicked a bug from his arm as his lips curled into a suspicious smile. "So you also know that I work out."

Inside, I burned. Outside, I played it cool. "Our yards do face each other, you know."

"Oh, yes. I know." He filled the gap between the two short phrases with all sorts of innuendo. Then he glanced from his house to mine. "With half a mile of water between. You must have quite the eyesight."

Time for either confession or diversion. I chose the usual. "So, what was this object you and Mrs. Elbee were haggling over? If you don't mind my asking."

"You're a reporter. You're obligated to ask."

I pulled a curious pucker. "You seem to have the advantage over me, Mr. . . .?"

"No *mister*. Just Rafe. Rafe Borose, rhymes with *morose*."

"Borose, okay. But *Rafe*? You don't hear that one too often. R-A-F-E?"

He seemed amused that I'd spelled it aloud. "That would be correct."

"An anagram of *fear*."

"Aha." He flicked the wild brows. "Not unexpected."

"What's not?"

"You process in words, letters, probably homophones and puns, too."

I shrugged. "Spelling bee champ." I raised three fingers. "Three years in a row."

"Image guy myself. Colors, diagrams, lots of mental swirling." He twirled a finger near his head. "Ideas form in three dimensions—not that they always make sense. Numbers float around like dots, and smells come to me in rainbow shades."

I bit down on my lower lip, intrigued. "Does sound ever come to you as a scent?"

He closed his eyes and sniffed the air. "Your voice is strawberry rhubarb pie, with a squeeze of lemon."

I smiled. As a fan of the sweet and tart confection, I found the comparison apt. "Very unexpected indeed," I said.

"What is?"

"You're a synesthete. I've never actually met one. Your senses are intermingled and cross-patched. Much more interesting than a girl who can memorize a dictionary."

"You're sitting in the middle of a swamp with a dead body for company. I'd call that interesting."

"But back to my question. Were you and Mrs. Elbee haggling over the last eggplant available?"

"Actually, we both wanted an amulet acquired by a decidedly strange vendor."

"Bruce?"

"I don't know his name. He barely spoke. Wore a funky braid halfway down his back, a flowing robe, and communicated mostly with gestures and grunts."

"That's Bruce. Big traveler, not a big talker. So what was the amulet for? Good luck?"

"No, that would be a charm or a talisman, both of which attract good things to their wearers. But an amulet"—he cut a serious glare in my direction—"is more of a defensive piece."

"Defensive? Who would Mrs. Elbee need defending from?"

He shrugged, and new muscles bulged before disappearing. "She mentioned that her husband died a few years ago. Maybe he was moving things around in the dead of night."

I laughed. "George Elbee didn't strike me as the haunting type. Unless he was haunting the fridge for a cold one." Guilt tapped me on the shoulder—bad taste to be making fun of the dead widow's husband right in front of her. Another round of my game lost.

"She told me she was worried about a restless spirit who was out to get her," Rafe said. "*Pissed off and petulant* was how she described it."

"Sounds like she needed that amulet more than you."

He rotated his head slowly in my direction. "You don't think I'm hauntable?"

"Are you?"

He thought about it. "I'd rather be the haunter than the hauntee. But I only collect the pieces for their beauty and history, so I bowed out of the bidding and let her buy it." He glanced at Mrs. Elbee's neckline. "I think she's wearing it."

I looked down to see a thin, silver chain around Mrs.

Elbee's neck. Carefully, I lifted one flap of her blouse and saw the head and horns of a ram with two cobras curling up from its forehead. "Is that it?"

Rafe leaned over and took a respectful peek. "Sure is. Made of ivory. It's a symbol of the Egyptian deity, Amun. Usually, you see the ram's head with one cobra, but the gods merited two. And Amun, he was king of the gods, according to some stories."

"I remember something about him from school. Wasn't he invisible?"

"Until you called him by his fuller name, Amun-Re. Then he'd appear. There's also a belief that he could regenerate himself by becoming a snake and shedding his skin."

"If only it were that easy."

Rafe gazed at me, but I gave him only profile.

"No idea who's handling Mrs. Elbee's arrangements," he said, "but I bet she wanted to be buried with that amulet. In Egypt, the dead were often entombed with them to ward off evil spirits in the afterlife."

I shivered as a breeze kicked up. "Poor Mrs. Elbee. Now she'll be in the same realm as that pissed-off spirit."

"She must have been carrying quite a burden." A quiet moment passed, and then he spoke again. "We must have spotted her around the same time. I had just gone back inside and was watching my favorite heron—pure spastic elegance when he swallows a fish—and I knocked my telescope with my elbow. The lens landed right on the body, and then you came into view."

I got a paranoid twitch in my gut. "You . . . have a telescope?"

Rafe pointed to his glass-encased residence. "Several. The most powerful is on the third floor, behind that dark window with the green shutters. Modern-day crow's nest, if you will." He fixed me with a penetrating but charmed gaze.

"That's how I know that you seek me out with your Porro-prism binoculars, if I'm not mistaken."

"I'm afraid you are mistaken."

"Really? I can usually tell from their shape. The Porro-prism binocs contain multiple reflective surfaces that determine the light's path, which is curved." He used his hands to illustrate. "The curved route forces the barrels of the binoculars to be wider. Makes them bulkier than roof-prism models that split the image but allow some light to escape."

I took a breath and huffed. "I didn't mean you were mistaken about the *model* of binoculars."

His tight smirk made him downright adorable. "I know."

"What makes you such an expert on the travels of light, anyway? Are you a scientist?"

"No, just a guy who's fascinated by splitting and interfering with light. It makes the real unreal and gives us a glimpse of other dimensions." He flicked a bug from his arm. "I'm hard-pressed to think of anything more intriguing. But back to you spying on me."

I considered diving headfirst into the swamp, to let the sun's rays on the water split my image a thousandfold, perhaps dissolving my embarrassment. But rather than death by a thousand refractions, I was saved by the arrival of Chad's Blazer on my driveway. The green, all-terrain vehicle moseyed to the water's edge at the same slow pace its driver usually walked.

"The law has arrived," Rafe said, rising and stepping back into the water like it was a second skin. "And you seem to have everything under control here."

"Yes, but," I said, inexplicably desperate for him to stay, "shouldn't you give a statement? They'll want to know what you saw."

Rafe smiled in a jaded fashion. "I find quite the opposite. They usually want you to verify what they already think." He slipped fully into the water. "But in this case, Chloe, tell them I saw the same as you."

His use of my name sent a shiver through my midsection. "Which was?"

"Mrs. Elbee's body racked with . . . something. But of course, I saw it in symphonic tones while picking up the scent of those garishly bright fingernails."

Part of me wanted to reach out and draw him back. "What did they smell like?"

"Oranges, of course," he said, flicking the brows as he skimmed away on the water's surface.

Chapter 9

Chad's perfect head of hair exited the Blazer first, followed by broad shoulders. The local barber had once described Chad's stiff black locks as tunnel hair, *'cause it don't matter if he's in a wind tunnel or a cyclone—not one strand of that stuff is goin' no place.*

With the exception of the bulky shoulders, Chad sported a runner's bod—narrow hips, sinewy legs, and minimal body fat. He'd drunkenly confided to me once that he viewed fat as a luxury of normal childhoods filled with cookie jars and birthday cakes. Denied the opportunity to indulge as a child, he felt a near-obsession to abscond as an adult.

He waved to me before turning to pull on his waders.

The Blazer's passenger door then opened to reveal Sherilyn, already wearing her pink waders. A couple months back, she'd painted large yellow daisies on them—*heck, my job needs a shot of joviality.* But when she grabbed her crime scene kit and stepped out of the Blazer, she looked like the interior of a Volkswagen exiting the wrong vehicle.

She strode toward the water with the same exuberance she showed for everything, from a hand of poker to a hand in a box—something she'd found last year after a loan went wrong between two oystermen—and she entered Black Swamp like it was a puddle. "Be right there!" she shouted.

"Couldn't you have floated Old Lady Elbee over here?" Chad yelled, approaching the water like it was acid. Most of his foster homes had been in cities; he much preferred the certainty of concrete over the swamp's shifting bottom.

"Keeping the body disturbances to a minimum," I yelled back, my voice finding no echo as Black Swamp sucked up everything in its path—except tourist dollars. Nearby Crater Marsh and Juniper Swamp had made a killing in recent years, offering air boat rides and bridge-walking tours during high-water season, but the residents of Back Beulah weren't nearly as eager to share.

Sherilyn and Chad's eventual arrival maxed out the population of my tiny island. "Who was that bushy-haired guy out here with you?" Chad said, sounding more like a jealous teen than a deputy with a dead body to manage.

I jerked a thumb toward Rafe's house. "Lives in the glass house. Saw the body same as me." I delivered my response like a sea-weary captain, trying to convey how much I couldn't care less who Rafe was; it only served to emphasize the opposite.

Chad harrumphed. "Maybe he knew where to look. I'll have to question him."

I waved away Chad's suspicions. "I think we all know this is most likely a suicide, Chad."

"I've seen that guy around New Beulah," Sherilyn said. "Yum-mee! Bit of a loner, though."

Chad ignored Sherilyn and smirked in my direction. "Looked like you two were getting pretty chummy out here."

"Yeah," I said, "we were just about to get into some ménage-a-trois necrophilia when you guys showed up."

"Eww," Sherilyn said before grinning.

"What's his name?" Chad asked.

"Rafe Borose. Rhymes with morose."

Chad snorted. "What the hell kind of douchey, prep-school name is that?"

"I don't know. Seemed to fit him, though."

"So he *is* a douche, then?"

I almost smiled at Chad's cute stripe of jealousy. He'd never gotten over our break-up even though he'd initiated it. Neither of us could put a finger on our underlying issues, but it probably had something to do with the fact that he was in love, and I only loved the sex. Poor Chad had no history of normal relationships on which to base the relative normalcy of ours, but he knew there should have been *more* to whatever we had. More depth, more honesty, more *something*, but with me, he was ramming his head against a wall and could barely make a crack. Warm and fuzzies weren't my strength. One thing I knew for sure, though: he shouldn't gauge *normal* by me. He deserved better than that.

I gestured to Mrs. Elbee who was starting to shrivel. "Shall we attend to the business at hand, Deputy?"

Chad forced his attention to the body. "So what happened to Mrs. Elbee? Her own bitterness come around and bite her in the ass?"

"Chad, please," Sherilyn said. "Let's show some respect."

"Sorry, Sherilyn. Just that Grace Elbee made my outlook on life seem bright and sunny. What've we got?"

"Hard to tell," Sherilyn said. "We'll give her a good once-over at the lab." Sherilyn lifted Mrs. Elbee's leg. "Ligature marks around her ankles but not very deep." She indicated the back of the ankle. "And very little on the back side. Kind of odd."

"You think she tried to drown herself by tying something to her ankles?" Chad asked.

"Maybe, but she did sort of a careless job," Sherilyn said. "Awkward way to go." She lowered Mrs. Elbee's foot and looked up at Chad. "Might want to check the river current, figure out how she ended up here. And if she *was* trying to kill herself with just her ankles weighted, you'll need to check water depths to see where she could drown with her body upright. If you can find her entry point into the water, it'll be easier to find the thing she weighed herself down with. How long has she been missing?"

"Few days," I said, ashamed for the entire town that it had taken so long for anyone to notice her absence. "I stopped by the other day to check on her, but when I saw that her car was gone, I figured she'd left town without mentioning it."

"The timing makes sense," Sherilyn said. "Usually takes a couple days for the bloat-and-float. She's lucky nothing took a bite out of her." Sherilyn glanced up and down the length of the body. "That nail polish is kind of loud for Grace."

I stared at the nails and reflected. "People don't always think rationally when they're out to kill themselves." My voice faded off at the end of the sentence and I didn't chance a look at either of them. One could never really be sure what stayed secret in Back Beulah.

"If Mrs. Elbee is here with us," Chad said, "then who took her car?"

"She could have driven to a different spot on the river before jumping in," Sherilyn said.

"But her house backs up to the river," Chad said. "Best lot in town. And no one's reported an abandoned car."

"Better put an APB out on that car," I said. "Just in case."

"Wouldn't hurt to seal off her yard, too," Sherilyn suggested. "She's got a lot of river frontage with heavy brush near the bank. If it was foul play, someone might've snagged a piece of clothing on a branch or left an imprint in the mud."

"Will do," Chad said. "Hey, Chloe, think I oughta tell my father to watch out?"

"What do you mean?"

"Seems like things aren't working out so well for the lottery folks. First Boyd and now Grace."

"Don't spread that around," I said. "I still have three interviews to do for my article."

Sherilyn clapped her gloved hands together. "Okay, let me get some pictures and we'll get Mrs. Elbee out of here."

Chad shook his head, disgusted. "Imagine swamp water being the last thing you taste in life."

I swallowed away a rush of queasiness. I often wondered if swamp water was the last thing Hoop tasted. Now, given what I'd seen in Boyd's basement, I kind of hoped it was.

"I gotta ask," I said. "Is Boyd Junior talking at all yet?"

"Not a word," Chad said. "Lawyered up real fast. The guy can hardly add two and two, but when it comes to his constitutional rights, he turns into a regular legal scholar."

I snorted my repugnance, the morning's roller coaster of emotions threatening a loop-de-loop.

"Chloe," Chad continued, "you want to come with me to Mrs. Elbee's? You've been in her house more than the rest of us. Maybe you'll notice if things are out of place."

"Sure thing," I said. I knew he was asking out of kindness, to offer me a diversion until some answers materialized about Boyd's basement, but I'd helped out on cases before. While a reporter's presence at two crime scenes in one day might not sit well with snooty townspeople, Beulah folks didn't seem to mind. Sheriff Ryker had even floated the idea of deputizing me once. Of course, that was before I'd assaulted his car with my foot.

The ambulance arrived, and Mrs. Elbee exited Black Swamp the same way her husband had—wet and dead.

Back on land, I peeled off my waders, wondering if I was being observed while performing the world's least sexy striptease. Was my image whole or split in a certain telescope across the way?

And then I wondered why the thought made me tingle.

Chapter 10

Chad and I found Mrs. Elbee's front door unlocked, a common condition in Beulah where robberies mostly consisted of teenagers filching beer from garage fridges. Sometimes, the delinquents even left a few crumpled dollars in exchange. We donned gloves and booties before entering, though I suspected we wouldn't find much more than a sad, strange note.

Whenever Mrs. Elbee had been *under the weather*—her euphemism for *depressed*—I'd do her grocery and drug store shopping. Even though I'd known her since I was eight years old, she never failed to count the change to make sure I didn't cheat her. Never bothered me; it was just her way. Although I considered her my closest neighbor, we still lived one mile and several social strata apart—me where the land stayed wet and the regulations required stilts, her on a beautiful lot that overlooked a wide expanse of river. When I was in high school, she and her husband had hired me to walk their collie while they took *international trips*. The phrase, in my mind, had sparked images of George and Grace Elbee donning royal clothing and riding camels through exotic lands. Having later seen pictures, I learned that it just meant tacky t-shirts, overpriced cocktails, and cheesy photos with a tour bus in the background.

"See anything unusual?" Chad asked as we stepped in.

I glanced around. No overturned furniture, broken windows, or spattered blood. No strange smells to indicate the presence of a stranger. Just a well-kept house decorated by people who'd become suddenly rich twelve years ago. They'd pulled decorating ideas straight from trendy magazines but had gone too far, making the place feel prematurely dated. I squatted down and ran a gloved finger along the foyer floor and first two stairs. "There's dirt here, like someone might have tramped up the stairs in shoes."

"Is that odd?"

"Mrs. Elbee was fastidious. Vacuumed every day and made me take off my shoes when I came over."

Chad pulled out an evidence bag and brushed the dirt into it. "We'll run it through the lab."

I followed him into the kitchen. He sniffed, four short snuffs. "Onions, garlic, a bit of fish," he said. "Three days old, maybe four."

"Strong work, McGruff. Case solved."

"Hey, you grow up hungry, you learn to savor smells." He turned around and checked the low counter where Mrs. Elbee kept a phone, notepad, and, apparently, her collection of amulets. I could see now why Rafe collected them; they were beautiful and varied with striking details and jewels, most containing carved symbols I didn't understand.

"This reminds me," I said, pointing to the amulets. "We've got to tell Sherilyn that Mrs. Elbee might want to be buried with the amulet she was wearing."

"Did she mention that to you?"

"No," I said, pretending it was my idea. "But she killed herself while wearing it. She might be trying to ward off evil spirits in the afterlife."

Chad gave me a strange look but let the topic go. He pressed the blinking red light on the answering machine. Only one message: from a telemarketer offering life insurance.

"Should have answered that one," Chad murmured while scrolling through the Caller ID. "She got a bunch of calls from California, always around noon on even days of the month."

"Probably her son," I said.

"Drying out in L.A. this time?"

"The best that lottery winnings can buy."

"Easy to find him, then." He jotted down the number in

the tiny notebook he always carried and kept scrolling. "You know anyone named LeGrange? First name starts with *M*?"

I whirled around. "What did you say?"

My clenched jaw and wide eyes told him he'd said far more than he thought. "*M. LeGrange*. It's on the Caller ID. He's called six, no seven, times recently."

I rushed over and looked at the display. "It's not a *he*," I said. "It's Macy LeGrange."

"Macy? The little girl that got killed on her bike?"

"What's the number?" I asked.

"South Carolina area code and a Beulah exchange, but could be a telemarketer from Timbuktu these days. They make the phone display say anything they want." He wrote the number down. "I'll check it out. If an *M. LeGrange* did speak to Mrs. Elbee recently, she might know something."

Transfixed, I scrolled repeatedly through the seven calls from *M. LeGrange*.

Chad touched my arm, the way he used to when I drifted into one of my dazes. "Chloe, it's just a name on a display. Not like there's only one *M. LeGrange* in the world."

I tightened my face. "Macy and I were friends. Good friends."

"I guess in a town this small, you knew every kid your own age, huh?"

His question was part filler and part ongoing investigation of what a normal childhood entailed. It was easy to forget how he'd missed out on the basics. "I knew every kid in town," I said, "probably well enough to blackmail them." I leaned against Mrs. Elbee's clean granite countertop and shook my head. "Macy was the type all the girls should have been jealous of, but none of us could get there."

"What do you mean?"

"She was beyond adorable. Blond hair, big dimples, huge blue eyes. But sporty and cool at the same time."

"A Shirley Temple jock."

"Exactly. The boys loved her, but she barely noticed. And she was funny without being catty or gossipy. Just . . . so damn happy, grinning at life even when it didn't grin back."

Chad smiled wistfully, and then started toward the stairs. "Come on, let's check out the bedrooms."

The second level of Mrs. Elbee's house smelled musty. Wouldn't surprise me if mold was painting the backside of her sheet rock with stubborn black grit. Out of some warped obligation to a fellow lottery winner, the Elbees had hired local developer, Richie Quail, to build their dream home. Quail was a gifted salesman who could close any deal, but his real specialty was screwing whoever was on the other end of the handshake—George and Grace Elbee had made the mistake of shaking his hand. Despite the house's external charms and great location, it was rotten to the core. Dozens of contractors had come and gone over the years, but none had been able to overcome Quail's shoddy work.

Chad and I entered the master bedroom. A slight whir of tension gripped me as memories of our own times in such rooms flooded back. I avoided looking at him—even if part of me did want to jump his bones.

The room was tidy, although the rumpled bedspread seemed out of place, and, upon closer inspection, the small clumps of dirt near the side of the bed seemed odd. I pointed them out to Chad.

"Maybe she went outside to find a rock to weigh her body down with," he suggested, "and then tracked dirt back in here to get something—or to leave a note."

We looked around. No note. On her nightstand was a paperback, bookmarked three-quarters of the way through: *Return From Death*. I glanced around, worried Mrs. Elbee might have already cashed in her return ticket and been hovering above us. After making sure Chad wasn't looking, I gave a quick smile and wave to the empty air above her bed, just in case.

As Chad bagged the second sample of dirt, I turned my attention to the tall dresser in the corner and checked out the happy family photos: Grace and George smiling in sunglasses and hats while floating on their boat; Eric, the son, waving as he opened the door to a new car; the three of them arm-in-arm in front of the house. The images were only a mirage, though, a creation of the life Mrs. Elbee had felt she deserved.

While I surveyed, Chad moseyed into the bathroom. "Whoa!" he said upon entering. "Now *that's* a little weird."

That registered as high emotion for Chad, so I hustled over to the all-white, marble bathroom. Even before entering, I could smell the mold that was multiplying aggressively in Mrs. Elbee's absence. Once in, I followed Chad's shocked gaze to the mirror above the sink and gasped. For a long stretch, I forgot to breathe.

I finally inhaled enough to speak. "That wasn't just an *M* on the Caller ID, was it?"

Chapter 11

"Macy LeGrange," Sheriff Ryker read from the mirror.

"Weird, right?" Chad said.

Strike Ryker stood between Chad and me as he repeated Macy's name. It was scrawled on Mrs. Elbee's bathroom mirror like some horror movie message, but instead of a drippy, blood-red font, the name reflected back at us in cheery, aqua shades of toothpaste. It was composed in tidy cursive, except for the *L*, which was somewhat smeared.

"That's definitely Mrs. Elbee's writing," I said. "That's how she wrote her big G's."

The stout sheriff rotated his head to me. His aggressive stance and accompanying frown made me wish I'd said *capital G* instead of *big* G, but too late now. Either he was still reeling from my morning antics during Boyd's arrest or he was simply being himself. Strike Ryker had to be the only lottery winner in history who'd grown crankier with each dollar of accumulated interest.

"We found an *M. LeGrange* on Mrs. Elbee's Caller ID," Chad said, gesturing to Macy's name on the mirror. "Seven calls over the last few weeks. Mrs. Elbee's phone kept track of call lengths, too. Looks like she answered the final call and talked for a while."

The sheriff grunted. "Take her answering machine in, and—"

"Already got it bagged," Chad said. "And I put in a request for all of her outgoing phone records."

The sheriff gave a subtle nod of approval. "Wasn't Macy's mom's named Melanie?"

"Yes, sir," I answered.

"She left town shortly after Macy's funeral," he said.

"Didn't *leave* so much as get booted out," I said. "Rumor

has it that Richie Quail kicked her out of her place just two weeks after Macy was killed."

The sheriff waved that sorry aspect of Beulah's history away, not in an uncaring way, but in a one-issue-at-a-time sort of way. He turned to Chad. "Probably Melanie LeGrange calling Mrs. Elbee, don't you think?"

"But the calls came from a local number," I interjected. "I dialed it with my cell while we were waiting for you to arrive. It's disconnected."

"People change numbers," the sheriff said unconvincingly.

"Any chance Mrs. LeGrange moved back here?" Chad said.

"I feel like we'd know if she had," the sheriff said.

"I'll track her down," Chad said. "Either of you know where she moved to?"

The sheriff and I both shook our heads.

"I'll find her," Chad said.

"Maybe Grace Elbee and Melanie LeGrange were commiserating over Richie Quail," I said. "Quail not only owned the duplex development where Macy and her mom lived, but he also built this house." I glared at the sheriff like it was his fault. "What a piece of work your friend is, Sheriff."

He turned and got right in my face. When questioned or accused, Strike Ryker had a way of sizzling before skewering. It didn't have to be a deep question, either. With a simple, *How do you take your coffee?*, his skin would crinkle and crisp while he searched behind the question. Then he'd spit out an answer like a dragon shooting fire. *Black* would have been the answer to that one because Strike Ryker, steadfast keeper of law and order, would always take it black—even if he preferred it light and sweet.

I stood my ground and held eye contact.

"Richie Quail is no friend of mine," he said, his voice

even and slow. "You'd do well to remember that, Chloe."

Instead, I remembered something that Chad had once told me: *Strike has limits, and you'll always find out what they are.* I'd just pressed up against an interesting one.

"You played the lottery with him," I said. "Figured you must be friends."

The sheriff's left eye narrowed to a razor-thin line, making his right one appear demonic. "Quail and I happened to be in Boyd's General at the same time that morning, along with Adeline DeVore. We all chipped in for Grace's ticket. And yes, we won, but that hardly established a basis for friendship."

"You know, Sheriff, I'd know all these details if you'd returned my calls last week. I still need to interview you for my article."

"Write it without me. I don't like that *Lucky Four* label and I don't like being called *rich*."

"No problem. Built-in Thesaurus on my computer. Plenty of other words for *rich*. But either way, you're in the article. You're pivotal to every event that happened that week."

He looked startled. "What is that supposed to mean?"

"You won the lottery. You found Macy's body. You called the ambulance for Avis Whitaker. You even visited Avis in the hospital every day"—the sheriff turned a mild shade of crimson upon learning that I knew that detail—"and you ordered the dredging of the swamp to find Hoop. And now, with Boyd's basement, you might be pivotal in finding out what really happened to him. You're every up and every down of that week, Sheriff. I don't have a story without you."

I glanced again at the name of my childhood friend—the one who could do more hula-hoop twirls than me but would tell everyone I did it with lots more style. Desiccated sections of the toothpaste had begun to chip off and float down to the sink. With the slow leak around the faucet, a bluish green puddle was forming around the brass fixture. I returned my gaze to the sheriff. "I don't know how this story ends, Sheriff, but given today's events, my article is shaping up to be a lot more interesting. I'm talking to Richie Quail this afternoon, and Adeline DeVore in the morning. That covers three of the four lottery winners. You're the only one left."

He looked taken aback, one jowl sinking lower than the other, his head jutting farther forward than usual. "I do not want to be the central point of your story."

"You won't be, if you agree to an interview."

His radio crackled. Chad and I exchanged a smirk. Strike Ryker was the *only* person in Beulah who refused to carry a cell phone—and that included the homeless-by-choice ex-banker who camped outside the firehouse offering raw hot dogs to passersby.

"Ryker," the sheriff barked into his radio.

The reedy voice of Annika, the department receptionist who still reveled in her Miss Beulah County title, came through the radio. "Sheriff, we got some mighty impatient FBI fellers here who are asking to see you."

"Details, Annika." The sheriff was not one for teasers or drama, preferring black-and-white versions of everything, including movies and squad cars.

"Something to do with Boyd's alleged goings-on in the basement," Annika squeaked. "Apparently, they'd been keeping an eye on him and they're none-too-happy that you interfered. That's all I got."

Chad and I exchanged a surprised glance that Boyd Sexton could rank on anyone's surveillance list, but maybe he'd done something stupid like cross state lines with his drugs or sell to an undercover agent.

The sheriff shook his head; he didn't need this particular brand of headache right now. "I'll be right over," he said into the radio, and then turned to me. "Did you interview Mrs.

Elbee for your story?"

"Yes. Last week. I recorded it."

"Gonna need a copy of that for the investigation. Maybe she said something that will shed light on"—he nodded toward the mirror—"this."

"I'll email it to you."

He sneered. "Can't you just bring me a tape?"

I smiled at Beulah's adorably old-fashioned sheriff. "I'll bring it over first thing in the morning—if you agree to an interview."

"Dang it all, Chloe. I'll just take possession of your tape by force if I need to."

"But that would require a warrant, Sheriff. Much easier if I just hand it over willingly after our interview tomorrow."

He sizzled. "Fine. I gotta give a talk at the high school in the morning. Come by around nine."

"I remember those *this-is-your-brain-on-drugs and this-is-your-butt-in-jail* spiels you gave, Sheriff. They stuck with me."

He grunted and turned to go but then craned his head back. "Ever think maybe your story's cursed, Chloe? Maybe you oughta just leave well enough alone."

"Thought you knew me better than that, Sheriff. That's exactly why I won't leave it alone."

Chapter 12

Four Days Before The Thump

"Chloe!" Macy shouted. "Over here!"

Fourteen-year-old Macy LeGrange waved her friend, Chloe Keyes, over from across the road, intermittently pointing to a group of kids who'd gathered on the cleared field behind Boyd's General. Chloe glanced around to make sure no cars were coming, and then she shifted her weight until her longboard made a smooth arc across the pavement. She glided over to where Macy was standing in frayed jean shorts, a gray baseball shirt, a blue cap, and formerly white tennis shoes.

"We're getting a softball game going," Macy said. "You up for catching?"

"Getting too tall to catch anymore. Hurts my knees." Chloe had grown four inches in the past year and, in her eyes, had become more awkward than pretty. Her mother kept reminding her that ugly ducklings turned into swans, but Chloe had despised that story as a four-year-old and really couldn't stomach it as a teen.

"No problem," Macy said. "Hoop oughta be by any minute. He don't mind catching. Think you can handle second base?"

When Chloe heard that Hoop was coming, she lit up. Heck, she'd have played ump if she had to. "Second's cool," she said. "I'll put Pete Rose to shame."

"Think he kinda did that to himself," Macy said, "but I hear ya." She smacked Chloe on the butt as she ran past. "Get out there, girl."

Chloe joined the ten other kids milling about. As she glanced at her teammates, she realized she knew enough about each of them to populate a cheesy novel. There was

Ronnie Fields who farted whenever he got nervous or laughed hard. His mom shoplifted the occasional steak and his little brother, Andy, still wet the bed. Casey stood next to Ronnie. Casey's dad gave his mom a black eye about once a year, usually around Christmas. Casey himself had cheated on every math test since second grade and recently claimed he'd felt up Katie Wossack twice. Katie denied it; said it was only once. There was Rory, with his gorgeous eyes, who couldn't read or spell but could fib his way out of anything. Maxine, approaching Ronnie, had stuffed her bra since fifth grade. And Lissette, who was retying her shoe, had a chemistry teacher for a mom. Lissette's mom had allergies—or a drug problem—that made her nose drip, along with a tendency to flirt with Maxine's dad, the history teacher. Chloe knew the other kids viewed her as that girl from New York whose crass but likeable father had moved the family here to escape the wrath of a powerful enemy. Apparently, while running his butcher shop in Manhattan, he'd refused to pay *protection* money to dangerous men. *"When's the last time you heard of a knife-wielding butcher getting held up for a side of beef?"* he'd argued. They'd responded by pressing his hand to a chopping block and removing the tip of his pinkie finger. Which is how a little girl who'd asked the Times Square Santa for a pet gerbil at age three had ended up in tiny Beulah, South Carolina, rumored to own a pet alligator.

Chloe high-fived her friends, thankful that everyone's problems disappeared on the field.

Two minutes later, a mint-green Cadillac with a dented door and over 150,000 miles on its odometer pulled up to the side of the road. It jolted to a stop just before a muddy ditch that was threatening to encompass the eastbound lane soon enough.

The passenger door opened and out stepped Hoop Whitaker, his dirty-blond hair peeking out from beneath a red and black USC Gamecocks cap. He had a sack full of bats and balls over his shoulder and a folded cardboard box under his arm. His trademark green-and-black flannel clung to his waist and fanned out like a peacock tail as he ran to the field. If anybody saw Hoop Whitaker without that flannel, they'd think something in the world had surely gone amiss. Even on hot days, he'd wear it in case he needed a pillow while napping on the edge of the swamp. Claimed it was a lucky shirt, but in Hoop's world, everything resonated luck, from a pen to a fishing lure to a smelly white sock he'd tied to the back of his bike like a challenge flag.

"Play ball!" he shouted as he threw the bag down and started tearing up the box to use as bases and home plate.

The group, which had somehow grown to thirteen since Chloe's arrival, let out a series of whoops and hollers and broke into teams.

Macy took shortstop because she played the position like nobody else. One thing about Macy, she never ducked—didn't matter if a ball threatened to break her foot in a vicious grounder or rocketed toward her face in a line drive. If it was in her vicinity, she'd grab it, seams, hide, and all. Boys teased her that she'd end up like a toothless witch if she didn't stop staring balls down, but in response, she'd rub mud on her front teeth, get up in their faces, and say, "What's wrong with a witch?"

Five minutes into the game, Chloe picked up a rare one that got by Macy, and missiled it to bucktoothed Ian on first for an out. Hoop came up to bat next. Chloe crossed her fingers that he'd hit a double.

Hoop, as always, made a big show of warming up. He got everybody laughing by pretending to trip over his own feet before transforming the fall into a flip. Then he joked about the batter's box being a literal cardboard box. While others were either enjoying the show or jeering at him to get on with it, Chloe caught a glimpse of Boyd Junior watching the game from the back of the store, a crooked face atop a crooked body. Reminded her of a scarecrow left hanging in a field too long, the pole jutting one shoulder up too high, the head skulking too low, and the sun taking its toll on all the mismatched parts. He had inherited the store eight months ago when his father died from a 4-pack-a-day habit. The cause of death hadn't made much of an impact on Boyd, obviously, because a cigarette hung from his thin lips. Despite the distance, Chloe could see the weathered twenty-year-old watching Hoop. Smoking and watching. Even when someone in the field yelled something funny, or when Maxine the cheerleader turned a cartwheel to kill time, Boyd never tore his gaze from Hoop.

Chloe knew from fierce, slightly jealous observation that most grown men, given their druthers, would stare at Macy, no questions asked, or at least at Maxine. So what was wrong with Boyd? A sensation of fingers grabbing her spine worked its way to the nerves in her stomach and made her feel queasy. She jerked her head away as Boyd let out a thin plume of smoke. Heck, he'd always given her the willies. Like her mom said, *every town has a few*. At least he never talked much. Took people's money and kept his thoughts to himself, however dark they might be.

Hoop finally made contact with the ball, hitting a solid double. Aaron Belfour chased it down and followed up with a respectable bullet to Chloe, but nobody and no-how could outpace Hoop Whitaker. The kid, according to his own legend, had outrun gators and jumped clear of rattlesnakes with time to spare, so getting to second base in a dusty patch of turf didn't exactly present a challenge.

Hoop overran Chloe's base by four steps, giving her a whiff of his strong, musky deodorant. She relished the smell, figuring he applied it more than once a day, even on top of sweat. She caught the ball and tossed it to the pitcher. Hoop returned soon enough, barely out of breath.

"Geez, Clover," Hoop said, "you're growing like a weed. Must have an inch or better on me now."

"Yeah," she said, unaware of her slouching shoulders, "I don't like it much. Seems flat-out weird to be taller than most of the boys."

"Don't worry," he said, patting her roughly on the arm. "When they catch up, they'll be after you sum'n fierce."

Chloe blushed, making it clear she didn't believe him for a minute, but loving that he'd said it.

"'Cept me, of course," he added.

Chloe's heart contracted. Her lungs followed suit and it became hard to breathe, but she hoped her fake smile covered the pain.

Hoop touched her arm again, then craned his head until she was forced to meet his gaze. She hadn't realized she was avoiding it, but once her eyes were locked in, she wished time would freeze and let her linger there forever.

He grinned shyly at her. "I didn't mean *except me* being after you. I meant *except me* catching up in height." He paused a moment in that thoughtful way of his. "I mean, you seen my old man? That guy is no great shakes in the height department."

Chloe didn't know what to say. She considered blurting out that even if Hoop were a foot shorter than her, she'd still marry him, but the crack of a foul ball sidelined the comment. "Maybe your mom was tall," she said a moment later, immediately regretting her insensitivity. She waited for the rebuke, but Hoop only nodded as if impressed by the idea.

"Maybe she was," he said. "Gonna have to ask my dad. Only pictures I have of her, she's either sitting on a motorcycle or perching on a bar stool. Hard to tell."

Hoop's mom hadn't been around since he was six or

seven, and no one in town knew the whole story. It was the rare topic Hoop didn't discuss openly, but maybe because no one felt comfortable asking.

Chloe and Hoop watched Lissette take her tenth pitch and then whiff her first strike, knowing two more would follow. Poor Lissette still wore her hair in the bowl cut her mom had inflicted in preschool, and her athletic skills seemed equally stunted. But she was a good sport, and on a dismal field in a swampy town, that's all it took to be part of the team.

Hoop nudged Chloe. "So I hear you got eyes on that leprechaun fella, Rory."

Chloe tapped Hoop hard with the tattered glove she'd pulled from his bag earlier. "Rory's nice," she said, blushing, "and he talks awfully cute, but you heard wrong on that one."

"So who is it then? Who you got eyes on?"

Chloe swallowed, barely able to look at the boy she'd had eyes on since second grade. Her smile found the ground. "Can't say."

"Come on, maybe I can make something happen for you," he said with his eternal grin. "That's my specialty, you know. Making things happen."

Chloe may have been lovestruck and shy and awkward, but once in a while, she could get some gumption going. "Doesn't look like you've made much happen between you and Macy."

Hoop waved away her comment as Lissette struck out and Ronnie came up to bat. "That don't mean nothing. She's just not in a place right now where she can fit me in. Lot going on at home." He wiggled around on the base, burning off excess energy and readying his legs for a sprint to third, maybe even a home plate steal. "But our time is coming, believe me." He winked. "It's her birthday real soon."

Crack! Ronnie smacked a solid one that sailed over the outfielders' heads and into the woods.

"See ya, Clover!" Hoop shouted as he took off for third.

"Hope you brought extra balls," she shouted, watching him move rapidly away.

He smiled back as he rounded third. "You know I did!" he shouted. "Hoop Whitaker is always prepared!"

The declaration made his team hoot and whistle as he sailed toward home plate.

It was the last run he'd ever score in Beulah.

Chapter 13

As Chad and I left Mrs. Elbee's house, his cell phone rang. A picture of Sherilyn with last year's orange hair appeared on his screen. "What's the word, Sherilyn?" he said into the phone, but his tone implied that he expected the word to be *dismal* or *dire.*

He listened, his face turning from casual to serious to confused. Without realizing it, he took several steps away from me and began to mumble. By the time he hung up, his head was hanging low.

"What'd she find?" I said, coming around and planting myself firmly in his sights. "It was Hoop's blood in Boyd's basement, wasn't it?"

Chad jerked his head up. "No, sorry. She doesn't know that yet. It's just . . . one of her staff found something weird."

Sure, to Chad, this whole thing could be passed off as weird, maybe even fascinating. He hadn't grown up in this thermos-sized town where good and evil commingled and gelled, sealed up like some Twilight Zone experiment until everyone and everything took on a hue of eccentricity and improbability.

"Tell me," I blurted while he fidgeted.

"She got partial DNA results back from that piece of duct tape."

I fought the sickness growing within me, ready to start a conversation about anything from aardvarks to xylophones in order to avoid hearing the results. A door was about to slam on my past, shaking the flimsy foundation upon which I'd built a tenuous adulthood.

"There are two sets of DNA on the tape."

"So one person put it on another person."

"Maybe." His face changed to one of hope, as if he'd just

found an escape hatch. "Or maybe one person ripped it off another person."

"Okay. So whose DNA was it?"

"One set belonged to my dad." He stepped back, waiting to see if I'd strike. I didn't. I didn't even know whether to feel relieved or confused.

"Your dad? That makes as much sense as Boyd Sexton's DNA at a nunnery."

"I agree."

Relief suddenly dominated my swirling emotions. I paced back and forth on Mrs. Elbee's front walkway. "All right, so if your dad's involved, maybe it's nothing." A frantic smile popped onto my face. "Maybe I blew everything out of proportion. I mean, it was just a piece a tape and a random piece of flannel." I worked hard to convince myself of what I was saying. "Even Boyd must have owned a warm shirt for cool nights. Maybe he tore it up, used it for dusting."

Chad remained silent, no doubt envisioning the same ridiculous scenario I was: creepy Boyd Sexton playing housekeeper and sprucing things up for demanding cannabis clients . . . dusting a metal pole in a dirt-floored room and leaving handcuffs around as a whimsical touch.

"What about the second set of DNA?" I said. "Anything on that?" My voice was losing the battle to keep things light.

"Nothing yet."

I waited. Something in his tone left the sentence hanging. And then he ran his perfect, proportional hands through his perfect tunnel hair—the same motion he performed before breaking up with me.

"There's more, though," he finally said.

My insides shrank to the size of a pebble, nearly doubling me over.

"There were hairs embedded in that strip of flannel. Hairs from a human head. The DNA from those hairs did match the DNA from the blood on the wall, and . . . "

"And what, Chad?"

"There were multiple sets of DNA on the handcuffs."

"Oh, God. Multiple people held down there over the years?"

"Not necessarily," he said. "Two sets belonged to prostitutes who were in the system."

"Are they both still alive?"

"Yes."

I felt relieved, not for the prostitutes, but for the as-yet-unidentified person. "And the third set?"

"The third set matched the hair and the blood."

I drew in a deep breath and winced. "So whoever was wearing the shirt was handcuffed to the pole, and also bled onto the wall."

"It's possible, yes. And all of them matched the second set of DNA from the duct tape."

My eyes remained open, but I saw nothing. My lungs emptied and felt hollow, drained of life.

"Listen, Chloe, it still doesn't mean anything conclusive. We have no idea who the other set of DNA belongs to. You've got to keep it together a little longer."

My voice came out robotically. "Theoretically, someone in that basement, probably wearing a green flannel shirt, had duct tape over his mouth, was cuffed to a pole, and then either bled to death or was tortured. But I should keep it together?"

"No one said anything about death or torture."

"No one had to. The blood is screaming it."

"The quantity of blood on that wall isn't even enough to suggest a serious injury, let alone death."

"How much blood got absorbed into that dirt floor? Or eaten by bugs and rodents? Hey, maybe Boyd used soil from that room to grow his pot. Maybe Hoop Whitaker's blood fertilized every joint smoked in Beulah for the last twelve years." I threw my hands up. "I've partaken a time or two. Think I got high off my friend?"

"For God's sake, Chloe."

I shook my head. "Could Sherilyn tell how old anything was? Was it from twelve years ago?"

"The tape is at least ten years old." He sighed. "Guess it stands to reason the blood would be, too."

At least ten years could sure as heck mean twelve. "So Boyd Sexton and your dad were somehow tied up in Hoop's—"

"Now hold on! No proof of Hoop's presence yet. Maybe Boyd kept a dog down there or something."

I smirked. "Pretty tough to handcuff a dog, last I checked."

"Maybe—"

"You'd better find out what's going on, Chad, and you'd better not cut me out of the loop. I know you're—"

"I won't, but—"

"But what?"

"You can't be jumping to conclusions. I don't need you . . . doing anything rash."

I glared at him, but I understood. Maybe certain rumors had found Chad, after all.

"Because right now," he said, "there's *nothing* tying Boyd or my dad to Hoop Whitaker, and nothing tying Hoop Whitaker to any of this."

"We need a sample of Hoop's DNA."

"It would help, but that won't be easy to find."

"Hoop's dad was in lock-up more than a few times. His DNA would be close enough."

"Nobody takes DNA samples for drunk and disorderly."

I gasped. "What about when Mr. Whitaker was in the hospital after the crash? They must have taken his blood."

Chad frowned. "I'm sure they did but that was over a decade ago. No one would have kept a tube of his blood around."

"It's worth looking into."

"Fair enough." He jotted a note in his little book. "I'll head over there, see what I can find out. But I'm not getting my hopes up."

"You never do, Chad."

Chapter 14

On my way to interview Richie Quail, a vicious caffeine headache clutched my skull. I never had gotten coffee today. My morning stop at Boyd's had always been a perfect, well-oiled, 50-second jaunt. Whenever I entered, Boyd would be stocking shelves. I'd leave a dollar on the counter and give a wave. He'd grunt or nod. That was it. Cordial enough to remain civil, cool enough to reinforce our distaste for one another.

A few minutes later, as an added insult to my throbbing head, I passed Boyd's. Crime scene tape surrounded the scarred remains of the store like a perverse Halloween decoration. Despite the flimsiness of the yellow barrier flitting in the wind, already torn and waggling in one section, a chill shot through me. Had crimes other than drug-related ones been committed in the bowels of that establishment?

A forensics team, basically two guys with gloves, bags, and cameras had violated the barrier with authority and were marching toward the building. Meanwhile, an unmarked car of an uppity sort sat perpendicular to theirs. It served as the leaning post for a dark-suited, trim guy in sunglasses. Couldn't the FBI at least switch up the look a little bit? Wouldn't surprise me to see J. Edgar Hoover saunter into view any moment.

I veered right and reluctantly steered my car over the bridge toward New Beulah, which had sprung up after The Lucky Four put Beulah on the map. The publicity after the big win had outed tiny Beulah as a business and tourist-friendly *destination* with good weather, great taxes, and an up-and-comer vibe. I turned right off of the bridge, my car juddering like a jackhammer because public officials had chosen cobblestone for New Beulah's busiest roads, claiming it complemented the cutesy shops that always made my stomach turn. The proprietors of the establishments struck me as phony come-heres who would use the town up before abandoning it like a spent hooker, desperate and worse for wear. The bars served cocktails called Angostura Alligator, Swamp Sucker Punch, and Pluff Mud-Slides, while the pubs concocted vegetarian versions of turtle and alligator soup. The *boutique* shops conducted most of their business on-line, yet managed to get written up as adorable whimsies that thrived on curious visitors and loyal locals.

I pulled up to Grinder Minder Coffee Shoppe, *built with reclaimed wood and recycled cork.* They charged oodles of first-world dollars for third-world coffee beans and tried a little too hard to be Charleston in Beulah.

I stepped out of my car and caught my reflection in a window. Not good. I looked too thin, with frown lines that ran too deep for a 26-year-old, and I'd forgotten make-up altogether. With a tired sigh, I headed down the sidewalk only to look up and see Rafe Borose-rhymes-with-morose approaching from the opposite direction. He'd already smiled at me, so I threw my shoulders back and marched on, determined to pretend I looked better than I did.

He grabbed the oversized pewter handle and held the door for me while simultaneously producing a yellow rose from his left palm. He presented it with a confident grin and I accepted with a smile. Sure, it was plastic, but a rose was a rose, and no one had given me flowers for a long time. Not knowing what else to do, I gave it a sniff but only caught whiffs of an essential oil—either patchouli or sandalwood—and realized I was probably smelling his cologne. It mingled with his natural scent, something reeking of confidence and danger.

"A rose for my neighbor who rescues the mournful," he said.

My reporter hackles went up. "Mournful? What makes you think Mrs. Elbee was mournful?"

"A woman who takes her own life surely mourns it before committing the final act."

I thought back to Macy's name on the mirror. "I'm afraid Mrs. Elbee might have been mourning more than herself."

"Herself, others, decisions. Life offers much to mourn."

"That's a dour outlook," I said. "I like it."

"I hope you won't embrace it." A look of warning flashed across his face. "Better to look forward brightly than to focus on the past through a dark lens."

My gut constricted. The comment hit unusually close to home. "Thank you for the rose. Do you give them to all the ladies?"

I hadn't intended the jealousy that tinged my comment, but I did feel oddly possessive of this new stranger, as if he were a plaything that existed solely to amuse me. Even when we met in the swamp, I'd felt a trace of resentment over Mrs. Elbee's intrusion.

"I give roses to ladies I admire," he said. "And I'm a big fan of your writing. You mingle hard-hitting facts with hard-won insights, and then sprinkle your stories with unexpected humanity."

"Unexpected?"

"Oh yes. From you, it can be rather unexpected." He grinned in such a way that I felt we'd shared an inside joke, but I was still stuck on the outside. "I don't know your plans for your morning libation," he continued, "but would you care to join me at one of the distressed tobaccowood tables in this pretentious establishment?"

His hypnotic gaze, coupled with the grin dancing on his lips, made me regret my answer. "I'd love to, but I've got an appointment."

"I understand," he said, as if he'd expected the refusal.

We ordered from Grinder Minder's thirty-item menu, which essentially broke down to coffee, coffee with milk, and coffee with flavorings. He insisted on paying, and I squelched an unexpected bolt of jealousy when the petite cashier flirted with him.

As we waited for our order, Rafe gazed at me unabashedly. "I've never seen you here before. Are you trying it out because of the fire at Boyd's?"

"Yes. You know all the sordid details?"

He leaned in confidentially. "Wouldn't surprise me if half the folks in New Beulah were customers of Boyd's basement business."

The mention of the basement made me stiffen, but I remained mute.

"I was there a few times," he said, and then clarified. "To the legitimate part of the store, I mean. Boyd carried great licorice but always struck me as an odd choice to run a neighborhood establishment."

"His dad died years ago and left it to him. I doubt it would have been his first career choice."

"Oh? What would have been?"

"Does it matter?" I said, bitterness lacing my tongue. "All his choices were bound to lead to *felon*."

Rafe flicked up his eyebrows. "Something personal between you and this Boyd fellow?"

"That's what I aim to find out. There was more to that basement than you know."

Rafe's rather expressive brows knitted together. "A reporter on a mission. How very Lois Lane."

"Well, as Lois would tell you, people don't just disappear without a trace." I regretted the comment the moment it exited my mouth, but something about this guy flustered me.

Rafe crossed his arms and cocked his head like a curious dog. "I'm not sure I follow. Did someone disappear?"

"I'm sorry. It's nothing."

A freckled boy with a half-inch ear gauge announced our order. As we grabbed our respective cups, I noticed a bandage on Rafe's forearm.

He saw me notice and smiled devilishly. "Dropped a mirror on a tile floor," he said. "And may I say it was none too pleasant having a hundred images of my own face staring back at me, all of them declaring me a klutz."

"Bad luck for seven years."

His inky gaze grew intense. "Broken mirrors or no, I believe we create our own luck."

"Really? Tell me how. I could use some today."

"Chloe, I would very much like to know more about what goes on in your world."

I plucked my cell phone from my pocket and checked the time. Fifteen minutes to get back over the bridge to Quail's office. "More than I have time to say, I'm afraid. But thanks for the coffee. I'm going to be late for an interview."

"With anyone interesting?"

"Richie Quail, one of the Lucky Four."

"Oh, I know Mr. Quail. We run in the same investment circles."

"Then you should probably watch your back." My eyes narrowed. "What is it you do for a living, Rafe?"

He smiled and sipped his beverage before answering. "I research, invest, invent, scavenge, and program. And, of course, I dabble in magic and rose distribution."

I twirled my yellow flower by way of acknowledgment. "And which of your many pursuits provides you a livelihood?"

"Is this on the record?"

"Is there a reason to keep it off the record?"

"Why don't I show you?"

"Show me what?"

"What I do. Tonight. Over a glass of pinot grigio. Six

o'clock?"

I had absolutely no time for a quasi-date tonight, and yet I knew my answer immediately. "Six thirty," I said. "But I'm more of a pinot noir girl. I'll bring it."

"Perfect," he said, and then he lowered his head but kept his eyes lifted. "You know where I live."

I flushed with embarrassment but gave as good as I got. "Yes, I do. One Porro-prism length away."

He beamed with delight.

"I've really got to go," I said, my frown lines reaching their usual depth as reality invaded the espresso-scented fantasy world of Grinder Minder. I turned to leave, but Rafe called after me, his warm voice encompassing every note of the octave. "If you don't mind my asking, Chloe, I'm dying of curiosity. Who disappeared?"

I stopped with my hand on the open door and turned back to him with a melancholy air. "Someone I wish I could stop looking at through a dark lens."

Chapter 15

Despite ownership of a dozen apartment buildings along the east coast, two high-rises in the Carolinas, fourteen Creamy Cow franchises, and three homes, Richie Quail still maintained his original office in the middle of Beulah's tiny industrial park—if a tile store, a drafting consultant, and a vague importer/exporter could pass as an industrial park. At least Quail seemed better tolerated in Beulah these days, perhaps because everyone had gotten used to his gregarious manner, his money-flaunting ways, and his lack of humility. Or maybe people were just kissing his ass.

About once a week, I'd see him promenading through town, usually running his mouth. And every time, his girth floored me. A swirl of nasty thoughts always crossed my mind: *Was he the best choice to be representing a high-fat ice cream franchise? When was the last time he'd seen the $800 loafers on his feet? And how in the world did he maintain his Top Five ranking at the tennis club?*

As I entered his office, a bell tried to ring out. No go. I glanced up to see its cracked shell, a crooked clapper, and an interior caked with dirt. Turned out, it was a proper precursor to the office. Coffee stains dotted a puke-green rug, brown blemishes marked the faded paint on the walls, and the receptionist's desk looked like a decades-old factory reject. The place also carried a mild scent of urine—I did *not* want to know.

In front of me, a full-bottomed, shapely woman stuck a leg into the air behind her as she leaned into the main office. She could definitely do justice to a mud flap. "Uh huh, uh huh, got it," she said as her foot waggled. Presumably, she was speaking to Quail. His voice bellowed back at her, something about a *Mr. Haverhill,* and *if Mr. Haverhill says it's so, then it must be so.* As he continued speaking, I gathered that Mr. Haverhill had made Quail some big bucks over the years. I wondered how many of those bucks had seen the underside of a table.

The secretary had now moved her ample backside all the way into Quail's office. She let loose with another round of agreeable *uh-huh's* before saying, "But ten million, Richie?"

"Ten million, yes, ma'am!" Quail said with a loud *thwack*, presumably a fist slamming a desk.

I considered myself a gifted eavesdropper, but my skills found no challenge here; these two were downright loud. I hoped Quail would specify ten million of *what*. Despite his alleged wealth, I could hardly imagine ten million *dollars* being bantered about in an office as shabby as this. I'd seen better while getting my oil changed.

"Awful lot of eggs in one basket," the secretary said.

"Do I pay you to make omelets, Sarah, or to look good and move my money around when I tell you to?"

Sarah sighed but with a giggle behind it. "I just don't feel like we've done our due diligence on this one."

"He hasn't steered us wrong yet. Now git."

Sarah sashayed into the waiting area and looked startled to see me. "Oh, hello. Didn't hear you come in."

"I'm Chloe Keyes from The Herald. I have an—"

"The lottery interview, right? People never do tire of that story." Despite Quail's office being only a few feet away, she turned and yelled as if he were across a football field. "Richie! Chloe from The Herald is here!"

I expected to be told to wait on one of the lumpy couches, but Quail appeared at the door instantly. Maybe that was how he kept his tennis ranking—quick on his feet. I worked to banish the surprise from my eyes as the forty-something man filled the entire door frame. He'd easily gained a hundred pounds in the last ten years. Still, I couldn't deny that his face looked good. Either the subcutaneous fat or an absence of stress made him glow. His smile caused the only wrinkles in his smooth complexion, and it provided a glimpse of crooked but shiny teeth. His plain brown eyes held decided warmth, and I wondered if I'd misjudged Richie Quail all these years, or if people simply became nicer when their bank accounts and stomachs were equally full.

"Chloe Keyes," he said as if we were old friends. "How are you?"

He didn't venture beyond the door frame, and it crossed my mind that he might be stuck in there. "I'm fine, sir, thank you."

"I knew your parents. Your dad was the butcher, right? Funny guy?"

"Yes, sir."

"And your mom was an accountant."

"Still is, but they're in Florida now."

"Florida? No thank you. Can't imagine leaving Beulah. We've got it all here."

Well, *he* had it all. Owned it all, in fact, although I'd heard rumblings of trouble from Larry Gentry, the Herald's business beat reporter. Larry did analytical freelance work for financial publications on the side, so his tentacles extended internationally. Told me that Quail was overleveraged and might well be living in a house of straw on a cotton candy foundation. Some of his investments had gone belly-up when the partners in his real estate trust had exhibited none of that quality. But the pending ten million dollar deal being bantered about the office belied that tale. Perhaps the mysterious Mr. Haverhill had saved the day.

"Sorry about this place," he said, waving a thick arm around. "Got nice digs all over the country, but here's where I get real work done."

"I understand. I work best in my cramped kitchen."

At his behest, I entered his tiny office. Accolades and awards decorated the walls—along with photos of him accepting those accolades and awards. One high-def image showed him in front of a building, plunging open-mouthed scissors toward a red ribbon that seemed to be attempting an escape. Standard photo for Grand Openings, but the ravenous look on Quail's face as his thick tongue licked his lips gave the image a grotesque sheen. I jerked my eyes away.

Quail walked around to his desk chair. It looked to be made of fibrous cobwebs and two hundred adjustment knobs. But when he sat down, it neither squealed nor dropped him on his ass. Perhaps that's what had sucked up the office decorating budget.

I made myself comfortable in a brown leather chair that exhaled as if I were the one north of four hundred pounds.

"You live in that stilt house, don't you?" he said.

"Yes, sir. Where river meets swamp."

"*Where river meets swamp!* Now that's a good tag line. Gonna have to put that on the brochure."

"What brochure?"

"I'm buying up some acreage over there to develop. You like living there, do ya?"

Develop? The word might have good connotations, but in Quail's lexicon, development meant destruction, delay, decay and *de uglies*. I'd lose trees, privacy, and salvation.

"I wouldn't recommend it," I said. "Lots of problems, unless you like unpredictable water levels, endless mud, mosquitoes galore, and if I'm not mistaken"—I knew I was—"the government is planning to take control of the water access. Going to make it illegal to put in docks and whatnot, so there goes your sales angle."

I looked straight at him. Damn! My lamentations paled in comparison to the greedy glint I saw in his eyes.

He leaned back and chortled. "Sounds like someone don't

want no neighbors encroaching upon her."

I shrugged, keeping up the façade. "Just wouldn't want to see an investment of yours go south, Mr. Quail."

A crack showed in his jolly armor. "Tell me more about this retrospective doodad you're writing."

"It's about the week of the lottery win, sir. I'm interviewing the Lucky Four—"

"Not Grace Elbee, I imagine. What a shocker, eh?"

"Terrible," I said, leaning forward and lowering my voice. "I'm the one who found the body, believe it or not."

I'd found in my short career that confiding something early on made subjects more likely to return the favor.

Quail's interest was piqued. "Now that would make sense, given where you and Grace live in relation to one another." He leaned forward but didn't get as far as I had. "What do they think happened exactly?"

"No official word yet, but I wouldn't be surprised if it was suicide."

"Now that's a damn shame. Gotta be said, though, Grace was getting a little . . . eccentric lately. And mighty spiritual on top of that."

I recalled the word I used when writing my post-interview notes with Mrs. Elbee. "I'd say mystical, putting faith in the idea of an alternative afterlife."

"No desire for an afterlife myself. Having too good a time in this one." A quick hammy fist slammed the desk in celebration. "Still, I had no idea the woman was so low. I built her house, you know."

I pulled out my notebook and then laid my phone on his desk, the recorder app switched on.

"Tried to tell her and George not to build on that lot," he continued. "Too much shrink-and-swell, too much settling yet to come, but George wanted that view and that water access so he could race around on those ridiculous cigarette boats. Me, I prefer an oar and a slow ride in the shallow water." He winked as he rubbed his stomach. "Not as buoyant as I look!"

"You were right about the Elbees' house, sir. Didn't they end up having some problems?"

"Did they ever! I tried to address each hitch, but I tell you, between Grace getting loopy and George not knowing how to manage much more than a bottle opener, it turned into a years-long nightmare. They even sued me." He said it with a surprising lack of rancor. Maybe because he'd won.

"I guess you didn't remain close to Mrs. Elbee after that?"

"Not true. She came to see me less than a week ago."

"Really? About what?"

He sighed. "I shouldn't say, and keep this off the record, but believe it or not, she wanted to borrow some money."

Wow. I'd have thought Mrs. Elbee would bow down to the devil before begging from Richie Quail, though some would argue six of one, half a dozen of the other. "Did you two strike a deal?"

"Told her I'd work something up, with generous terms, of course. I mean, what the heck. The lottery bonded us for life, right?"

The sheriff might beg to differ. "I hate to say it, but the police will want to know about your meeting with her."

"They already do. Indirectly, at least. The day Grace came by, Chad Ryker was here dropping off Sarah after lunch."

A twinge tweaked my gut. "Your assistant is dating Chad?"

"Little bit, I suppose. You know Chad? What am I saying? A girl your age, of course you would. Good-looking fella, am I right?"

I gave a polite smile.

"Anyway, Chad and Grace would have run into each other in the waiting area. Of course, Chad probably wasn't real eager to stick around and hear what Grace's candlestick had to say!" Quail laughed hard enough to turn his forehead crimson. "And don't think that candlestick didn't give me second thoughts about lending her money. I mean, what if it told her to burn the money, am I right?"

I transitioned to my basic questions about how the lottery changed his life. I let him go on about investments, job creation, and *respectable housing at reasonable prices*. He peppered it with ample mention of his charitable giving. I nodded and let it all pour into my recorder. When he wound down, I changed the topic to *The Week's* lowlights.

"You have close ties to the tragedies that occurred that week."

"I do?" He doubled down on his chins and crossed his arms so that they rested atop his belly. "How do you figure?"

I counted off his tragedy links on my fingers while answering. "You owned the complex where both the LeGranges and the Whitakers lived. Macy LeGrange was the girl killed on her bike. Mr. Whitaker hit her, and Hoop Whitaker disappeared."

"Guess I never thought of me being tied to it that way, but you're right. You know, I came up through school with Melanie LeGrange. And that Avis Whitaker—smart as a whip when he wanted to be, and hands-down hilarious when drunk. Came up with some hoot-worthy excuses for being short on rent, I tell ya."

"Did you collect the rents yourself back then? Before the lottery?"

"Who else was going to do it? Let me tell you something, darling. People loved to paint me as the evil landlord, but if I didn't collect rent, how could I keep the buildings up to code?"

"Did you?"

"Never failed an inspection. But try explaining that to people. They throw down a few ratty couches and think they're entitled for life. But Richie Quail don't run no squatter operation. Heck, there was a time or two I forced my way into people's units and removed belongings myself. I'd put their stuff in storage and use it as leverage until I got my money."

"Interesting tactic. Did it work?"

"Every time."

"Did you know Hoop Whitaker?"

Quail scrunched up his thick, red lips, a droplet of spit hanging from the lower one. He leaned back. "It was a long time ago, but I think I did. Little wheeler-dealer, that one, which I actually admired. Skinny, wise-acre kid, right? Kind of scruffy?"

I couldn't decide whether to smile or cry. Hoop wore the swamp like a badge of honor. If he finished the day covered in mud, bugs, and swamp stink, he considered it a boastworthy accomplishment. Wouldn't have thought himself scruffy for a second.

"That was him," I said.

"Everything kind of blurred together back then with the excitement of the win, but I guess it was all the same week, wasn't it?"

I decided to push, reminding myself never to play this tape for the sheriff and Chad, as I might be dangerously close to defying their trust. "You bought the winning ticket at Boyd's General Store, right?"

"Yep. Boyd Junior sold it to us. Shame about the fire this morning."

"Yes, it was. How well do you know Boyd Junior?"

"Not too well. Knew his dad, of course, but Junior keeps to himself. Can't say as I see him out in town much, with a pretty girl on his arm or anything."

"Were you aware of any relationship between Boyd Junior and Hoop Whitaker?"

"Relationship?" Quail looked confused, but then smiled

knowingly. "You mean like drug-dealing? Because I heard tell of what they found in Boyd's basement."

"No, I don't think Hoop used drugs." I made sure Quail was looking me right in the eye. "But you mentioned how you never see Boyd with a girl on his arm."

It took a moment, but Quail's lips curled in disgust. "Now hold on a second. I don't like where this is going. Thought you were here to talk about the lottery."

"The article covers the whole week, and now tragedy has struck two of the people involved in that week: the ticket seller and one of the winners. Just as tragedy struck back then. I'm curious about your insights, as landlord or otherwise."

He glanced at the recorder, and either paranoia or confusion flashed in his eyes. The shine dulled from his skin. "That best not be the angle you plan to play up in your article, young lady, making me look like a greedy ogre while others were suffering."

I planted both feet firmly on the floor and leaned forward. "May I ask you a controversial question, Mr. Quail?"

Skepticism jerked on and off his face. He hesitated, but then leaned his beefy arms on the desk and forced an air of joviality. "You don't ask questions, you don't get answers. Shoot."

"It's said that you evicted Melanie LeGrange, your former classmate, shortly after Macy's death. Do you have any explanation for that?"

Quail remained frozen, his seersucker jacket straining as it puckered at the shoulders like the wrinkled mouth of an old man. Then he inhaled with ferocity, as if surfacing from a near-drowning, and pounded his fist again. "I'm glad you asked that! About time I straightened out that misinformation."

I held my tongue and waited. I was good at waiting.

"Like I said, I knew Melanie and that no-good husband of

hers, Darrell." Quail screwed up his face as he said the name; if he could have spit on it, he surely would have. "And I did go to her place a couple weeks after her daughter died. I was newly rich and she was newly alone. But if you were to investigate, which is part of your job, you'd find that I certainly did *not* kick her out of her place. Quite the opposite. We talked for a good long while, and in the end, let's just say she had the means to move on from the town that had buried her daughter and seen her husband leave her for some hussy." He threw up his hands in disgust. "I mean, how was she supposed to stay in a town that allowed Avis Whitaker to stay on the road after multiple driving offenses? I think it's fair to say she wasn't going to find happiness here, not with reminders around every corner."

"And yet, you said *you'd* never leave."

Quail's round nostrils flared into disquieted ovals. "Beulah has both its charms and foibles, Ms. Keyes. Just as every couple isn't meant to be together, neither is every person and place."

"So you gave Mrs. LeGrange money to start over someplace else?"

"I ain't saying nothing, and I sure ain't saying nothing on the record. But you infer what you want."

How had Quail just become the good guy in this scenario? I stared at him in unabashed awe. It was like seeing him through a funhouse mirror—or perhaps seeing his true colors for the first time. What had I built my beliefs on anyway? Childhood rumors? Prejudices against his appearance? I'd bought into the worn stereotype of the evil landlord from those who'd failed to live up to their end of the contractual bargain. I felt duped. I just wasn't sure by whom.

He smirked and nodded. "Not what you were expecting, eh, darlin'?

"I delve into my stories with no preconceived notions,

93

Mr. Quail."

"You'll forgive me if I call B.S. on that one. Because everyone in town has notions in their head about ol' Richie Quail here." He worked his lips around his face and finally settled on a confidential pout. "You want the real skinny on me, young lady—no pun intended?"

I nodded.

"I'm all business, all the time. Life ain't nothing but one big deal, and in every deal, someone comes out on top. Why shouldn't it be me?"

Cold and straightforward. Couldn't say I didn't like it.

"You ever heard of a coral snake?" he said.

I recited the childhood rhyme that distinguished harmless snakes from those that would send a person into paralytic shock followed by death. "Red next to black is a friend of Jack; red next to yellow will kill a fellow."

"That's right. Your mama taught you well. But people up north," he said with a wink, "they don't learn such things. My first day showing an apartment, I was barely twenty-one. Had this weasel from Connecticut giving me a hard time. So we walk into the bedroom and he opens the closet door and BAM! Staring back at him was a big ol' thick-as-your-arm snake. Yellow, red and black stripes, five-footer at least. Scared the bejeezus out of him! I swear he wet his pants. So I went over, grabbed that snake by the tail, and let it do its little dance for a while, you know, upside-down, wriggling like a ribbon in a storm. Then I marched over, popped open a window, and dropped the little fella outside. Everybody happy. And you know what?"

I couldn't imagine. I was still stuck on the image of a prospective tenant standing in urine-soaked pants. "What?" I managed to say.

"He signed the lease that day. Said he liked how I handled myself and wanted a landlord who took care of things head-on."

"Why weren't you scared of the snake?"

He pushed his chair back and laughed. "Wasn't nothing but a harmless ol' milk snake, red next to black! Couldn't have hurt me if it wanted to. But I didn't tell him that." A guileful smile crossed Quail's face. "Know what else I didn't tell him?"

I shook my head.

"That I'd put that snake in there not ten minutes earlier so I could play the hero. Heck, I'd raised that snake up since it was no bigger 'n my finger. Fed it bugs, crickets, and the occasional frog. Freddy, I called him. Closed quite a few deals together, me and Freddy." He pointed a thick finger at me and punctuated the air with it several times. "And *that*, li'l darlin', is how you do business."

Quail had himself another hearty laugh, even pulling out a picture of a thinner version of himself holding young Freddy. I didn't know whether to be impressed or horrified, but as I appreciated how quickly Quail's own stripes could change, the picture of the snake in front of me set off an urgent thought in my head.

"Mr. Quail, you mentioned putting tenants' items in storage."

"Not official storage, but sure. Never cost me nothing."

"How'd you pull that off?"

"Early in my career, I bought a historic property over in Flinton. I'd planned to fix it up and turn it into a B&B, but later inspections revealed it to be unsound. I sued the seller and lost." He leaned forward again and winked. "I've upgraded lawyers since then." Then he sat back in his chair, not overly distraught about his bad investment. "Would've cost me a bundle to get the place in shape, and with the inspection on the record, I'd've lost money selling it. But I found plenty of uses for it over the years."

I admonished myself for daring to hope. "What about the

Whitakers' stuff, sir? What would have happened to their things after Avis Whitaker died?"

"What would have happened," he said. "I sure don't know."

My optimism deflated. Something of Hoop's—something containing a trace of his DNA—would be the only way to link him to the grisly evidence in Boyd's basement. Or better yet, to *not* link him.

Quail then lit up with a duplicitous sparkle. "But what *did* happen, I know exactly. Their stuff's in the attic of that house. Been meaning to clean it out for years."

My breath caught as hope shot through me. It ignited a pain in my head but a warmth in my heart. A link to Hoop, after all this time. One that might finally reveal his fate.

Chapter 16

Twenty minutes after leaving Quail's office, I turned off a somewhat busy road in Flinton and wound back to the three-story Victorian that he'd left to rot. It resembled a gingerbread house from which someone had taken a few bites. It sat at the rear of a 1500-acre farm, half of which had been subdivided into lots now hosting cookie-cutter homes with identical trees, mailboxes, and fences. The house had once belonged to the matriarch of a family that made its money in tobacco. Her great-grandchildren, far removed from any sentimental attachment to the place, had sold it to a young, naïve Richie Quail.

Quail told me there might be workmen lurking about doing some repair work, but from the looks of it, only one workman was needed: a wrecking ball operator. While the house's core surely held promise, the exterior, and presumably the interior, had been left to the mercy of the elements for quite some time.

The steeply pitched, uneven roof lines gave it a severe appearance, though the porches on the lower level softened that impression. The former green and pink exterior paint had faded to foggy reminiscences of their original shades, while the coned roof of the tower had begun to sink on one side, as if tipping its hat to visitors. But I didn't feel welcomed. Instead, I sensed the cold glare of a discerning eye beneath the hat rim, determining my worthiness to enter and likely deeming me unfit.

Shaking off the feeling, I followed the long, looping driveway around to the rear. The pretty stone pavers that marked the first half gave way to a muddy path that ate my tires. As my tread got a grip, I glanced at the note Quail had scribbled for me: *Back door, yellow, 31-8-17-20-5.* The five digits represented the combination to a padlock that would grant me access to the Whitakers' things.

I made the final turn to the back of the house . . . and nearly hit Chad's Blazer. Worse yet, Chad was still in the driver's seat, talking on his cell. When he glanced over and spotted my Subaru, his jaw stopped moving, and then his head tilted as he shoved the phone back in his pocket. I parked nose to nose with him before we both exited our cars and met at my front bumper.

"Remind me, Chloe. Who's the deputy sheriff and who's the reporter?"

I smiled apologetically but in truth, I hadn't wanted to share Hoop's belongings with anyone else. At least not yet. "Richie Quail just told me about this place," I said. "How'd you find it?"

"Not from you calling me."

"Sorry."

"Nurse at the hospital used to work for Quail," he explained. "She mentioned it, so I called Quail's office and got the details." From hot little Sarah, no doubt. "Figured there might be something inside with Hoop's DNA."

"Any luck at the hospital with Avis Whitaker's DNA?"

"No, but they'll be sending his old medical records to the station once they dig them up. You never know."

I glanced at the back door. It may once have been yellow, but now it looked more like a white door someone had peed on. Moisture—hopefully not urine—had taken a toll on its flushness with the frame, thus the need for a padlock. Seemed like the entire house was nothing but a flimsy layer trying vainly to shield its contents from critters, rain, and humidity.

"Be amazing if anything inside is intact," I said.

"DNA's like a good postman," Chad said. "Neither dust nor heat nor termites nor moths . . ." The sentence faded. "Well, maybe termites."

As he worked the rusty wheel mechanism on the cheap lock, I wondered why Quail had saved the Whitakers' belongings at all. Had he thought *the scruffy kid* would return to mourn his father or to claim his junk? Neither had happened. The sad truth was that hardly anyone had shown up to grieve for Avis Whitaker. My parents and I made up most of the crowd, alongside Strike and Jacqueline Ryker. Difficult for most folks to well up sympathy for a drunk driver guilty of vehicular manslaughter, but we'd attended for Hoop's sake.

Chad yanked the lock open. The snapping sound made me start. Why had I never thought to search for Hoop's things before? Discovered earlier, they might have hinted at his fate or provided a clue as to his whereabouts. Instead, I'd wasted time mourning him, contenting myself with the few treasures I did possess: an orange-checkered snakeskin he'd given me, now crumbled into grey powder in a shoebox somewhere; an alligator tooth necklace he'd sold to every girl in the class; and, an essay he'd written about his future. The latter was my most treasured.

Three weeks before his disappearance, our English teacher, Miss Farlow, had stapled his *My Future* essay to the cork board in the hallway. In red ink, she'd written, "So imaginative!" After *The Week*, I'd forced myself through the minimal motions of life, but one day while staying late at school, the empty halls had beckoned and drawn me down the halls toward the English classroom. My chawed fingernails dug behind the staples and peeled Hoop's essay from its cork backing. His words and dreams didn't belong to the school, and certainly not to the students and staff who breezed past them every day without due amazement. No! Hoop's future belonged with someone who would both revere it and lament its loss. It belonged with me.

I'd secreted all three pages of the essay away in my

backpack, stashing the staples in my pocket. Those staples had poked and scratched me all the way home, but I didn't adjust them; instead, I welcomed the pain. I deserved it for letting him disappear. In one fell swoop, he'd lost his father and his favorite girl when the two collided like sin and purity, in the most cataclysmic way possible. It annihilated his world. What kind of night must he have spent? Had he been at home? On the banks of the swamp? Had he run, blind from tears, and drowned in treacherous waters—or had he been kidnapped and handcuffed by Boyd Sexton, Jr., overpowered by a lesser being while at his lowest point?

At home, I'd flattened the wrinkled essay and tucked it into a drawer beneath my pajamas. I'd left the staples in my pocket for days, until my leg bled through. It wasn't the last time I'd bled for him.

Now, staring at the dilapidated house that held whatever remained of him, I realized the pain had never really stopped.

I reached in front of Chad and pushed the door open.

Chapter 17

Wisps of sunlight cut through the unshaded portions of the multi-paned windows in the front of the house. Dense, twirling dust danced in the shafts of radiance, giving the dank place an illusion of life. But the stale odor of deterioration made it clear that the structure was but a sarcophagus for forgotten projects and displaced objects.

We'd entered into some version of a family room. Two sprawling tables that would normally be found in a kitchen occupied most of the floor. They were covered in blueprints, sketch books, stacks of files, and random office supplies, as if Quail had actually done some work here—or plotted his next money-making scheme. But even from a distance, I could see that the files hadn't been touched in years, and the paper clips had probably rusted into permanent closure.

"What a waste," I said to Chad. "With the high ceilings and huge rooms, this place could be gorgeous."

Chad took a step and the floor sank beneath his weight. "Christ," he said, "I feel like I'm in the swamp."

A drip of water fell on my head. I stepped aside and gazed up at a bowing-ball-sized hole in the ceiling. Water was actually falling from the ceiling of the floor *above* that one. Didn't seem promising for the contents of the attic.

Chad and I made our way to the front of the house and up a flight of warped stairs. Immediately to our left was the door to the tower. To our right was a long hallway with eight doors, including one in the ceiling that provided attic access. Neither of us was pleased to discover the ancient pull-down ladder that did everything in its power to discourage us from entering the attic. Chad finally got it to a point where we could hoist ourselves up, but the rickety structure seemed more suited to a dollhouse. No way Quail had ever climbed up here.

With a few additional struggles, we entered the attic, not entirely certain we'd make it back down. I glanced around. Some poor schlep had indeed been tasked with lugging a lot of junk up here. Some of the items were large—chairs and mattresses—and roof leaks had decimated them, but the miracle of plastic offered hope for the bins stacked against the wall in back. Someone—a person more thoughtful than my fourteen-year-old self—had actually stored the Whitakers' possessions in sealed, labeled containers. Had that someone yet given up hope, as years mounted to a decade and the black ink of the labels faded to gray?

I reached toward the first bin cautiously, like a kid in a poisonous candy shop.

"Hey," Chad said, nudging my arm, "you've got to wear these." He held out plastic gloves. "If it turns out there *were* nefarious goings-on in Boyd's basement, this stuff might become evidence."

I resented the forced layer of sterility but understood its necessity. Chad slapped the gloves into my hand and I slid them on, but the idea of Hoop's personal items becoming evidence made me squirm. While I wanted justice, I hardly wanted his life on display for a jury to ogle or some reporter to romanticize. Already, the grief-filled territory I'd carved out in my heart felt trampled upon by outsiders.

"You know what to look for," Chad said. "A hair, particularly with the shaft and root, or maybe a trace of blood. Personal items, like a toothbrush or a fingernail clipping. Anything that might contain DNA."

"How come you didn't send a forensics team to do this?"

"We're overwhelmed. Sherilyn can't rule Mrs. Elbee's death a suicide yet, so they're turning her place over, and we've got the FBI and DEA down from D.C. looking into Boyd's mess. Would you believe he had a false wall on the east side of that basement? He was running a pretty big operation.

Little more to Boyd than any of us gave him credit for."

I snorted my disgust. "Guess he kept the store as a front."

"Maybe. They had him under surveillance for a while."

"If the Feds knew about his operation, why didn't they act?"

Chad shrugged. "Maybe they were hoping to lure in a bigger fish. They won't say much."

"Did they at least *surveil* whoever started the fire?"

"Apparently not. More of a remote, on-and-off surveillance."

"What tipped them off in the first place? High electricity bill?"

"No. Anonymous tip a few months ago."

"When it rains in Beulah, it sure as heck pours, huh? Did these Feds know anything about Boyd keeping people captive in his basement?"

"No," Chad said. "And believe me, I asked. But we'll figure it out. I've got my best investigator on it."

"Who?"

He smiled. "You."

With that, we dug in. My first bin contained Hoop's clothes. No green flannel amongst the piles, but I was knocked out by a whiff of the cheap deodorant Hoop used to wear. It never did stand a chance against his energy, but here it was, twelve years later and still going—unlike its wearer. I checked the clothes for blood but came up short. Just in case, I bagged a pair of dirty socks.

The next bin contained a wooden train set, painted by a child's rough hand. The globs of red and black on several cars contrasted with the jagged strokes of green and yellow on others. Orange dots boldly mixed themselves with purple swirls and uneven diamond shapes, letting the painter's passion shine through. I knew exactly which train Hoop had been trying to paint, though it looked like he'd been subconsciously influenced by a pack of Animal Crackers.

Chad looked over my shoulder and caught me playing with the giraffe car. "Barnum and Bailey?" he asked.

I whipped around, feeling sad for my ex. "You don't know, do you?"

"I didn't have the most well-rounded childhood, Chloe, but I know what a circus is."

"You didn't know *our* circus."

He leaned back on an end table and gestured for me to enlighten him.

I held up the train engine and pointed to the red and black *FG* painted on the side. "The Forenza-Galasso Circus," I announced. While setting up the cars one by one, I related the best part of Beulah's history, a part that had nothing to do with illicit drug schemes, missing children, or manslaughter. "We didn't have much to brag about here in mosquito-infested Beulah, but we did have something most kids would have given their left arms for: the Forenza-Galasso Circus. It was huge in the southwest but very secretive in its recruitment, its schedule, everything. Every year, on the third Sunday in May, it premiered in Beulah for its trial run, sneaking into town under cover of darkness on those old train tracks."

"The abandoned ones? Thought the money ran out in 1910 and those tracks never got finished."

"True. Nothing but two wavy strips of rust, but the Forenza-Galasso train would detour off the main line to test their wares here in Beulah. Probably illegal, but the carnies always carried this air of skirting the law. They were like this crazy band of gypsies. And when the show was over, they'd back that train out to the main line and go on their way. Finished up their season in Texas or something."

"Pretty big deal, I imagine."

"When the old red-and-black squealed into Beulah, it

was like a breath of life inflating a long, flat hose. Acrobatic acts, crazy contortionists, eye-assaulting freaks, and, of course"—I pretended to be speaking through a megaphone— *"feats of daredevilry never before performed in front of a live audience."*

I smiled like I had when I was a kid and it seemed to surprise Chad.

"They were on their way to bigger, better venues," I continued, "but they wouldn't dare perform in front of a live audience without testing everything here, away from critical eyes and bad press—or people who expected more. We were their sounding board, and our applause or silence refined them into something better." I swung a toy trapeze that hung from a tall train car. "For an hour and a half every May, our mouths hung open and our fingers turned white as we clutched our seats because the Galassos and Forenzas . . . they were downright certifiable."

"Carnies often are."

"But I tell you, when they descended on Beulah, you could stick a finger in the air and get shocked by the tingle. We'd all sit on that half-built train platform for hours, and when we felt the first vibration of the track, we'd all jump around and wouldn't settle down until the show was over."

"How come they stopped coming?"

My mood plummeted from elation to ice-cold anger. Silently, I recalled my final memory surrounding that wretched train platform, and I found myself glaring at Chad. "They never showed . . . after."

"After . . . *the week*?"

I averted my eyes. "Yeah."

"Guess all I've ever known is post-lottery Beulah."

I glanced at the green and orange caboose in my hand. "Hoop always planned to join them."

Chad snorted. "Doing what?"

"Snake charming. Determined to impress people with the first Hoop Snake ever found. That's how he got his nickname."

"But those snakes aren't real. They're an embellishment of mud snakes."

"Hoop believed in them."

Chad stared at me with concern, shaking his head slightly. "Is that what you're always searching for? With the binoculars? Are you seriously frittering away your life looking for a hoop snake?"

"What? No. Why would you even say that?"

"I used to sleep at your place, remember? Every morning, you'd be on the deck, but you were never just observing. You were *searching*. I used to wonder what for."

"I was looking at the swamp. Is that a sin now?"

Chad shook his head. "For God's sake, Chloe, you're trying to live his dream. He was more than just a friend, wasn't he?"

"Drop it, Chad."

"I've seen it, Chloe. That look in your eyes when you're—"

I wheeled on him, throwing the caboose to the floor. It broke into pieces and I feared I'd set off some ancient Forenza-Galasso curse. "Thought we were here to find DNA, or do you want to talk about fairies and elves next?"

He held my eyes. Something heavy passed between us, and then we both spun on our heels, our backs facing each other as we searched through more junk. Ten minutes passed as the modest possessions of the Whitakers grew less impressive: a toaster oven; a boot brush; a calendar with no appointments. Finally, I opened one container and old classmates gazed up at me with dated hairdos and clothes. It was my fourth grade class picture. A single tear slid down my cheek and splashed onto the image.

In the photo, I stood at the end of the second row next to the teacher, back when I gave a hoot about what teachers thought of me. I wore pink hoop earrings, dull brown pants, and a lacy green blouse. I smiled obediently—a pasted-on grin held too long while the photographer fiddled. In contrast, Hoop knelt in the front row with a wide smile, outshining the boys that flanked him. If he'd spun around, he could have been proposing to Macy who stood behind him in a pale blue dress. She beamed with an open-mouthed giggle on her face, her eyes huge as if caught by surprise. Even though I had a copy of this photo at home, it wasn't until that instant that I noticed Hoop's left hand snaking behind him, grabbing Macy's ankle. The photographer had captured their moment of contact, the mutual delight of prankster and prankee. Hoop never did squander a chance to remind Macy that he was alive and coming for her, full-force and guns a-blazing.

Beneath the photo lay a yellow envelope with Hoop's fiddlestick handwriting. A single word on it: *Macy*. The envelope was clipped to a smaller box within the bin. I greedily reached for it.

"What about that?" Chad said. I jerked my hand back and followed his pointing finger to a tiny, plastic container with a faded white design on it.

"What is it?" I said.

"I might be wrong, but in one of the homes where I lived, this kid who was meaner than a wet badger kept his pulled tooth in something like that."

"Never heard of the tooth fairy?"

"Kid was dumb as a rock but not stupid enough to believe in the tooth fairy at age thirteen."

Chad reached down, grabbed the container, and popped it open. There, inside, lay a tooth.

I gasped. "It's Hoop's. It'll definitely have his DNA."

"Could've been his father's."

"No, I remember the day he got it pulled."

Hoop had skidded to a stop on his bike after his dentist

appointment. *Clover*, he'd said, t*he good Lord knew how much talking I'd do, so He gave me some extra teeth to work with. And can you believe it? That dentist saw fit to mess with the good Lord's work.* He'd made the declaration with a hole in his grin and a fishing rod in his hand.

I looked at the tooth. Maybe the Lord did work in mysterious ways.

Chapter 18

Four Days Before the Thump

Hoop slung the bag of bats, balls, and mitts over his shoulder and headed down the road. His team had lost, 8-5, but he still felt like he'd won. After all, he'd made two outs, two runs, and had worked up a respectable sweat killing time with friends.

"Hey, Hoop," Ronnie Fields shouted from his bicycle. "Ain't your dad picking you up?" Ronnie was peering around his little brother who was climbing onto his handlebars for a ride.

"Not likely," Hoop said, "but it ain't far."

"I'd give you a lift, but my mom says I gotta give Andy here a ride home. Too stupid to find his own way."

"Am not!" Andy protested, his legs kicking frantically while he locked his butt into place.

"It's all right," Hoop said. "Good game, by the way. You knocked that one ball clear to West Virginia!"

"Thanks," Ronnie said. "Got some solid contact." He wobbled down the road with his unsteady passenger, waving as he went.

Hoop ambled on, kicking pebbles while wondering about the friction between stones and macadam. The bats clanged against his bottom with each step, urging him on like a racehorse. His shirt was covered in sweat, but the cool evening air would dry it soon enough. He wouldn't have minded a ride, but his dad was busy doing something with a wagon—either falling off it or fighting to stay on it. He smiled as he remembered how his dad had surprised him this morning with fried eggs and hash browns, three of each.

\#

"Why three of everything?" Hoop had asked.

"Celebration," Avis said, showing the grin he'd passed down to his son.

"Three days sober?" Hoop said, keeping his voice measured in case it was three hours until a bar opened up.

"Yessiree," Avis said. "Turning a corner. And not just a ninety-degree corner, Hoop. Going the whole one-eighty."

"Think they call that a U-turn." Hoop raised a hand toward his dad with pinkie and thumb curled in. "Gimme three," he said, and Avis slapped the fingers with three of his own.

"Remember when I didn't come home a few nights ago?" Avis said.

Hoop nodded while shoving a hash brown into his mouth.

"That's because I hit what they call rock bottom, and in my case, it was pretty literal."

"How so?"

"Blacked out. Woke up cold, wet, and dirty in . . . you know what? You don't need the details. What you need to know is that I'm climbing my way back up. Sound square to you?"

"All kinds of square," Hoop said.

Avis rustled Hoop's hair like he used to.

Hoop dug in to his eggs, thinking how it'd be a storybook life like this every day if his mother had stayed in the picture. But she'd edited herself from the pages long ago. On her worst days, Jessica Whitaker had made her husband look clean and sober, but on her best, she'd made Avis and Hoop feel like the luckiest people in the world. Hoop's last memory of her revolved around a tattoo she got a week before hitting the road: *Better Without*, it had said, inked in a circular design of rose, emerald and black, near her shoulder. *Better* had formed the top half of the circle while *Without* scraped the bottom.

Hoop had traced it with his finger, impressed with the curly letters and the smooth blending of colors. Back then, he and his dad had been too thickheaded to get it, but now, as a fifteen-year-old, he understood that his mother had been sending them a message: *better without her*.

"Macy swung by," Avis said as Hoop scraped up his last egg. "She's getting a game going this afternoon. Said she'll take shortstop if you bring the game."

"I always bring game, Pop."

"I'll drive you over."

Hoop hid his surprise at the offer. Usually, his dad was too inebriated to drive, at least with anyone else in the car. "Thanks," he said.

Avis shoved aside a pile of dirty clothes and sat down on the fold-out chair where Hoop was supposed to do homework, though that hardly seemed possible with the array of boy-treasures covering his desk. "You ever gonna ask that Macy girl out, Hoop? They don't wait around forever, you know."

Hoop heard the underlying message: *they don't stay around forever, either*. Hoop wiped his mouth with the back of his hand and grinned. "I got plans in motion, Pop. Big plans. Don't you worry about me."

"I rarely do, buddy. The good Lord knew just how much I could handle this go-round, so he gave me exactly one serving of it."

"*This* go-round?" Hoop asked. "You planning on coming back?"

Avis thought about it, his mouth squaring up. "I'd like to think so, now that I've worked out some of the kinks."

Hoop sat back and contemplated. "I like the idea of circling back. Takes a little of the taint off death, don't it?"

"Sure does, but in my opinion, you should still treat every day like it's your last."

"Doesn't everyone?"

Avis rubbed his bristly stubble. "I've had too many near-last days myself. Wouldn't mind this being the start of some firsts."

"It will be, Pop." Hoop got out of bed, set his breakfast dishes aside, and pulled his blankets up to his pillow. In the old days, his mother would work half the night as a bartender, drink three male co-workers under the table, and then near-kill herself on a motorcycle on the way home, but she always got up in the morning and made her bed. Claimed it started the day in a fresh manner, which could never be a bad thing.

Avis cleared his throat. "That box you been keeping in the closet . . . got anything to do with your plans for Macy?"

Hoop gave his dad a guilty glance. "Meant to tell you about that. And yeah, it does."

Avis rose up and headed to the kitchen with Hoop's dishes. "You just be careful, y'hear?"

"Always am, Pop."

#

A bat and ball shifted in Hoop's sack and banged him in the hip. He switched the load to his other shoulder, then spoke without turning around. "I know you're there," he said. "You got that smell."

"Good smell or bad?" Macy said. She'd been following him on her bike for a good fifty yards now.

Hoop sniffed like a wine expert sticking his nose in a goblet. "Downright evil," he said, "like a femme fatale going for the kill in one of them noir movies."

Macy pedaled to catch up to him. "Honestly, Hoop, I don't know what you're talking about half the time. But it always sounds good." She pulled her bike to a stop. "Hop on."

Hoop assessed the rusty blue bike. The foam filling on its green banana seat had popped out from the vinyl covering in three places, like the first mushrooms of spring. "You're gonna need good balance with me carrying this bag and all."

Macy accepted the challenge with a snort. "Get on. Can't have you supplying the game and carrying it home, too."

Hoop swung a leg over the seat, adjusted the bag, and rested a hand on Macy's hip. He couldn't have been happier.

Macy lifted herself up on one pedal and pressed down hard. The muscles in her arms and legs strained slightly as she got the heavy load going, but after a few rotations, she cruised along with ease. As her ponytail swung like a pendulum along her back, Hoop imagined it counting down the seconds of their life together. But then he remembered the conversation with his dad and decided that the ponytail was counting *up*, toward the seconds he and Macy would be spending together in multiple lives.

"April Fools' Day is coming up," Hoop said.

"Yep." Macy turned her head a quarter way round. "You getting me something good this year?"

"Getting you something? For what?" The tease in Hoop's voice came through loud and clear. "Oh, wait. Is it your birthday? 'Cause seems to me I gave you a custom-made alligator tooth necklace last year."

"Yeah, me and every other girl in the class."

Hoop smiled and squeezed her hip. "But I gave you the sharpest tooth—and I didn't charge you."

"Last I checked, birthday gifts were *supposed* to come free of charge." She cruised around the bend and let the bike glide as they coasted along a downhill slope.

"Mm, I mighta got you something better this year."

"Not something gross like a beaver tail, is it?"

"Don't see what's wrong with a quality beaver tail, but nope. For starters, I got you a card."

"A real card? Like from a store?"

"Got the receipt in my back left pocket. Same place you keep yours."

He watched her neck grow longer as she craned her head

113

up in surprise. "How do you know where I keep my receipts, Hoop Whitaker?"

"You'd be surprised what I know about you, Macy LeGrange."

"Do you know why I save receipts?" she asked.

"In case you wanna return something?"

"Nope. I do origami with them. Receipt paper's real thin, so it folds tight. And after a while, the ink fades to awesome shades of violet or green."

"Well, I'll give you the receipt for my card, then. Found the perfect one at Boyd's."

"Didn't know Boyd carried cards."

"He's got everything. You just gotta dig."

"Sometimes, that Boyd Junior gives me the creeps, but then he turns around and helps Momma and me out. Lets us pay on credit and whatnot. Which reminds me, I need a card for Momma's birthday."

"When is it?"

"I'll put it this way. We were born four minutes apart but in two different months."

Hoop needed less than a second to process. "March thirty-first."

"You got it. She was born one minute before midnight; I came along three minutes past."

"The original April Fool."

Macy steered the bike onto the rutted dirt road that led to their duplexes. The bats clunked and the balls shivered, but Macy kept her balance. Hoop wouldn't have traded the bumpy ride for anything.

"I'm looking forward to the card," Macy said, her voice vibrating with the ruts. "I don't get many real ones."

Hoop leaned forward and spoke into her ear. "It ain't the card that matters, Macy. I mean, heck, you're finally gonna be fifteen."

Macy hoped he couldn't see the deep blush of her cheeks, but she was pretty sure the heat of it had traveled clean up to her forehead. She smiled from ear to ear, realizing she was going to get exactly what she wanted for her birthday.

Chapter 19

"Is it all right if I take a few things from this bin, Chad?" The bin held the old class photos and the yellow envelope addressed to Macy. Guilt and desperation were undoubtedly glazing my features, so I remained facing the wall as I made the request.

Chad sounded pained to answer. "I can't let you, Clo."

I spun around accusingly. "Why not? In case it's relevant to a *murder*?"

Chad suddenly took a deep and awkward interest in the floor. "Not like we're in a wrecked old attic digging up DNA samples for fun, now is it?" His eyes lifted and found mine.

"I'm sorry," I said. "You don't deserve the brunt of . . . all this."

"Apology accepted. Now come on, let's get out of here."

The flimsy attic stairs served their purpose and we made our way down the wide hall. As we passed the entrance to the second-story tower, Chad pointed. "Betcha that's where the poker games are held. I think it used to be a library."

I tried the door but it was locked, and the frosted glass denied peeping eyes. But when the scent of cigars, smoky bourbon, and dashed dreams entered my nostrils, I knew Chad was right. This was the room where men forgot their daily worries and dreamt big—until departing with a hole in their pockets.

After we descended the stairs and exited to the weed-filled back yard, Chad's cell phone rang with an upbeat bird-tweet. He looked embarrassed, as if he'd been caught feeling hopeful while I was feeling anything but. After he answered, he listened and nodded for at least two minutes, taking notes with the half-sized pen from his pocket.

"Anything?" I said as he hung up.

"They found Melanie LeGrange. She works at a travel agency in Chicago as"—he referred to his notes—"an international liaison for high-level business executives."

"Whoa," I said. "Guess she finally got on the right meds."

"What do you mean?"

"Mrs. LeGrange used to lie in bed for days, claiming migraines, but we all knew it was more than that. One summer, she got so emaciated, you could almost see through her. And you could tell she was stunning once, but somewhere along the way, a demon must've grabbed hold of her beauty, wrung it through hell, and spit her out on the other side."

Chad looked mildly horrified. "Where do you get your images, Chloe?"

"I'm just saying, when the bad stuff took over, it took a toll. That's when Macy ran things. Laundry, meals, forging signatures." I knitted my brows and thought back. "Guess the last time I saw Mrs. LeGrange was at the funeral."

"That must have been awful."

"You never saw a person more shattered." I cocked my head at him, feeling like I owed him something positive. "I bet you didn't know it was your dad who paid for Macy's funeral."

"That was nice. Guess he could afford it, right?"

"No, he offered that up *before* he knew about the lottery. Beautiful casket. Ivory and gold with a cushiony purple lining." I swallowed hard, but emotion overtook my voice. "Macy looked amazing, like getting thrown from a bike didn't even faze her. It was a proper send-off, even if she would have hated the froufrou nature of it."

Chad looked lost, and I suddenly realized he'd probably never been to a funeral. That would have required knowing people in a permanent enough way to mourn them. Still, he tried to empathize. "Must've been a huge turnout."

"It was. Minus one."

"Hoop Whitaker?" he asked, something less than

sympathy in his words.

"That's when we knew something had happened. Because if Hoop were alive, he would have been there." It was only as I heard the words aloud that their meaning clocked me in the brain. I folded my arms in front of chest and swallowed the lump in my throat.

"Anyway," Chad said, clearing his throat, "Melanie LeGrange says she didn't call Grace Elbee. Hasn't thought about her in years. Assuming she's telling the truth, couldn't have been her on the Caller ID."

A strange tingle swirled around my body and then whooshed away, like an evil spirit had dropped in, checked out the goods, and deemed me useless. I shivered. "Then who was calling Mrs. Elbee?"

Chad glanced at me cynically. "We'll find out, but pretty sure it won't turn out to be Casper the Friendly Ghost, if that's what you're thinking."

I couldn't shake the ominous feeling, and then something bubbled up in my brain. I took out my phone. "What was the number that the *M. LeGrange* calls came from again?"

He flipped a few pages back in his notebook and read: "843-7526."

As I looked at the numbers on my keypad, the earlier tingle crushed my chest. "That was Macy's number."

"Come again."

"That was Macy's number when we were kids. I should have realized it when I saw Mrs. Elbee's Caller ID."

"How do you remember Macy's number?"

"I don't know. I spell things in my head, and I have a weird memory for phone numbers and stuff. Macy's number spelled THE SLAM."

Chad looked at his own phone to verify, then sighed. "So big deal. Some telemarketer got hold of an old phone book and programmed in local numbers with the hope that some sap would answer."

I smirked. "Did that telemarketer also plan for the sap to write the caller's name on a mirror and end up dead in a swamp seventy-two hours later?"

"Good point, but it's less of a stretch than believing that a ghost is using Ma Bell to haunt earthly beings." He shook the tooth container. "I gotta get this to Sherilyn."

"Hey, did you tell your dad about his DNA on the duct tape yet?"

"No. Guess I'll do it now."

"I'm coming with you. I need to see his reaction."

"What? Why?"

"Come on, Chad. Isn't it strange how Boyd's troubles with the law always disappeared? Seems to me something must have happened in that basement that compromised your dad."

Chad's turn to cross his arms. "You know what? You *can* be there when I tell him. Because I guarantee you, there's a simple explanation. Old Strike is not one to be compromised."

He leaned down to get in his car but then popped back up. "By the way," he said, "you heard anything about a magic show coming up?"

"Magic show? No."

He glanced at his ever-present notebook. "Mrs. LeGrange just got an invitation in the mail for a magic show here in Beulah. She thought it was weird to get a call from one of our investigators the very next day."

"You have any more details?"

"She read the invitation to my guy over the phone." He recited from his notes. "*Never-seen, never-imagined marvels that promise to leave Beulah on tenterhooks.*"

"Tenterhooks?" My face knotted up. "Sounds painful. Maybe it's a prank."

"Could be, but who would have known to mail it to her in

Chicago? We had trouble finding her ourselves." The sun reflected off his watch as he checked it. "After we talk to Strike, you wanna grab a drink and hash through some of this stuff?"

I remembered my commitment to Rafe, but instinct told me not to mention it to Chad. "Can't tonight," I said. "Gotta prep for an interview in the morning—with the dreaded Adeline DeVore. The deadline for this story is crushing me."

"Okay, sure," he said. "I should keep working these cases, anyway. See you at the station."

With a stilted wave, he got in his car and drove off. Dried mud spewed up from beneath his tires like a lazy dust bunny before settling back into place. After watching his car disappear around the corner, I turned and stared at the padlock on Quail's back door.

I wanted that yellow envelope addressed to Macy. And I knew the padlock's combination.

I glanced around. No one but me and some tobacco-farming ghosts. Might as well give them something to talk about over their evening smoke.

Chapter 20

No sooner had I grabbed the yellow envelope and the box it was clipped to than I heard a door slam downstairs. Dang, I'd been caught. I stashed the goods in my backpack and went to the opening in the floor. The stairs hung down like the gaping jaw of a dragon.

"Chad?" I called out reflexively.

"Hey! Who's here?" It wasn't Chad's voice. "This here's private property. You best get yerself outta here 'fore I call the police." The voice carried a decided drawl and sounded vaguely familiar. I racked my brain to put a face to it but only came up with one impression: smelly. Maybe it was just some local workman Quail had hired. He'd probably spotted the open padlock and had come in to check it out. No problem. Quail had given me the combination and I had every right to be here.

Determined footsteps clomped up the stairs and then the voice came again. "Ain't nobody supposed to be in here, and I got a gun!"

Shit. I didn't. And then my mind matched a face to the voice. Oh no. The tables were about as turned as they could be. This would not play out well. I got on my belly and frantically reached down to the attic stairs, trying to yank them up. If I could just grab that cord . . . and if the stairs would just cooperate by oiling their own hinges, I could—

Crash!

I plummeted ten feet. Not too horrible of a tumble, though, and a fairly competent landing. I'd toppled out of the attic head-first but had grabbed hold of the pole-thin railing accompanying the stairs, so I'd flipped midair. Still, I landed hard on my elbow, hip, ankle . . . well, just about everything that sat to the right of my belly button. By the time I got my bearings, I was staring straight into the homely, gaunt face of Zeke Carver, my malodorous, early-morning visitor.

"Well, looky here," he said, his eyes glinting with devilish delight.

Thankfully, he was holding a toolbox, not a rifle.

"Hey, there, Zeke." I rose up and tried not to ache in every single place in my body. "I was just—"

As I tried to formulate some reasonable excuse for being here, Zeke placed his toolbox on the floor, reached into it, and pulled out a compact .38 revolver. "Now if this ain't the cat swallowing the canary," he said.

I let it go, lessons on idioms probably not my strongest play here.

"You following me or something?" he said.

"No, absolutely not. Why would I be following you?"

"That's right. Why would you? You got nothing on me."

Paranoid much? But I didn't care. Odds were that I could encounter Zeke on any day of the week and he'd be within seventy-two hours of either committing a crime or planning one.

"I don't have squat on you, Zeke. You are absolutely right." I watched for signs of shock, certain that he'd never heard those last four words before. He seemed okay, so I continued. "I'm here on behalf of Mr. Quail."

"Whatchu talking about?"

I pulled out the note Quail had scribbled for me and thrust it forward, but Zeke frowned and looked suspicious. "Crumple that up and toss it here," he said. "I don't trust any high-falutin' chick that makes guns appear from her nether regions."

I suppressed a grin. Had he assumed I pulled this morning's .22 directly from my ass? *Ouch.* I crushed the notepaper into a ball—it even had *Quail Realty and Development* printed on it—and threw it at him. He leaned over to scoop it up, all the while keeping a wary eye on me.

Unsure if he could read, I blurted out its contents. "See? Mr. Quail told me to use the back door and he gave me the combination."

"You could've written this yerself, for all I know." He took a step closer.

"Yes, but how would I know the combination?" I said, moving back.

"I don't know how you know stuff. All's I know is I got hired to work on the roof in this-here house, and I was told ain't nobody else gonna be here." He took another step, taunting me with the potentially hot end of his revolver. The suspended attic steps hung between us. "But let me tell you something, missy. Me and my brother, we don't like being threatened. And we sure don't like no woman getting the better of us." He smiled in a deeply unfriendly way, his tongue bulging out through the toothless space. "Way I see it, it's just you and me here, and ain't nobody the wiser."

A deep-seated survival instinct took over. *Fight or flight*, it said. *And he's way bigger than you.*

Like a good reflex, my response allowed no time for additional analysis. My body took charge, leaving my mind in the dust. Next thing I saw was Zeke's gun-toting hand rushing to his mouth, trying to stop the bleeding from where the hinged portion of the staircase had smashed him in the teeth. Might be room for his whole tongue to wriggle through that unsightly gap now.

By the time he could even think to react, I was midway down the stairs pulling off a ninety-degree turn on the landing. As I whipped around, I glanced up and caught a glint of the gun in his hands, but if his aim sucked as bad as his idioms, he'd miss by a mile. Still, I made it to the first floor in two seconds flat and flew through the living room. Hadn't moved this fast since a copperhead had greeted me in my laundry basket four years ago.

Halfway through the big room that contained Quail's old tables, I heard Zeke scuttling down the stairs. "You'll pay for that, you bitch!"

I overturned a chair behind me to block his path and kept on keepin' on. If he did follow me out the back door, I never knew about it. I was in my car, slamming the key into the ignition, and skidding around to the front of the house faster than a rabbit with a wolf on its tail. I took the corner on two tires, swerved around his blue pick-up, and kicked up a wall of dust. As my tires chewed up driveway like a ravenous hound, I thought I heard what sounded like the report of a wild gunshot. I braced for it, but my windows and tires remained intact, the bullet no doubt landing somewhere in an abandoned tobacco field.

Sure hope it didn't hit any of my ghosts.

Chapter 21

"Is he here?" I asked upon seeing Chad behind his desk and reading through a file. I'd decided to keep my Zeke encounter quiet since I didn't feel like explaining how I'd reentered Quail's Victorian to steal potential evidence in a case.

Chad glanced up, his mind still linked to whatever he'd been reading.

He and Strike occupied a small space here at the station, along with Annika, the receptionist who was nowhere in sight. It was an area far more compact than I would want to share with my father, but Chad lacked the childhood baggage that the rest of us accumulated in the teen years.

"He should be here any second," he said as the sheriff barged in on cue, treating the door like a thickset opponent in the ring.

"Tell you what!" Strike declared to whoever happened to be in the room. "Someone needs to take a belt to the bottoms of half the kids in this town. Would save a lot of trouble down the road."

"What happened?" Chad asked.

"Bunch of skateboarders doing graffiti on the bridge again. I pulled over and they took off, leaving one of their idiot friends dangling sixty feet in the air."

"What'd you do?" I asked.

"Reeled his butt up. And guess what comes falling out of his pocket?" The sheriff produced an evidence bag containing a bottle of bright orange nail polish.

I stepped over to take a closer look at the small, pricey bottle of DeVore Long-Lasting Nail Lacquer. "That looks like the same shade Mrs. Elbee was wearing," I said.

"Gonna need Sherilyn to verify that," the sheriff said,

"but sure looks like it, don't it?"

Chad tapped the file he'd been reading when I came in. "According to this report, there was no orange nail polish found at Mrs. Elbee's house."

"So it was missing," I said. "Makes you wonder where the tagger got the polish."

The sheriff set the small bottle down. "Idiot said it fell out of his uncle's truck and he thought it would add the perfect detail to his bridge art. *Bridge art* . . . you believe that?"

"Hmp," Chad said with a disapproving frown. "Not what I used to use."

"Kid considers himself some sort of Pee-casso. Up there drawing a deformed-looking woman, and I am not about to mention the parts he used the polish for."

Thank God. No one in Beulah needed to hear the sheriff struggling for euphemisms for female parts that merited neon.

"Who's his uncle?" I asked.

"That idiot, Zeke Carver."

"You're kidding," I said with enough shock that both Chad and the sheriff craned their necks and waited for an explanation. I swallowed and went with the only thing that came to mind. "I sort of pulled a gun on him and his brother this morning." At their bewildered expressions, I added, "What? They broke, they entered, I pulled. At least I didn't point."

They shook their heads but didn't seem too surprised. Meanwhile, I felt compelled to say something about Zeke's current location, but how to present it without implicating myself?

"By the way," I finally said, "Richie Quail mentioned that he hired Zeke to work on that Victorian house in Flinton. You should look for him there, Sheriff."

"All right," he said. "We'll see what Sherilyn finds first, but I swear, I'm not sure my I.Q. can dip low enough to handle a conversation with one of them Carver brothers." He suddenly shifted moods and frowned at me. "What are you doing here, anyway? Thought our interview was tomorrow. You bring me that Grace Elbee tape?"

"Not yet, but Chad was just telling me about an interesting detail Sherilyn discovered. Something involving you."

Chad glared at me. I caught it with my peripheral vision but kept my eyes averted.

The sheriff turned to Chad. "Well? What is it?"

Chad cleared his throat, not quite as confident as he'd been earlier. "Darnedest thing, Strike. That duct tape they found in Boyd's basement room, you know—"

"Yeah, what about it?"

Chad blurted it out. "They found traces of your DNA on it."

The sheriff looked as excited as a sloth awakening from a nap. "And?"

"And it was in a sealed room with someone's blood and a set of handcuffs—"

"Handcuffs that were most likely securing Hoop Whitaker's wrists," I finished accusingly.

"So?" the sheriff said. He shifted his gaze repeatedly from Chad to me with a menacing expression. It was probably a good thing Strike Ryker had never raised small children. "You two cook up this little presentation to make me cower in a corner and confess to something? Because that simply ain't happening."

Chad looked relieved, but I didn't quite buy it. "Care to explain, Sheriff?"

"It's a piece of duct tape," he said. "Been using it all my life, some of it right here in this office. Years back, I used it in those school demonstrations. Even fixed my mower a time or two with the dang stuff."

"Then what was it doing in a room you supposedly didn't know existed?" I said.

"A yank of tape in some rotten old basement? How should I know? Could've been there for years."

"It was," Chad mumbled.

"Funny how it was your lottery winnings, Sheriff, that paid to create a top-of-the-line forensics lab, but when the evidence points to you, the results mean very little."

The sheriff frowned, harder than usual. "It means there's a piece of tape in a room in a building where I've been a thousand times. But you can't jump from that to whatever's going on in your head, young lady. You're hardly objective here, and I think we both know that."

His voice had adopted an unexpected air of pity, and I didn't like it.

"I'm stating facts," I said, "and they need to be explained."

The sheriff harrumphed. "That tape could've been there from when I helped Boyd Senior with an addition twenty years ago. Or maybe I dropped it once while getting coffee. What does it matter?"

Chad shifted uncomfortably as the sheriff continued. "Y'all are coming off like two terriers going at the last bone— and I'm the bone." He put his hands on his hips. "I don't like being the bone."

I took the lead. "We need to know exactly how you were involved with whatever happened in that basement. Because honestly, it rings a little false that you didn't know about Boyd's drug operation all this time. Boyd's troubles have always had a way of vanishing into thin air, don't you think?"

The sheriff's expression grew as dark as I'd ever seen it. He whirled toward his desk, not knowing where to vent his anger when his fists were compromised by decorum. "For God's sake, my DNA is probably wallpapering this town." He grabbed a garbage can from the floor, turned it upside down, and shook the contents onto his desk. From the pile, he pulled a used Band-Aid. "Here! How 'bout this? I threw it out yesterday. Maybe you can use it against me! Or how about every crime scene in Beulah over the last twenty years? I must've left a hair or a trace of spittle at each one." He snatched a pen from his desk and thrust it in my direction like he wanted to plunge it between my ribs. "What about this? Go throw it in the swamp! Maybe you can accuse me of drowning Mrs. Elbee!"

Well, I'd clearly struck a nerve—but I couldn't deny enjoying the scene just a bit.

"You know what, Chloe?" the sheriff said, suddenly softening in tone in a jarring way, leaving me shifting uncomfortably from foot to foot. He took a quiet step in my direction. "Enough is enough. You see, Jacqueline told me how everything that went down twelve years ago was extra hard on you, particularly. And she had to tell me again last year when Chad here got all sweet on you."

"Strike!" Chad said, horrified that he was now a pawn in his father's defense.

"Shush, now," the sheriff said, walking over to within arm's reach of me.

I burned inside. Strike's wife, Jacqueline Ryker, had been the K-8 school librarian. She was as perceptive as she was caring. Whenever a student had become upset or disruptive, Mrs. Ryker could settle matters with a few wise words, gently delivered. She seemed to know things about people they barely knew about themselves, but I sure as hell did not want my secrets revealed by Sheriff Strike Ryker. Not here, and least of all in front of Chad.

"I don't know what you're talking about," I mumbled.

The sheriff exhaled deeply, as if working out a cramp. For a man who best expressed himself through fists and feints, this was clearly a difficult conversation. "Come on, Chloe. You lost Macy and Hoop in a single day. You got crushed by tragedy from both sides."

My hands flew up defensively. "This is a nice diversion and all, Sheriff, but we're straying from the fact that your DNA—"

"With Macy, you lost a close friend, and with Hoop, you lost the boy you were in love with. All in a single day."

I tightened my fists, and the pressure of my clenched jaw worked its way to my ears. It filled them with a pounding deafness, as if I could block the truth from entering. I'd sealed off my feelings for Hoop at every pass and could not fathom my barricades being knocked down by the likes of Strike Ryker.

"Hoop and I were only fourteen, hardly—"

"And you knew Hoop only had eyes for—"

"Stop it!" My voice blazed with fury, the tension in my neck traveling through my body. I glanced at Chad, then back at the sheriff. "You have no—"

"You could barely imagine life continuing after they both—"

I shoved the sheriff, but it was like a butterfly ricocheting off a concrete pillar. The emotional onslaught, fueled by shame, transformed me into a combustible mess. "Stop trying to change the subject!"

"It's time someone said something! That week threw you into a vicious cycle." He grabbed my right arm, turned it palm-up. "Believe me, I know."

I jerked my arm away, torqueing my shoulder, but I remained silent, defenseless.

"Why do you think you're still dredging all this garbage up?" he yelled. "Still writing about the damn lottery and things that happened twelve years—"

"Strike!" Chad shouted, his voice more defiant than I'd ever heard. "Cut it out! Right now! This is cruel, not to mention irrelevant. If Chloe has a personal agenda, it has nothing to do with Sherilyn's findings."

Despite the harshness of his voice, Chad sounded disheartened. Strike's revelations had been news to him, or at least a confirmation of something he'd suspected.

Strike Ryker turned to his son and showed the worst emotion possible to someone who shunned the sentiment: abject pity. "I'm sorry, Chad, but she's been searching for that boy her whole life. That's why you and her never worked out. A living man can't compete with a ghost. It's impossible. Because a living man has faults."

Chad glanced in my direction for an awful moment, seeming to hold out hope that I'd rebut the comment. But Wizard of Oz, indeed, a curtain had been pulled back to reveal an advantaged rival—one he hadn't even known existed. The truth showed in the rapid rise and fall of my chest, the quick swallows of guilt, and my too-fast blinking as I stifled tears. Finally, I raised my eyes to the sheriff, my resentment falling squarely on his shoulders.

"Keep trying to spin it, Sheriff. Keep trying to take the focus off yourself. But you can't explain the DNA. Maybe that duct tape will end up explaining why you never found Hoop, or why Boyd was allowed to thrive as a drug dealer and destroy our community. I'm not sure what-all went on in that basement, but I will find out."

I spun to leave.

"Now wait a gosh-darn minute," the sheriff said. He took two deep breaths, in and out. "I'm sorry, Chloe. I am. Maybe I shouldn't have said everything I just did."

I stopped, moved by the sincerity in his voice.

"But here's the God's honest truth. I wish to hell I

131

could've found that boy. You think it shines high on my list of accomplishments that I let him disappear without a trace while his father was laid up? I tell you, I couldn't stop picturing Avis regaining consciousness—learning that he'd not only killed a girl but that his boy had gone missing, too. Despite everything, I really liked Avis. That's why I visited him every day. I mean, how was he supposed to handle everything when he woke up? What was his future gonna hold?" The sheriff's face bunched up, emotions pushing against the surface.

As if to counter the display of vulnerability, his next words spilled out. "I don't know what happened to Hoop, but believe me, no one wanted to find that boy more than I did."

I glared. How dare he claim that title? The mystery of Hoop's vanishing had left a hole so gaping in my heart that its rough edges had hardened and sealed over with the thickest of scars. Yet here stood the sheriff—now linked to the case— proclaiming desperation to solve the mystery. I shook my head—*No!*—and stomped to the door as Chad's desk phone rang.

"Hold up," he said. "It's Sherilyn."

The sheriff and I stood awkwardly and waited while Chad took the call. When he hung up, he looked from one to the other of us.

"It's about Mrs. Elbee," he said, his handsome face taking a decided twist toward the confused. "There were significant traces of Ambien in her system but she didn't have a prescription, and no sleeping pills were found in her house. There was also petechial hemorrhaging around her neck, a stress fracture on her collarbone, a bump on the back of her head, and multiple bruises on her arms. Sherilyn's ruling it a homicide."

Chapter 22

Three Days Before the Thump

Macy listened to the pounding on the door. She knew who it was. She considered ignoring him, but better for her to deal with the situation than her mother. With a sigh more befitting an older soul, she hoisted herself from the kitchen table to handle the 300-pound problem on the stoop.

At the second hammering against the door, Macy glanced at her mother's bedroom and hoped all would stay quiet within. Then she crossed the rectangular room that served as the hub of her life. At least her father had left the old television behind; it gave her and her mother something to watch while eating dinner. On the day Darrell LeGrange had stormed out of the duplex, he'd cracked the screen with his size eleven boot and assumed it was ruined for good. It wasn't, as long as nothing important was happening in the upper left hand corner of whatever program was on.

When Macy pulled open the front door, the bright sun forced her eyes into a squint. The hour had crept to near eleven, but with all the blinds pulled to minimize Momma's headaches, Macy hadn't realized the time. At least there was a huge gut in front of her that blocked most of the sun's rays. She raised her eyes to the owner of the gut.

Quail the Whale wheezed as if he'd just climbed three flights of stairs, rather than three cracked steps.

"Good morning, Mr. Quail," Macy said with characteristic exuberance. "How are you today? Did you hear that thunder last night?"

"What's your name again?" Quail asked, his face not altogether unpleasant and his manner mild compared to his knock.

"Macy, sir."

"That's right. Well, Macy, I did hear that thunder last night, but I tell you what, it didn't wake me up."

"It did me, sir, that's for sure."

"Well, see, I was already awake, worried about making payroll this week. Do you know how a person makes payroll, Macy?"

"No, sir, I sure don't."

"Let me enlighten you. I collect money from people who live in my apartments and townhomes, and then, I give that money to other people who take care of the apartments and townhomes."

Macy's eyes brightened with optimism. "Sir, if you got those people on your payroll, we sure would appreciate you sending them over here because we ain't had hot water for days, and when we do, seems like all the cockroaches like to swim in it anyway."

Quail sucked in a breath that so filled his stomach, it almost blocked out his face. "Now listen here, little girl, I don't need to be hearing no complaints from the likes of you. People who pay their rents"—he waggled a hot-dog-length finger at her—"they're the ones who get the attention."

Macy giggled. "I feel like you give Momma and me plenty of attention every month, sir."

Richie Quail looked unsure how to respond to Macy's lingering smile. He finally just huffed and shook his body from head to toe. "Why don't you go get your mother for me? Tell her I'm here for the rent, and I'm not leaving until I get it." His last words made him sound like a stubborn teenage boy—and Macy sure knew how to handle them.

She let her shoulders drop and her head droop. "I'd sure like to, Mr. Quail, but Momma's out looking for a new job. Just like every day. Said to tell you she'd have that money by tomorrow, that's for sure."

Quail looked both impressed and skeptical. "Really? Now that's good news. Where's she looking?"

"Where *isn't* she looking? The diner, the theater, the school, the library, and that new place that opened up with the funny lights and the motorcycle parked out front."

Quail drew back. "The tattoo parlor?"

"That's it. Inks and Kinks, right?" Macy found herself unable to stop some fabrications once she'd gotten started. It was the reason Miss Farlow often chose Macy's stories to read aloud in class, although one of Hoop's had really shined recently. But something about this Richie Quail character just begged to be lied to, so Macy didn't fight it. "Momma said she hoped she wouldn't have to get a tattoo to work there, but she was willing to do whatever was necessary to land the job. *Whatever* was necessary."

Quail's face knotted up as he tried to process Macy's meaning. "I certainly hope she's not coming across too desperate. She could get into trouble, you know, a woman as attractive as your mother."

"That's what the man told her." Macy conjured an imaginary, tattoo-shop owner—rangy, too tan, and confident as all get-out. "Told her she was real attractive." Macy watched as the deep, parallel lines between Richie Quail's brows dug in and held on.

"What man told her that?" he said, the rattling wheeze in his voice increasing a notch.

"That man that runs Inks and Kinks. You know him? He looks like he's seen more than his share of the sun. He ran into Momma in the grocery store last week and he said she could make men pitch tents or something like that—if she prettied herself up some." Macy had heard the phrase from two high schoolers in town last week. She knew darn well what it meant, but her innocent grin and dimples implied otherwise. She watched Quail's lips twist into a mushroom shape and quiver. "And that's what she did, Mr. Quail. She prettied herself up right fine this morning. Put on some heels and a skirt and more make-up than I seen her wear in a good, long time."

"Hmp, well, I don't like the sound of that one bit, but a job's a job, I suppose." Quail glanced over to Hoop's unit, scoping out his next victim, and then returned his gaze to Macy. "You know, your Momma and I went to school together. I was in better shape then, but I never did..." He waved away the rest of his statement.

Macy suspected he might be blushing, but it was hard to tell given his splotchy skin. Then his eyes assumed their usual, coal-like aura, and he continued. "Used to think she'd amount to something, but look at her now. Damn jock husband left her high and dry, and she can't even pay a lousy rent."

The stinging words lashed Macy, but she'd learned a lot about survival since her dad had walked out. She shook her head as if commiserating with Quail, then she bit down on her lower lip and glanced at him confidentially. "I shouldn't say— well, no, I'd better not."

Quail leaned his 6'3" frame down to Macy, but only as far as his stomach would allow. "Go ahead. You can tell me."

Macy lowered her voice. "Well, a few times, when we've been sitting around trying to figure out how to make ends meet, Momma mentions how she sure chose the wrong guy in high school, and if only she had it to do over again . . ."

Quail pulled his melon head back far enough to rest it atop his mishmash of chins. "Is that so?"

"It's so. Says she wishes she'd chosen the guy who liked her better than all the rest but was too shy to act on it." Macy twinkled and batted her eyelashes. "And she never fails to mention the success you've become. *That Richie Quail*, she says." Macy stood on sturdy ground now, certain that Quail had no idea of her mother's acidic tone when mentioning him.

Macy watched the big man's ego swell. She could practically see him swimming around in his inflated self-image, soaking up the adulation like a cockroach in a warm bath.

Quail pulled himself up to full height. "You know, doesn't surprise me one bit your Momma feels that way, not one bit. But that's neither here nor there now." His words argued against the grin trickling across his floppy lips. "So you don't have that money, then?"

"Sure don't, but I can run it by your office in the next couple days. Might even be cash if they give tips at that tattoo place. You must know if they do."

Quail was caught off-guard with that one, unaware that Hoop had taught Macy the advantage of keeping people off-balance by a degree or two. *Never hurts to rattle someone's foundation, Macy. You'd be surprised what can happen.*

"What? No!" Quail said. "How would I know? You think I have tattoos?"

Macy simply stared, her blue eyes more blameless than anything going on behind them.

"What's your name again?" Quail said. "Stacy? Gracie?"

She smiled as if he'd paid her a compliment. "It's Macy, sir, just like the parade."

"All right, Macy. You bring me that money within two days, y'hear?"

"I'll deliver it myself, Mr. Quail. Promise."

Quail descended the stairs and mumbled to himself as he trudged toward Hoop's door, his footsteps surprisingly light for such a heavy load. As Macy watched him go, she wished she hadn't added that *promise* bit. She hated breaking promises, but not as much as she hated for her mother to be tormented.

She closed the door. There was no way to come up with that money.

Chapter 23

My airboat had never before delivered me to a date, but driving to Rafe's would have meant a fifteen-minute trip, even longer if the bridge was up. By boat, I was but a quick sneak-peek away, and I really needed something to end this day on a good note.

It did feel silly, however, to step onto my refurbished 1994 Cottonmouth Airboat in three-inch heels. Definitely an insult to the nature of the craft. When I bought it used, the engine had forty hours on it; I'd added over two hundred since then and would gladly relive every one of them. I might not have been the biggest fan of Beulah, but the swamp and I had a mutual understanding: I would love and respect it, and it wouldn't kill me.

I cranked up the fan and felt the hum of the craft as much as heard it. The sound of the huge whirring blades lulled me into a tranquil state. Then I reached over and switched on the light—didn't want to hit a gator, after all. They were easy to spot by the reflective shine of their eyes at night. Always came in twos—except on Old Bastard, of course, an ancient mainstay who'd met with a nasty enemy or vicious fishhook somewhere along the way. Last time I laid eyes on Old Bastard's eye, Hoop had rowed me out in Mr. Swanson's canoe, a vessel he'd adopted as his own because Mr. Swanson had graduated from canoe to cane and rarely left his porch anymore.

\#

"There he is!" Hoop had said. "Old Bastard in the flesh!"

Hoop always threw him a fish—against the recommendations of experts—but Old Bastard never bit.

"You ever get scared he's gonna eat you alive, Hoop?"

"Nope. I've sat with him plenty. Had some of my finest

conversations with Old Bastard."

"About what?"

"Life. The future. The secrets of the swamp."

"And he never gets carnivorous during these chinwags?"

"Nah. Gators are ectotherms, Clover. They got low metabolic rates—unlike your humble captain here—so they don't eat much. A big dog'll eat more in a year than an eight-hundred-pound gator does. That's why, for insurance, I toss a fish or two at him before settling in to partake of his wisdom."

"How long you think he'll live?"

Hoop blew air out between his lips. "Good question, Clover. Can't say as I know, but there's this gator over in Serbia, hails from Mississippi, believe it or not, and he's been around since *before* World War II. Goes by the mighty cool name of Muja. Still kicking as far as I know, and I figure Old Bastard'll smash Muja's record by a landslide."

#

I realized I hadn't seen Old Bastard in over six months. I really needed to pay him a visit.

With my left hand on the rudder, I cruised along, my stomach churning as fast as my blades. Was it possible I was nervous? I gazed at Rafe's house. A single lamp shined from his living room, but as I got closer, I spotted random beams of light radiating in various directions inside the house, flashing on and off at inconsistent intervals. A vision of a disco ball and strobe light popped into my head, and for one irrational moment, I worried Rafe might answer the door in a white tux, breaking out vintage John Travolta moves.

Still, despite a legitimate fear of hearing *Night Fever*, I made a smooth landing, hobbled onto his deck in my heels, and tied up my boat.

I grabbed the wine I'd brought and traversed the beautiful stone walkway that would lead me to the front yard. It wasn't until my fourth step that I noticed how the path automatically lit up in front of me while the stepping stones behind me extinguished themselves into darkness. The effect was both charming and sinister. Were there cameras out here, too? Were upskirt shots of my thong underwear going viral in real-time? As these irrational thoughts crowded my head, I wondered why I was even going to a near-stranger's house when I feared both disco and voyeuristic perversion.

I reached the front of the house, ascended the eight bluestone steps, and stood immobile under the eerie glow of two yellow lights. My hand, moist with sweat, remained clasped in front of me, refusing to reach out and ring the doorbell. What had gotten into me? I'd been on plenty of dates and besides, this wasn't really a date. It was two neighbors—

The door opened. No creaking or scraping. It simply opened. I pasted on a smile like the one in my fourth grade class photo and almost fell back when I saw Rafe's feet—dangling in the air. They hung at knee level. I tried to scream, but the sound got lodged in my throat, ballooning down and outward with such force that I feared a flesh-and-blood explosion right here on the porch.

But Rafe's feet were moving, and not in a random way. They were doing some sort of creepy box dance, with no floor. I couldn't stop staring at them. They were clad in expensive loafers, a single leather tassel on each. My throat suddenly clamped shut, and my legs turned to lead before the back of my neck tensed up so hard that it caused an instant, blazing headache to flare. Finally, despite my temporary paralysis, my eyes rose up and my scream became all too real.

Chapter 24

Rafe was not, in fact, dangling from a noose as I'd feared. He was smiling down at me, gesturing for me to enter. His lips moved, but no words escaped. As I stared with one part fascination and two parts horror, I searched desperately for wires, projectors, or any logical explanation, but my speculation was cut short when the upper left quadrant of his head evaporated, as if taken out by the silent heat of a sniper's bullet. It happened with no blood—and no apparent consequences—because his mouth kept moving despite the lack of a frontal lobe. I felt like I'd landed in the middle of some badly dubbed, Japanese zombie movie.

Suddenly, my fear and panic vanished. In their place blossomed anger and rage. I recalled the strange lights from earlier, along with Rafe's fascination with lenses and light-splitting, not to mention the magical appearance of a yellow rose from his duplicitous palm.

This was some sort of trick.

I shouted at the apparition that now bobbed in midair like an elevator attendant unable to decide on a floor, "Screw you, you weirdo! I should have known you'd be a warped son of a—"

The door flew open all the way. A desperate, panting Rafe stood before me, his feet planted firmly on the floor, his head in one cohesive piece. Beads of sweat sprinkled his forehead; half-headed Rafe had somehow disappeared.

Instead of melting into a grateful puddle of relief or rushing into a fit of trembles as my adrenaline subsided, I coiled up and struck, using words in place of a forked tongue. "You thoughtless son of a bitch! You evil, inconsiderate lowlife! I knew you were different, and undeniably strange, but I hadn't realized you were a diagnosable psychopath."

I smashed the neck of the wine bottle against his doorframe and poured the dark red contents onto the absorbent bluestones of his front landing. It would stain permanently.

"Chloe, I am so sorry," he said, the grin on his face belying his words. Even as he tried to repress his impish expression, it shone through in the delightful crinkles that highlighted his dark eyes like snappy jazz hands.

I reached down, whipped off the shoes I'd regretted putting on anyway, and began the humiliating march back to my boat. But in a flash, Rafe dashed down the steps ahead of me and blocked my path.

"Get out of my way," I said, my voice flat but promising a roller-coaster of an encore if necessary.

"Please, Chloe. That went horribly wrong. I'm working out some final kinks in a project, and I got wedged inside my control room in the rush to get to the front door. I must have nudged a mirror and God knows what it did to my hologram."

I narrowed my eyes. "I'll tell you what it did. It evaporated your brain, although I suspect that organ may have taken its leave long ago."

Again, he could barely contain his spirited smirk despite a valiant effort. His irrepressible joy was hard to ignore, but my rage kept firing fresh jolts into my system. I poked him hard in the chest. "You don't do that to a person."

"I beg forgiveness," he said, bowing with a swirl of his fingers. He continued his downward spiral into a one-kneed pose as he reached for my hand. "Please . . . give me another chance? You're the last person I want to hurt."

Although my wrath was quelling, the sentiment hadn't quite reached my larynx. "Who's the first?"

He smiled and lifted his eyes to mine. "You see? It's always words with you, and you do delight me with your choices."

"All right," I said. "Get up. I don't like anyone that close to my feet."

He kept his eyes high. "Remarkable arches, though. A silhouette of your foot could easily pass for an alligator sunning itself on a warm rock." At my disgusted expression, he added, "That's a high compliment, you know."

I pulled on his hand until he stood all the way up. With him situated one step lower than me, we stood face to face, our eyes and mouths exceedingly close, and I resented the rippling sensation it sent through my body. Because our hands were still linked, he took the opportunity to amend his initial greeting. He pumped my hand up and down several times. "Chloe Keyes, I am so glad you could join me tonight. Won't you please come in?"

I could never explain why I left my hand in his and allowed him to lead me into his contemporary home with the Frank Lloyd Wright vibe, but even as it happened, I knew I wanted it to. We crossed the two-story foyer decorated with steel tables and huge quantities of camellias, tulips, and roses. No sign of a Rafe avatar. I followed him into a cavernous room with a painted cathedral ceiling. It seemed as if Rafe had contracted Michelangelo himself to enhance the décor, and I definitely wanted a closer look.

The steel theme flowed throughout his home, combined with exposed beams, sleek black furniture, and a massive amount of high-tech astrology or photographic equipment. The latter was strewn about in a careless but sterile manner.

I dropped my shoes on a beautiful area rug and let him lead me to the kitchen. Despite the scene at the front door, I felt instantly comfortable with my host and sensed that he felt the same way. He released my hand at the precise instant I expected, and, as if choreographed, he placed the stem of a poured glass of pinot noir into my waiting fingers. Had he known I'd be painting the porch with the bottle I brought?

I sipped the wine and relished its subtleties; it had been a very trying day. When I turned to face the main room, Rafe flowed over and stood next to me. "Chalet Borose," he announced.

"Rhymes with morose," I said.

He swept his hand to encompass the magnificence, including the vertically intimidating windows that faced my house. I noticed that I'd left a bathroom light on, but more consequentially, I realized how my juvenile spy charades with clunky binoculars were mere child's play to him. And for God's sake, I really needed to stop walking around naked on Sunday mornings.

I stepped into the living room with its vast array of telescopes, lenses, and things I couldn't name, letting my hand stroke the top of one piece as I spun toward him. "Care to explain?"

"That?" he said, pointing to the phallic equipment beneath my fingers. "That is a high-level Celestron telescope, capable of seeing everything from the notches of Orion's Belt in December to the crack in the left pillar supporting your house."

If circumstances were anything close to normal, I might have found the comment disturbing; circumstances, however, were not even orbiting normal. "When I asked you to explain," I said, "I wasn't referring to this telescope, and I think you know it."

"Ah, you meant Hologram Rafe." He strode over and stood across from me, the telescope jutting upward at an angle between us. "He's quite handsome, isn't he?"

I sipped my wine in response.

"It's a hobby of mine," he said. "Splitting light, as I mentioned in the swamp, and interfering with it. That's really all holograms are. But I've got a nasty habit of taking hobbies to the extreme. Three pending patents for my work in the area, in addition to four I already hold." He gestured to the water between our homes. "Sometimes, I think it's all a hologram."

"The swamp?"

"No, Beulah. Back Beulah especially. With its homey charms untouched by modernism and its quirky, workaday vibe. But then, there's a darker aura."

"I don't disagree."

"An aura of having been secreted away like the naughty child you don't acknowledge when guests visit. It strikes me as a place with sharp edges, ruthlessness, and self-delusion—the idea that everyone should act and believe one way while those in power act and believe otherwise."

"What does any of that have to do with a hologram?"

"If I can split the light that creates the illusion of a place like Beulah, then it's within my power to reveal the deeper, darker layers."

"Why would you want to?"

"Because while everyone's staring at the hologram and believing it's real, their souls are being picked like a pocket."

"Picked of what?"

"Decency. Humanity. Truth. All pilfered by the man behind the curtain."

The Wizard of Oz reference threw me, as if Rafe had plumbed my recent thoughts. "And who is this man?" I asked.

"Remains to be seen, I suppose."

I stepped away from the telescope and ventured into the heart of the high-ceilinged room. "For a newcomer," I said, "you have a very sober take on Beulah, but I see it differently. To me, it's a jaded snow globe, a joke designed by Norman Rockwell on his worst day. Beulah gets shaken up now and again, and maybe the world glances our way, but then it all settles down and excitement floats to the bottom, until nobody cares anymore. Nobody gazes in. We return to stillness and isolation." I turned to take in the view of my jaded town. "But I don't mind. I like it better when it's settled and established."

"Why?"

"The shaking has never brought good."

"What about the lottery winners? That brought good to the town."

"It was the snow in the snow globe, maybe. But you know what happens to snow after a couple days. It turns black from exhaust. Becomes a burden if it doesn't melt."

He snickered. "A wet blanket, so to speak."

"Yes. Our little flurry of winners came with a wet blanket of tragedy. That's what my upcoming article is about."

"I can't wait to read it."

"Soon enough. But first, explain this gadget-filled room. Most people have a new-model smartphone. You've got Q's laboratory from James Bond."

"Ah, Q. Clever fellow, though I could teach him a thing or two." He touched a button on a nearby remote control and made Hologram Rafe appear, motionless and daunting. "The name of my game is illusion. The details involve mirrors, beams of light, and utter stillness. But knowing what's behind it detracts from the magic."

"You said you'd show me which of your many pursuits helps you make a living." I gestured to fake-Rafe. "Is this it?"

"No, my livelihood is rather boring, bordering on shameful. But it has allowed me the freedom to pursue my passions." He gestured halfheartedly toward his laptop. "There. That's how I make my living."

"Must be more to it than that."

"There is. Have you ever heard of the Forenza-Galasso circus?"

My shock was such that the swinging breeze of an empty

trapeze could have knocked me over.

Rafe gaged my reaction and smiled. "I'm afraid it's not as exciting as you might be imagining."

"But the circus used to perform here."

"I know. That's why I'm here. My uncle, Berrio Forenza, knew the place and recommended I put down roots. I have clients in the area."

I swallowed hard. "You're a Forenza?"

Rafe grinned. "No, if I were a Forenza, I'd probably be a Galasso, too. They've created rather their own scary species—intermarriage and all that."

I laughed, but internally, my mind buzzed. I'd tried for years to find an insider with the circus, but like a magic trick, they'd disappeared without a trace, physically and virtually.

"I'm a Forenza by employment," Rafe explained. "But if you can tolerate their eccentricities and caginess for more than a few weeks, they essentially adopt you and become your uncles, aunts, and cousins."

I tilted my head. "You don't strike me as a carnie."

"Far from it. Like you, I grew up in a small town where the circus made one of its stops. For three seasons, I even smoked the good stuff with Sacchi, one of the more rebellious Forenza boys. He'd sneak out with his spider monkey on his back, meet me in the woods, and we'd create all sorts of havoc. Amazing what a spider monkey will do with cannabis smoke in its system."

"That's cruel."

"We didn't do it on purpose. That little guy would lean forward from Sacchi's shoulder and inhale as if a cloud of gold was floating by. Anyway, when I got out of school, through a rather circuitous route, I got hired to hide money for both families."

"Buried treasure sort of thing?"

"Money laundering sort of thing."

147

"Was your degree from the Tony Soprano School of Finance?"

"Impossible to learn the good without knowing the bad."

I took a moment to process. "So staying off the SEC's radar requires knowing what puts you on it?"

Rafe smiled and shot a finger in my direction. As he did, he used his other hand to steer his hologram self around the room. Was I only moments away from some kinky twin orgy? I didn't tell him to turn it off.

"Ever notice that if you research the Forenza-Galassos," he said, "you don't find much?"

"Yes. I tried several years ago. It's impossible."

"Let's just say I introduced them to the dark corners of the internet."

"Didn't know it had corners."

"Far more than four. Ever hear of TOR, the onion router?"

I shook my head.

"It was founded by the Naval Research Laboratory to help people in oppressed countries stay anonymous yet provide a way for them to get word out to the world. The onion router can bounce signals to five-thousand relays if it needs to, to help mask online identities. Quite intriguing, really."

"So . . . the money I spent on cotton candy and peanuts . . . did it travel along this onion thing and get laundered?"

"Not directly. Laundering requires that the money be dirty first, but I can't say much more than that. Unfortunately, TOR is now exploited by sex predators and drug dealers, and it's one of the things that helps me make a living."

I cringed, fearing he was about to reveal a life of crime.

He knitted his bushy brows, the thickness of which now seemed to fit better on his face—a match for the intensity of his eyes. "I shine light in the dark corners."

I brightened. "You work for the good guys?"

"Among other things, I act as a consultant, combatting those who exploit the dark side."

"And this justifies the money laundering you did?"

Rafe narrowed his eyes and reflected. "Both professions involve cleaning up." He made his hologram sit on my other side and put an arm around me. I blushed. "I also do significant investing for a few wealthy clients. But these topics are so boring. Tell me, Chloe, why did you try to contact my uncles in years past?"

"I was searching for a friend." I shifted to face him more fully on the couch, turning my back to the hologram as I grew more interested in the solid version. "Do you by any chance have a roster of performers, anything like that?"

He grinned. "A circus that swings beneath the radar, deals in cash, and specializes in breeding people with inhuman flexibility, does not keep a roster."

"But you must have known everyone. Were you there twelve years ago?"

"Ouch. Do I look that old?"

I sighed. He looked thirty at most, making him eighteen or younger when Hoop went missing—just entering school, not finishing it. But perhaps Hoop was still there when Rafe arrived, having become a full-fledged carnie under a different name. As I tried to hope, images of blood and green flannel streaked my thoughts. Optimism won out, so I asked. "Did you ever come across a boy named Hoop Whitaker? He might still have been there."

Rafe tilted his head and paused. "Hoop Whitaker," he repeated. "Good circus name."

Hearing the name uttered with no trace of sadness seemed odd. It had been so long since anyone in Beulah had been able to do that, but Rafe had used an upbeat tone that Hoop would have appreciated. "I'm sorry," he said. "It doesn't ring a bell." He leaned in closer. "Is he the one you mentioned at Grinder Minder, the one who disappeared?"

"Assuming it was only a disappearance."

He reached out and pushed a strand of hair away from my face, the tips of his fingers caressing the edge of my skin. Incredibly intimate, strongly reassuring. Shockwaves reverberated through me and almost created the illusion that life was normal and unscarred.

"I'll tell you what, my intrepid little reporter. My uncles can be tough to get a hold of—they stay away from all modern trappings—but if you give me a few days, I promise you an answer on your Hoop Whitaker."

I wanted to feel elation but couldn't banish the chilling reality of Boyd's basement from my mind. "That would mean a lot. Thanks."

"I'll get back to you by"—Rafe glanced at the huge, multi-function watch on his wrist—"April Fools' Day. Deal?"

My gut clenched. April Fools' Day was Macy's birthday. But it seemed as appropriate a time as any to hear the truth. I touched his hand and a charge shot through me. "Thank you, Rafe. Truly."

The hologram floated in front of us. Suddenly, in Rafe's voice, it said, "You're welcome."

I nearly jumped out of my skin. "It talks?"

Rafe chortled. "The house is laden with speakers, and *you're welcome* happens to be one of the phrases I programmed in."

I gestured to the apparition. "Why don't you make this your profession?"

"I've helped at concerts and done plenty of private projects, but I plan to use my holograms for much more than money."

"Hopefully not for spying on neighbors."

"I think one spy is enough for this swamp, don't you?"

I blushed again. "Hardly my fault if you're exercising when I'm gator-gawking. Besides, I think you like that I watch."

He stroked my face again. "I'd much prefer you watching me without those silly binoculars between us."

I resisted the urge to lean forward and kiss him. "How are you controlling your hologram, anyway?"

He held up the remote in his hand. "I've custom-programmed this. Click here if you want it to do something, and here if you want to do something to it."

"It's that easy?"

"It is if you think of the remote as a supercomputer with a billion lines of code and patentable technologies that the government would ban if they knew existed."

After some struggles and corrections from Rafe, I made the hologram float to the ceiling and back down. "What do you plan to use this handsome guy for?"

He stood and grabbed the wine bottle, then gestured dramatically to the ceiling. "For disillusionment."

I arced my neck up to take in the details of the fresco, but Rafe extended his hand toward me. "Easier to appreciate if you lie down."

I hesitated but took his hand and stood. He put down the wine and reached into a wooden chest, pulling out a thick blanket and one pillow.

"Why do I get the feeling you've done this before?"

"Because I have. But notice, only one pillow. I usually gaze up there when I'm alone and need inspiration."

He spread out the blanket and positioned the pillow. We lay down together, our heads close, but my feet pointing at seven o'clock, his at five. I looked up and felt pummeled in the heart by the beautiful but harsh montage above: flowing robes; shining swords; bright blood; a brighter sun; manes of hair on full-busted women; layers of muscles on barely clad men. All of it violent, passionate, and demanding. "What exactly are we looking at?"

"Betrayal."

"More specifically?"

"Over there, Medea killing her own children to get back at the husband who betrayed her. There, the sons of Pelops, Thyestes and Atreus. The latter killed and cooked the former's children—and fed them to him—but of course, Atreus had slept with Thyestes' wife who bore a child that was raised to kill his uncle."

"And these scenes are your *inspiration*?"

"There"—he pointed to a depiction of the poet Horace with a feather pen—"is my favorite. 'Nec deus intersit, nisi dignus vindice nodus'."

"I'm afraid my Latin is rusty."

"*That a god not intervene, unless a knot show up that be worthy of such an untangler.*"

"I remember that. Referring to the old Greek plays using deus ex machina, right? The god machine?"

He swiveled his head to look at me. I could feel his warm breath on my neck. "Not so rusty, after all. Yes, in the old plays, they used cranes to lower gods who, in turn, would extricate the characters from all sorts of treacherous and convoluted situations. Horace, however, found the arrival of the gods a weak solution to a story's problem."

"I kind of like the idea."

"Horace believed such a device should be limited to difficulties so insurmountable that they were worthy of a god's unraveling."

"Do you agree?"

"Well, we don't have the option of lowering a god from the ceiling, do we? But it reminds me to be my own god, my own problem-solver."

I pointed. "What about that section, there?"

"My tribute to Judas, of course, and next to him, a montage of images from King Lear. Brothers betraying brothers. Children betraying fathers." He turned to me again, but I kept my eyes upward. "They say that at the heart of every betrayal lies a warped set of values, which in the end leads to the betrayers betraying each other."

"But you said this was about disillusionment. All I see is betrayal and cruelty."

"It disillusions *me*. Reminds me what people are capable of, how they are not always what they claim to be. I use it to keep myself grounded. Believe me, it's an ongoing battle."

I leaned up on one elbow, not realizing until I was facing him how intimate it made the space between us. "Rafe, you have such a dire outlook. Who betrayed you?"

"No one, really. Not me."

I narrowed my eyes in doubt and indicated the ceiling. "A man doesn't turn his heavenly view into a constant reminder of betrayal because he likes the red hue of the blood."

He leaned up on his elbow, the distance between our bodies narrowing to a thin slice. Heat ricocheted between us. Had we been standing, one of us would have lost balance and leaned on the other for support. "The art depicts duplicity and depravity," he said, "but its purpose is to counteract the human tendency to fill in the blanks with goodness. We do that instinctively, and in ignorance, to compensate for breaches of the soul so deplorable that we can barely fathom them."

I felt lost but struggled to stay afloat. "You mean we try to deny the worst evils, even in the face of facts?"

"Exactly. We assign good. We rationalize. It's a coping mechanism."

"I disagree. I've dedicated a career to the opposite. I don't sugarcoat things. I report the facts, on the guilty as well as the innocent. And when people read my articles, they tend to believe them."

Rafe smirked, and I felt like a sucker continually guessing the wrong cup under which the truth was hidden. "What if the news you report is wrong?"

"Then that's my fault. But you can't believe that people choose to see goodness in evil simply because the evil is unexpected or inhumane. The world is overrun with sickos doing unimaginable things every day. If anything, we're all too aware of it."

"And from sickos, we expect sick deeds. It's tougher to accept those we admire as evil, those to whom we have lent credence."

He reached behind him and opened a low drawer from a jigsaw-like table. From within, he pulled two six-inch square cards, and then resumed his position across from me. He held up the first card. It showed four black circles, one in each corner of the card. Within each circle were three other circles, growing progressively smaller in diameter

"What do you see?"

"Four individual circles with concentric circles inside them."

He held up the second card. It showed the same circles, but with a sheer blue circle overlying their centers:

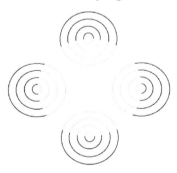

"What do you see now?"

"A large blue circle covering portions of the black

circles."

"And yet, there is no blue circle."

I reached out and touched the card. "It's right here." I traced its outline.

"Your mind created the blue circle because you expected it to be there. You filled in the blanks."

"What blanks? There are no blanks."

He pointed. "Here. In the empty space between each of the black circles. It's still white, still empty, but your mind completed the image you're comfortable with. The only real blue in this picture is where the black lines have been colored blue."

I took the card from him.

"Ah," he said, "the reporter needs her hands-on proof."

I stared, using my hands to block out parts of the image, verifying that the portions that appeared blue were actually white. I thrust the card back at him and spoke like a bratty teen. "Okay, you win. But so what? Eyewitness testimony is the weakest form of proof."

Rafe stared, his black eyes sucking mine in, perhaps deeper than I wanted to go. "So true."

He dropped the cards behind him without breaking our visual connection. "It's hard enough to convince our eyes of horror when it's right in front of us. Much harder to convince our minds and hearts. Ever see a wife defend a husband after he's obviously battered their child? She's desperate to believe in his goodness. She married him, after all, so she fills in the warm blue parts and refuses to see the cold red or the blank whites. The mind-torque required for her to veer so far from her core beliefs, well, it's soul-wrenching. Once illusions like that are dispelled, it doesn't leave a person normal."

I felt my jaw go tense beneath quivering lips. I felt fear, a dread that I was alone with a man who might not have been left normal. "Is that what happened to you?"

Rafe didn't respond, but didn't necessarily seem averse to responding, either. He simply stared.

"I understand if it's personal," I said, "but something must have happened."

There was lightness in his expression as he reached out and laid his hand on the side of my neck. His fingers were hot, almost blazing, his touch gentle yet imposing. The pressure of his palm felt powerful against my skin, and suddenly, my increased pulse rate became an exposed, throbbing heart in the veins of my neck. I no longer cared about the fear. We were entangled on a level I'd rarely achieved with anyone. Some might call it spiritual—I certainly had no name for it— but we were uniquely intertwined at that moment, as if he were conveying a secret directly to my soul. I struggled to decode it.

The past became trivial, as if all moments had been leading to this culmination—but a culmination of what? Had I only ever existed to be delivered to this point in time? My soul swam in the murkiness of his eyes. I became hypnotized, captivated, no longer an individual composed of my own dreams and history, but one swept away beneath his strength. Something gripped me inside, tethering me to his truth, and it became vitally important that I learn it.

"I understand," he whispered.

"What do you understand?" My voice barely broke the surface of the dark waters under which I was flailing.

"The unimaginable strength it takes to be patient, to still the waters of your wanting."

I could only feel: his palm on my neck, my blood against his palm, the rhythmic throb between his thumb and forefinger conducting the tempo of my heart, subduing my body. "This isn't about me," I said.

"It is, Chloe. Haven't you waited? Sacrificed? Haven't you dug, relentlessly, like a prisoner with only a single pebble to chip away at the wall denying your destiny?"

I swallowed. He stroked my throat with his thumb.

"I don't know what's happening," I said. Apprehension overtook my entangled feelings from earlier. My breathing grew erratic, and with a force that burrowed up from deep inside me, I forced his hand from my throat, breaking the spell. "No," I said. "Whatever this is, I'm not ready for it."

"You will be," he said. "I promise. You've waited as long as anyone."

I remembered his story about the amulet—a conduit from another world. Had he cast some sort of spell on me? Drugged my wine? I wanted to stand, to confront him, but weakness overwhelmed me. I became the white parts of a blue circle—not really there, not seen by anyone, lost in a mirage. And then an idea struck me. *The answer had to be above.* I needed to look again, to see not what my mind had filled in, but what was really there.

I lay back down on the floor, staring upward. He watched, sitting up, unmoving. I gazed at the images, felt myself swirling in the brushstrokes of the paint, the taunting edges of the subjects' robes. I felt the glistening points of their weapons, tasted the coldness of the metal. A dismal gloom surrounded me, and suddenly, I spotted something disturbing in the image, something anachronistic and haunting, but I couldn't be sure.

"Binoculars," I whispered. "I need binoculars."

He reached for them.

The doorbell rang.

We both froze, pulled from the surrealism of the past few minutes, and we looked at each other accusingly, as if each had plotted for the doorbell to ring at precisely that moment.

It sounded again. I sat up and shook my head to indicate that I had no idea who it was. Rafe broke into a grin, then, as if enthralled by the prospect of more fun and games. Part of me wondered why he wasn't more disappointed that our evening alone, filled with such disturbing potential, had been interrupted. As he sprung up to answer the door, I stayed motionless. It was all I could do to breathe.

"Let's keep this between us, Chloe," he said as he crossed the room. Then he turned back and winked. "I know you can keep a secret."

Seemed to me that a secret was the least of what had transpired between us.

He strode to the foyer and opened the door. From where I sat, I couldn't see him, but the acoustics in the vast space allowed me to hear everything.

"Evening, Deputy Sheriff," Rafe said. "It's Chad, isn't it?"

Chapter 25

I stiffened. What in the world was Chad doing here? I forced myself up and straightened my dress. Then I primped my hair and prayed that my face would go pale. But I felt flushed and downright post-coital—a look Chad was intimately familiar with.

Please don't invite him in. Please don't invite him in.

"This was on your front door," said Chad's voice, and I heard a crinkle of paper exchanged.

A quiet moment passed. "A magic show?" Rafe said with boyish delight. "Sounds intriguing. Won't you come in, Deputy?"

"Sorry to bother you like this unannounced," Chad said in his easy way, "but you don't have a land line, and I knew where you lived, so I took a chance."

I could hear him wiping his feet on Rafe's sisal carpet.

"No problem at all." The front door closed.

I willed Rafe to tell Chad that he had company, that he was busy, anything but—

Chad entered the living room. I forced a smile, my hair tousled, my lips shaky. Chad's expression left no doubt that I looked all sorts of not right.

My hand strayed to my neck, touching an area that still felt tingly. For all I knew, Rafe had left a handprint there—or a psychic hickey. Then I patted down a strand of hair, but none of it did anything to lessen the aura of guilt wafting off me like an animalistic pheromone.

"Chad. Hey." Awkward, fluttery wave. "What are you doing here?"

His face darkened and he actually ignored me, turning back to Rafe who'd remained standing at the edge of the room. "I'm sorry, Mr. Borose," Chad said. "I didn't realize you had . . . company. We can talk tomorrow."

"No worries. And please, call me Rafe." He flowed into the room then, his bare feet silent against the floor, as if awkward situations actually made him cooler. "I believe you know my neighbor, Chloe Keyes."

"Neighbor?" Skepticism filled Chad's voice. "As the crow flies, I guess."

"May I get you a glass of wine, Deputy? Chloe and I were just discussing betrayal. We'd love to hear your take."

Chad looked pointedly at me while answering. "It happens. That's my take."

Rafe laughed—a fine, gentlemanly laugh, rich with color. "A succinct answer. I like your style."

Chad folded his arms in front of him. "As I told Chloe earlier, turns out Grace Elbee was betrayed more than we originally suspected."

"How so?" Rafe said.

"Evidence of foul play. That's all I can say."

Rafe pulled his head back. "That's disturbing."

Chad adopted a confident, nonchalant manner. It was his best persona—the one that had turned me on most when we dated. "So, Rafe, I need to know how it is you came to know where Mrs. Elbee's body was the moment it surfaced."

"Certainly. If you'll excuse me just a moment." Rafe glided into the kitchen, leaving Chad and me alone to stare at each other. He made a show of noticing my bare feet, which stood only inches from the single pillow on the floor. It seemed that his heart broke a little then.

Rafe appeared between us with a glass of water for Chad and a refilled glass of wine for me. He gestured for Chad to take a seat. Chad chose a wide chintz chair with enough room for two while Rafe chose a curved, short-backed sofa, leaving me with an awkward decision.

I chose the pillar between them, leaning against it and

sipping my wine defiantly.

"I'm afraid I won't be of much help as far as Mrs. Elbee goes," Rafe said. "But I'm happy to give you my statement."

Chad gave an encouraging nod. "Please."

"I got on my computer around 4 a.m. I do a lot of futures trading at night and a fair bit of monitoring of the Asian markets. At sunrise, I took a break and played with my cameras—I'm a bit of a technology wonk—and later, I went outside to do some yoga." He sniffed deeply. "I do love the smell of swamp in the morning."

I glanced at Chad, knowing how pluff mud's stew of decaying odors made him feel like he'd stuck his nose in a pile of dirty socks.

"When I came back inside," Rafe continued, "I bumped my telescope and it landed on Mrs. Elbee's body." He gestured to his telescope. As Chad glanced over, he surely appreciated how the phallic lens offered a perfect view of my house. "Shortly afterwards, I spotted Chloe entering the water in her waders." He smiled at me as if we were an established couple sharing an intimate memory. "Very flattering by the way."

I cast my eyes to the floor, pissed. He had no reason to hurt Chad. But Chad surprised me by letting out a chortle. "I used to tell her she looked like a walrus in those things; she thinks they're slimming."

He and Rafe shared a chuckle over that one and I ended up feeling like an idiot.

Rafe continued. "I calculated that Chloe would reach the body before me, so I called 9-1-1 to report it in case she hadn't."

Chad's head cocked just enough to be noticeable. He'd be verifying that call.

"And then I swam over to see if Chloe needed any help."

"Did you know Mrs. Elbee?" Chad asked.

"Only briefly. We tried to get our hands on the same

amulet at the Farmer's Market." Rafe got up and plucked an amulet from a display case against his wall, dangling it like a hypnotist's watch. "Very similar to this one."

He handed it to Chad, who examined it closely and then placed it down. "Since you're into this stuff . . . what about writing a dead person's name on a mirror? What does that mean?"

I was surprised Chad revealed that detail, but at least he hadn't related it directly to Mrs. Elbee.

"A mirror?" Rafe said, sitting down and crossing his legs while splaying a long arm across the back of the sofa. "Attraction, clearly. Think about it. We use mirrors to enhance our own attractiveness. Images multiply within them, many times over with the right angles." He looked at me to convey the next thought. "Mirrors can also split light and create images that seem ghostlike or real. They're used for deception and trickery, even spying. I can't imagine a more attractive surface for drawing the attention of a spirit than a mirror." He looked pointedly at Chad for his next question. "Was the mirror in a room with other reflective surfaces?"

Chad glanced at me, no doubt thinking of the sterling silver candleholders in the bathroom, the shiny porcelain vanity, the shower's glass door, and the echoes of our own images in the reflective light fixtures. He returned his gaze to Rafe, his suspicions far from allayed now. "It's just a hypothetical situation," he said.

"Well, the more times a reflection is projected into the world, the more dimensions it reaches. Better odds of connecting with a particular spirit."

I couldn't help but interject, although I needed to phrase my question carefully. "But if someone were wearing an amulet to repel evil, why would they want to attract a spirit?"

Rafe slowly turned his head to me to answer the question. "You know what they say. Keep your friends close, your enemies closer. I've always believed in it." He punctuated his statement with a satisfied smile before continuing. "The amulet would still protect its wearer from the evil intentions of the spirit, while simultaneously bringing the spirit closer . . . either to be destroyed or to receive a message. Most commonly, one attracts a spirit to renew love and ask it to stay, or to make amends and ask it to leave."

Chad cleared his throat. "And if this spirit got the message, how would it respond?" He smiled, but insincerely, and I sensed it was meant for me. "Not like it could call on the phone, right?"

Rafe leaned forward and seemed to take the question more seriously than it had been rendered. "We humans think it's harmless to shoot all sorts of rays and waves around the world with our cell towers, microwaves, electromagnetic pulses, radios, you name it, but spirits savor such waves." His eyes narrowed and his enthusiasm grew. "Think about it. There are colors on the visual spectrum we can't see, depths of odor we can't decipher, frequencies we can't hear. Why wouldn't there be hitchhikers out there, invisible to us, traveling on the waves we take for granted?"

Chad threw his hands up, palms facing Rafe. "Whoa. Getting a little out there for me."

"Deputy, if the voices of everyone from Elvis to Justin Bieber can travel on waves to either delight or haunt our ears, why wouldn't we believe those same waves might be carrying uninvited guests? And why wouldn't those guests travel on such easy, pre-established conduits like the telephone line you mentioned?"

"Tell you what, Rafe, if you believe in ghosts, you got your choice of 'em in this town." He glanced from Rafe to me. "Now, when was the last time each of you had interaction with the victim?"

I started at Chad's use of the word *victim*, realizing that despite my neutral post against the pillar, teams had been chosen: Chad versus Rafe and me.

"About ten days ago," Rafe said. "Mrs. Elbee was walking through New Beulah with a candlestick, using it as a microphone of sorts."

"How about you, Chloe?"

"That would be this morning, Chad. When I dragged her body out of the swamp for you."

He smiled patiently. "And before that?"

"Am I a suspect now?"

"Haven't ruled anyone out yet."

"Then don't leave yourself out," I said. "You saw her when you were picking up Richie Quail's secretary for your lunch date. Does that help?"

He nodded, ever so coolly. "Noted, thanks."

Rafe then gave a formal statement. By the end of the conversation, I'd had quite enough of the evening. I thanked Rafe for the wine and stepped onto the porch with Chad, who noticed the red stains there with a curious eye. He then reflexively took my arm and offered to escort me to my boat, but I told him I'd be fine. When we reached the bottom of the stairs and stepped onto the lawn, Rafe called after me. "Chloe, I don't know when I'll see you again, and there's a magic show coming to town." He held up the flyer and shook it. "Would you do me the honor of being my date?"

Did Chad feel my forearm tighten in his grasp? "That sounds lovely, Rafe. Thanks."

I pulled my arm from Chad's grasp, mumbled a quick good-bye, and we went our separate ways.

Chapter 26

Two Days Before the Thump

Macy smelled bacon. She leaped out of bed and grabbed the aluminum Louisville Slugger leaning against her wall. She gripped it like someone who meant business as she tiptoed to the door, pressing her ear against it. Was that humming? Coffee dripping? If it was a robber, he sure was making himself at home.

She loosened her grip on the bat and inched the door open. Her mom smiled at her.

"Morning, sleepyhead," Melanie LeGrange said.

Macy shook her head to be sure she wasn't dreaming. Her mother noticed the reaction. "I know, I know. But I woke up feeling good today, and as they say, take 'em when you can get 'em."

Macy ran over and hugged her mother as if they hadn't seen each other in weeks. In essence, they hadn't. "We celebrating something?"

"Baby, in my world, I celebrate if I don't wake up feeling tired."

"Is it that new medicine Doc West prescribed? Thought you were ready to give up on it."

"He told me to stick with it for a week, so I did. Eight days today. I may not be feeling quite as chipper as this bacon sizzle suggests, but whaddya say we do something fun?"

"Anything," Macy said, beaming.

Her mom opened the refrigerator. "Looks like we're out of cream. You okay with milk in your coffee? Or maybe you can take it straight, like your momma."

Macy had been drinking coffee since the age of ten. Her mom probably didn't realize it, but most days they couldn't afford cream. Milk was all she'd ever used.

"I'm fine with milk."

"Let's stop by Boyd's later and pick up some cream. Can't have my girl starting her day off with a compromise."

After breakfast and showers, with only a few cockroaches for company, Macy and her mom went window-shopping at the scant stores Beulah Proper offered. They stopped by the park and swung on the swings, and when Melanie leaped off her swing just to prove that she could, Macy laughed for a solid minute as they both brushed sand from her mother's bottom. Afterwards, they grabbed a bite to eat at Tupelo's Lunch Counter where two people could split a sandwich and stick two straws in a shake for less than five dollars.

As they walked over to Boyd's to get cream, Macy told her mom how she'd lied to Richie Quail about her getting a job at the tattoo shop. That cued Melanie to laugh for a solid minute. "And what did Richie say to that?"

"Let's just say I wouldn't be surprised if he walks his wide tush over there in search of you."

Melanie shook her head. "I sure hope the owner doesn't talk him into a tattoo."

"Momma, be serious. I do believe they'd run out of ink."

As they reached Boyd's parking lot, they ran into Chloe Keyes who was tying a plastic bag to the handle of her bike.

"Hey there, Chloe," Mrs. LeGrange said. "You buy much more, you're going to need a basket on that bike."

Chloe jerked her head up at the sound of Mrs. LeGrange's voice. She looked stunned to see the woman out and about. Subduing her reaction quickly, she converted it to a smile. "Hi, Mrs. LeGrange. Hey, Macy. Just picking up some butter for my mom. She's a pretty bad cook, but butter makes it better, as my dad says, so we stay stocked."

"I agree. A little butter and salt never hurt anything," Mrs. LeGrange said.

Chloe indicated Boyd's store with her thumb. "Boyd Junior's in a sour mood today. Better watch out."

"I'm sure it's been hard on him since his father passed," Mrs. LeGrange said.

"Still," Chloe said, "I was a lot fonder of Boyd Senior. Used to throw hard candies in my bag, just to be nice."

"Junior's not so bad," Macy said. "Maybe he's embarrassed because he dropped out of school and such." She nudged her mother. "Hey Momma, you should ask for a job in there. You could probably double Boyd's business in a week."

Her mother grinned. "Maybe I will, sweetie. Especially if it comes with a store discount."

Macy pointed to the A-shaped sidewalk sign outside Boyd's. It read: *Egg Special $1/Duz.*

"Look at that, Momma. Eggs are on sale and we used ours up this morning. Must be our lucky day."

"If it's our lucky day," Mrs. LeGrange said, pointing to the lower half of the sign, "then we ought to buy a ticket."

The second message on the sign, hogging most of the space, read: *Power Pot Lttery. Now 16,0O0,000 $. Tix here BYD'S GENERAL Stre.*

"Looks like he ran out of zeroes," Macy said. "Bet he's never needed that many before."

"Tickets are five bucks a pop," Chloe said.

"Maybe we should have skipped lunch," Mrs. LeGrange said, her voice projecting a trace of regret.

When Macy glanced up, her mother was smiling, but it seemed to require more of an effort than it had this morning. "Absolutely not," Macy said, rubbing her stomach. "Best lunch I had in weeks. Besides, Hoop promised me when he grows up, he's gonna make more money than every Power Pot winner combined."

Mrs. LeGrange looked instantly anxious. "That's not a plan, Macy."

167

"What do you mean?"

"You girls need to remember one thing, if you remember anything at all." She pointed at each of them with her slim finger as her expression grew taut. "Don't you ever depend on any man to help you make it in life. Depend on only one person in this life, and that's yourself. It's all well and good if some boy plans to make himself a million dollars, but you need to go out and make your own million. Or at least enough to get by, with or without the likes of him."

Macy and Chloe stayed silent, both surprised at the lecture when everything had been so lighthearted a moment earlier. Then Macy put an arm around her mother's tiny waist and pulled her in close. "Doesn't mean you get to go back on your promise, though. I'm still allowed to date when I turn fifteen, right, Momma? Millionaires or no."

Mrs. LeGrange put an arm around Macy. She sniffed and blinked before answering. "Of course, but I sure don't recommend it." She turned to Chloe. "Did your parents make you wait before dating, Chloe?"

Chloe scratched her head and hoped it was only the sun's heat burning up her cheeks. "Uh, no, ma'am. They never really said. Can't say it's mattered much either way."

Macy waved away her mother's question. "Chloe's got bigger concerns than boys. She stays real busy studying and writing for the school paper, ain't that right, Chloe?"

"That's true," Chloe said, averting her eyes. She climbed onto her bike, scraping her calf against the pedal but ignoring the pain. "I'd better head home before this butter melts."

"Tell your mom and dad hello for me now," Mrs. LeGrange said.

"I sure will," Chloe said, seeming in a rush to get away. "See you at school next week, Macy."

They watched her pedal off. "That girl's got a good head on her shoulders," Mrs. LeGrange said. "She'll get out of this town, just like you, baby."

"She wants to be a reporter for a big city paper."

"How about you? Where do you want to end up?"

Macy looked off into space. "Can't say as I know yet, but I sure wouldn't mind staying here, close to you."

Mrs. LeGrange's expression grew panicked. She leaned down and grabbed Macy by both arms, probably harder than she meant to. "No, sweetie. You're going places, you hear me? You've got to set your sights well beyond Beulah."

"All I meant was—"

"Beyond South Carolina. Heck, maybe beyond the United States, because it'll be over my dead body that I'll have you living and dying here in Beulah. Over my dead body."

Macy winced and felt her heart contract. "Don't talk about dying and such, Momma. I don't like thinking about that stuff."

Mrs. LeGrange blinked rapidly again, trying to smile, hoping the moment would pass. Then she stood and patted down her hair. "Let's go get us some eggs and cream."

They joined hands and entered the store, ready to take on Boyd.

Chapter 27

The next morning, I startled awake to my alarm and seriously considered cancelling my interview with Adeline DeVore, by far the sexiest of the Lucky Four lottery winners. No way could I tolerate her patronization this morning. But then I remembered something. If she'd been a regular at Boyd's back in the day, maybe she knew of a link between Boyd and Hoop. If anyone knew dirty little secrets in Beulah, it was DeVore the Whore; heck, she'd been one herself more often than not.

I forced myself from bed and dug out my old coffee maker because tramping over to Grinder Minder every day was out of the question.

An hour and a half later, caffeinated but not enthused, I found myself knocking on a seemingly impenetrable mahogany door, the sound barely piercing the wood. The crest on the door matched the marquee on the outside of the six-story building: two sexually suggestive green leaves sprouting up and out to form the letter *V* of *DeVore Cosmetics,* with caramel-colored swirls above and below the name. The *V* screamed *vagina* so loudly that it could have scored the cover of Maxim.

Adeline DeVore's long-nosed assistant looked at me with minimal tolerance, the same attitude she'd conveyed when I entered the office wearing no mascara.

"I said she was ready for you?" the assistant whined. "That means you don't have to knock?"

I shot a withering glance at the fashionista-wannabe, tempted to respond in the same grating Valley Girl tone, but instead, I pushed down on the door handle, shoved, and let the door hang open a few inches. The assistant looked panicked. She waved her black-lacquered nails for me to *go in, go in,* both hands flapping desperately, as if the worst thing in the world was to keep Adeline DeVore waiting for three more seconds.

What she didn't realize was that Adeline DeVore needed me more than I needed her. DeVore Cosmetics had suffered a slow drip of bad publicity lately, leading to suspicions of a mole within the company. Rumors that DeVore cleansing oils weren't as pure as advertised, and their creams not as naturally sourced as claimed, hadn't yet affected share prices, but DeVore Cosmetics needed to plug the leak soon, before it became a deluge.

I stepped into the office and slammed the door.

Adeline DeVore, 44, but highly-maintained, sat behind a smudge-free glass table, her long legs crossed beneath— something they'd rarely been as she'd risen to prominence, at least according to Beulah lore. Supposedly, the only reason she'd been in Boyd's General to buy the winning lottery ticket was because she and Richie Quail had stopped in for a post-coital cruller.

"Good morning, Ms. DeVore," I said, ignoring the floor-to-ceiling, triple-pane windows that offered a stunning view of the Nuckatawny River. A tiny condo with such a view would easily run north of a million dollars here in New Beulah. I couldn't imagine how much lipstick had been sold to afford this building.

"It's Chloe, right?" she said in a voice that could hold its own as an emcee of a burlesque show or as a keynote speaker at a shareholder meeting.

"Yes," I said, crossing the room. "Chloe Keyes. You used to be a customer of my father's."

"Who was your dad?"

"Eddie Keyes, *Beulah's Best Butcher.* Moved to Florida a few years ago."

"Eddie," she said with a smile. "Used to give me the

thickest steaks. Said I needed the calories."

She rose up on five-inch, acrylic heels from an already considerable height, and we shook hands. Pouty lips anchored her angular, flawless face, and she pursed them while making a show of studying me through tiny, diamond-encrusted glasses.

"You're pretty," she said. "Great skin. Dramatic bones. Do you use my products?"

"I'm afraid I don't use enough of anyone's products, but I have tried your foundation."

It was true. My mother had scored a sample bag as a luncheon prize and had immediately regifted it to me. Convinced that Adeline DeVore had hit on my dad, my mom wouldn't wear anything created by *that DeVore hussy*.

Adeline smiled, showing choppers I didn't recall from twelve years ago. "You wrote that article last year," she said. "About the new bridge between Back Beulah and New Beulah." She lowered herself back into her seat. "Who knew a story about a bridge could be so dark?"

"Everyone, I hope, by the time they read the last paragraph." I smiled and took a seat.

"Makes me wonder how you'll spin this lottery story."

"To tell you the truth, it's more than a lottery story. I'm after the essence of the Lucky Four, as well as the effects of that week on the winners and on Beulah."

"Oh, that week. Not a great time, was it?"

I pulled out my phone, tapped it to tape recorder mode, and laid it on her desk. She reached out, stroked the screen, and deactivated the recorder. Clearly not her first time dealing with the press.

"I have a bone to pick with your type first," she said, arching a brow that looked like the elegant wing of a tern in flight.

I wondered what my *type* was. Plain? Possessed of

morals? I waited for her to go on, but she looked at me expectantly.

"The article?" she finally said in a tone reminiscent of her assistant's. "In the personal section of your paper this morning? I don't know why your editor would run it and then send you here expecting cooperation."

"I'm afraid you've caught me unaware." Sadly, I barely read my own paper.

She grabbed a copy of The Herald from the black slate credenza behind her, whirled back, and slid it to me. The *article* proved to be nothing but a full-color, close-up photo of her exiting the office of Dr. Smithson, a local dermatologist. In the photo, she sported a tiny bandage on her forehead and a series of red bumps above her brow line. The headline read: *Injections for Natural Make-Up Queen?*

I stared at the photo longer than necessary in order to avoid doing the predictable—gawking at the accused forehead eighteen inches from my face.

"We just introduced an all-natural, plant-based wrinkle serum sourced from the Hottentot Sugarbush in Africa. And now this?"

"I see," I said lamely. "Maybe the national papers won't pick it up."

"You're *owned* by a national paper. Besides, it already hit the internet. My people spun it by claiming migraines, but I need you to find out who took this picture."

"It's not credited?" I said, glancing again at the photo.

"It's a pseudonym, and there's no record of payment, according to your editor." She tapped the photo with a hard nail. "Dr. Smithson lets me park in the back, before office hours, in a spot reserved for his nurse. It's very private. So who took this picture? I need a name."

"I'm afraid I don't know."

"But you'll let me know." It was an order, not a question.

"Absolutely," I lied, jotting what looked like a reminder but was actually a note to pick up protein bars; I'd been running low. Given the things I needed to *look into* in this town, Adeline DeVore's Botox stalker was not high on my list of priorities.

"I appreciate it. Now, let's talk lottery." She swiped my phone again, restarting the recorder.

"I'd like to start with a mundane question," I said. "How did the four of you come to buy the ticket together?" I already had Mrs. Elbee's version of the story but wanted a different perspective.

"It all started with Grace Elbee, bless her heart." She shook her head. "I just heard about what happened to her. So sad."

We did the sentimental exchange thing for a minute, but I decided to keep the homicide ruling to myself.

"Grace was at Boyd's picking up a few things," Adeline said, "and she'd forgotten her wallet. Boyd Junior wouldn't give her a break, but Grace was *not* leaving without that lottery ticket. She rambled on about how she was in there all the time and how Boyd's daddy used to spot her money if she was short."

"Boyd still wouldn't budge?"

"No. Just stared at her with those dead shark eyes of his. Seemed extra ornery that day but probably because the sheriff was in line behind Mrs. Elbee and Boyd didn't want to get into trouble. Of course, I don't think Strike Ryker could have cared less what they did. Had bags under his eyes big enough to hold Mrs. Elbee's entire order. He just wanted to pay for his things and get out."

"That was the year Jacqueline Ryker was finishing her cancer treatments."

"It sure was. So after a minute, the sheriff tapped Mrs. Elbee on the shoulder and said he'd lend her the money if they could just move things along. But that was all Richie Quail needed to hear—"

"Richie Quail—you were there with him, right?" I asked innocently.

Adeline shot me a scowl. "No. Contrary to rumor, your headline will not be *DeVore the Whore Admits Shagging Quail the Whale.*"

My eyes bugged out. Apparently, there was more to Adeline DeVore than I'd realized.

"I was there by myself," she said. "Stopped in pretty often, actually."

"My mistake. So, what was it Richie Quail did when the sheriff offered to pay for Mrs. Elbee's ticket?"

"He stomped right over—a big bear claw in his hand— and smacked his palm down on the counter. Declared he was feeling *right auspicious* that day." She leaned forward. "Keep this off the record, but I thought he meant *suspicious.* Thought he was accusing the sheriff and Mrs. Elbee of being in cahoots, but turns out, it means lucky."

Adeline threw her head back and laughed, and I had to admit, everything about the woman surprised me. From her self-deprecation to the warm, throaty chuckle escaping her lips, to her general openness. It was a wonder my father had limited himself to offering her only thick slabs of meat.

"Richie wanted in on the action," she continued. "Said he'd pay for Mrs. Elbee's ticket if she'd go fifty-fifty on the winnings."

"Why did he involve himself?"

"That man could never stand to be one-upped. Just the *idea* of someone else pitching in on a ticket was like a slot machine showing two cherries and dangling the promise of a third. He couldn't resist."

"How did *you* end up in the mix?"

"Well, Grace Elbee turned down Richie's offer. She said

the sheriff's money would do just fine. But Richie was adamant. I think he knew Mrs. Elbee didn't care for him much, so he made the deal less exclusive. He hollered out for everyone in the store to *gather 'round*, but the sheriff and I were it. Richie convinced us all to buy the ticket together and split the pie. I tell you, that man could sell a fur coat to a polar bear."

"How did you all pick the numbers?"

Adeline went blank, and then shrugged. "You know, I don't remember. I think Grace had already selected them."

Time to steer the conversation to my advantage. "So you went to Boyd's often?"

"Too often."

Her short answer was filled with seedy promise. I tilted my head and nudged her with silence.

"Off the record," she said as if we were sisters swapping secrets, "I was *alone* in that store too often. This will sound vain, but back then, men used to undress me with their eyes all the time. But not Boyd Junior. He always made me feel like I was interrupting something more important."

The shared confidence made me feel ill. It did not bode well for a young boy held captive in his basement.

"A few days before the whole ticket episode, I was the first customer in the store and Boyd had to practically drag himself up from that basement. He looked like bloody hell."

"Literally? Was there blood?"

"No, he just looked . . . battered. I asked him if everything was alright, and he mumbled something about unloading crates. I let it go, but now, with this drug-dealing story coming out"—she shrugged—"pretty obvious what was going on."

I cocked my head. "What was going on?"

"A transaction gone bad, no doubt. You remember Avis Whitaker? The man who hit the little girl on the bike?"

"Yes." I swallowed.

"Well, when I was checking out that day, Avis Whitaker suddenly straggled up to the front of the store."

"Avis Whitaker?" I repeated. "Are you sure?"

"Positive."

"Did he come from the back of the store or the basement?"

"I don't know. Appeared out of nowhere and tramped on by. He and Boyd shot each other dirty looks. Let's just say it was a look I did not like being in the middle of. The whole thing stank to high heaven."

To me, it stank of a place due south of heaven. If Boyd Junior and Avis Whitaker were on the outs over some drug deal gone bad, that would've provided Boyd a motive to kidnap Hoop—as collateral—to make Avis square up on a deal. Adeline DeVore had just opened a big can of worms, and the worms were slithering over the rim and squirming around the floor. I didn't like it.

"That poor girl," Adeline was saying. "You know, I bet Avis Whitaker was on drugs or something when he hit her. It just wasn't right, was it?"

"No, definitely not."

Adeline looked off into the distance, toward the river. "One minute, you're riding your bike, the wind whipping through your hair, and the next, you're flying through the air and . . ."

Adeline looked like she might tear up. She couldn't finish her thought, and I didn't blame her. What were the possible endings to her sentence? Not one of them could convey the impact of death visiting too soon and too permanently.

Hoop had once confided something to me about his father; I decided to share it with Adeline. "Avis Whitaker used to drive that road on purpose when he'd been drinking because hardly anyone used it. Thought he was being smart, lowering his risk of hurting anyone."

"It's a terrible, curvy road. I don't go on it anymore." She shook her head as if to clear it. "You know, DeVore Cosmetics gives seven percent of its profits to charity. I made it part of our mission from day one. Five percent to underprivileged, undereducated girls, and two percent to organizations like MADD, SADD, and AA. All because of what happened that week."

It was moving to know that the powerful Adeline DeVore thought about Macy LeGrange up here in a spectacular office that seemed to deny the more banal reality below. But I wondered if Macy would appreciate being associated with *underprivileged* or *undereducated* girls. In her view, she'd had it all.

"Ms. DeVore, how would you describe—"

"Miss DeVore!" the assistant's voice screamed through the intercom. A red light started flashing on Adeline's phone. "Miss DeVore, oh my God! They stormed past me!"

Before either of us could react to the frantic screech, the doors of the office burst open and three dark-suited men rushed into the office. "Adeline DeVore," said the first man. "I'm with the FBI and you're under arrest." As she rose and simultaneously reached for a black panic button beneath her glass desk, the burliest of the three men rushed behind her and cuffed her slim wrists. Although it surely wasn't the first time Adeline DeVore had donned handcuffs, it had to be the first time it wasn't voluntary.

"Plenty of time to panic later," said the burly agent, eyeing the futile panic button.

I met Adeline's eyes as she was manhandled behind her desk. It was like watching a person shatter in slow motion. If she had pulled a Dorian Gray and turned into a wrinkled wreck of an old woman, the sight couldn't have been more pitiful. She moved her lips several times as if to speak, but nothing came out. She looked confused yet resigned, like she knew this day would come but had no idea it would be so ugly. Worst of all, she was failing to do the one thing everyone would have expected of her—scream out in defense.

I did it for her. "I demand to know why Ms. DeVore is being arrested."

Steely eyes bore into me from the tallest of the men. "Who are you?"

"Chloe Keyes from The Herald. Ms. DeVore has the right to know the charges against her."

He narrowed his eyes and seemed to take pleasure in answering. "Conspiracy, mail and wire fraud, insider trading, violations of the Toxic Substances Control Act and the North-Stephens-Cooper Act. That enough to get you started on your exclusive, Chloe Keyes?"

"I'm not asking because of—"

"Look, *reporter*, I don't care why you're asking. Time for you to make yourself scarce. Your friend here is in a lot of trouble. Next time you talk to her, it'll be through a different kind of glass." He rapped his knuckles on her desktop, creating the only visible smudge on the whole surface.

They hauled Adeline DeVore away in cuffs and heels. I couldn't bring myself to take a photo. A section of her hair had fallen in front of her face, and her mascara had begun to run. As they marched her across the office and shoved her through the door, she glanced back at me, forlorn.

My editor would kill me for not getting a picture.

Chapter 28

The elevator to the Devore Cosmetics lobby stopped three times to let on no-nonsense, silent agents carrying DeVore computers and files. I sneaked peeks, wondering what secrets the confiscated goods might hold, but inside, I was thankful my job didn't involve combing through all that mundane information to find violations of Yuppie-named federal acts.

Still, I'd have to reference the raid in my article, so I took a shot, delivering a question to the elevator populace. "This the kind of thing that destroys a company? Or do the principals just end up with a slap on the wrist?"

A woman with stringy, pulled-back hair and a sour face glowered at me. "If you're a loyal DeVore customer, you might want to look elsewhere for your lip gloss."

"So this is a big deal, then."

She sneered. "Uh, we don't exactly form multi-agency task forces for a tube of mislabeled mascara."

Her coworker nudged her to shut up. Whatever. I texted all I could to Larry before we hit the lobby. Told him to break the speed limit getting here if he wanted the scoop of his career.

The elevator doors opened. Puss-face did not offer me the courtesy of stepping off first, so by the time they removed all their boxes and computers, the doors were trying to close again. A perfectly manicured, male hand reached inside to keep them open. As I exited, the owner of the hand entered and we collided.

"Chad, what in the world are you doing here?"

He stepped back into the lobby with me. "Chloe, I was coming to find you."

"Seems you're doing a lot of that lately."

"About that, I had no idea you'd be at that Rafe guy's house last night." Then his voice assumed a more acerbic tone. "I'm sure he was helpful in preparing for your interview this morning. That is what you said you needed to do last night, right?"

Ouch. He got me. I took it like the lying sack of garbage I was.

"Listen," I said. "I was just about to text you. I found a connection between Hoop Whitaker and Boyd. A possible motive for Boyd to have kidnapped him."

Chad looked suddenly sad, like someone had just stuck a pin in his last balloon. Slowly, his eyes clouded over but no words came.

And then I knew.

"Oh no," I said, crumbling from within even though I'd expected the news.

"Perfect match," he said. "Between Hoop's tooth and the blood and the hairs in the green flannel. Everything. There's no question. Hoop was in that basement."

I staggered to one of the four sofas that had the perverse DeVore logo etched into every cushion. My head sunk into my hands as Chad sat down next to me. I vaguely felt his hand holding my arm.

"He was down there, Chloe, but there's still no proof he's dead."

I pulled my arm away. "Let's review, shall we?" My eyes turned moist and my words spit acid, but I didn't care. "We can conclude that Hoop Whitaker was in that disgusting pig pen against his will, his mouth taped shut, his wrists handcuffed to a pole, his shirt ripped from his body, and his blood on the wall. Need I go on? Because I will. The last time anyone saw Hoop Whitaker—quite possibly me—was the same morning Macy was killed. He was seen pedaling his bike in what everyone assumed was the direction of the swamp, but if we extrapolate that route by half a mile, we can conclude that he was headed in the direction of Boyd's General Store around the same time the store opened. How do I know this? Because I opened my front door as Hoop pedaled by, to let out our stupid cat who always woke me up at the same time—that cat was like a frickin' Timex. Hoop waved. I waved back. But I was really waving good-bye, wasn't I? Because he was never seen again, and that puts him at Boyd's General right after it opened." My eyes ripped into Chad. "You'd better have interrogated Boyd about this already."

Chad sucked in a wheezy breath before swallowing hard. His Adam's apple rose up and down like a carnival sledgehammer game, hitting the bell and then some. "Something I need to—"

"And I told you, we have motive now. According to Adeline DeVore, Hoop's dad had a messy confrontation with Boyd shortly before Hoop disappeared. He must have been holding Hoop in order to—"

"Chloe, stop! Somebody posted Boyd's bail this morning. He's out."

My world spun. "What? No! That's insane! You've almost got him on murder now."

Chad shook his head. "When his bail was set, all we had was possession of illegal substances with intent to distribute, and he had no priors. Sherilyn didn't finish the DNA analysis until this morning, but even if she had, it would be grueling to prove murder with no body and no witnesses."

"How could you let him go, knowing the test results were coming?"

"I didn't, and neither did my dad. Boyd got out through some narrow slice of time when Abe was on duty."

"I don't understand."

"Abe had just started his shift and no one told him about—"

"Who posted the bail?"

"Hold on a second. There's more."

"Jesus, Chad, how can there be more?"

"Last night, three guys came to the station to interrogate Boyd. One from the DEA, two from the FBI. They said Boyd had offered them information that would make the drug dealing look like jaywalking. He said if they gave him immunity and got him out, he'd spill his guts."

"About what? How he murdered Hoop?"

"No, not a confession. Sounded like he had the goods on someone or something else."

"Here in Beulah?" I wondered if it had something to do with the early-morning raid on Adeline DeVore, but it seemed unlikely that Boyd would know anything about the cosmetics industry.

Chad shrugged. "You know how these Fed-types are. Real tight-lipped. Wouldn't even give us a hint. But they needed to clear the deal with their superiors. They were supposed to get back to Strike this morning."

"So *they* posted his bail?"

"No. That's the thing. Strike was at the high school and I had a mandatory county meeting. By the time we got to the station, Boyd was gone. I called the DEA agent and he was beyond pissed. Said neither he nor the FBI guys had anything to do with Boyd getting out."

"Then my question stands. Who posted Boyd's bail?"

Chad pulled out his notebook. "A guy named Clive Haverhill. Sent a courier with cash. I've got Annika checking out who he is, but I was worried about you, given as how you and Boyd didn't part on the best of terms when he was arrested."

Something detonated in my head. "Did you say Haverhill? Richie Quail was talking to a *Mr. Haverhill* when I interviewed him. Quail was planning to invest millions with him. Could it be the same person?"

Chad frowned. "Hard to imagine Quail posting bail for Boyd Sexton."

"Boyd got a nice chunk of change for selling the winning lottery ticket. Ten, twenty thousand, at least, right? Maybe he and Quail ended up using the same financial advisor."

"It's a stretch, but I guess it's possible. Sad to think the lottery funded a drug operation."

I shook my head, still in disbelief that Boyd was roaming around free. "Can you or your dad rearrest Boyd today on new charges? Or at least bring him back for questioning?"

Chad lowered his eyes and ran his fingers through his hair. "We don't know where he is."

My body began to quake with rage. "So you guys let a child-molesting murderer go free, and then you don't even keep tabs—"

"Hey, we didn't know about any of this in time. You need to step back."

Chad was pissed, but I figured that was a good thing. Negativity tended to motivate him.

"Now what?" I said.

"Strike's off searching for Boyd, and the Feds are beating the bushes, too. They'll find him. In the meantime, we'll build our case, but you've got to keep your expectations in check. It's going to be a tough case to prove, especially if the Feds give him leniency in exchange for information."

I sat back and smacked the sofa with my hands. Chad was right. Even without the Feds involved, the case against Boyd was circumstantial at best.

"There is one possibility," Chad said, but the hesitation in his voice told me I wouldn't want to hear it. "I've got an excavation team coming over from Newbury. They're bringing dogs and the whole bit. I've asked them to dig up Boyd's basement."

I sucked in a gulp of air but only used it to suppress my nausea. "Jesus, Chad . . . do you really think . . .?" My hand flew to my mouth. "I'm going to be sick."

"No one's asking you to watch, but you were right. No one ever saw Hoop again after that morning, and no one saw Boyd carry out a body—or bury one. It makes sense. If he was holding Hoop down there, and something happened, he might have just . . ." Chad gulped a breath of courage. "You saw that floor. It was dirt. It's what I would've done."

I went numb.

"Meanwhile," he continued, "you need to stay away from your house today. Boyd knows where you live, and while he's probably making himself scarce, he might have it in his mind to come after you."

"I hope he does."

Chad rolled his eyes, perhaps wishing he hadn't shared the information with me. But my energy surged as thoughts dinged frantically around my head. I wanted to plunge neck-deep into this case, dig up bodies, find weapons, and uncover lost video footage, but there was little I could do. Chad was right. In his mellow, pessimistic way, he was right. Without a body, Boyd would never be brought up on anything but drug charges, and maybe not even those.

Then suddenly, a memory flooded in from the back of my mind: a ride in a canoe, a trek into the woods, a secret place.

My energy had just found an outlet, and I had a new mission: find Boyd Sexton. If anyone was going to hear his secrets, it was going to be me—before he made some deal with the Feds.

"Thanks, Chad. I'll be fine. Touch base this afternoon?"

"Definitely. Sooner if the excavators find anything."

Our eyes hung together in some dismal purgatory, both of us regretting what he'd just said, neither of us sure what to hope for.

Chapter 29

I ignored Chad's advice and headed straight home. God help Boyd if he was waiting there for me. Lucky for him, he wasn't. A few minutes later, I was buttoning up my camouflage shirt and reaching into my nightstand. I pulled out the knife my father had given me and clipped it to my belt. As a butcher, my father believed every problem met its match at the end of a blade—a theory that hadn't helped him much in New York, but one he clung to nonetheless. My mom had not been the least bit pleased with my father's gift to me, but she'd held her tongue.

Next, I pulled out my 9mm Glock 26. Despite my dad's philosophy, I tended to believe that a bullet kept you farther from a problem than a blade. The Glock was too heavy for my morning runs, but where I was headed, it would prove more intimidating. After all, Boyd might not be feeling too chatty.

I snapped the gun in its holster, slipped my cell phone in my pocket, donned a jacket, and headed to my canoe. I rowed deep into the swamp, following the same route Hoop and I had used years ago. First thing I passed was Black Swamp's welcome sign—a gum tree with a huge, heart-shaped hole. It had formed long ago when the bark split and rejoined, working its way around a detour and ending up all the stronger for it. Macy and I used to ping rocks toward the heart's center with our slingshots. She once said it should remind us to be patient with love because it had taken so long for that heart to form its solid message. Would she be disappointed that I only felt solid emptiness where my heart-shaped hole used to be?

I continued rowing through the swamp's wonderful illusions, thinking how Rafe would love it out here. Maybe I could take him along this route someday and change his perspective on things.

The best sources of illusion were the cypress knees—the colorful, cone-shaped knobs that projected upward from the cypress trees' submerged roots. The roots were mostly orangey but contained a magical fluorescence whose source I didn't want to know. They poked out of the water like so many delicious lollipops. While suburban kids grew up looking at clouds and turning them into dinosaurs, birds, and fire-breathing dragons, we in Beulah had our cypress knees. Imagination transformed them into anything from a big mother beaver hovering over her babies to the profile of an angry goblin, or even a whole family of meerkats leaping out of the water, all scrambling to return a volleyball over a net.

Cypress knees weren't the only springboard for the mind's eye. There were baby turtles with patterns on their undersides prettier than anything found in a kaleidoscope, and moss that grew on trees like a velvet curtain. Forget Scarlett O'Hara's dress of green drapes; I'd take a rich layer of moss any day.

My vessel floated past desiccated bark and sand that uncannily mimicked rows of alligator scales. Hoop used to say that nature was as consistent and methodical as it was violent and unpredictable. He harbored no doubts that it always knew exactly what it was doing. I rowed past a bale of turtles sunning themselves. They were brave enough to mingle with a gator on the same log and clever enough to have ensured the gator's satiety as they all chilled out and warmed up together. As for the turtles that weren't as clever, well, they learned soon enough. If the swamp was anything, it was Darwinian in its pronouncements.

My favorite game on canoe rides involved pareidolia—that human tendency to see faces and familiar shapes in everything. I'd point out a grumpy old man high above us on a tree knot, insisting it was a spirit warning us to turn back, and

Hoop would say, "There you go, Clover, paradoling again." But even a formal label couldn't stop me from spotting smiling angels in the vines or scary demons in root outcroppings. The swamp was full of faces, and the sooner you learned to smile back or run, the longer you survived.

The near-mile journey proved tranquil, the antithesis of what might follow. I tied up on the same tree where Hoop and I had secured Mr. Swanson's canoe years ago. After all, I had the same destination in mind: the place where Boyd might be hiding.

#

A Month Before the Thump

"What's this big secret, Hoop?"

"Not that big a deal, Clover, but it's pretty cool and I'm only showing people I trust. Can you keep a secret?"

"Does a gator like to lie in the sun?"

"All right, then," he said with a nod. "Found it the other day when I was out exploring. So far, I've only told Macy and Ronnie, and you're the first one I'm actually showing."

"Cool. Thanks."

"Figured a few of us might have a party here sometime— and you never know when you might need to hide out for a few days."

We tramped through the thick underbrush, pushing away the Spanish moss that hung from the oaks like the hair of a banshee—old and gray, a little crazy and wild. "My mom used to make voodoo dolls from Spanish moss," Hoop said, grabbing a few locks.

"Of who?" I asked with concern.

"Can't recall, but she would hand me a pin and tell me to poke it. Then she'd have herself a good laugh."

"I love the moss," I said. "Makes it seem like Halloween year-round."

Having forgotten bug spray, we suffered a hundred mosquito bites between us before reaching our destination, but it was worth it.

"We're here," Hoop announced with a wide grin.

I peered around, saw nothing. Even when I looked up, I didn't notice anything out of the ordinary. "Um, the woods?"

"Honestly, Clover, you'd think you were raised in a city or something. First of all, these ain't just woods. These woods, as you call them, are home to several champion trees of North America."

"What's a *champion* tree?"

He rolled his eyes but in a patient way. "The largest documented specimen of its type. We got a record cherry oak bark, a loblolly pine, and a sweetgum. Hasn't your dad ever taken you on a tree tour?"

"Like that's a thing."

"Did it with my dad when I was seven."

"Well, my dad's only here because he's in some kind of witness protection program, but without being a witness and without protection. Only champions he cares about are the Yankees and I'm not real sure they've been champions much lately."

Hoop laughed. "Well, I'll take you on a tree tour someday. But what you're looking at here is one of the best-camouflaged tree forts ever."

I gazed up again. "Where?"

"Right there, between this tupelo and that oak." He pointed straight above me but I still didn't see it. "Helps if you lie down and stare."

"Is that how you spotted it?"

"Sure was. I was having myself a good think on this nice patch of dry ground here."

I smirked in his direction. "Is this a trick?"

"Nuh-uh." He got flat on his back to prove it. I lay down

next to him and crossed my feet at the ankles. Then I cushioned my head with a dirty hand and stared upward. "Holy moly!" I shouted when I saw it. "That's amazing!"

"Might go so far as to call it a tree *mansion*."

Hoop and I were staring at the base of a tree fort covered in real tupelo bark and branches on one half, and real oak bark and branches on the other. It looked like the natural intersection of two trees fighting for space. The structure itself rose up eight feet on all sides, and from what I could tell, it was roughly pentagon-shaped on the exterior.

"Figure it's dang near 150 square feet inside," Hoop said.

"Who built it?"

"Boyd Sexton and his dad. Least from what I can figure. Found some magazines inside addressed to B. Sexton, along with tools that got B.S. scratched on 'em."

"Does Boyd Junior still use the place now that his dad is gone?"

"Dunno, but there's no reason we can't use it when he's not."

"Except I wouldn't want to go getting on the wrong side of Boyd Junior."

Hoop waved away my concerns. "He's harmless as a house cat. Not a whole lot of IQ points getting a workout in his head, but if you leave him alone, he'll leave you alone."

"Breaking into his fort ain't exactly leaving him alone."

"Come on, chicken. I'll give you a tour."

We clambered up in no time flat. "Dang," I said, "It's a regular palace."

The structure boasted solid walls, a dry interior, two camping mattresses with protective covers, a tiled table, oodles of canned goods, two beanbag chairs, and even a fancy skylight and small slitted windows. Blushing, I pointed to a magazine with a naked woman on the cover. "What's the date on that magazine?"

"The date?" Hoop said, grinning. "Pretty sure that's the last thing most people are interested in."

"I know." My pink cheeks now glistened. "But I'm curious if Boyd was up here recently."

"You see? That's why I call you Clever Clover."

"I've never heard you call me that."

"I just did. And who's to say I don't talk about you behind your back?"

The thought made me deliriously happy, even though he no doubt talked about me platonically—and probably to Macy.

He grabbed the magazine and, perhaps out of a sense of courtliness, did not let his eyes linger on the cover photo. "It's from last month."

I frowned. "Still active, then."

"Not surprising. I mean, who would ever give up a place like this?"

He leaped up and landed with a soft squish on a beanbag chair. "So what do you think, Clover? Party here next month?"

"Can't imagine a single reason not to."

\#

Turned out there was plenty of reason not to; two of the planned party guests were either dead or missing by the next month, and I'd hardly wanted to be alone with Ronnie Fields in Boyd's tree fort.

All these years, I'd only returned to the fort once—to search for Hoop a week after he'd disappeared. But the emptiness of it had proved so daunting that it had stripped all the magic from the first visit. I'd vowed never to come back, but here I was, tramping through a forest *with champion trees*, hoping Boyd Junior had taken refuge in his wood palace. If I could catch him off-guard and at gunpoint, maybe he would tell me the truth.

When I got within a quarter-mile of the fort, I hunkered down, remembering well the peekaboo slits on each side of the pentagonal structure. Although I wasn't the experienced hunter Hoop had been, he'd taught me how to move quietly. Patience, controlled steps, sharp ears, and good eyesight went a long way toward remaining undetected. I chose a route far from the main path, just in case Boyd was using it.

I tiptoed, crawled, and scurried from tree to tree until I was within twenty yards of the fort, far enough to stay hidden, close enough to detect activity. It didn't take long. Four footsteps thudded out from above, and then four more, again and again.

Boyd was in there. Pacing.

I considered the best approach. Sneak up and in? Wait until he descended to ground level? Flush him out with a few gunshots?

I was settling on a strategy when something hard and metallic pressed into my head.

"Well, well, well," said a scratchy, quiet voice. "If it ain't the rabid dog still infringing on my rights."

Chapter 30

My heart thudded in panic, and every survival instinct in my body escalated to DEFCON 1, but still, a calm thought occurred to me: If Boyd was standing behind me with a lethal weapon against my head, who was pacing inside the fort?

It might mean help was nearby. It might mean trouble. I could call out, but who knew who was in there? Could be some drugged-out loser. Could be the FBI. Best to remain silent because I still wanted Boyd alone. I raised my hands.

He backed the weapon off my cranium and I slowly turned to face him. It was hard to see his face given the large crossbow between us, but there was no mistaking this crooked scarecrow for anyone else.

"Look, Boyd," I said quietly, surprising myself with an even-keeled voice. "I just want to talk."

"Yeah? You always bring a gun and a knife to talk?" He grabbed them both from my belt, swiftly, like a man accustomed to handling weaponry and double-crossers.

I shrugged. "Wasn't sure you'd be in a sociable mood."

"Lucky for you, I am. Let's go."

That was suspiciously easy. "Where?"

"Away from here."

"Why do we have to go anywhere?" I said as he grabbed my arm and shoved me along a side trail. "Can't we talk here?" I figured it wouldn't hurt to keep the person inside the fort within shouting distance . . . just in case.

"How'd you find me?" he barked as we lumbered along the path. "D'you find my boat? Follow my tracks?"

A light bulb went off. Boyd didn't know I knew about the tree fort. It was even more camouflaged than it had been years

193

back. He thought I'd tracked him. "Yeah," I said. "I tracked you. Could've found Butch and Sundance if I'd been around back then."

"Figures," he mumbled. When I paused at a fork in the path, he gestured with his loaded crossbow and I obeyed. A gun or knife can intimidate, but nothing really compares to the sharp, metallic tip of a crossbow bolt loaded with a hundred-plus pounds of tension and aimed at one's head.

"Where are we going?"

"You wanna talk? We'll talk. Can't hurt to have a reporter on my side."

I marched in front of him, taking cobwebs and twigs to the face while he grunted out directions here and there. We reached what seemed to be a random spot next to a boulder and he told me to stop.

"Look," he said. "I got no reason to kill you. Truth is, I ain't never killed no one and I don't wanna start now."

"Forgive me if I'll need some confirmation on that."

"What are you talking about?"

"What happened with Hoop? Did you kidnap him to get back at Avis Whitaker?"

"Avis? What in the hell does he have to do with anything?"

"He came up from your basement a few days before Hoop went missing. It looked like the two of you had some kind of fight."

Boyd shook his head. "A fight? No way. Avis got stone-cold drunk one night, stumbled into the store and somehow ended up passed out in the basement. I didn't find him till the next morning, and if I remember right, I had a pretty rough night myself. When I tried to wake him, he freaked out, started hitting me. Still drunk or something."

"But I know for a fact Hoop was in your basement. His DNA was all over the place, along with his shirt and blood."

"Huh? Well, shit." He spat a wad of phlegm to the ground. "I ain't hardly been in that room all these years. Never even thought about cleaning it up. I mean, why would I? Nothing really happened."

"Come on, Boyd. You used to stare at Hoop in a weird way. Like pedophile weird."

"Pedophile? Jesus! I got enough problems with *women*. Why would I mess with a kid? A boy, no less." He kicked at the ground and a hint of sadness tinged his narrow face. "Maybe I did used to look at him, yeah, but only 'cause I wondered how he did it."

"Did what?"

"Hell, I don't know. Made everything look so easy, 'specially when I knew he didn't have it all that easy."

Despite the circumstances, I pressed my lips together and held in a burst of sad yet joyful emotion. It hadn't been lust or perversion I'd seen in Boyd all those years ago; it had been envy, maybe even admiration, for a boy who'd lived life at the top of his game. Boyd just hadn't known how to express it, let alone achieve what he'd longed for.

"Then tell me what happened down there," I said.

He paced back and forth, his limbs jerking wildly as if he were fighting out an issue with himself. Finally, he pivoted to me and blurted out his thoughts. "Look, I can tell you some stuff, but there's things I can't say, and you don't strike me as the type that's happy with half a story."

"I'll take whatever I can get."

"Truth is, I don't need no murder rap following me around, so you just report this: Yeah, Hoop Whitaker *was* in my basement."

My knees went weak and for a flash, my vision blurred. I fought it by concentrating on breathing.

"Stop panting," Boyd said. "Sound like you're gonna have a damn baby or something."

I regained control. "Sorry. Go ahead."

"He came into the store, and yeah, I locked him in that room. I ain't proud of it, but I kinda panicked."

"You cuffed him to the pole?"

"Only because I needed answers."

"About a drug deal?"

"What? No." His frustration showed in the way he kept smacking his dried-out lips. "Look, you gonna let me talk or what?"

I nodded for him to continue.

"So yeah, I cuffed him to that pole. Them cuffs were down there from these ladies my father used to . . . Hell, I don't know what he did with 'em, but that's what that was about. I never used 'em before, and when I went back into that room, well, shit, I don't know what happened, but Hoop, he—"

"Boyd Sexton! Put down the weapon!"

Both Boyd and I jerked our heads toward the voice. It was the sheriff, no doubt having played the role of tree fort-pacer a few minutes earlier. The sheriff looked downright terrifying, dressed in full law enforcement regalia. On his belt hung his Sig Sauer .45, a police baton, cuffs, a flashlight, pepper spray, and a radio. Meanwhile, his Remington tactical shotgun pointed squarely at Boyd's chest, and his aggressive upper body lean—legs hip-width apart, one foot slightly in front of the other to help absorb recoil—showed pure inclination to act. One of his eyes squinted while the other remained peeled on his target with zero wavering. I'd never seen Strike Ryker look so ominous and powerful, but then, I'd never seen him draw on anyone before.

The next move happened so fast that I'd swear I flung myself into the action. Boyd grabbed me by the arm and whipped me in front of him, thrusting my body between him and the sheriff. He held me fast with a surprisingly strong arm, his fingers digging into my shoulder. With his other hand, he aimed his crossbow at the sheriff.

I did not sense this ending well.

Chapter 31

"Let the girl go, Boyd. I just wanna talk." Strike Ryker took several confident steps forward and I began to question his tactics. A lawman with a pierced heart wouldn't be of much use to me—and Boyd wouldn't be of much use to anyone if the sheriff got off the first shot.

"You don't wanna talk," Boyd said. "I know what's going on."

"Come on now, Boyd, let's make this easy. I gotta bring you in for questioning."

I wanted to scream out, to tell the sheriff that Boyd was already talking, but my larynx was crushed beneath the force of his arm.

"That your personal hunting rifle?" Boyd said. "Or police issue?"

Well, if we were all going to shoot the shit about personal weapon choices, maybe I should get a campfire going. But Boyd's wild heartbeat against the ribs of my upper back told me this was more than idle chitchat on his part.

"Truth be told," the sheriff said, "I'd prefer using none of it today, okay? Now put down your weapon and let the girl go."

The more the sheriff talked, the more frantic Boyd's heartrate grew. I might not have had a lot of experience in police standoffs, but I knew one thing for sure: things were not tipping in the sheriff's favor.

He took another step, leaving only eight feet between his rifle barrel and my chest. "Let's all take it easy," he said. "Now Boyd, I'm going to overlook you drawing a weapon on an officer of the law, and I'm going to overlook—"

Nope. Things getting worse. Heart more erratic. My own breathing grew nonexistent, but with a surge of adrenaline like I'd never felt, I grabbed the bowed limb of Boyd's crossbow with both hands and yanked down. At the same time, I smashed my captor's shin with the heel of my boot.

"Bitch!" he yelled out.

He yanked his arm back and his finger must have pulled the trigger because an arrow slashed through the air with a wicked *whoosh* and buried itself in a tree thirty feet behind the sheriff. Boyd pulled at the weapon to get it back under his control, but my hands—out of paralysis or fear—held on as if welded.

Boyd, in what had to be the fastest calculation of his life, released his grip on the crossbow and darted into the thick of the woods, zigzagging like a gazelle with a hunter on its tail.

"Chloe!" the sheriff said as he sprinted after Boyd with remarkable agility. "What in tarnation?"

"Don't shoot him, Sheriff!" My voice came out hoarse, pained. "He knows what happened to Hoop!" The message died in my throat.

I glanced around. In what had been a very bad move, Boyd had put my gun and knife down on the boulder. I grabbed them and dashed after the two men in time to see Boyd pull a sharp right onto a path—a route I was familiar with. It would veer left in twenty yards and then head down through a gully. Negotiating that gap would be no picnic. Boyd better hope he either had a big lead or that the sheriff wasn't feeling trigger-happy. Beyond the gully, the trail would lead to one more turn that offered a straight shot to the water's edge.

But I knew what waited there.

I figured I could help the sheriff close in on Boyd by taking an alternate route. It would put me on a bank of sturdy roots just upwind of where Boyd would emerge—possibly before he arrived. I scrambled over rocks and silent patches of pine needles, and then through an ungodly amount of thorns and vines before gaining access to my chosen path, but once I did, I whipped along. Within three minutes, I'd situated myself on my expansive root perch where it jutted out over the water.

I scanned the area, surprised to see that *he* wasn't there—and I wasn't talking about Boyd. I was talking about the other regular resident of that particular real estate on the swamp's bank: Old Bastard.

Damn! Old Bastard's lolling presence would have sent Boyd straight back into the sheriff's arms. Where was my old ectothermic friend? Never had I passed by here and not seen him in position. My heart sank for a moment as two possibilities filled my mind: Old Bastard had finally cashed it in and floated off to alligator heaven—or Boyd had killed him so he wouldn't have to face him while holed up out here.

Bastard!

When I heard rustling, I drew my gun and waited. Suddenly, from a patch of low-hanging branches and vines that formed a vertical curtain, Boyd burst forth like a late night TV host, his arms spread as if greeting an audience. He leaned over on his knees to catch his breath, looking exhausted and petrified—and guilty as hell. So, he thought he'd just skirt by, feed me his line of bull, and then skip town, but now he'd have to fill in the gaps of his lameass story—as long as the sheriff agreed to question him before letting the Feds know.

Panic shot through me. What if the sheriff turned Boyd over too soon? No, I couldn't—wouldn't—let that happen. I glanced at my gun and decided that if I had to, I'd hold them both at gunpoint until I got the truth.

A still-panting Boyd turned to face the trees from which he'd just emerged. He had no idea I was watching. I waited in silence, using the time to extract my cell phone from my back pocket and turn on the recorder app, just in case Boyd confessed to anything in the pending confrontation.

A gun and a phone—all a 21st century girl needed to survive.

The sheriff's voice suddenly penetrated the air with an unexpected calm. "Come on now, Boyd, I'm too old for this malarkey. I just want to talk."

Boyd glanced at the water, his eyes shooting in the direction of my canoe two hundred yards away— out of his reach and way slower than a bullet. *Think again, buddy.* He looked around desperately, even skyward, perhaps hoping that a giant-taloned hawk—or a Greek god on a crane—would reach down and save him.

"Leave me alone, Sheriff," he shouted. "I ain't saying nothing. Got nothing *to* say."

The sheriff finally emerged through the draping branches, his face flushed, sweat glistening in the small space between his hat and furrowed brows. He held his gun steady, the muzzle pointed straight at Boyd's unprotected chest.

"You made a deal with those government men, Boyd. You promised them a conversation. Now I got to imagine that's going to be one heck of a chat."

"But I'm out of jail! Mr. Quail got me out! Said everything would be alright. Besides, I ain't talking to no one. I was just bullshitting those government men, stalling for time." His breathing became jagged, his motions spastic and desperate.

So Quail *had* posted the bail. What a snake.

"You think those men are just gonna let you walk away, Boyd?" the sheriff said. "Come on. You're smarter than that. They're expecting something big."

Boyd raised both hands and took three slow steps back. Two turtles peeked their heads up at him, motionless, curious if the human would be joining them for a swim.

"I got nothing to tell nobody, Sheriff, I swear. I just wanna get out of this town. You tell those government men you couldn't find me. Besides, Mr. Quail, he checked with everyone. Told me everything was square."

"That don't make you square with me. Now it's too hot for running. Let's head back to town and have a conversation."

"No! You're just trying to get me where"—Boyd stumbled on a rock, caught himself. He took one more cautious step back, his foot entering the water. Behind him, a flash of dark gray bumps, punctuated by long, curving rows of short wide spikes launched out of water. It hadn't been two turtles watching Boyd, after all. It had been an eye and an empty eye socket.

Old Bastard propelled himself at least four feet into the air, revealing ancient, muscled armor backed by eight hundred pounds of hunger and ferocity. The legend was far from down and out . . . he'd simply gotten hungry. His jaws unhinged soundlessly and rejoined to clamp down on Boyd's outstretched left arm. Then, with a jerk of his powerful neck and a serpentine twist of his spine, Old Bastard yanked his prey into the murkiness below with blinding speed.

Boyd never yelled out. Never really had a chance.

Alligators don't chomp their prey to death, Clover. They grab hold of somethin'—harder 'n a crane claw lifting a two-ton car—and then they drag it underwater and thrash it around until it drowns.

"Sheriff!" I yelled, startling the hell out of a man who must already have been on pins and needles.

"Chloe, what in the hell?"

The water above the area where Old Bastard had disappeared looked calm, but several yards downstream, the surface wriggled, offering evidence of a struggle below.

It pained me to say it, but I did. "Sheriff, you've got to shoot Old Bastard!"

The sheriff staggered to the water's edge, searching

frantically for any sign of Boyd.

"Shoot Old Bastard, Sheriff! Now! He's trying to drown Boyd. Boyd might lose an arm, but it's only been a few seconds. He's still alive."

The sheriff looked as panicked as I felt. "I can't just start shooting willy nilly! What if I hit Boyd?"

BANG! I took a shot. It had to be done. The bullet exploded out of the gun and hit the rustling waters, but it dissipated in ferocity the moment it made contact with the liquid.

"For God's sake, Chloe! You're more likely to hit Boyd than anything else."

I geared up to take another shot but stopped myself. The sheriff was right. Not only could I get arrested, but if Boyd died at the receiving end of one of my bullets, so did the truth about Hoop. I'd been so close! I couldn't risk killing him now.

"You're closer to them!" I shouted. "Look for your shot and take it if you get it. They're going to surface again soon and Boyd will still be alive. Old Bastard's the bigger target, so be ready!"

The sheriff raised his gun.

I didn't know where my sudden knowledge of reptilian carnivorous habits had come from, but I knew there'd be one more chance if Old Bastard surfaced in the right spot. I readied my gun, just in case, and locked my eyes on the water, waiting for the tussle between man and beast to make itself airborne. But my concentration wasn't what it could have been because inside, I was cursing the sheriff for not having questioned Boyd when he had him in custody the first time, and for allowing today's situation to escalate to whatever this mess was.

Whoosh!

Old Bastard's tail shot out first. It smacked down in order to propel the long, unwieldy body out of the water with insane force. With the body came the struggling, pathetic prey, whiplashed into the air like a rag doll, an entire human body flailing like a ribbon tied to the end of Old Bastard's snout. The lightning-fast jaunt above the surface was wild and frantic. No way for the sheriff or me to get a shot off, but it sure sufficed for Old Bastard to get a breath.

Oh sure, Clover, ain't no problem for a gator to hold its breath for fifteen minutes if it wants to. Got all sorts of flaps it can close—ears, nose, throat. Might as well be wearing a set of scuba gear.

Old Bastard wouldn't surface again for a good, long while, certainly not before Boyd succumbed.

The sudden stillness of the water contrasted sharply with the violence below, increasing my awe for Black Swamp—and I'd already revered the damn place.

I waited several more minutes, and finally, with my head and spirits as low as they'd been in a long time, I made my way back into the forest. It would take me five minutes to swing around and meet up with the sheriff. On the way, I called Chad, explained what had happened, and told him to send reinforcements. I knew what the call meant for Old Bastard's fate, but to delay the call was only to delay the inevitable.

By the time I reached Strike, I could see the water patrol on its way over in an air boat that made mine look like a toy. Still no sign of Boyd, although that didn't stop the sheriff from searching. He couldn't seem to wrench his eyes from the water, and he looked all sorts of torn-up inside.

I touched his shoulder to make sure he knew I was there—didn't want him turning his rifle on me in a panic. But he didn't turn around or even glance in my direction. He merely let out a heavy breath that reeked of despair.

"You kidding me with this, Chloe?" he finally said. "What in tarnation were you doing out here, getting between two men with weapons? Sometimes I think you're as crazy as they say."

"No crazier than you, Sheriff."

"I was here to bring Boyd in for questioning, something *you* don't have the clear and stated authority to do. So, really, I'm at a loss as to why you're here."

Boyd's backpack suddenly surfaced, both straps shredded, the contents peeking out through tooth-sized holes in the canvas. Alligator tooth-sized, that is. At least the bag's built-in flotation device had remained intact.

"This is horrible," I said. "I never . . . I mean . . ."

"I know," he said, softening. "I ain't never seen nothing like it. I don't reckon Old Bastard eats more than once or twice a year." He sighed. "Boyd just put a toe in the water on the wrong day."

The police boat arrived as a huge shadow appeared forty feet out in the water before disappearing like a wisp of dark smoke. They'd probably hunt him down and slice open his stomach. I hoped he could outwit them, but I doubted he would. What a sour last meal it would prove to be for the old guy.

Chapter 32

I pounded on Richie Quail's office door but received only echoes in return. Quail was my sole connection to what Boyd had been ready to tell me. Plus, I needed to know why he'd posted that bail. Seemed like he wanted Boyd sprung before the big conversation with the federal boys. So what did Quail have to hide? If it had anything to do with Hoop—and I was beginning to think it did—I'd have to do to Quail what they were planning to do to Old Bastard.

I called Quail's main office number, hoping it would forward to wherever he was today, but it only made the phone on Sarah's desk ring—a persistent, old-fashioned jangle that grated against my every nerve. Sarah was proving unreachable, too, and I wondered if that was Quail's doing.

Wait a minute. I had one more lead. I sat down on the industrial park's chipped concrete curb and pulled out my tablet. I searched the internet for the person who'd actually posted the bail: *Clive Haverhill.* Only seven results, but none of them related to an actual person named Clive Haverhill. What was he—some mysterious stranger who posted bail on derelicts and invested millions for the morbidly obese?

Chad had mentioned that Annika at the police station was trying to dig up details on the elusive Mr. Haverhill, so I got in touch with her, but she'd come up as empty as me. I considered narrowing my search parameters, but in today's world, it didn't get much narrower than seven results. Frustrated, I banged my tablet against my forehead and actually came up with a new lead: Rafe Borose. If anyone could help me track down a person hiding behind the slick layers of the internet, he could.

I grabbed my phone but ended up staring at it blankly because I had no contact information for the man I'd lain on the floor with. Did that make me some sort of twenty-first century harlot? No matter, I'd been called worse. Fifteen minutes later, I was over the bridge and knocking on my second door of the afternoon, this time with success.

A haggard-looking Rafe answered, sans hologram doppelganger. He sported a knee-length blue robe—and not much else as far as I could tell.

"Chloe," he said in a tired voice. "What a pleasant surprise."

I double-checked my watch. Yep, two in the afternoon. I glanced back at him. Still a robe and slippers. "Sorry to interrupt your busy day, but I didn't have your number."

"I really need to start scratching it onto more bathroom stalls." He reached into his robe pocket and plucked out his phone. "Let's remedy the situation now." He swiped and tapped his phone screen and held it out to me. "Here, put your number in."

I entered my digits. Our fingers touched when I handed it back, causing a rush of flurries in my stomach.

"Now give me your phone," he said.

I complied. He called my phone from his so that his number would automatically be in my database. Then he turbo-tapped his name into my *Contacts* and handed it back. "There," he said, "now we're in each other's devices. I believe that counts as some level of modern-day intimacy. Maybe the new first base?"

"More of a second-base gal myself," I said without thinking.

"Hm. Well, I'll see if I can hit a double."

More flutters and flurries, along with a blush, but I pushed it all aside.

He gestured for me to enter, and I immediately got hit with the intoxicating scent of coffee. Almost before I could think to ask for some, he led me to the kitchen and placed a heavy mugful of the elixir in my hand. When he gestured to the cream and sugar, I partook in both and felt like my day was starting anew. "So," I began by way of explanation, "you probably don't know what happened yet."

"Old Bastard feeling a tad peckish, I heard."

My jaw went slack. "How did you know?"

He sat on one of three stools at his granite counter. "There's this thing called the internet, and on it, there's this thing called news. Tends to skew towards the sensational. An AARP-eligible gator chomping down a wanted felon definitely qualifies as sensational."

I smiled while sipping the delicious coffee. "I sometimes forget that Beulah keeps up with the internet. Usually feels like we're a century or two behind."

He narrowed his eyes. "I heard there was a reporter at the scene of this breaking gator story."

"I seem to be at all the breaking news lately—while taking little interest in it as a reporter."

"Doesn't bode well for your career."

I shrugged and sat on the stool next to his, facing him. "I know our relationship only extends as far as lying on the floor, sharing a pillow, and being mutual suspects in Mrs. Elbee's murder, but I need a favor."

"Anything."

"I need to know who Clive Haverhill is."

His head jerked back a few millimeters, and then he stuck out his hand as if to shake. Was he inviting me to tango?

"I'm Clive Haverhill," he said. "Pleased to meet you. And color me impressed that you tracked me down."

Chapter 33

I stared, ignoring Rafe's outstretched hand. Then I swallowed the gulp of coffee in my mouth with great care, lest I spit it all over his counter. "Excuse me?"

"Clive Haverhill, financial investment advisor and all-around smart guy. At your service."

"You can't be serious."

"I'm not sure I see the problem." He shrugged. "It's just a pseudonym."

"You posted bail for Boyd Sexton this morning."

Rafe's thick brows came together while his full lips puckered with interest. His eyes, however, remained red and tired. "Technically, yes, but at the behest of a client. That seems like a full day's work ago." He let out an exhausted breath. "Busiest week ever, but I knew it would be."

At my look of exasperation, he continued. "One of my clients requested that I wire money to a courier. I vaguely remember that the money was to spring Boyd Sexton from the confines of his prison cell. All legitimate and aboveboard as far as I could tell. Seven or eight o'clock this morning."

I still couldn't decide if this was a bad joke or a horrible coincidence. "*Who* is your client?"

"I'm not supposed to say, but what the heck? Richie Quail, of course." He almost laughed. "You don't think I'd locate myself in Beulah as an investment expert to the wealthy without a few key clients in the area, do you?"

"Thought your circus uncle recommended the place."

"He did, as soon as he found out who my clients were."

"Somehow, you failed to mention that the richest man in Beulah was your client when I told you I was working on a story involving him."

"I did mention that he and I ran in the same investment

circles, but in general, I'm supposed to keep things under wraps. Besides, what I do is so sterile; it's just moving money around, a game of numbers, that's all. He's been my client for years."

"It occurs to me that there are only so many wealthy clients for you to cater to here in Beulah. Do you have other big ones in town?"

He grimaced. "I don't think I should say while you've got hot coffee in your hand."

My nostrils flared, but I kept my voice level. "The cream cooled it. Start talking."

"Adeline DeVore is also my client," he said, raising his hands in mock defense.

I seriously considered throwing the coffee at him, but it tasted too good.

"Chloe, what's the big deal? I told you I handled money for wealthy people. You just happen to be working on a story about lottery winners. Logically, they're the ones with money to invest. What's the harm if I invest money for people you know through work?"

I set my mug down, hopped off the stool, and paced. "The harm is that you posted bail for Boyd Sexton who is now dead but who was ready to spill serious information about what we found in his basement—and I'm not talking drugs. Boyd Sexton may have killed . . . he might have . . . for God's sake, he was the only one who knew what happened to the boy I loved!"

I had huffed and puffed myself right into Rafe's face, and then suddenly, I gasped as I heard what I'd said aloud to a near-stranger. "I mean . . . I didn't mean that I—"

Rafe reached out and grabbed me by both arms. In different circumstances, I felt certain he would have kissed me, but right now, he didn't dare. We stayed motionless for a long moment, my jagged exhalations becoming his inhalations, our eyes glued together. My wounded expression surely conveyed how much his actions had hurt me.

He didn't back away. He didn't try to make excuses. What he did do was close his eyes as his face knotted up, seeming to repress his own urge to cry. By the time he opened his eyes, he'd regained composure but continued to look personally pained. "I didn't know," he said. Then he seemed to go distant for a flash before an awkward half-smile formed on his lips. "I guess I didn't think of everything."

"No, you didn't."

He released my arms. "Can you ever forgive me? You have to think back to our conversations. You never gave me all the details."

"But how could you not know that you were doing something underhanded by posting that bail at the last possible second? Right before the Feds got their claws in him."

"I process a hundred transactions a day, all over the world. It's sort of why I'm in a robe at whatever time it is now. I'm buying real estate, selling stock, finding partners for trusts, trying to come out on the better end of a short sale. Something as trivial as sending money to a courier"—he raised his hands innocently—"I don't even know the story behind the transactions most of the time. Perhaps that's a fault, but . . ." He gestured to his living room. "Do you have time to talk now?"

"It's too late. Boyd's dead. There's no other link, and no one else knows what happened to Hoop."

"Hoop," he repeated. "The boy you think is with the circus."

Reality finally took its full and oppressive toll. I could feel wrinkles of weariness forming on my face as I accepted a truth I'd denied for years. "That was nothing but a fantasy," I said. "One I've finally given up as recently as today."

Rafe gently grabbed my hand and turned me toward him. "Don't give up yet." I could feel his strength and optimism traversing between us. "I've already made contact with my uncles, and I promised you an answer soon enough. Can you hold out a little longer before giving up?"

I swallowed and fought the urge to take comfort in his arms. "April Fools' Day, right?"

"Without fail. Listen, it was never my intention to hurt you. If I'd known that a simple transfer of money would result in this much pain for you . . ."

"What I don't understand is why Richie Quail bailed Boyd Sexton out at all."

Rafe released my hand and shrugged. "The possibilities are endless, right? Did Quail owe Boyd a favor? Did Boyd have dirt on Quail? A drug history, perhaps, or proof of an unsavory liaison. Surely, with your knowledge of Beulah, you must have a theory or two."

He was right. All I needed was the connection. Who better than a reporter to uncover it? I told him I had to go and he walked me to the door, his robe hanging carelessly at his sides, revealing black gym shorts topped by ripped muscles that looked more defined than ever. A primal part of me wanted to run my fingers over the hard mounds of his stomach and chest, but I resisted.

Damn, I'd been looking too long. I jerked my eyes up. Too late. He was grinning, and then he slowly, teasingly, tied his robe shut.

"All that from yoga?" I said.

"All that from discipline, along with an unstoppable, obsessive desire."

"To do what?"

He smiled. "Absolutely anything."

"You scare me."

"I doubt that. But thanks."

"I have one more question," I said. "Why the pseudonym? Why Clive Haverhill?"

"I keep personal and professional separate, and *Clive Haverhill* reeks of blue blood and polo. The funny thing is, clients must rarely read what I send them because I usually sign things using my full, legal name."

"Which is?"

He spoke as if revealing a royal secret. "Rafe Ogden Borose."

"Couldn't slip a simple *John* or *Sam* in there somewhere?"

"Definitely not. Far too square."

I smiled at his choice of words and wanted to ask him the origin of *Ogden*, but my phone rang. It was Sherilyn, so we parted company at the door with a wave and a promise yet to be fulfilled.

"Hi, Sherilyn," I said into the phone as I headed to my car.

"Girl, you are so gonna owe me a cocktail. Get your skinny butt to the lab pronto. Need to turn this evidence over to the sheriff, but he can't get here for an hour. Hurry!"

Chapter 34

I barged into Sherilyn's lab in loud, unsterile fashion.

"People with sharp instruments here!" she shouted while lifting her scalpel. "Could you keep the startling noises to a minimum?"

Her eyes—the only feature visible behind her surgical mask—rolled when she saw me, but in a friendly way.

"Aw, Jesus!" I yelled when I saw what was on her table. I spun away as fast as I could. "Is that him?"

Lying in front of Sherilyn was a body with a rough semblance of a head, the face scraped off, and a multi-punctured, banged-up, beat-to-hell-and-back torso with only one leg and one arm attached: Boyd.

"Looks like Old Bastard was in the mood for bones," she said. "Maybe he needed to clean his teeth because he left the meatier parts for me."

"Can't believe they recovered the body so quickly."

"Old Bastard took off with what he wanted, left the rest behind."

"Do you really need an autopsy?" I said. "I can tell you the cause of death."

"Drowning?"

"No, being a degenerate idiot who stepped into a swamp backwards."

Sherilyn laughed. "That's the God's-honest truth, but I don't think we have a code for that. I'm eager to write this one up, though. Death by alligator is pretty rare around here. This'll be a great teaching case." As she whipped a white sheet over what was left of Boyd, I turned around to see her peel off her gloves, lower her mask, and reveal a glowing grin. "Chad's been keeping me up to date on everything," she said, "but I wasn't sure how much he was keeping you in the loop. That's why I called."

"Why would Chad *not* keep me in the loop?"

She gave me a playful sneer. "Lingering jealousy, of course."

"Over what?"

"Honey, you think that boy ever got over you? Get real."

"*He* broke up with *me*."

"Because you shut him out like you do all men."

"What are you? Chad's counselor now?"

"We talk. But admit it, he's only now learning what he was up against. Or should I say *who*?"

"Yeah? Then why do I have a sudden and abiding interest in someone else?"

Sherilyn's eyes went bigger than their usual round discs. "The hottie from the glass house, right? Mm, wouldn't mind throwing a few stones at him myself."

"Stay clear, Cougar."

Sherilyn clawed the air before adding, "Just remember to go easy on Chad."

I shook my head. "You're wrong on this one, Sherilyn, but thanks."

"Let's go." She clapped her hands together. "You won't believe what I've got. And I sure shouldn't be showing you, but since you found Mrs. Elbee's body and all." She gestured for me to follow as she banged through two swinging doors and looped around to the other side of the building. "I'm telling you, Chloe, un-freakin'-believable."

I knew Sherilyn well enough not to push for more. She was all about dramatic revelation. She kept a huge collection of horror movies at her 1800's Southern Antebellum house, and she preferred to watch them alone—with all the lights turned out.

We finally entered a small, dim room loaded to the gills with audio-visual equipment, computers, monitors, and a tangle of wires. But the main attraction was Sherilyn's irreplaceable asset: Charlie West. Sitting on a blue exercise ball and perched in front of a computer screen, he watched as numbers and symbols flashed before his eyes in rapid succession. Upon our entrance, he slammed a finger down on the keyboard, stopped the progression, and twirled to face us. I had to repress my surprise at the thickness and distortion of his glasses. Without them, Charlie was a remarkably handsome, light-skinned black guy with jutting facial bones and a body that could launch a hipster clothing line, but with his intense, almost frightening eyes—now magnified fivefold—and his nervous tics, he would hardly be a photographer's dream.

"Chloe, long time, no interface," he said in his usual clipped speech. With no artifice, he looked me up and down twice, his mouth twitching to the left while his bug eyes lingered longer than social norms allowed. After rocking his head back and forth a few times, he said, "You look defeated, and in desperate need of a good night's sleep. You should try this new tea I created. All-natural, even if the FDA says otherwise. Brings on the alpha waves and knocks you *out*. You won't even stir if an intruder breaks in."

It would never occur to Charlie, whose brainwaves were undoubtedly off the charts, that oblivion to intruders might be a problem for a swamp-dwelling, single female.

"Remind me to give you a pouch of it before you leave," he said.

"Will it make me look less defeated?" I said.

He shrugged. "Might get rid of those bags under your eyes."

"You dating a lot these days, Charlie?" I said with sarcasm that he missed.

"Believe it or not, no."

"Hm, who'd a thunk it?"

Sherilyn put an end to our banter. "Did you eliminate the distortion in the video, Charlie?"

He whipped his head around to her and they shared a manic grin. "Looks like we caught ourselves a couple murderers, Sherilyn. Pretty as a picture and scary as heck."

Sherilyn gestured to a huge monitor in the corner of the cramped room. "Let's cue it up over there."

Charlie rolled his seat to the corner and brought the screen to life.

"What are we about to see?" I asked. "Do I need any set-up?"

"Remember that amulet Mrs. Elbee was wearing when you found her?" Sherilyn said.

"Of course."

"Turns out it had a built-in video camera."

Charlie spun his head around. "Serpent's view!" he shouted. "The amulet had two tiny snakes on it, and the camera was in the left snake's bejeweled eyes. How cool is that? Remotely activated. Previous content was uploaded to somewhere, but this final scene, and I do mean *final*"— Sherilyn cackled at that—"was inaccessible because the camera was underwater."

"Don't tell me we're about to see—"

"Yep!" Charlie said.

The video began and I heard the familiar, loud voice of Mrs. Elbee. The scene showed an unsteady view of her bedroom, as if someone were pacing with a low-quality, hand-held camera. First it would show Mr. Elbee's bureau—the one that contained the family pictures—and then it spun dizzyingly to show the door to her master bathroom. The top inch of a slim red candle hovered in the forefront of the shot. Mrs. Elbee must have been pacing while wearing her amulet. She was talking to herself, as usual, and most likely holding that stupid brass candlestick.

217

"Look, Macy," Mrs. Elbee said on the video, "the afterlife is not so scary. I've been reading about it, and my husband loves it there—we chatted in a dream just last night. Did you know they have boats there that run without water? Imagine, Macy! Imagine that. A dry-land boat."

"It's called a car," Charlie interjected.

"Good one," Sherilyn said. "Now hush."

Grace Elbee continued speaking. "Mr. Elbee will show you around, Macy. You just need to go to him, y'hear? It's time." Her voice grew more frantic, and the candle began to tremble. "You've got to go! You hear me? Just go! You know how I feel. I won't go over it again. Now git!"

The camera closed in on the bathroom door, which opened, and suddenly, we were looking at the interior of Mrs. Elbee's bathroom. She hummed a bit to herself, and in the next shot, her face filled the screen, blurry at first, but then the snake eye camera must have focused in on her reflection.

I gasped. Wow. Talk about looking defeated. Life had clearly trounced Mrs. Elbee in her final week. Looked like she could use all the tea in Charlie's stash.

"She's in front of the mirror," I said, mostly to myself, somewhat in awe as I tried to understand what was happening.

Charlie hit pause. "It gets a little disturbing from here on. You sure you want to go on?"

"Of course she does!" Sherilyn said, smacking Charlie on the shoulder.

I nodded, the gesture conveying a weak and unconvincing *yes*.

Charlie pressed *Play* again.

Mrs. Elbee leaned to the left, mumbling while rummaging through a drawer.

I could pick up snatches of phrases: *read about this; power of reflection; universe; your destiny.*

When she fully faced the mirror again, she was holding a thick tube of toothpaste. She reached high up on the mirror and started to write Macy's name, saying quite clearly, "Power of reflection, shine out into the universe. Go, Macy. Find your destiny." When she finished, she gazed at her work, looking both proud and unburdened.

"There," she said. "That ought to help. Ought to help, indeed." Then, as if writing dead girls' names on mirrors was just another daily task completed, she reached over, grabbed her toothbrush, and started to brush her teeth. Oh sure, perfectly normal to send a frustrated spirit out into the netherworld, and then stare through the spirit's name while cleaning your gums and evaluating your skin and wrinkles.

A series of small noises rang out in the background. Mrs. Elbee's face reacted in subtle ways but not with fear. At the fourth noise, she turned her head, cocking an ear in the direction of the sounds. Hearing nothing else, she gave a half-shrug and returned her attention to her foaming mouth.

She turned on the faucet and let the water run while hitting her back molars. Finally, she leaned over to spit, and when she rose back up—

"Holy moly!" Sherilyn shouted. "Great quality, Charlie!"

"Oh my God!" I screamed as the camera fully refocused. "That's—"

"So much clearer now," Sherilyn was saying. She gave Charlie a friendly smack on the arm.

Charlie had frozen the video on Mrs. Elbee's shocked face, framed by the minty *G* of LeGrange. Behind her and to the right, near the final lower-case *e*, stood a tall, scraggly, divot-faced dude who looked like he'd already seen the inside of a casket—or at least the inside of an emergency room on occasion. Worst of all, I knew him. Zeke Carver.

To Zeke's left, over Mrs. Elbee's other shoulder, stood a woman. Fewer divots, greasy blond hair, and in desperate need of a burger—preferably super-sized to match her dilated pupils. Her sunken cheeks made the skin on her face look like poorly-hung sheers, and any spark of life in her had long taken shelter in the crazed azure of her irises.

"That's Zeke Carver," I said. "I had a scary encounter with him, and he and his brother were at my house to fix my foundation."

"I hope he's better at foundations than at pulling off crimes," Sherilyn said.

"I wouldn't know. I booted him and his brother out under threat of testicle removal." They both glanced at me, so I explained. "I don't like smokers."

"My guess is he smokes more than Marlboros," Charlie said. "I've seen him hanging around Boyd's. Always loitering outside, looking shifty. Never met him, but it's hard to forget someone this gangly." He poised with his hand over the computer mouse. "Here goes nothing."

He clicked *Play* and I felt my body stiffen from stem to stern. I'd never watched a snuff film and I sure didn't want to start now. Sherilyn, on the other hand, gripped my arm and leaned forward, eager and excited.

Onscreen, Mrs. Elbee didn't scream or show the alarm that would have overtaken normal people. Instead, she slowly turned around until her amulet brought the bony woman into focus. Then Mrs. Elbee's age-spotted hand reached out and stroked the woman's hair, pushing a few stringy strands behind her ear. "You're so much older now, Macy. Still pretty, though."

The woman snorted and grinned, revealing zombie-like teeth. "Yeah, sure," she said in a voice that held traces of youthful sweetness, before harsh chemicals had stripped her vocal cords dry. "Why not?" She guffawed and twirled around the bathroom, waving her hands in the air. "Look at me, I'm Macy! I'm Macy! I'm a fucking Thanksgiving Day Parade." She nearly doubled over laughing and the gesture couldn't be described as anything but graceless.

"You need to go, Macy," Mrs. Elbee said calmly. "I'm glad you came, but you need to move on, okay?"

"Yeah, I'll go," the woman said. "Fact is, I think you're going with us, right, Zeke? Won't she be coming with us?"

"That's right, baby," Zeke said. "That's right."

A wet, choking sound filled the next audio portion of our entertainment. The focus of the camera jerked back to the mirror, revealing Zeke's grimy arm around Mrs. Elbee's throat in a choke-hold position.

"Oh my God!" I shouted. "He's killing her! He's killing her!"

"Nah," Sherilyn said, casually plucking a fuzz from her jacket. "She really did drown."

Mrs. Elbee's face, fully visible in the mirror, turned red and seemed to swell. Her small hands tried to pry away the arm locked tight around her neck. Though I couldn't see the lower half of her body, I could only imagine that Zeke was lifting her into the air while her feet kicked futilely below.

Drool dripped down Zeke's chin as ten seconds turned to twenty. It landed on the side of Mrs. Elbee's neck. He no doubt smelled vile and deathly. Perhaps it was a silver lining that Mrs. Elbee couldn't inhale whatever horrid odors were wafting off him.

Zeke's own breathing soon grew ragged, his eyes turning spastic, as his arm squeezed the struggling Mrs. Elbee.

While his prey suffered, he gestured with his head toward the message on the mirror. "Ha! That'll work as a suicide note, don't you think, Etta Lee?"

"I don't see why not," Etta Lee responded.

She entered the shot immediately after as she swiped the L of LeGrange, cutting a finger-wide slice through it. A moment later, she could be heard smacking her lips together and laughing. "Fucking spearmint suicide note."

In the interim, Mrs. Elbee went totally limp against Zeke, who had finally loosened his grip. In what had to be an undignified exit from the bathroom, we heard only scratchy sounds and grunting while getting an eyeful of blue cotton blend. The amulet must have gotten tucked behind Mrs. Elbee's blouse.

The next shot showed a ceiling. The assailants had presumably placed Mrs. Elbee on her bed. An elegant light fixture, purchased with lottery winnings and the promise of a bright future, filled most of the screen—until Zeke stuck his face in. Gravity took a grotesque toll on his skin as he looked down at Mrs. Elbee from above. His unkempt, overlong hair fell forward like a menacing hood.

"Charlie, turn it off!" I shouted. "I can't watch if he rapes her."

"No, nothing like that," Charlie said, his composure off-putting as he waved away my concerns.

Zeke's face jiggled in the unsteady frame as Mrs. Elbee began to cough. She was coming around. Zeke held up a tiny pill, no bigger than the tip of a pinky nail. "Now yer gonna have yerself a nice sleep, y'hear?"

"She don't look tired, Zeke," Etta Lee said.

"Etta Lee, sometimes, I swear, you're dumber than a bag of rocks."

"What is that?" I said to Charlie. "Can you zoom in?"

"Already confirmed," Charlie said. "Ambien pill. Ten milligrams. He gives her forty."

"Forty pills?"

"Forty milligrams. Definitely enough to knock out someone as small as Mrs. Elbee, especially if she's not used to them."

As promised, the video showed—or provided the sound effects of—the despicable Zeke forcing pills down Mrs. Elbee's throat. She tried to fight it, but it looked like he clamped her mouth shut. At one point, a cup of water flashed into view, handed from Etta Lee to Zeke, and it was empty by the end of the sequence.

Five unbearable minutes passed, most of which Charlie fast-forwarded through. Zeke and Etta Lee were either unnaturally quiet during the interval, or they'd left the room and done God-knows-what God-knows-where in the house, probably having secured Mrs. Elbee to the bed. I thought back to the dirt Chad and I had found near Mrs. Elbee's staircase and bed. At least now we knew its source.

When Charlie stopped fast-forwarding, Mrs. Elbee was still alone—and still awake. She was mumbling to herself in a barely audible whisper, no doubt pondering her fate, when Etta Lee returned alone and peeked down at her. The picture bounced a bit as Etta Lee must have seated herself on the edge of the bed. "Hey, Lady," she said, "you mind if I have these?" She dangled two diamond earrings above Mrs. Elbee.

"Take whatever you want, Macy. It's all yours. All yours."

"Thanks." Etta Lee must have tried to put the earrings on, because the next audio was, "Damn if these holes ain't closed up. Now I gotta get Zeke to poke 'em again." She leaned over Mrs. Elbee's face and grinned confidentially. "Least he's good with needles. Ha!" Etta Lee disappeared from the frame, but stayed near as her voice came through. "Your nails are a mess, lady. I can fix 'em up for you, real pretty-like if you want."

Mrs. Elbee heaved out a sigh. "Sure, sure. But then you'll go see Mr. Elbee? He's waiting for you."

"Whatever. This okay?" Etta Lee held a bottle of neon orange fingernail polish above Mrs. Elbee's face.

"I didn't do anything wrong," Mrs. Elbee said. Her slurred voice was showing the effects of the pills. "Not . . . I mean . . . along for the ride." Her voice withered to breathy notes. "And boom, and then boom, and then boom."

Mrs. Elbee's respirations grew steady and deep. Three minutes of silence followed, interrupted only by Etta Lee muttering to herself, complaining about Zeke-this and Zeke-that, and then a more voluble, "There. All done."

Suddenly, the frame filled with Mrs. Elbee's fingernails being proudly displayed above her face, held in place by Etta Lee's scrawny hand. Both hands quickly disappeared from view. "Hey Zeke! Zee-eeke!"

Zeke entered the room, or rather, the sound of his voice did. "Quit yer yapping, Etta Lee."

"She's asleep. Can we go?"

"Not yet. He said to wait till dark."

"Whoa!" I yelled. Sherilyn smiled and nodded the same way people do when they've already seen a movie and like to take credit for its surprises.

"Who's he talking about?" I said. "Who said to wait until dark?"

Sherilyn shook her head. "Can't be certain, but it sure implicates someone. My money's on Gator-Bait out there." She jerked a thumb toward the other room, presumably to the slab holding undigested portions of Boyd. "He was the big dealer in town, and these two have a direct connection to him. But it could be Zeke's idiot brother, too."

"Anybody could have hired these morons," Charlie said. "If you needed cash, wouldn't you hit up a crazy old widow?" Charlie hit *Play* again.

"Yeah?" Etta Lee's voice said. "Well screw his stupid ass. She's ready. Let's do it before she wakes up. And hey! You gotta punch holes in my ears again."

"Always something with you." Heavy footsteps indicated Zeke was leaving the room.

Out of the corner of my eye, I noticed Sherilyn tensing up with anticipation. I braced myself for another surprise, dreading it but keeping my eyes glued to the screen.

Etta Lee must have untied Mrs. Elbee at some point because a few moments later, the camera view whooshed up and showed a large, standing mirror near the foot of the bed, thereby also showing Mrs. Elbee's frenzied reflection.

"Damn clumsy idiot!" Mrs. Elbee screamed. She looked like something out of The Exorcist—contorted face, harsh eyes, and rigid body. She stared straight into the mirror and shouted again, perhaps believing it would carry her message to the universe. "Curse you and your fidgety fingers! May you rot in hell!" Then she whipped her head to Etta Lee, grabbed the wispy girl by both shoulders and shook her. "Now go, Macy! I've taken care of it. I've cursed him to hell. You must go!"

Zeke rushed into the scene, showing the same fleet-footedness he had when chasing me through the Victorian. The video images cut in and out, as if there were a tussle, but best I could tell, Mrs. Elbee went immediately back to sleep after her outburst, sparing Zeke from forcing more pills down her throat.

Charlie stopped the tape. "There's more," he said drily, "but it's just them transporting her to a pick-up and driving to the river. Not much dialogue. From what I could figure, they tie her feet to a couple cinder blocks and dump her in the water." Charlie let a muted half-giggle escape his lips. "It's the most incompetently executed crime you'll ever see, accompanied by the most incriminating video ever made. Too lame for words, really."

"Charlie wants to release it on YouTube," Sherilyn said. "But I told him the sheriff would skin us alive!"

"It would rank in Crime Fails for at least a month," he said. "And my channel could use the viewership."

I had to agree with Charlie; I couldn't imagine any crime-fail topping these idiots. Then again, they almost got away with it.

"What was that about *fidgety fingers* at the end?" I said.

Sherilyn gave a big shrug. "I just *find* the clues, honey; I don't process 'em. Maybe her husband was clumsy in bed and never got her off. Who knows? You seen enough?"

"More than. Hey Charlie, Mrs. Elbee had that amulet for a while. What happened to everything it recorded before this final scene?"

"It only retains the last thing recorded until the material is uploaded. After that, no record of it."

"Except on the computer of whoever accessed it," Sherilyn added.

"No idea who would have been interested in Mrs. Elbee's daily rants," Charlie said.

"How did the camera know when to start recording?" I asked.

"Remote control. The only limitation would be distance."

"What was the range?"

"About five miles, any direction."

Projecting outward in a five-mile radius from the Elbee house would cover all of Back Beulah, plus New Beulah and portions of neighboring towns. Pretty big pool of suspects. "At least we know it was someone local," I said. "Any way to trace the remote's location?"

"Only if it's activated again, which doesn't seem likely," Charlie said.

"In the rest of the video, did you see any stolen property in Zeke's truck? To establish motive? Maybe he loaded up when he was off-camera. There must be something missing besides those earrings."

"No visible stolen goods," Charlie said, "but I could only see what the amulet camera picked up, which wasn't much."

"Plus," I said, "they could have returned to her house after they dumped the body."

"Where'd she get the amulet, anyway?" Sherilyn asked.

"Farmer's Market," I said. "That guy with the long braid—Bruce."

Sherilyn lit up. "I've been out with him a couple times recently." She held up an index finger and made a raspberry sound as she let it flop down. "Erectile dysfunction unfortunately, but what a character."

Only Sherilyn would date a near-mute ex-hippie who chose potato sacks for his attire—and only she would broadcast his bedroom challenges so casually.

"He's on his way here now," she continued, "to return some earrings I left in his tent."

"His *tent*?"

She smirked. "Right, like you've never dated a survivalist. He's only been doing it for a couple years, but I think he might score a gig on one of those reality shows—a naked one if he gets his way."

"You know what, Sherilyn?" I said. "The less I know, the better."

"Okay, then," she said, clapping her hands together again. "I've got half a corpse to finish."

As I followed her back through the lab, a heightened feeling of disdain washed over me for Boyd. In his final hour, he claimed he'd never killed anyone, but was it possible he'd hired those junkies in the video to do his dirty work?

"What Old Bastard did to Boyd," I said to Sherilyn on my way out. "You know what I call it?"

"What?" she said.

"A good start."

Chapter 35

A paper flyer, pinned beneath my car's wiper, fluttered in the wind. I grabbed it and read: *Beulah Magic Show! Come witness mystical, captivating wonders!*

It gave the location of the event as The Pavilion on Dirt Hill. The Pavilion was an indirect creation of Richie Quail's during his pre-lottery years. In a story that never quite rang true, he'd cleared land and dug foundations for one development while leaving a huge pile of low-quality dirt near the swamp, allegedly for a second project that never panned out. Eventually, he convinced the county to let him build a pavilion atop the pile—for rental income, of course—rather than remove the dirt. The board members fell for it or, more likely, received a tidy payoff to approve it. Since then, The Pavilion had hosted dozens of weddings and holiday parties, serving as a preferred location for ritzy events that needed a quaint, small-town feel. The place offered a stunning view of the swamp, along with prizewinning sunsets, but its crooked history had never sat well with swamp purists.

For the last six months, though, The Pavilion had not hosted a single event. Some out-of-towner had supposedly rented it at twice its usual rate for the entire duration. Ever since, two swarthy-looking men, solemn as Buckingham Palace guards, stood watch over the area 24/7. Rumor had it that a reality show was in the works—hopefully not naked Bruce's—but Quail would never confirm or deny. Larry and I had delved into the mystery, but we'd run into such a tangle of red tape and dead ends that we'd given up by month two. Periodically, however, a burst of activity would occur. Short, muscular men would scale the hill in delivery trucks, and drapes would cover whatever they transported inside. Additional workers would show up once in a while and stay for several days, but no one ever saw them around town. Despite a stakeout by a determined intern on The Herald staff, their mission remained a mystery. By the fourth month, everyone had lost interest, settling for the idea that Quail had bound himself to silence via contract and would reveal the truth in his own sweet time.

Would it all now culminate with this magic show? I glanced at the flyer again. It was a bit of a graphical mess, unable to decide what it wanted to be. The center showed sketches of floating ghosts, one of whom vaguely resembled our own grumpy sheriff, and another looked like a buxom woman of the night. In the lower corners were rabbits popping out of hats. Along the top, rows of black and red stars floated amidst bursts of yellow light. A Roman chariot raced through all of it, while a bejeweled snake slithered along the bottom, its tongue caught in the act of smelling the atmosphere. I wouldn't mind asking that serpent what he could sniff out on this pamphlet, because it confused the heck out of me.

"Hmm. Magic." The gravelly, deep words came from behind me. I jerked around to see Bruce standing there, apparently reading over my shoulder. Silver hoop earrings shimmered in his hand. "For Sherilyn," he said by way of explanation.

"I know," I said. "I just met with her."

He stepped forward to go around me, but I blocked his path. His reaction was to stop in his tracks and fix me with a glower from beneath wisps of his graying hair. He wasn't a big man, but something about him reeked of strength, while something else about him reeked of moldy bread. I desperately warded off images of Sherilyn bumping parts with this primitive being.

"Bruce, do you remember selling an amulet to Grace Elbee in the past month?"

"Dead now."

"Yes, but do you remember the amulet?"

He nodded.

"Where did you get it?"

"Cuthbert's. Every third Thursday."

Cuthbert's Pawn Shoppe had been around for ages, operating on the edge of town and the edge of legality. Sherilyn's mom had worked there as a teen and shopped there as an adult. *No idea why they got the extra letters on Shop,* her mom would say, *but it sure adds a touch of class, don't it?* I didn't think so. The place gave me the willies, as did most of the folks who worked there.

"Is that when you go to Cuthbert's, Bruce? Every third Thursday?"

He nodded and tried to pass again.

"Do you know who the original owner of the piece was?"

"Just brought in. By a gypsy."

My cynical look said it all. The ethics of Cuthbert's employees were highly questionable, but they were stellar salespeople. They'd no doubt seen Bruce coming from a mile away. *Yes, Bruce, and this one was brought in by a real, live gypsy.*

"Is that what you told Mrs. Elbee when she inquired about it?" I said.

"Told her what I knew."

"Which was?"

"Owned by a gypsy to whom no evil had come," he said as he shuffled past me.

I tossed the flyer onto my passenger seat, but even as I tried to dismiss it with a wave of cynicism, a flurry of excitement gripped me—because inside, I was amped to be attending the show with Rafe. On top of that, there was a palpable buzz in town about the event. Nothing permeated Beulah's collective consciousness like this since the

Forenza-Galasso circus. I wouldn't mind losing myself in it, too, but for some reason, the thought of the show made my tattoo sizzle. Besides, I needed to forget about it for now and head home. Grace Elbee's memorial was tonight, and I looked a wreck.

Due to Grace's case remaining officially unsolved, her body would not be in attendance at the service; however, due to recently adopted spiritual beliefs, she'd arranged with the local pastor to "see her through" to the next dimension within thirty-six hours of her death. The pastor, through no fault of his own, had clearly missed that deadline, but he had managed to throw together a service for tonight, complete with a lowcountry boil.

When I pulled into my driveway ten minutes later, my phone vibrated. I answered as I ascended the stairs to my deck.

"Hey, Chloe," said Larry Newsome on the other end of the line. "Thanks for all the DeVore Cosmetics scoops. The story's growing every second. You sure you don't want in?"

"Got a full plate right now, Larry, but thanks."

"Listen, I went through your taped interview with Adeline DeVore, but I still have a question. Did she give you any inkling that she knew who the company mole was?"

"The only thing she said was that whoever was behind the corporate leaks might also have taken that photo of her at the Botox appointment."

"That mean anything to you?"

"Maybe that it was getting personal?" I said.

"I agree. If I find the Botox photographer, I bet I find the blogger."

"What blogger?"

"You don't know? There's a blog called *Abhor DeVore*. It posts a bunch of negative information on DeVore Cosmetics. Been active for a year. Can't believe Adeline didn't get it shut down."

"Maybe that would have served to promote it."

Larry chortled. "Believe me, she wouldn't have wanted to do that, especially if what's on there is true."

"Did it have a lot of followers?"

"No. The posts are like a slow drip of disparagement designed to take the company down implication by implication. Not a lot of solid proof behind the claims, though."

"Solid enough for the FBI to take an interest."

"Sure looks like it. Thanks, Chloe."

"Good luck, Larry."

I hung up and entered my house, smelling the sweet smoke a moment too late.

Chapter 36

"I was just enjoying the view," said Levi Carver from the center cushion of my sofa. "That's a real purty house across the way. Mite big for my tastes, of course." He sucked on his cigarette. "Mind if I smoke?"

My mind jumped around frantically. Damn! I had no gun. But Levi did. Matter of fact, he had *my* gun. My cute twenty-two. Larry's phone call had distracted me and I'd stupidly left my Glock and knife in the car.

"Thought I made my feelings clear last time you were here, Levi. I do mind."

"Yeah? And what are you gonna do about it, sweetheart? Got another surprise for me there in your pants?"

His lewd tone reminded me of his brother Zeke's threats in the mansion. These Carver brothers were becoming a serious pain in my hide.

I considered my options: dash back out the door; work my way to the knives in the kitchen; or talk my way out of this mess. Then a new idea hit me. It might just work, but I'd have to move fast because it would only be a second before Levi thought of it, too.

As he made some smart-ass comment—something about how smoking both calmed and excited him—I snaked my thumb along my smartphone screen and stroked it to power, thankful that the sounds were turned off. Then I tapped the lower left corner where my *Contacts* icon was located and hoped for the random best.

"Now I heard you yapping to someone as you came in," Levi said. "Why don't you put your phone down so's we can talk uninterrupted-like?"

I placed my cell on the small table near the door. When I vaguely heard a voice say, "Chloe?" I went off into a loud rant, knowing I was speaking for an audience of two. "Listen, Levi," I said, "I don't know why you broke into my house, but I have nothing to say to you, and in case you're not aware, I've got deep connections to the sheriff's department."

"Oh, I know. That's why I'm here. We need to talk."

"Well, I'd appreciate you getting off my couch and giving me back my gun. Then maybe we can have a civilized conversation."

"Well, ain't you the chatty one today?"

"What is it you want to talk about, anyway?"

"I need to know what my brother's gotten himself into—and what the cops know about it."

I smirked. "You mean Zeke didn't share his criminal mastermind strategy with you?'

"All's I know is the police been knocking on my door, knocking on my sister's door, and harassing my kid about graffiti on the bridge. Then a buddy of mine on the force calls to say they're putting out an APB on Zeke. Murder one or some such nonsense."

"So why come to me?"

He waved the gun. "First off, I needed a piece, and I figure this shitty little thing'll do in a pinch."

"I find it hard to believe you don't own a whole rack of guns."

"I own plenty, but the cops took 'em when they came to the house asking about some damn nail polish my kid had."

I faked a gasp. "You mean you had unregistered guns in your domicile, Levi?"

He sneered. "Don't go using your fancy reporter-girl words on me. Now rumor has it you're involved in this case against my brother, and I ain't talking to no cops till I find out what's going on. You need to tell me what they got on him—and then we're going for a ride."

"To where?"

"Start talking " He cocked the pistol. I was one redneck-twitch away from a hot piece of lead cooking my insides—or at least putting a hole in them. I started talking, hesitating a few times when it came to the specifics of the case against Zeke, but Levi pressed.

"What kind of video?" he said. "Where'd they get it?"

I vaguely explained about the amulet, while expounding upon Etta Lee's intellect and the value of choosing girlfriends more wisely.

"Get on with it. Where's this video now?"

"They've probably made multiple copies by now."

"And maybe they haven't." He waggled the gun, his finger trembling. In a different time and place, I might have been moved by this show of fraternal concern, but as things stood now, I was hoping Levi would shoot himself in the foot and die from a slow-creeping gangrenous infection. "Where is it?" he repeated.

"At the forensics lab."

"That's attached to the sheriff's office, right?"

"Yes."

"I done work on that building. There's a back entrance."

"It's incredibly secure," I lied.

He smiled, and I resisted the temptation to lecture him on how smoking discolors the teeth. "The security guard's my cousin. I can get us in."

"The place is swarming with cops," I said.

"Them cops all seem to like you, from what I hear." He assessed me up and down, much like he did at our first encounter. "Don't see the big attraction myself, but you'll do to get us where we need to go."

"And then what? You think we're just waltzing out with a big handful of evidence?"

"From what you said, there's no witnesses, and ain't no jury gonna convict my brother over a few specks of dirt he mighta tracked into some old lady's house. If I get ahold of that charm necklace—"

SWOOSH!

Poor Levi. All he got ahold of was a bullet to the hand. As he yowled in shock over the damaged stump at the end of his wrist, the gun crashed to the floor. He leaped up from the sofa and had a downright conniption fit, but I had no time for sympathy or disgust. I dove, sliding right through a slick puddle of his blood, and extended my arm for all it was worth. The moment my fingers touched the twenty-two, I flipped over and aimed straight at the one-handed dude still shrieking in my living room.

The whole scene was pitiful, but my primary thought was how uncool Levi would look trying to light his ciggies from now on. He dashed out the door, gripping his bloody paw, just as sirens approached, accompanied by the mad scrape of tires skidding to a stop on my driveway.

I stood and took in the scene surrounding me. Gross. The splattered blood against the taupe couch looked like a flock of red ducks scattering skyward after a hunter's stray bullet. Thank God *my* hunter's bullet hadn't gone astray. I turned around, faced the *purty* house across the way, and waved my gratitude with a smile. Then I walked over, picked up my cell, and returned to the window. Rafe's voice came through from the other end of the line.

"Thank God you never put curtains on that window, Chloe."

"Why would I? They would block my view."

"And mine," he said suggestively.

"Thanks, by the way, for saving my life. I had no idea you were such a good shot."

"Quite good, as a matter of fact."

I turned and glanced at my couch. "So I see."

"Good thing we exchanged phone numbers, eh?"

"I'm just glad yours was the most recent number in my contacts."

"Glad to be of service. By the way, I understand Mrs. Elbee's memorial is tonight. Want to head over together?"

"Are you seriously asking something as casual as that after what just happened?"

"Want me to call back?"

I laughed. "No, it's fine. Pick me up at six."

"See you then."

Chapter 37

Half an hour later, everything was cleared up with regard to Levi. Something told me I wouldn't be seeing either Carver brother again for a long time.

"Thanks for getting here so fast, Chad," I said.

"Good thing Rafe thought to call it in so fast," he said with only the merest hint of resentment.

"Still, I'm sure this was the last thing you needed on your plate," I said.

"All in a day's work. But these last couple days have been awfully strange."

"You going to the memorial tonight?" I asked.

"Yeah. Picking up Melanie LeGrange at the airport, believe it or not, and then heading over."

"What? Mrs. LeGrange is coming all the way back to Beulah for Grace Elbee's service?"

"No. Get this. Someone sent her a first-class ticket to fly in for that magic show tomorrow night."

My open-mouthed gape replied in full.

"I know, right?" he said. "Anyway, when she heard about the memorial, she decided to fly in a day early." Chad shifted and looked uncomfortable. "Listen, Chloe, something I've got to tell you."

My heart lurched to a stop.

"The guys finished the dig in Boyd's basement. There's nothing there."

I allowed myself to breathe again.

"Couple bones," he said, "but they're from a dog. Other than that, we're going through the soil with a fine-tooth comb, but there's no body."

I told Chad what Boyd had said in the woods, about how he admitted to cuffing Hoop in that room, but that he denied killing anyone. "Boyd actually seemed surprised about the blood and other evidence down there," I said. "Claimed he never even thought to clean up that room because nothing really happened."

"And you believed him?" Chad said.

"No, but why admit to cuffing Hoop at all? Why not just keep denying it outright? It lent a grain of truth to his story."

Chad and I lamented Old Bastard's unexpected appetite and then said our good-byes. It took me over an hour to clean up the mess Levi had left. Seemed I was always cleaning up after the Carver brothers lately—from Zeke's bathroom stench to Mrs. Elbee's body to Levi's blood. And if I wasn't mistaken, I was staring at a fleshy wedge of fingertip in the corner of my living room. I hoped that was the last I'd see of either of them.

As I brought my stained sofa cushions to the laundry room, I caught a flash of yellow in my open book bag. My eyes went wide with surprise. It was the envelope from Hoop addressed to Macy. I'd forgotten all about it after clocking Zeke with the attic stairs. I dropped the cushions and unclipped the envelope from the box to which it was attached. It wasn't in the purview of good taste to rummage through a dead kid's memorabilia, but I'd gone to an awful lot of trouble to do otherwise now.

And then I gasped. I'd never thought of Hoop as *a dead kid* before, and yet, I'd done it so nonchalantly, so carelessly. Had I become that jaded? Or was it finally getting easier to accept because I'd always known—since the day they found his Schwinn in the swamp? Or when he hadn't shown up at Macy's funeral? Or maybe from the moment I waved to him that final morning, when a horrible sense of foreboding had crushed me?

Clutching the card in my hand, I sat down. I hesitated before opening it, even checking over my shoulder for Macy's ghost. For her sake, I sure hoped Hoop had written something worthwhile inside. I removed the card from the envelope. The front showed a picture of two birds holding a wavy, pink banner in their beaks as they flew skyward. It declared: *Happy Birthday to a high-flying girl!*

The sad irony was that Macy *had* ended her life as a high-flying girl. Unless I'd always imagined it wrong. Maybe Avis Whitaker's old Cadillac had jolted her sideways, or straight to the ground. I'd never asked for details. All I knew was that the car was found with her left pedal hooked in the fender, and the marks in the road showed that Mr. Whitaker, the bike, and the car had all skidded a hundred-fifty feet before crashing into the oak.

I opened the card. It contained a preprinted message: *You've already taken off with my heart*. On the other side was Hoop's heavy, dark handwriting. I knew it better than my own. That same scratchy penmanship had shouted back at me every time I'd read his final essay—and I had read that thing a hundred times over.

The note said:

April 1 . . . 15ᵗʰ Birthday . . . 12:03 a.m.

Happy Birthday, Macy! It's a big one because . . . <u>you can finally date!</u> And that leaves just north of 105,000 hours till our wedding day, and then we got forever, which is a few more seconds than I can put a number to, but I'm sure going to try:

We'll be together longer than the human race survives. Longer than the moon shines and the earth rotates, but not longer than the stars because we'll be two of them, forming our own constellation: the Double-Macy-Hoop! (If only other humans had survived long enough to see it!) The Double-Macy-Hoop will of course be in the form of two hoop snakes who've accomplished the rare state of ouroboros—that perfect symbol of eternity, rebirth, perfection and balance. Yin and yang. And that sure is us. Me as one circle, you as the other. But we won't be concentric. In our own way—a way I can't even imagine—we'll be coiled together, two perfect circles entwined, forever.

Heck, we'll be our own fire in the sky. But if you don't want to wait that long . . . then for your one and only fifteenth birthday . . . my gift to you . . . Look up!

I reflexively looked up, futilely hoping—for what? For Hoop to be holding an engagement ring? To be juggling two rings of fire? All I saw was blurriness filling my own eyes. My God, he loved her. He loved her purely and unconditionally. Why had I never accepted it?

I let my tears flow before closing the card. There was a note on the back: *P.S. Please wish your mom a Happy Birthday for me—only four minutes belated!*

It took me longer than it should have to understand the postscript. Mrs. LeGrange's birthday must have been the day before Macy's. If Hoop had planned for Macy's card to be read at 12:03 a.m., as indicated, he'd only have missed Mrs. LeGrange's birthday by a few minutes. The last time I'd seen Mrs. LeGrange, in front of Boyd's General, it must have been close to her birthday. Our encounter had only lasted five minutes, not the type of meeting anyone would remember . . . but I did. It was the last time I'd seen Macy alive. I could still conjure the raw emotions I'd felt when Mrs. LeGrange mentioned how Macy would be allowed to date soon. Like a selfish brat, I'd pedaled my bike home and cried until my pillow was saturated. I'd cried out of self-pity, knowing that Macy and Hoop would become official. And then I'd cried for being such a horrible friend.

I slammed a fist down on the table. If only they'd lived! Maybe Macy would have become a stuck-up homecoming queen, and Hoop a raging jerk or drunk like his father. I might have grown to despise both of them. Life would have been so . . . *normal*, with reputations growing soiled and realistic, rather than purified and flawless through the filter of death. Childhoods weren't supposed to end abruptly, freeze-framing people in innocence and perfection. They were meant to peter out slowly so that adults could look back and wonder when they'd become so jaded.

I knew exactly when I had.

I pulled out the box that had accompanied the birthday card and lifted the lid. Fireworks. A hundred dollars' worth or more. Of course. That's what Hoop had planned to give Macy for her birthday: a fireworks display. Fire in the sky.

I reached into the box and picked one up. It fell apart in my hand, corroded and ruined.

Chapter 38

Grace Elbee had apparently planned every last detail of the memorial with her pastor. Not surprising. She'd been talking about her death for years and had been prepared to go—just not in the precise way she'd gone.

A small tent had been erected outside the church, the chairs lined up, and the stage set. Grace had pre-purchased a bottom-of-the-line casket. *"I'll be dead. Why delay the decay?"* she'd once told me.

Rafe and I took seats near the back so I could watch the comings and goings. I was especially curious to see if Richie Quail would show.

Grace's son, Eric, sat in the front row with a dour-looking gentleman—probably a sponsor or a guard. Grace had always claimed Eric was in rehab, but some of us believed it was a facility of a more restrictive nature.

Next to Eric were Grace's friends from before her candlestick days. They periodically approached Eric to offer condolences, but he kept his head lowered. Probably Jonesing for a drink or a ciggy.

Rafe nudged me and nodded to the right, toward the center aisle. A rotund barrel of gregariousness had made its entrance: Richie Quail. He'd returned to town after all. A burning fury rose up within me. It was all I could do to keep from storming the aisle and throttling one of his necks. Thanks to him, Boyd would never reveal his secrets, never reveal Hoop's fate.

Quail's second wife hung off his arm like a cheap accessory. She was some Russian babe he'd mail-ordered like a toy off a cereal box. She averted her eyes from all who glanced in her direction—which was everyone, because she was ridiculously gorgeous. Just the thought of Quail and her in bed together made my stomach feel nauseous. Quail made a big to-do of his arrival, waving and shaking hands with people as if it were a wedding and he was the father of the bride. Christ, he could have been the father of *his* bride.

Rafe patted my arm and only then did I realize I'd balled up my fists and raised my shoulders. "Plenty of time to talk afterwards," he said with a hint of a grin on his face.

I'd barely gotten over the revulsion of seeing Quail waddle down the aisle when Chad walked in with Melanie LeGrange on his arm. Wow—still stunning. Chad gestured for her to enter the row immediately in front of ours. Not until he was seated did he realize his proximity to me. He almost smiled, but when he saw my seatmate, he adjusted his reaction to a curt nod. And when he sat and faced forward, I thought I saw his superhero jaw tense up and set itself for the rest of the evening.

Mrs. LeGrange took her seat, but immediately turned around. She lit up upon recognizing me. Despite more wrinkles around her eyes and mouth, and slightly thinner lips, there was no denying her beauty. She seemed much healthier and happier than I remembered. Even with additional weight, she remained thin, but all hints of her former frailty had vanished. My assessment was confirmed when Rafe got a full look at her; I'd swear I heard him stifle a gasp. Who could blame him? Her good looks were of the Hollywood type, rarely seen in person and never seen in the likes of Beulah.

"Chloe Keyes," she said with a gleaming smile. "My goodness, is it really you?"

"It sure is, Mrs. LeGrange." I leaned forward and hugged her, forcing Chad to lean right. She squeezed me tightly—a real hugger's hug—and when we let go, she gazed at me as if in awe, no doubt wondering what Macy would have looked like at my age. "It is wonderful to see you. Truly."

"And you as well," I said. "You look amazing."

"It's been a long road," she said, her eyes warm and full, "but I've survived. Finally got where I needed to be."

I smiled in response, unable to fathom her travails along the way.

"Is this your husband?" She glanced at Rafe and extended her hand. I could only imagine the grating toll the conversation was taking on Chad.

"Oh, no," I said, my face growing hot, "this is my friend, Rafe Borose. Rafe, this is Melanie LeGrange."

Rafe, still wearing a reverential smile on his lips, reached out and shook her slim hand. "Mrs. LeGrange," he said. "Enchanted to make your acquaintance." Then he either closed his eyes or did an elongated blink as he bowed his head in her direction.

Mrs. LeGrange tipped her head a bit, too, her silky blond bob falling slightly to the side. "Lovely to meet you, Rafe. Did you grow up in Beulah? I don't recall your name, and yet, it's so unusual."

"I live in New Beulah, actually. One of the recent transplants."

"Well, I'm glad you found us. Chloe here was a wonderful friend to my daughter, Macy." She glanced down but then back up, quite deliberately, as if a therapist had taught her that small trick for finding courage. "She passed away many years ago."

"My condolences."

Mrs. LeGrange nodded in appreciation, then turned back to me. "It's still hard for me, of course, and I didn't think I'd ever return to Beulah, but I received the strangest invitation. A magic show, believe it or not, and my curiosity got the better of me. Do you know anything about it?"

"Only that I'm going, too," I said. "The whole town is. Where are you staying, by the way? I can offer you a great Murphy bed at my place."

"Thanks so much, but everything's been taken care of by whoever invited me. I'll be at the Hilton in New Beulah." She leaned forward and spoke confidentially. "Personally, I suspect Richie Quail is behind all of it. He was very generous to me when I left town, and I don't have many connections left here. It's got to be him."

"Richie Quail is actually here," I said. "Up front. Perhaps he can explain afterwards."

"Oh, I doubt it," she said. "He's kept the whole thing very secretive. Probably wouldn't do to spill the beans the day before. I just hope it doesn't have anything to do with . . . well, the day after tomorrow would have been Macy's birthday. And tomorrow is the anniversary of her"—she smiled awkwardly— "well, anniversary doesn't seem like the right word. I just hope the date is a coincidence."

"I'm sure it is," I said. "By the way, that means your birthday is tomorrow, right?"

She looked baffled that I knew, and I saw Rafe looking more than a little surprised.

"How in the world did you know that?" she said.

I didn't want to admit that I'd read a private card meant for her deceased daughter, so I went with an old standby, which happened to be true. "I have a weird thing for dates and phone numbers. Macy must have mentioned it when we were kids."

She smiled. "It's true. *Four minutes apart*, Macy used to say, *but in two different months*. My husband would get jealous because his birthday was half a calendar away—in late October sometime." She stifled a giggle. "You know, I can't even remember which day now." The last sentence came with a hint of pride; she really had moved on.

I moved off of Macy-related topics, but we got cut short when the memorial began. Strike and Jacqueline Ryker arrived just in time to scoot in next to Chad. Jacqueline, always poised and gracious, gave Macy's mom quite an embrace and welled up immediately. Then they all sat quietly as the music started.

The preacher dominated the memorial, as Eric Elbee clearly had no intention of speaking. Toward the end, two of Grace's bolder friends approached the podium and shared stories, reminding us all of the few times, long ago, when Grace had actually lived up to the spirit of her name.

Chad spent most of the time staring straight ahead, a smirk covering his face, and his mind clearly occupied by murder, arson, and armed Feds swirling about town. Meanwhile, the sheriff held Jacqueline's hand throughout and managed to look unfailingly miserable. It couldn't have been easy for him watching his town spiral out of control like this.

Afterward, everyone hustled out to enjoy the lowcountry boil provided at Mrs. Elbee's expense. It may well have been the most generous thing she'd ever done, but I couldn't bring myself to enjoy it. When Rafe began conversing with Mrs. LeGrange about Chicago, I drifted over to Chad who was struggling with a crab leg.

"Is your dad going to talk to Richie Quail?" I asked. "About why he posted bail for Boyd?"

Chad gave up on retrieving anything edible from the leg. "I don't know, Chloe. Why don't you do it? You're so on top of everything lately."

"What's eating you?"

"Gosh, I don't know. Here we are at a memorial service for a long-time neighbor." He gestured to the crowd. "Guess I didn't realize it was a date sort of thing."

"Seriously? That's what's bothering you? Rafe knew Mrs. Elbee, too, in case you—"

"You know what, Chloe? I don't care. Rafe saved your life today. Maybe that's your cue to jump in bed with him."

"Where's all this coming from? You and I broke up

almost a year ago."

"And I only recently found out why."

"Chad, please."

He picked up an ear of corn but only used it to point at me. "You and me, we had a great thing going. But when the relationship hit a point where it had to get serious or die, you headed straight for the off-ramp."

"People break up, Chad. It happens. Get over it."

"That's rich, coming from someone who can't get over a teenage crush."

My tattoo suddenly scorched and my ire erupted. I wanted to grab that corn and shove it in his ear. "That's a new low, Chad. It was more than a crush, and you know it."

"Only because of how it ended."

"And you're speaking from what? All your *normal* life experiences?"

"Looks like we're both hitting new lows tonight."

"News flash, buddy. You barely knew me, so there's no way you loved me."

"You got that right. Because love goes two ways and we sure didn't have that. But neither did you and Hoop. You wanted it to be love, but news flash back at ya—it wasn't."

I stepped toward him, ready to lash out, but my anger suddenly receded while curiosity took its place. "Why is all this coming up now?"

"Because seeing you with that Rafe guy really pisses me off. I didn't get a fair run, and now he's moving in when there might finally be an opening."

"An opening? Because Hoop might be dead? Is that how you're viewing all this?"

"That's not what I meant and you know it."

"What did you mean then? That it's a job position to love me?"

"Felt that way to me sometimes." He dropped the corn

back on his plate and sneered. "I got into your lockbox, you know. The one you keep in your closet. I mean, Jesus, is that what I was up against?"

I shook my head compulsively, trying to prevent Chad from talking about the one item that laid bare my soul. I rubbed my arm, wishing it could scald him to keep him from revealing how truly barren I was.

"You ever think about it anymore, Clo? Huh? So maybe you can join him in some warped way?"

My eyes seared him. Then I put my lips within licking distance of his ear. "You know what, Chad? I do think about it. Every. Damn. Day."

He stepped back, his surprise dwarfed by his anger. "Honestly, Chloe, I don't know how you do it. I don't know how you keep the spark alive for someone who never lit theirs for you."

"You don't know that."

"Yeah, I do. It's like you're the one who died that week."

I flashed a disconcerting smile. "At least you got something right."

I spun away and my eyes landed on Quail as he stuffed a sausage into his mouth. *Why not?* Wife-nikov was nowhere in sight—probably in line preparing another overloaded plate for her living, breathing ATM. If the sheriff and Chad weren't going to do their jobs, I'd get the ball rolling.

Chapter 39

I marched over and scowled at Quail until he finally dismissed the junior councilman who'd blown enough smoke up his ass to set off an alarm.

"Ms. Keyes," Quail said, his greasy lips glistening. "I'm guessing you either want a word, or no one's ever taught you how to mingle."

I unclenched my jaw. "You put up Boyd Sexton's bail."

The duplicitous twinkle in his eye said it all: he sure had. "Not a big secret," he said, shoving a potato into his mouth. "Anybody could trace it back to me if they wanted to."

"I wanted to. Tell me, why the big rush to get a lowlife drug dealer out of jail?"

"Rush? There was no rush. Boyd was in there a good bit of time, you ask me."

"And you got him out just before he planned to spill his guts to the FBI."

"Did I?" He rubbed his bulbous hand along his chin and pulled his lips into a mound of bewilderment. "Didn't realize that. Must be why he sounded so frantic when he called. 'Spect he didn't really want to talk to those fellas."

"More likely, he was planning to tell them something *you* didn't want them to know. What was he going to reveal, Mr. Quail?"

"My goodness, Ms. Keyes, you're filled with vim and vigor today. Or is it venom and vigor?"

"It's suspicion, and you didn't answer the question."

He grabbed a large shrimp off his plate and took it with one bite. This seafood-as-stalling-tactic game was growing beyond lame. Couldn't he at least fake a heart attack? Apparently not. He took his sweet, Southern time licking three portly fingers and then declaring, "Mm, mm, mm. That

Grace sure knows how to throw a boil." Eventually, he acknowledged my presence again by muttering, "Heck, Ms. Keyes, I don't have the faintest idea what was running through Boyd Junior's mind. The boy wasn't exactly Nobel Prize material, am I right? All's I know is he called and I answered."

"Of all the people he could call in town, why you?"

"Why not me?"

"Because you barely knew one another. You said as much in our interview."

"In my world, when the son of a good ol' boy asks for help, you respond. But perhaps I put more stock in a promise than you do."

"What promise would that be?"

"The one I made to Boyd Senior on his deathbed." He leaned down to confide in me, his spicy breath doing him no favors. "Between you and me, Boyd Senior knew that Junior wasn't the slickest fish in the school. So when his lungs were crackling like a spent log, he pulled me in close and said, 'Richie, promise me you'll take care of Junior. Not in a day-to-day way, but if he gets into trouble, I'm gonna need you to be there.' So I gave my word, and I'm sure as heck glad I was there when Junior finally called."

What a load of meadow mayonnaise. I felt like the sucker opening a closet door and yelping at a harmless milk snake. "Your loyalty's inspiring, Mr. Quail, but before he became gator mash, Boyd Junior said that you *made everything square* and that you'd *checked with everyone*. I need to know: what was square? And who did you check with?"

Quail pulled himself up to his full height and forced an exhale through his nose, the stream of wet air repulsing me. "That sounds to me like a question a sheriff should be asking, not some podunk reporter for the local paper."

"The sheriff's got his hands full. Podunk will have to do."

He lowered his voice, and the affable veneer he'd been wearing dissolved into one of cold hostility. "Are we on the record?"

"Nope. Just you and me chattin' it up at a boil."

He leaned down until his face blurred into a soft pile of gelatinous jelly. "Then screw off. You got nothing on me and I don't appreciate your tone."

I didn't back away and I sure as heck didn't screw off. Not even a little. "I see your stripes, Mr. Quail, and I'm not buying what you're selling."

"You'd be the first. Now if you know what's good for you, little lady, you'll take your leave."

"Know this, Mr. Quail. I do put stock in promises, and I promise that if you had anything to do with Hoop Whitaker's disappearance, I will find out, and you will go down for it."

Melanie LeGrange suddenly materialized to Quail's left. "I'm sorry to interrupt," she said sweetly, "but I just had to say hello, Richie. Is this a bad time?"

The abrupt change in Quail's demeanor would definitely qualify as a freak occurrence of nature. His pallor returned to normal and his smile came across as genuine. He turned to Melanie LeGrange with a beaming expression. "Melanie, my goodness, you look as lovely as the first time I laid eyes on you in middle school."

"I owe that to your generosity, Richie. I've never forgotten what you did for me. Leaving Beulah turned out to be the healthiest decision I ever made."

"You know, there's folks around here who find it hard to believe, but sometimes, old Richie Quail here's got good instincts about the heart and soul—and how to heal them."

If he could have, he'd have patted his own back and topped it off with a hand-job.

"I'll spread the word," Melanie said with a smile.

"Tell me, Melanie, what brings you to town? 'Cause you

can color me surprised to see you here."

"Oh, come on, now. I suspect you know why I'm here. A little something to do with a magic show?"

Quail looked pleasantly puzzled. "Think I saw a flyer about that. You planning to attend?"

Melanie smiled like a cunning co-conspirator. "Matter of fact, I am. I've been promised a delightful spate of shocking surprises, or something to that effect."

"All this way for a little show, eh?"

"Of course. You paid—I mean, *someone* paid for my ticket." A delicate frown marred the still-taut skin between her brows. "You know, if you're really not the person behind all this, then I'm a mite concerned. Perhaps I shouldn't have come."

"Nonsense," Quail said with a chortle. "Fun to have a little mystery in life. You know, Melanie, I'd be honored to escort you to the show. Been curious about the goings-on in my pavilion myself, and it's not the sort of thing my wife would be interested in."

Mrs. LeGrange narrowed her alluring eyes and grinned playfully, clearly suspicious that Quail was putting on a front. "Okay, then. As you may or may not know, I'm staying at the Hilton. Pick me up at eight?"

Chad approached our trio without a single glance in my direction. He asked Mrs. LeGrange if she was ready to head to the hotel because he had to get going. As they said their good-byes and departed, Rafe came over and stuck his hand out to greet Quail, who looked surprised to see him.

"Evening, Clive," Quail said, using Rafe's financial advisor pseudonym. "Didn't expect to see you here."

"I had the pleasure of meeting Mrs. Elbee shortly before her untimely passing."

Quail, still shaking Rafe's hand, pulled him in close. "Everything go okay with our recent transaction?"

"Of course, Mr. Quail, but surely, we shouldn't discuss business in front of Miss Keyes here."

"Oh," Quail said with a wicked twist of his lips. "You two know each other?"

"Quite well," Rafe said. "You might say we're both swamp rats. We drove here together."

Quail looked down his nose at Rafe. "Then I suggest you keep your date under control."

Rafe cocked his head and took his time before speaking. "And I suggest you behave like a gentleman."

Quail snorted. "Now listen here, boy—"

"I don't think so," Rafe interrupted, stepping into Quail's personal space. "It's you who listens to me. It's you who heeds my advice."

Quail took his time wiping his mouth with a napkin. "Let's be clear on one thing, Clive. In life, there's the prize-winning stallion and there's the lackey who picks up after him. The lackey might enjoy some of the glory, but at the end of the day, he's still holding a bag of horse hockey."

"Well, as they say in hockey, Mr. Quail, sweat more in preparation, bleed less in battle. And I've been sweating."

Quail's features bunched together. "Didn't realize we were in battle, Clive."

"Then consider the lines drawn. With that bail transaction you asked me to post, you cost Miss Keyes here valuable information. I don't appreciate being made party to deception."

Quail's nostrils went as wide as a pig's stuffed cheeks. "Fortunately for you, Clive, I'll consider this friendly social banter."

Rafe leaned forward. "Unfortunately for you, I won't."

The pissing contest was growing too wet for my tastes. Besides, it wasn't worth Rafe losing a top client; Boyd was already dead. "Come on," I said, nudging Rafe. "Let's get out of here."

He glanced at me, his expression a complete surprise. No coursing testosterone. No meteoric plunge from an adrenaline high. Instead, just pure joy.

He extended an elbow in my direction. "Shall we?"

I looped my arm through his and we showed our back sides to Quail as we departed. Just before we exited the tent, I glanced back and noticed the sheriff finally heading in Quail's direction. About time. But from the sheriff's slumped posture and lowered head, I sensed he was in for a losing round.

Chapter 40

One Day Before the Thump

The morning sun promised an unusually hot March day. Macy couldn't believe the beautiful weather they'd gotten for Spring Break from school. As she pedaled her bike faster than usual, the air whistled through the hole in her sneaker, cooling her foot. She sure wouldn't mind an air vent in the other shoe, but yesterday's practice on Ronnie's skateboard had only taken a toll on the one. Besides, Momma would have a fit if she came home with holes in both shoes—not that Momma would notice things like that again for a while. Her sky-high mood of yesterday had vanished in a dark instant this morning, just after a call from a collection agency. She'd barely gotten the phone back in its cradle before returning to bed, complaining of a headache.

In response to the complaint, Macy was now on her way to Boyd's General to pick up some aspirin—*the generic*, her mother had specified. As she coasted around the final curve to Boyd's, she checked her watch. Eleven minutes flat. A new record. *Let's see Hoop beat that!* She parked her bike in the rack that Boyd kept in the rear of the lot. Glancing around, she was surprised to see no customer cars. For a split second, she worried about being alone in the store with Boyd, but she ignored the feeling, and it passed when she pushed the door open and heard the familiar bell overhead.

No Boyd in sight, so she started her shopping. After locating the aspirin, she searched for birthday cards and found a small selection below the cleaning supplies. Hoop was right—Boyd did have a little bit of everything if you looked hard enough.

Crouching down, she opened and read them all, smiling

as she wondered which one Hoop had chosen for her.

"Help you?" Boyd Junior said in a scratchy voice. Probably his first words of the day. He was standing at the end of the aisle, clearing his throat and averting his eyes when Macy looked over.

"Morning, Boyd. Just picking out a card for Momma. Birthday's tomorrow."

He grunted and cleared his throat again before walking away.

Macy chose a card with pink flowers and water droplets that said *Happy Birthday* in bright green lettering. She brought her items to the register and then reached into her pocket for the crumpled dollars she'd grabbed from the kitchen counter. When she pulled out a ten dollar bill, she gasped.

"Something wrong?" Boyd said, looking all caved-in on himself.

Macy had completely forgotten about the money she'd earned babysitting last week. Finding it again was like getting paid twice. Her eyes grew huge, and she bit down on her lip while she debated. Finally, she fixed Boyd with a mischievous grin. "Is it too late to buy a lottery ticket?"

"Drawing's tomorrow," he said.

"I know." She waved her ten dollar bill. "Can I buy a ticket?"

"Uh, *people* can, but *you* can't."

Macy looked down at her body, clear to her feet and then back up at Boyd. "Last time I checked, I was still people."

Boyd showed no trace of amusement. "You gotta be eighteen."

Macy kept smiling and sparkling, though her charms were mostly squandered on Boyd; his eyes stayed locked on the register. But heck, if Macy LeGrange gave up that easily, her report card would reflect the actual grades she earned rather than the ones she talked her teachers into.

"Boyd, you know how sometimes you let Momma buy things on credit?"

"Sure."

"And sometimes you let me buy things on credit while Momma's in the car?"

"Yeah."

"And we usually pay up within a week or so, right?"

"I guess." He seemed to be growing less comfortable, and Macy worried he might fold himself right into an origami swan, but she kept going.

"And since those tickets are still for sale, you'd sell Momma one if she were here."

"But she ain't."

"Only because she's laid up with a doozy of a headache." Macy shook the aspirin bottle but stopped when she saw that the sound made Boyd grimace. "Momma told me just yesterday that she sure doesn't want to miss out on a chance to win that jackpot. I mean, if anyone in this town could use that money, it'd be Momma and me, don't you think?"

Boyd shrugged.

"Well, today's situation is even better than Momma being here herself, because I can actually pay—without using credit." Macy glanced around the store and gestured to its emptiness. "There's nobody here but you and me, Boyd, and no one will ever know if Momma was in the parking lot or not."

Boyd frowned and looked lost in Macy's triple-negative plea.

"What I'm saying is, can you just sell me the ticket and we'll pretend like Momma's in the car waiting on me?"

He glanced toward the parking lot, and then back at Macy, perhaps expecting Melanie LeGrange to have materialized. Then he reached below the counter, unlocked a drawer, and pulled out a lottery ticket. "Anybody asks, your momma bought this, y'hear?"

Macy beamed. "Thanks, Boyd. I knew you were cool."

Boyd blushed a bit, but Macy didn't notice. She was grabbing a pen from the yarn-covered can next to the register. The pen she selected was burgundy in color with white lettering that read: *Richard Quail Realty and Development*. She hesitated, hoping it wasn't bad luck to let Quail the Whale's ink darken the circles on her ticket.

"Hurry up now," Boyd said, glancing toward the front door. "Don't need no one seeing you."

Macy quickly picked her numbers and slid the ticket to Boyd. He rang up her order and she paid, feeling like Charlie from *Charlie and the Chocolate Factory* as she watched her money disappear into the register. Boyd made change, but before handing over the receipt, he copied her lottery numbers onto it. "Have your Momma sign the ticket, and don't lose it. But just in case, I always write the numbers on the receipts."

"Thanks, Boyd. Wish me luck."

He stared at the register again, but as she exited, he gave a small wave. She took it as a positive sign—until she looked up and saw Quail the Whale pulling into the parking lot. Dang it all! She'd promised him a hand-delivered wad of rental cash, and here she was with nothing but a few dollars in her pocket, and Momma still without a job.

Quail pulled in two spots down from the front door. He was spitting into his cell phone as he talked, waving his free hand all over the place—probably yelling at somebody to cough up their rent *or else*. He definitely hadn't noticed Macy yet, but there was no way for her to get to her bike without him spotting her. Then, another car pulled up and parked between her and Quail. The driver was that big-bosomed lady, DeVore the Whore, who acted like the answer to every man's prayers. She exited her car and dashed into Boyd's with only a quick, dismissive glance in Macy's direction.

Macy wasted no time in crawling along the length of the woman's car, hopping on her bike, and getting the heck out of there. As she rode home, the wind kicked up and whipped her hair in three directions at once, making her laugh out loud. Hoop would no doubt deem this a what-a-day, and he'd be right, too, because she had a chance in her pocket, a wish in her bag, and a big old heaping of hope in her heart.

Chapter 41

My phone rang at 7:00 a.m. I startled awake to find myself lying on my quilt, still dressed in last night's memorial clothes. My laptop, two pens, and a notebook covered the bed, the latter having left a spiral zig-zag indent on my arm. Like a whiny boyfriend, the phone just kept ringing, so I slapped my hand around until I found it. *Chad Ryker*, said the Caller ID.

"Morning, Chad," I said, trying to unstick my lips. I sat up and felt an urgent need for coffee. "Did I dream it or did we end on a really sour note last night?"

"Yeah, sorry," he said. "I mean, I'm not taking it all back, but wrong place, wrong time, wrong everything. My only excuse is that I've been living on like three hours of sleep a night."

I got up and staggered to the kitchen. "Maybe we can talk stuff out again when all this settles down."

"Agreed. Listen, I thought of something last night. Since we didn't find anything in Boyd's basement to indicate that a body was buried there, I figured Boyd might've, um . . ."

"Transferred the body?"

"If there was a body."

"Okay, but if he whisked Hoop away in his car, we don't have the car to—"

"Wrong." He waited and tried to suck up a bit of glory through the phone line—which I selfishly withheld. "Boyd sold his old Chevy to Doc West's daughter years ago. She moved to West Virginia, but she still has the car, believe it or not. The forensics lab there has agreed to—"

"Chad, allow me to be the bigger pessimist for once. What are the odds? You think nobody's cleaned that car in twelve years? Replaced the floor mats? Had it detailed?"

"DNA sticks around, Chloe," he said with anger-laced

grit.

"I guess it's worth a try, but—"

"Look, if there's any chance I can prove Hoop Whitaker's body was in that car, I'm going for it. I'm ending this thing once and for all."

I frowned as hard as my coffee was percolating. "Jesus, Chad. For who?"

"For both of us. And for him. You know what, Chloe? I'm doing my job. Isn't that what you want? Isn't that *all* you want from me?"

"Are we starting again?"

"No. Sorry. Hey, Strike was up most of the night. He tracked down Zeke Carver's girlfriend around midnight—the one who polished Grace Elbee's nails. Found her asleep in Grace's car at a campground in Revel Park. He's got her in custody now."

I wanted desperately to win a round of *Dammit, Be Nice, Chloe*, but it just wasn't in the cards today. "Tell him to make sure her bail is over a billion. Even Quail can't swing that."

"You're a piece of work, you know that?"

"I've been called worse."

"Yeah, by me."

I smiled, and so, I think, did Chad.

"Gotta go," he said.

"Hey, did Zeke's girlfriend say anything useful? Like who hired them to take out Mrs. Elbee?"

"No, she clammed up real tight, plus she was high on something when Strike brought her in. But guess what?"

"What?"

"She was wearing those earrings she stole from Mrs. Elbee."

"Priceless."

"Not really. They were fakes."

"Mrs. Elbee, ever frugal."

We hung up. I desperately needed to put in a couple hours on my article, so I gathered my notes and threw them down on the kitchen table. When I opened my laptop, I realized how little work I'd done. With no impressive sentences coming to mind, I stared mindlessly at the first line of my document: 03-08-10-28-31-41—the winning lottery numbers. The more I stared, the more the numbers filled my head, and for the first time, I experienced something akin to a synesthetic thought.

Twelve digits, sixteen million dollars, four winners, one ticket seller, one murder, one fatal accident, two arrests, ninety-nine numbers for PowerPot players to play. The ninety-nine numbers took on a purple hue in my head while the winning numbers assumed a yellow shade. In the old articles I'd researched, the winning numbers were always listed in this ascending sequence, but had the Lucky Four chosen them that way? Seemed odd. Maybe the lottery officials had released them to the public in that order. And why did I still not know how the winning numbers had been chosen? Would I ever find out? If they'd been meaningful to Grace Elbee, she sure wouldn't be able to tell me.

I dug through my files to find a close-up of the winning ticket. There it was. *Aha*, the numbers had not been chosen sequentially, but rather as: 41-03-31-10-28-08. All below fifty. If they'd all been twelve or lower, I'd have guessed they revolved around hours on a clock. If they'd been 31 or lower, I'd have guessed dates, anniversaries, birthdays, but 41 was the outlier there.

And then, without any provocation from my conscious mind, the 41 split itself violently in two. Each digit grew huge and throbbed in my mind's eye, changing from simple butter-yellow to blinding, sunburst-yellow.

Four. One.

Holy. Shit.

263

Chapter 42

I dialed the number again. Pacing. Frantic. Confused.

No answer.

"Come on!" I said aloud. "You just called me! Answer!"

Disconnect. Tap. Ring. Disconnect. Tap. Ring. Repeat. He finally answered. "Hey Chloe, can this wait? I'm kind of busy."

"Chad, you're not going to—"

I froze. What was I doing? I couldn't tell Chad. Of all people, I couldn't tell Chad. Now that I thought about it, I couldn't tell anyone. At least not yet.

"Uh, sorry," I said. "Not important."

"*Not important* enough that you called me five times?"

"I'll try you later. Bye." I put my phone down, then sat at the kitchen table and contorted my body into a pretzel. Staring at my notes with laser-like focus, I waited for more answers to bubble up. Nothing, except the earlier answer that kept hammering at my skull from the inside out.

No doubt about it: the winning lottery ticket had belonged to Macy LeGrange. Wouldn't hold up in court, but give me a jury of twelve, and they'd be convinced.

The 41 was Macy's birthday—April 1st. The 03 and the 31 were her mother's birthday—March 31st. Oh geez, that was today—and wow, Melanie LeGrange might have a heck of a present coming. The 10 and the 28 had to be Macy's father's birthday. Mrs. LeGrange had mentioned it was in late October, and I'd already confirmed it with a quick internet search on *Darrell LeGrange Bail & Bond Services*. The 08, I wasn't sure, but the number on Macy's volleyball jersey had been 8, and Hoop's birthday had been the eighth of January. Either one would fit the bill.

I pounded my fist on the table. Oh, how I'd love to hear

the Lucky Four try to explain this one away. Maybe Adeline DeVore could tell me her bullshit story again—how they'd all chipped in to buy the lottery ticket to help out poor Mrs. Elbee. Funny how Adeline had been able to remember a bear claw in Quail's hand, but couldn't recall how the numbers had been chosen. Liar!

If my suspicions were right, then the sheriff must have stolen the ticket initially because he was first on the scene after Macy's accident. But that would be highly un-sheriff-like. And then, why involve Quail, Adeline DeVore, and Mrs. Elbee? It was as if severity, greed, desperation and nastiness had all gotten into bed together and birthed out ugliness and depravity. What the hell kind of kinky quartet were they, anyway?

I got up and poured another cup of coffee. Two so far, and I was just getting started. I sucked it down and poured another while leaning against the kitchen counter, my mind on overdrive, my jitters in turbo mode. Disgust and horror hovered around me like a personal thundercloud—and I had no idea how to shake it.

I imagined one way the scenario could have played out . .
.

Macy would have been riding her bike the day of the lottery drawing, perhaps doing an errand for her mother. Maybe she knew her ticket was a winner by then; maybe she didn't. People always forgot to check. She was pedaling along Old Pleasant Road, where few cars traveled, probably humming or singing, and Avis Whitaker would have cruised around the bend near the edge of the swamp, maybe coming off a long night of drinking. He got distracted by something— maybe a dragonfly thudding against his windshield—or maybe he fell asleep—who knew—but he never saw Macy.

The tip of his already-bent fender, courtesy of a drunken run-in with a fire hydrant, would have caught the edge of

Macy's pedal with just the right force and angle to send her soaring into the air, landing in the one position that, instead of causing a broken clavicle or sprained wrist, had snapped her neck and resulted in immediate death. Then Avis rammed himself into a tree and an irreversible coma. That much was certain.

What wasn't so certain was the aftermath.

The sheriff, on routine patrols, or on his way to Boyd's, would have spotted Macy's body and seen Avis's car. He'd have swerved to a stop and rushed over to feel for her pulse, knowing full well from the angle of her neck that his fingers would feel nothing but his own blood racing through his veins. He'd have rested his head in his hand, his mind disbelieving, his heart disconsolate. He'd have glared, then, at Avis Whitaker's car with a rage so extreme that Avis would have considered himself lucky to be in a coma. The Caddy's horn— probably still blaring. Smoke—still rising from under the hood. And a transmission transmitting only misery. What a scene for the sheriff to take in.

His thoughts would have drifted to Macy's mother, the lovely and sorrowful Melanie LeGrange. How would he ever tell her about this?

And then, out of the corner of his eye, he'd have noticed the Power Pot ticket, perhaps peeking out of a bag or clutched in Macy's hand. He'd have picked it up, glanced at the numbers. At first, he wouldn't believe it . . . *weren't those the numbers he'd just heard on the radio, or seen in the paper?* Even if he didn't remember all of them, Macy's ticket would have matched enough numbers to make a significant dent in Jacqueline's medical bills.

Before talking himself out of it, he'd have pocketed the ticket while visions of Jacqueline's kerchiefed head flooded his mind. *We deserve it. Why not us?* The cold thought would have arrived with guilt and mournfulness—but still, tinted with a tempting silver lining.

And then, for some reason, as events unfolded—maybe his hand was forced or he needed co-conspirators—he shared the wealth with three others. Did they also share the burden of guilt? It would seem so, given Grace Elbee's mirror writings. Yes, all the winners were part and parcel to the deception. They'd stolen and profited from the dead, and they knew it.

My hands trembled so badly that I spilled coffee on the floor. I glanced around, my eyes unfocused, my mind a mishmash of possibilities. Had Hoop been at the swamp? Had he witnessed Strike's pilfering? No, if he'd been there, at his favorite swamp spot, he'd have tried to save Macy—or his father. Hell, he'd have tried to save both.

But what if Hoop *had* run to help Macy and Avis—*before* the sheriff arrived? And what if he'd decided that their only chance depended on him getting help? He didn't own a cell phone. What would he have done?

I knew the answer. He'd have hopped on his bike and pedaled his heart out.

And where would he have gone? No houses in the vicinity. No passing cars. He'd have headed for the nearest phone . . . at Boyd's General Store.

Oh no.

If Macy had already been to Boyd's to confirm her winning ticket numbers . . . and if Boyd knew that she'd pedaled away with a winning ticket . . . and then Hoop had burst into Boyd's shouting about Macy lying on the side of the road . . .

Had Boyd tricked Hoop into entering the basement, holding him captive until he could get his own greedy hands on the ticket? Had Boyd colluded with the sheriff, who later put duct tape on Hoop's mouth to stifle his cries for help, his cries of mourning?

I spun around—literally—and grabbed my hair, ready to

pull it out as I dropped to the floor in that lonely corner of my kitchen. Inside, I screamed. I screamed for Hoop's pain. I screamed for the pain of the truth.

Five minutes later, I rose up and wiped the salty tears and misery from my face.

I could play guessing games all day. I needed facts and confirmation. I needed to go to the source.

Chapter 43

"You know what, Annika?" I said. "I don't care where the sheriff is or what he's doing. I need to speak to him now."

As I leaned over the desk of ex-Miss Beulah County, I distracted myself from wrapping my fingers around her neck by counting the layers of make-up on her skin. I gave up after four.

"For the third time," Annika whined, "it's not like I'm hiding him under my desk. That would be gross. We got like a hundred cases going on and I honest-to-God don't know where he is. Not my fault he ain't answering his radio."

"Is that really the only way to get in touch with him?"

"Like I'm supposed to take the blame because we got a dinosaur for a sheriff? You know, maybe you should work here for a week. It ain't exactly sunshine and roses. Got Chad walking around with a broken heart for like a year now, and the new guys always quit after a month because the sheriff stomps around here like he ain't a friggin' millionaire."

At the moment, I needed to compartmentalize, so I set aside her comment about Chad. "Does anyone here know where he might be?" I asked.

She shook her head.

"Hey," she said, dramatically changing her tone, "heard you're with that new guy—the cute one from New Beulah. He got any brothers?"

I saw my angle and played it. "I can ask him . . . *if* you help me out. Might be fun. We could even double date."

Bait cast. Fish hooked.

Annika cocked her head and thought hard. It looked painful. "Now that I think about it, I did hear the sheriff answer his phone this morning. He said, 'Hi, Sarah' or 'Hi, Susie.' Something like that."

"Could it have been the Sarah that works for Richie Quail?"

"Oh, yeah, probably. She's been calling Chad a lot, so maybe she was calling the sheriff to get a message to him or something. But then the sheriff said something about *a dumb-ass hick* and how he'd get right on it."

"Anything else?"

She shook her head, but then piped up with one more thought. "Oh, wait. He also mentioned how he lost his pants there and hadn't been back since. That's when he hung up and hightailed it outta here."

"*Lost his pants*? You sure that's what he said?"

"Yeah, I remember, because the last thing I wanted to imagine was Sheriff Ryker with his pants off, getting a happy ending somewhere." She threw up her hands defensively, warding off the image. "No thank you."

I smiled. I knew exactly where Strike Ryker was. "Don't worry, Annika. No happy endings in store for the sheriff today." I winked. "I'll see what I can do about that double-date."

Chapter 44

I pulled up to Quail's Victorian mansion for the second time in a week. The tire tracks from Chad's Blazer and my Subaru were still visible in the muddy trail that looped along the side of the house, but evidence of our previous adventure had begun to petrify. Now, two additional sets of tire prints zippered the terrain—one set thin and shallow, the other wide and deep, probably from a truck. And the new tracks weren't the least bit hardened.

I suspected that the sheriff was here following up a lead on Zeke Carver—the "dumb-ass hick" Annika had mentioned. And the house's library-cum-gambling-den was the only place I knew of where a cautious man like Strike Ryker might have "lost his pants"—when he'd kissed away big bucks in that poker game years ago.

As a nod to safety, I'd texted both Chad and Sherilyn to let them know where I was going. I'd said that if I didn't call back within a half-hour, to come running. I'd had more than enough of rednecks pointing lethal weapons at me lately.

I parked on the side of the house and proceeded on foot. I peeked around the corner toward the back. Yes! Strike's car was there. No sign of a pick-up truck, though. Hopefully, Zeke had already taken off. With my gun at the ready, I squished through the mud to the pee-yellow door, careful to crouch low, out of sight of anyone inside.

I strained my ears for sounds from within the house. Got nothing.

The padlock dangled open. Still crouched, I nudged the door with my shoulder, cursing every decibel of its creaking hinges, and crept in.

Silence for three seconds, followed by heavy footsteps and a door slam, possibly the front door, but I couldn't tell.

More muted footsteps followed. From someone descending the front porch steps?

I sucked in a gulp of air and waited. Nothing.

Crash! Something had fallen to the floor upstairs.

I pressed myself flush against the wall and let my heart settle. Hard to tell where upstairs the noise had come from.

A car door then slammed outside. I instinctively patted my pocket to make sure I had my car keys, but the sound hadn't come from the direction of my car—or the sheriff's. Was it possible there'd been a third vehicle out there that I'd missed? Moving quickly and quietly, I ventured toward the front door, near the bottom of the stairway. As I did, a loud engine roared to life outside. Damn, someone must have been parked on the far side of the house, behind the jutting screened porch. There was no window on that side of the house for me to peek through.

I glanced up the stairs. No motion. No sound. I made a dash for one of the small windows flanking the front door. The sound of tires grappling with mud filled my ears. Before I could move the curtain aside and wipe clean a spot to see through, the tires outside caught hold and thrust into motion. The vehicle revved and peeled away, its rumble growing faint fast. I saw only the rear of a blue pick-up blazing down the long driveway. I cursed myself; I'd just let Zeke escape, but that might be a good thing. Hadn't really wanted to get between him and the sheriff.

Smash!

This time, the noise upstairs was followed by the tinkling of broken glass. Given my position at the base of the stairs, I knew exactly where the sound had come from: the poker room. With my gun raised, I took the stairs two at a time and squatted near the door. It was open a half-inch, but I couldn't see much.

A low moan reached my ears, and the scent of the room

hit me hard. Pungent, slightly sweet, with a touch of baked-in sweat.

Another moan. "Sheriff?" I called out, without much thought to the risk.

"Chloe?" said a weak voice followed by a cough. "What in . . .?" The voice faded to nothingness.

"Are you alone?" I said.

No answer.

"Sheriff?"

Silence. My heart galloped, but in a good way. It sharpened my thoughts. The sheriff wouldn't have given up my name if someone dangerous were lurking in there. He would have told me to run, even if it wasted his last breath. I burst in.

The sheriff lay on the floor, the front of his shirt covered in fresh blood. It bubbled up like a dying fountain with each shallow breath he took. The first surreal thought that entered my head was: *Jacqueline's never going to get that stain out.* Then my subconscious took in the heavy lamp on the floor near the sheriff's foot—the source of the first crash. A shattered bottle and a puddle of whiskey surrounded his other foot—second crash. The sheriff had been kicking things over, hoping to alert someone to his situation. And from the looks of it, each effort had cost him another pint of blood.

"Sheriff, don't worry. I'll get you through this."

No response. I got down on my knees and peeled back his shirt. One bullet wound to the gut. I whipped off the scarf I'd been using as a belt and applied pressure to the wound. With my other hand, I called for help. In all, it took less than fifteen seconds from the time I entered the room to the time help was on the way. What followed was harrowing nothingness: reassuring words falling on deaf ears; me peeling off additional clothes that did nothing to staunch the sheriff's bleeding. I was about to rip off my pants—fully appreciating the irony of *losing my pants* in this room—when a spark of memory ignited.

Macy had once told me how her bounty hunter father had chased down a Lebanese bail jumper who'd accidentally shot himself in the leg. The criminal had taken refuge in a neighborhood store. When Macy's dad had burst through the door, he found the guy with a pile of fresh coffee grounds pressed into the wound to stop the bleeding.

I glanced around. On the low table next to me was another bottle of whiskey, eight chipped glasses, two ashtrays, a coffee maker, and a canister of Maxwell House Original Roast—all the makings of a late-night game, minus the cards and cash. I couldn't remember the exact outcome of Macy's story, but the sheriff's blood was begging for a dam.

Holding my shirt against the sheriff's abdomen with my foot, I stood and grabbed the coffee. As I packed it into the unnatural hole in his body, I did something I hadn't done in years: I prayed. Why not? The Big Guy had pulled off a miracle for me once before, and He'd kept me alive all these years for some reason. Maybe our connection was still intact.

After two serious prayers, recited frantically in my head, the smell of the blood started to make me punchy. "Heavenly Father," I finally said aloud, "I need you! Make these grounds good to the last drop."

The bleeding slowed so dramatically, it almost frightened me. Prayers and coffee—who knew? Not only that, but the sheriff opened his eyes—wider than I'd ever seen, even on his best days.

"Chloe," he said in a voice that wasn't much more than a muted vibration in the back of his throat. He reached up to grab my arm, but strength eluded him for perhaps the first time in his life. I lowered my ear to his mouth.

"Get out," he said. "Had to be Zeke. He's desperate. He'll—"

"It's okay," I said. "He's gone. They'll get him."

And then, with strenuous effort, he muttered, "What are you doing h—?" But he passed out, the rest of the sentence proving too much for him.

I stayed quiet, knowing the answer would really prove too much for him.

Chapter 45

Trying to explain to Chad why I'd gone to Quail's old mansion in the first place didn't prove nearly as difficult as I'd imagined. I couldn't tell him I'd gone to accuse his dad of robbery and fraud, but another answer came practically gift-wrapped. "I was returning the stuff I stole from the Whitakers' bin the other day."

"Are you serious? You went back and tampered with evidence after I told you not to?"

"At least I was returning it."

Chad killed the next couple minutes by lecturing me on the sanctity of evidence. I let him ramble; it kept his mind off his father.

Jacqueline, Annika, and Chad, along with two deputies and I, had spent the last hour and a half listening to a cheap clock ticking on the wall of a dreary hospital waiting room. It had been a dismal fifty-four-hundred ticks of feeble encouragement when there wasn't a deep well from which to draw. I was feeling particularly awkward with Strike's blood turning up in weird places on my body—under my nails, crested across my elbow, and woven into my hair. I tried to keep Jacqueline from noticing, but every so often, I caught her glancing in my direction, tears brimming near the lower lids. At least the nurses had given me a patient gown that covered the upper half of my body, plus a portion of my stained jeans.

Finally, a doctor with weary eyes and a jarringly young face entered the room and bucked up his lanky frame as best he could. Jacqueline disengaged herself from Annika whose nonstop whimpering had shown that she cared more about *the old dinosaur* than she'd let on.

Jacqueline, Chad, and I huddled around the doctor. He asked if I was family, and Chad blurted, "It's fine. She can stay."

The doctor provided a highly technical update, as if by doing so, he could spare himself from delivering the simple message lurking behind the Latin: *It doesn't look good.*

Apparently, the bullet, due to its angle of entry and Strike's muscular frame, hadn't gone as deep as expected, but it had struck his liver and nicked his small intestine. He had a chance, just not a big one.

Jacqueline grabbed Chad's arm, while Annika, who'd heard every word, latched onto a chair and looked close to collapsing. Chad remained stoic, his eyes locked onto mine, seeking my strength. I gave it to him.

"Applying the coffee may have turned out to be a life-saver," the doctor said to Chad.

Chad jerked a thumb in my direction. "Thank the reporter here."

The doctor turned to me. "Did you do an article on survivalist first aid or something?"

"No," I said, realizing the irony of Macy's words having been the ones to save the sheriff. "A friend of mine told me a story once."

We sat again, but Chad implored me to go home; I sensed it might be better for everyone if I disappeared and took Strike's blood with me. I hugged them, went to my car, and cried. Not only for the Ryker family but for my secret. What was I supposed to do with it now? Would Strike take it to his grave? Would I let him?

I released a sigh as I punched the steering wheel. Then I went home and showered. By the time I wrapped my hair in a towel, Chad had left me a voice mail with some good news. Strike had turned a vital corner and was doing better than expected. The hospital would be providing an overnight room for Jacqueline. Chad, meanwhile, would be spearheading the effort to track down Zeke Carver, who, by the look of things, should have stuck to *doing foundations*; his own was looking pretty shaky at the moment.

As soon as I tossed my phone down on the bed, it rang again. The Caller ID read: *R. O. Borose.* It took my overloaded mind a few seconds to realize it was Rafe. He must have typed his name into my phone that way, using his initials.

I reached down to answer, but my brain suddenly jolted me to paralysis. Horrid chills rippled across my skin, one by one, each sending a new wave of disbelief through my beleaguered body and mind.

I read the name on the Caller ID again. I juggled it in my head, trying to convince myself it wasn't possible, yet hoping it was.

My heart pittered.

I spoke the name aloud.

My breathing slowed and my heart pattered.

I repeated the name, this time with a shaky voice: "R.O. Borose."

No. Not possible. No!

The phone kept ringing. The Caller ID kept flashing.

So much for giving up hope and moving on. I freaked the hell out.

Chapter 46

A Month Before the Thump

Chloe rowed Mr. Swanson's canoe through the swamp as Hoop's head lolled back and forth against his balled-up shirt. Twenty minutes earlier, she had lost at Spot-It-First, thus making her the designated rower. She and Hoop had made up the game on their way back to the canoe. In the final round, Hoop had been the first to spot a squirrel with a chunk missing from its tail, putting him way ahead of Chloe, who'd scored only one point with her discovery of tree sap sticky enough to hold an acorn.

The sun's rays were long upon the water, and a cool breeze came up unexpectedly, blowing Chloe's long hair and dropping the temperature a couple more degrees. She rowed hard enough to keep herself warm and to get home in time for dinner. She and Hoop had spent a full hour in Boyd's tree fort, during which she'd learned more than she wanted to from those risqué magazines. *Why would a man buy a vibrator for a woman? Didn't it kind of defeat his purpose?* She considered asking Hoop, but her ignorance in such areas was too mortifying to reveal.

"Now that there, Clover," Hoop said as he lazily lifted his head and pointed to the edge of the swamp. "That there is pluff mud."

"Yeah, Hoop, I live here, remember? I've seen the airboat patrol pull more than a few fishermen from the pluff over the years."

"You like the smell or not?"

"Love it. Whenever we go on vacation, or even into Charleston, I always know I'm home when that rotten-egg smell hits me. Stings my nostrils but tickles my heart."

"That's real poetic, Clover. Me? I always think the pluff makes Beulah kind of exotic. Like our own brand of quicksand. Puts us on the same footing as places like Egypt."

"Except *footing* is the last thing anybody gets once they're in the pluff," I said.

He grinned. "My pa taught me only to wade where the grass is short."

"Because you can't see too well if grass is in your eyes?"

"No, because the shorter the grass, the harder the bottom; the taller the grass, the deeper the mud. Head-tall grass means head-deep pluff. More like thick water than soft dirt; it'll swallow you whole."

"Guess I never thought of it that way. You ever heard the legend of The Cane Man?"

"Sure," Hoop said. "He spent decades tapping that cane ahead of his steps to make sure the swamp bottom was solid enough to hold him."

"Till one day, he happened upon a familiar gator—a gator whose mate he'd killed with his bare hands twenty years earlier."

"Old Cane Man," Hoop said, "he mistreated a lot of gators over the years."

"That's right. So this particular gator rose up and knocked Cane Man's cane right out of his hands. And Cane Man, well, he'd been mighty attached to that cane, hand-carved and aged as it was. And didn't he get down on his hands and knees and search for that cane with all he had."

"And down on his hands and knees like that," Hoop said, "he never realized how tall the grasses were getting, towering over him five, six feet at least."

"And didn't he happen upon a big patch of pluff mud while doing so."

"Sure did, Clover. Which is when he made the awful, terrible, rookie mistake of standing straight up. Full-on panicked, he did. Heard he sank faster than—"

"Than a fool in the pluff?"

"That'll do, Clover. Works for me."

"That was the last anyone ever saw or heard of Cane Man. But his cane, they found it years later, chomped in two, next to a big ol' gator."

"Gator with a smile on his face, I heard."

"Ashes to ashes," Chloe said. "Or in Cane Man's case, ashes to pluff." They both laughed. "Isn't that all pluff mud is, anyway? Decay and the bacteria that feeds off decay?"

"Yep," Hoop said, "along with the bacteria's waste products. But it supports all the life in the swamp. One big cycle. *Ouroboros*, I call it."

Chloe frowned. "A row of what?"

"Not *a row* of anything, Clover. Ouroboros."

"Still don't know what you're trying to say."

"I ain't *trying* to say it. I *am* saying it."

"Spell it out then. I can't know a word till I see it in my head."

"Really? Okay, then." He spelled it out as Chloe nodded along, engraving it in her mind.

"Pronounce it one more time," she said when he finished.

"It's easy," Hoop said. "*Errrrr*, like a dog growling. *Row*, like a boat. *Brrrrr*, like you're cold. Then *ros* rhymes with dose. Er-ROW-brrrrr-ROS." He fake-shivered during the third syllable.

"Got it. Ouroboros. It's mine forever now."

"Guess that's how you win the spelling bees, huh? 'Cause you spell things in your head?"

"That, plus I read like a book a week."

Hoop lay back in the canoe, his head resting against his shirt, a wisp of a twig clamped between his teeth. "I like reading true stuff, like about gators and ouroboros." He stuck a finger in the air like an enthusiastic professor. "Did you know that the symbol for ouroboros is a snake eating its own tail, representing the eternal cycle of life?"

Chloe smirked. "Thought you said you read *true* stuff."

"I do."

"Not sure most people consider a snake eating its own tail to be true, seeing as how no one's ever seen one. But far be it from me to mess with your obsession."

"At least give me this: it's true that there's a *legend* about hoop snakes. And the ouroboros legend goes back to Egyptian times, maybe even earlier."

"Okay, I'll give you that." She rowed harder on the right to make the vessel turn. "Can't say I don't learn something every time I'm out with you, Hoop."

"I probably oughta be a teacher, but I gotta make more money than that."

"Your dad did okay with teaching."

"Sure, but what did he have left when the hard times came?"

Chloe hesitated. "That what you consider your life now, Hoop? Hard times?"

"It ain't easy. I mean, we get by, but it's like the difference between climbing onto a cushiony mattress at night and pulling a rucksack over your body in a dirt hole. Either way, you sleep, but one sure is easier than the other."

"We got an extra mattress in the attic . . . if you or your dad wants to use it."

Hoop lifted his head and grinned. "You sure are a softie, Clover. I wasn't hinting around for no mattress."

"Well, it's there if you need it."

He tossed the twig at her and sat up, all smiles. "You're sweet. It's a wonder Rory McShane hasn't scooped you up. But I was just making an analogy, or a metaphor, or one of them things Miss Farlow's always going on about."

Chloe felt herself turn red, but with the sun casting

everything in a crimson light, she knew Hoop wouldn't notice.

"You figure we'll be friends when we're grown up?" Hoop asked. "'Cause I sure don't."

Chloe's heart shattered, but she held out hope that Hoop would declare they couldn't be friends because they'd be husband and wife.

"And here's why," Hoop continued. "'Cause I'll be so rich, I'm gonna have to refuse your calls on principle."

Chloe laughed, relieved. "That ain't gonna work, because I'll be your boss and you'll *have to* take my calls." She splashed him with a flick of her oar.

Hoop cackled. "Ain't gonna have no boss. Heck, I'm gonna own the likes of Richie Quail. You'll be talking to my secretary like, 'Tell him it's that girl he used to call *Clover*,' and my secretary will be all like, 'Mr. Hoop says if you keep calling here, he's gonna renew that restraining order against you.'"

Chloe splashed him again. "I'll still barge into your office and fire you. Somehow."

"Won't matter. I'll still be rich—'cause I'll be ready for the hard times." He flicked the water with his fingers. "See what I did there?"

Chloe rowed them up to Mr. Swanson's dock. "What?"

"I brought the conversation full circle, just like ouroboros."

He splashed her one final time, and they laughed.

Chapter 47

Despite the short distance of the trip, I gunned my boat, skipping it through the water. I looked like all-around hell, but I didn't care. Let the wind whip my wet hair into a frenzy. Let the water splatter my face. Didn't matter what a girl looked like to face the living dead.

I cut the motor, lashed my boat to the dock, and sprinted up the walkway to the front door. The doorbell light glowed, but a visit of this magnitude required serious pounding. I raised both hands and pulverized the thick slab of wood like a madwoman. When an answer didn't come immediately, I kicked the metal plate at the base of the door. "Answer this door, dammit! Let me in!"

And then, slowly, evenly, as if he'd been standing on the other side the whole time, Hoop Whitaker pulled the door open. He wore a body-hugging workout top and loose black pants. He held the same mug he'd drunk from the afternoon before, when he'd programmed his name into my phone as *R.O. Borose.* His face, flushed, held a concerned expression, shaded with devilish delight.

I analyzed that face now, from follicles to earlobes to Adam's Apple, and then I did it again, from forehead to nostrils to lips. The nose, the eyebrows, the cheekbones, the jawline, the clavicle, the hair. None of it fit, or rather, none of it fit perfectly.

He gazed back the whole time, pinning me with his hypnotic eyes, and then he broke into a smile, broader and more sincere than I'd seen from him so far—and I knew it was true.

"Color contacts?" I said.

He winced guiltily. "They're prescription. I'd take them out, but I really do want to see all of your reactions while we talk."

My nostrils flared. "Hair dye?"

He tousled the brunette waves on his head. "It darkened naturally over the years, but I did take some Nice 'n Easy liberties with it."

I gawked for another fifteen seconds before swallowing a huge lump in my throat. I wanted to speak but ended up simply breathing, long and deep, before finally expressing my deepest, most heartfelt sentiment.

"You bastard."

"Clover," he said, setting down his mug and pinching his lips together as if to keep emotions at bay. He stepped onto the porch and pulled me in tight, catching my bent arms between us. I longed to become lost in his embrace, to feel the joy that should accompany this moment, but I beat him away with both fists, until finally, under the strength of his grasp, I gave in, releasing years of heavy, salty tears, and saturating my old friend's shirt. The tears reeked of joy, rage, elation, relief, and far too much misplaced grief. I made sure he felt every drop, and a good part of me hoped they stung.

Finally, I pulled back and touched his face. He let me. How had I not seen it? The man in front of me may not have looked much like the thin, boy-faced teen I'd known, but his core had stayed true—same person, same soul, same energy. I shook my head in confusion. "You must have known when you programmed your name as *R.O. Borose* that I'd figure out who you were."

"Of course. I mean, who programs their name with first and middle initials?"

"Those who want their names to sound like ouroboros."

"One thing I knew for certain," he said. "You'd never forget a good word."

I sniffed away fresh tears and, like the gentleman he'd become, he produced a tissue from his pocket. "That word won me a jeopardy tournament in college," I blubbered. "Daily Double and everything."

His thick brows shot up, impressed, and I noticed that one eyebrow wasn't sitting right on his face. I fixed him with a look of exasperation and ripped off the caterpillar-like creature. "Really?"

He cringed in pain and peeled the other one off himself, dangling it like a worm. "Everything else is real, so please, no more yanking." He tapped his nose. "Got the new nose after a kick in the face from Petunia, a spunky baby elephant." Then he circled his face with his finger. "The rest was very late puberty, and either good or bad genes, depending on what you think."

I touched his face, still unable to fathom that he was alive. "All good," I said.

At some point, he led me inside and we sat on the couch, our hands entwined. My mind flooded with twelve years of questions.

"Why didn't you just tell me from the get-go?"

"I had to be sure I could trust you, and that I could keep you safe. Sometimes, ignorance is a strong shield."

I wanted to cry again. How could Hoop Whitaker not have trusted me?

"You made it to the circus, then? Because the average person doesn't encounter baby elephants."

"I told you I'd join."

"You told me a lot of things."

"And many have come true."

I sighed, still struggling. "Why? Why all this?" I gestured to the grand room in which we were sitting. "Why the deception?"

"Now that, I can't tell you. But I will. Soon."

"No." I pulled my hand free from his grasp and pounded it on my leg. "No more secrets."

"But they're for your own good. Your own safety."

"My *safety*? Why? What have you gotten yourself into?"

"Absolutely nothing. But others, they've gotten themselves into quite a pickle."

"Others? Who?"

"Come on now. You're the reporter. It's all in front of you, ripe for the picking." He leaned back and gazed at his ceiling fresco. "You just have to know where to look, and how to see through the façades others have erected."

I gazed up, remembering my fixation on the fresco from my first night here. "Binoculars," I said. "You never gave me the binoculars."

He rose, retrieved a sleek pair, and pressed them into my hands. "Shall I get you a pillow?"

I shook my head, put the viewfinders to my eyes and gazed up. I could barely remember what it was that had struck me the other night, but as I searched from tableau to tableau, face to face, I saw it: Macy LeGrange's face on the tiny, near-translucent angel hovering above all the scenes.

"This whole elaborate guise," I said, "whatever it is you have going on here, it has to do with Macy?"

He looked at me as if I'd gone daft. "Of course."

"And her stolen lottery ticket."

He smiled, pleasantly surprised. "Clever Clover."

The glint in his eyes held a trace of the demonic, and suddenly, I worried about his grasp on reality. Maybe Rafe wasn't so far removed from the likes of the mirror-writing, candle-talking Mrs. Elbee. Maybe his interest in phantom-repellent amulets wasn't simply of the collector variety.

"You can't change the past," I said. "You know that, right?"

He assessed me in a clinical manner. "I have no intention of changing it. I don't need to. Because in a circle, past is future's future and future is already past."

I stared at him, wobbling between staying put and running for my life. Who knew what had happened to him in the years since the accident? Or what toll his obsession—and losses—had taken on him.

"What's going on?" I said. "I feel like the answer's hovering in front of me like a hologram, but I can't see it."

"That's because you, like everyone, accept things at face value. You fill in what you expect to be there."

"The blue circle," I said cautiously.

"Precisely." He smiled in a somewhat sinister way. "I intend to destroy the illusion that the blue circle exists at all. To peel away, at any cost, what the collective mind has filled in."

"The collective mind? Whose?"

He sat down again, leaned back, and filled his body with a full and potent breath. "The audience's." His voice and manner were nothing like the innocent, hopeful Hoop I'd known—the Hoop who would gaze at a gray day as easily as a sunny one and declare it spectacular.

"I need a clue here," I said.

"And a clue you shall have, Clover. But not yet." The corners of his lips curled up and the edges of his eyes lowered to meet them.

"Boyd's basement," I uttered with caution, lest it raise painful memories for him. "Obviously, you're alive, but . . . were you . . . ? Did Boyd . . . ?"

He put a reassuring hand on my shoulder. "Yes, I was in Boyd's basement. I'd ridden my bike there to get help. The details are foggy now, but he must have knocked me out and dragged me to that room, or told me that's where the phone was. I don't remember. Either way, he cuffed me until he could figure things out. But sometimes, Clover, when you're fishing, a reel refuses to do what its very name suggests, in which case you check for line that might be caught in the bushing."

"What does that have to do with—"

"As any good fisherman will tell you, it's best to use a tiny, flat screwdriver to get under the line and pry it out."

"You picked the cuffs?"

"Child's play, really. They were like something a dominatrix would pick up at a novelty shop."

"And you picked the lock to the door to get out?"

"No, I tore off half my sleeve, and when Boyd came back in to do whatever he planned to do, I jumped him from behind, wrapped the cloth around his neck and pulled for all I was worth. When he fell unconscious, I took my leave."

"What about the duct tape?"

"Believe it or not, that duct tape must have fallen out of my pocket when I jumped him."

Like a circus clown, Hoop used to store one of everything in his pockets. He could have produced a rabbit from them if he'd wanted to.

"Remember that demo Sheriff Ryker used to do at school?" he said.

"He just did one." And suddenly, I knew what had happened. In the old days, before the sheriff had to cover topics like bath salts and huffing, he spent more time on bullying. For one demo, he'd called Hoop forward, and Hoop had made the entire class laugh by putting duct tape over his mouth. The sheriff ripped it off—thus leaving his DNA on there—and sent Hoop to the principal. Hoop no doubt pocketed the tape and forgot about it. It had been the final day of school before spring break—and *The Week*—had begun.

"But the blood," I said.

"Planted that a few weeks ago, along with the skull pocket watch. Needed to kickstart this thing."

"What *thing*?"

He smiled and it scared me. "Answers are imminent."

"Who else knows who you really are?"

"In Beulah? Only you."

"I don't get it. Why allow us to believe you were murdered?" My emotions surfaced again as I discussed the murder of the man sitting next to me. "Why let us dig for your bones and test for DNA? I don't—"

"An old circus principle, Clover. Make the audience believe so ferociously in the illusion that it will curl their brains and shrivel their last doubt. They must believe that the tightrope walker can fall, that the lion can maul the trainer's neck on a whim." He let out a snort of amusement. "The audience thinks the clown on the unicycle is the one struggling for balance, but an audience—*an audience on edge*—they are the ones fighting to stay balanced. In the end, you must make them question every rational thought they ever accepted as truth. And . . . if you succeed . . . things happen."

"Such as?"

"The bored become anxious. The calm grow agitated. The agitated grow irate. Doubters believe. Dismissers embrace. And betrayers betray in new and fascinating ways."

A realization washed over me like a slow, thick liquid poured from above. The fresco. "Betrayers," I said, glancing up. "The ones who destroyed your faith in decency and humanity."

"Precisely."

"But have they destroyed *your* humanity, Rafe? Your decency?"

A placid smile grazed his face. "I wish I knew, Clover. I barely remember the feeling of the old days anymore. I've dwelled so long on the other side."

"Why come back now? Should I be worried?"

He touched my hand. "You? Never. I've merely tweaked the balance. But once a wheel is rolling, you can't anticipate every hurdle it will encounter, or how people will react. I did get things rolling, didn't I?"

"Oh my God. You placed those calls to Mrs. Elbee—from M. LeGrange."

"I had hoped to inspire her to behave nobly. It almost worked, too."

"And the fire. Did you set fire to Boyd's?"

"In my defense, I called the fire department in advance, and I didn't intend for it to grow quite so large. My only error." He must have seen the horror on my face. "Come now, Clover. You're in the inner circle—best seat in the house. The fun is just beginning."

"Fun? This has been fun for you? Watching me squirm while I believed that my friend was tortured and murdered in some underground cell?"

His eyes warmed, despite the false layer of color between us. "Make it two errors, because I never, ever meant to hurt you. For that, I am truly sorry." He glanced at the floor in either shame or embarrassment. "I guess I never fully understood how you felt about me." He reached up and stroked my face. "I did try to reach out once, knowing you were the only person I could trust." His face tightened and his lips twitched. "But that . . . didn't go as planned. I'm sorry. My uncles forbade further attempts to contact you. Too dangerous."

"You never got to say good-bye to your father."

"Oh, I didn't leave town right away. My father's room, on the second floor of the hospital—I must've been in and out of that window a dozen times."

"So while the whole town was searching for you, you were hanging out at the hospital?"

"Whenever I wasn't hiding."

I frowned, letting empathy and selfishness fight it out inside of me. The selfishness won out. "Do you have any idea what your disappearance did to all of us? To all of us who adored you? I know that what happened to you was infinitely worse, but every kid in this town was devastated. Bad enough we lost Macy, but at least her death was . . . manageable. We had a service, we buried her, and it was horribly tragic, but kids get hit on bikes, you know? To compound it with the loss of *you*, and how much you must have been suffering, not knowing if you were alive or dead. It was like we couldn't mourn her properly without you to lead us. And we wanted to be there for you. You were our energy—the class clown *and* the class genius, the one we all wanted to be. You and Macy were even voted Prom King and Queen—*four years later*. Do you have any idea how depressing it is to watch an empty dance floor with an honorary black spotlight floating around while they played—I don't even remember what they played. You know why? I was too busy staring at a speck of dust on the floor, figuring out the best time to kill myself."

"Don't say that, Clover. Don't—"

"Don't what? Tell you that I tried to kill myself six weeks after you disappeared? That I have this tattoo on my arm because it looks good? No, Rafe! It covers my scar." I thrust my arm out in front of him. "I did it the right way. No horizontal, cry-for-help slice for me. I went the full enchilada." I shook my head then, confused to this day. "But I wasn't as alone as I thought. When I came to, I was being wheeled into the hospital, my arm bandaged, my head pounding—and my heart still beating."

"I know."

I jerked my head toward him. "What do you mean—*you know*?"

"They must have torn off the bandage I put on, before you got a chance to see it."

"See what?"

"The clover. I drew a clover on your bandage while my

uncle drove you to the hospital. I was trying to let you know I was still alive."

"*You* saved me?"

He smiled sadly and nodded. "You were so pale. Even in the dark, under that weird, sputtering light above the train platform, I could see how much blood you'd lost."

"But the nurse said a small man who spoke broken English brought me in, and that he'd disappeared without a trace."

Rafe grinned. "The Galassos are masters at disappearing. And he was small because his wife used to shoot him out of a cannon. He told them that he saw you fall from the platform, and that your arm was sliced open by a rusty nail on the way down when you tried to catch yourself."

I harrumphed. "My dad convinced himself to believe that; not sure my mom ever did." I gazed at Rafe. "But why were you at the train platform that night?"

"It was the night the circus was supposed to come to town. I knew you'd go. Just didn't know you'd be bringing whiskey—and a knife."

"I still don't see how you—"

"I just knew. That you'd want something positive, like the circus train, to be a connection between *life before* and *life after*. You used to be such a hopeful girl, Chloe. I pestered my uncle to take me, and when we got there, we found you bleeding. I was so upset; I couldn't lose another person I cared about." He swallowed the lump in his throat. "After we dropped you off, my uncle and I returned to the platform. He kept screaming at me, but I wouldn't leave until I scrubbed away all your blood. To make it like it hadn't happened. Never could find the knife, though."

"It was in my shoe. Can't believe the nurses didn't find it." I glanced at him shyly for a fleeting moment, feeling like an awkward 15-year-old again. "I still keep it in a lockbox."

"Why? As a reminder?"

"No. To finish the job it was supposed to do."

He grabbed me by both arms. "Chloe, why? You have so much to live for."

"They say time heals all wounds. I say bullshit. I've lived life, but from very far away as it passes me by, like I'm watching from a distance. Words can't explain what I felt when you and Macy were both just . . . gone."

"Let me try. Rotted and dark. Ripped apart in places you can't reach or pinpoint."

"A pit so deep, you forget to remember the way out," I added. "I couldn't get a full breath most days, not without it crashing up against my insides. Figured it had to be better wherever you and Macy were." I forced a lame smile and made jazz hands. "But I'm still here. In this dirty snow globe of a town, still searching for a reason to go on."

Rafe failed to sniff back his tears this time, letting them fall. I'd never seen Hoop Whitaker cry. Was I seeing it now?

"Your tattoo," he said, tracing the pattern along my arm. "I know what it is."

"It's just a random design I sketched to cover the scar."

He shook his head. "Look at it, Chloe." He forced my arm up. For once, it didn't burn. "It's a bike chain. Anyone can see that. It's a bike chain."

My face went slack. He was right. "Sometimes, it moves," I whispered. I'd never admitted that to anyone but myself.

"Of course it does. Your mind is fulfilling your fondest wish. For Macy's bike to still be pedaling. For the pedaler to still be alive. For my bike to still be whooshing down Old Pleasant Road." He stroked my arm, a single finger traversing the length of the pattern. "I saw your tattoo through my telescope the day I moved in. Reminded me what a rough go you'd had of it. It's why I suggested the twelve-year anniversary story to your editor."

"*You* are making the anonymous donation to the paper?"

"Thought you might finally write yourself an ending. And I do intend to give you an ending. One in which you can spell out every single word in that crazy brain of yours."

"Tell me now."

He gestured to his ceiling. "The final scene is being written. The stage is being set."

I glanced up at King Lear. "Is a god going to fall from the ceiling?"

An eerie ring tone sounded on his phone, accompanied by a picture of the caller: a narrow-faced woman with a ghastly pallor, jet-black hair, shadowed eyes, and a nose that ended in a severe point. The wicked witch?

He glanced at the phone. "I have to take this. It's my aunt."

"Shocking," I said with a healthy dose of sarcasm.

"I must bid you adieu now, Chloe. Until tonight. My car will be in front of your house at eight-thirty."

"I really don't think—"

The phone, which had ceased its ringing, started up again. The picture of the same woman appeared, but somehow, she looked angrier.

Rafe ushered me to the door and blew me a kiss. "Until tonight."

As I descended the stairs, I heard him mumble something into his phone before calling out to me.

"Clover?" he said.

I turned back. "Yes?"

"I know you can keep a secret. Keep ours. For just a little while longer."

Reality roiled with confusion in my head; my old friend had left me hanging, a fool twisting in the wind, battered like a piñata, for almost half my life.

He noticed my moment of hesitancy. "I know. You think I

betrayed you on some level. But I promise to regain your trust." He stared at me, the honest and open face of boyhood peeking out from behind the man.

"I'll keep your secret," I said.

He stepped back into the house and closed the door.

I shivered as I ran to the dock. What had happened to the boy? I thought of the lonely nights lying in my bed thinking how he couldn't possibly have dealt sanely with the dual loss of father and girlfriend, how such a tragedy would permanently alter a person.

I feared I was right.

Chapter 48

When I reached home, still reeling from Rafe's revelations, I remembered that the dress I wanted to wear tonight had been sitting at the dry cleaners for a month, unretrieved. It would require a quick trip across the bridge, but the distraction would be a welcome one. I combed out my hair, made myself somewhat presentable, and picked up my dress. The man behind the counter gave me only a couple nasty side-eyes while mentioning that he was running a cleaning business, not a storage facility.

While crossing the bridge to return home, I caught a glimpse of the graffiti on which the Carver boy had used nail polish for certain anatomical details. Did the kid really think the more sensitive parts of the female body would cast a neon glow in order to show him the way? *Sorry, kid, gonna have to hunt and peck like the rest of the male population.*

From the apex of the bridge, I spotted a flurry of activity on Dirt Hill, with three shiny trucks climbing to the peak. Out of curiosity, I drove over and encountered several dozen men, women, and children, all of whom resembled one another like a tight-knit camp of gypsies. They looked eerily familiar—a childhood memory streaked with a dose of nightmare—and when I spotted a jagged scar on one man's neck, I realized I was looking at the remnants of the Forenza and Galasso families sans make-up and costumes. Carnies in their natural element. What a sight to behold.

About a month ago, a tent the size of a football field had been erected next to the main pavilion on Dirt Hill. From street level, it hadn't looked quite so enormous, but up close, it resembled a stadium. It consisted of heavy white material with multiple tips trying to poke the sky, but without colorful balloons or flags adorning those tips. The whole structure looked like a flavorless lemon meringue pie—with the peaks of meringue not nearly browned enough.

"Excuse me," I said to a wisp of a man who repeatedly dashed in and out of the tent. "Can you tell me about tonight's show?"

He smiled and pantomimed something that looked like an explosion, then returned to his task. The responses I got from others were equally as perplexing. In absolute silence, they functioned like a colony of ants, transporting myriad equipment into the tent: mirrors, lights, chairs, projectors, screens, and all manner of paraphernalia. None of it hidden. None of it under wraps. I felt like I was watching the deconstruction of a jigsaw puzzle, and from it, I was meant to decipher what it had once been and what it might be again.

I feared I might know.

An hour later, I understood that I, Beulah's humble crime and features reporter, needed only to do my job for the rest of the evening. News was about to unfold in a way this town had never seen.

Back at home, I called the hospital to check on the sheriff—awake and doing well. I gave silent thanks that he and Jacqueline and Chad would be absent from tonight's show. Then I charged my camera and phone batteries, stocked my briefcase, and called every reporter and photographer on The Herald staff to make sure they'd be on the scene. I donned my lavender dress, dug up some rarely-worn three-inch heels, and applied enough make-up to make Adeline DeVore proud. Then I waited with a nervous energy I hadn't felt in years.

At precisely 8:30 p.m., on what had turned into a beautiful, clear night, a stretch limo pulled into my driveway. No Rafe in sight, but a professional and courteous driver emerged from the front seat to open the rear door for me.

"At your service, m'lady," he said with a knowing smile and a gallant wave of his arm. I sensed he was more than a chauffeur, and as he pulled out of the driveway, I heard the squeal of a small monkey from the front seat.

The driver took a right, and we were off to the show.

Chapter 49

Short, raven-haired men and woman stood at each entrance of the tent's perimeter. As they ushered in the many hundreds of guests, they displayed the grace and confidence of seasoned performers. My driver pulled up to a dark entrance that no one else was using. No sooner had he opened my door than a waif of a woman with a penetrating stare appeared. I felt sure I had seen her face earlier today—on Rafe's phone screen perhaps? She indicated with the subtlest of motions that I should exit the car and follow her into the tent. Somehow, it became clear that I, and only I, would be permitted access via her entryway. She emitted a matronly air, and despite no words passing between us, I got a strong sense that she was Rafe's circus mother—a woman who had loved him as her own.

The moment I entered the huge structure, a young man who could have passed for my driver's twin extended his arm and escorted me toward the stage. From the bland, nondescript exterior of the tent, one would never anticipate its interior. It resembled a beautiful, stately theater, with professional lighting, an elaborate wooden stage, a thick velvet curtain, and loads of high-tech equipment, most of it suspended from above.

The young man showed me to the second row and flitted away before I could thank him. I took my seat in the center, noting the sign: "Reserved for R. O. Borose and Guest." Inside, I felt a rush of pride; of all the people here, I alone understood the meaning of my host's name.

The chair next to me, I knew, was destined to remain empty.

I was seated for less than the duration of two short breaths when I was pulled back in time to the Forenza-

Galasso Circus—to the parade of elephants making an entrance in showy fashion, displaying the promise of their performance in bejeweled capes. Groomed and shimmering, they'd always been magnanimous in their power and size. Tonight, however, the crowd was treated to only one elephant—one that might require the dreaded hook—for our sole elephant was none other than Richie Quail.

Melanie LeGrange clung shyly to his arm. She looked even more beautiful than she had the night before, in a form-fitting red dress with small pleats on the skirt portion. She wore a gold shawl, elegant diamond earrings, and a delicate pendant necklace. Quail wore a rancher's hat with a silver buckle, a pair of snazzy, alligator-skin shoes, and a bespoke suit that actually slimmed his frame. The two of them were escorted down the center aisle by a short man in a classic tuxedo. Beneath the man's penguin suit, however, I detected layers of muscle, strength, and self-reliance, and I wondered if he doubled as a bodyguard. He showed his charges to the front row, two seats over from me. With all the hubbub, they didn't notice my presence, and I chose not to alert them to it.

The prime location of the seats seemed to both surprise and please Mrs. LeGrange, though she appeared somewhat uncomfortable with the attention—or perhaps envy—from those in the audience who weren't quite so lucky.

I felt a sympathetic ache for her. As she glanced at the stage, she seemed both awed and perplexed. After all, as far as she knew, no other attendees had been flown in first class to bear witness to the events about to unfold. And on her birthday, no less. But unfortunately, what was about to unfold would most likely devastate her.

Quail slung his arm across the back of the empty chair next to him, creating a gust of fruity cologne that he'd no doubt broken out specially for his old high school crush. He took note of the sign on the empty seat next to him. I'd already caught a glimpse of it. It read: *Reserved for Strike Ryker.* Quail turned to his date and spoke in his usual booming voice. "Poor Strike, it ain't looking too good, and he sure ain't gonna make it tonight. Might as well get comfortable." He proceeded to spread his legs wider and stretch out his arm more fully.

Mrs. LeGrange at least had the wherewithal to look horrified by Quail's nonchalance in regard to the sheriff's condition.

The crowd was soon seated, but we were all treated to one final pièce de résistance: the arrival of Adeline DeVore—cuffed and coiffed. And dang if she didn't look pulled-together despite metal rings around her wrists and a female court appointee leading her down the aisle. Still, the dismay on her face gave the impression of a caged alien being brought forth for public examination. She looked so out of sorts that I surmised she hadn't been told of her destination or why she'd been granted temporary reprieve from federal interrogation.

The court employee shoved Adeline rather unceremoniously into a seat beside Mrs. LeGrange, who looked more than affronted by the intrusion. Upon noticing the new arrival, Quail quickly glanced at the *Reserved for Strike Ryker* sign on his other side, and then took a renewed and horrified interest in Adeline's presence. If my profile view of him didn't deceive, I saw something in his expression I'd never seen before: fear.

Adeline returned the look, but they seemed to make a silent pact to face whatever was coming together, in stalwart fashion, full denials at the ready.

Quail faced forward again, inhaled deeply, and gazed forward. His frightened yet stoic expression was the last thing I saw—for the tent suddenly rocketed us all into alarming darkness. The crowd hushed, and the stage was set for revelation, drama, and most of all, for truth.

A single, narrow spotlight hit center stage like a bolt of lightning. A moment later, from the invisible slit separating the two halves of the curtain, Rafe Borose appeared in full tuxedo and tails, stunningly handsome as he emanated elegance and grandeur. Like the born master of ceremonies he was, he commanded every iota of attention in the room—the ultimate feat of the skilled ringmaster.

My heart leapt onto stage with him.

Chapter 50

"Ladies and gentlemen, boys and girls, thank you for taking a chance tonight." Rafe's voice reverberated through the tent, from the meringue peaks of the tent to the sleek wood flooring below. "A wild chance! A questionable chance, and yet, you already know you have made the right decision. This night, I promise, will fill you with heart-palpitating disbelief, stun you with the unthinkable, and force you to imagine the unimaginable. Not your typical magic show because, gentle people of Beulah, it is not magic at all, while at the same time, it is the best magic there is. I call it . . . disillusionment."

The crowd rumbled with murmurs of intrigue mixed with disappointment. They'd hardly gathered their little ones and trudged up Dirt Hill to be *disillusioned*; they wanted clever deception to carry them away from dull reality.

"You will be transported," Rafe continued. "That I can assure you. You will see things in a way you've never seen them before, and you will be startled beyond belief, because sometimes, truth proves the mightiest trick of all."

Rafe extended the fingers of his right hand. Sparkling shards of light seemed to burst forth from them in every color of the rainbow, ending with a burst of illumination so bright that it blinded and became almost painful to the retina.

"But first," he continued as our eyes adjusted, "some tradition and a little fun."

At that, the curtains parted and the spotlight zeroed in on an eight-inch-wide round table, supported by nothing but a rail-thin pedestal. On it sat a black top hat from which Rafe pulled a huge white rabbit with glistening fur that looked softer than any cloud God had ever created.

When the applause and amused laughter died down, a

hand other than Rafe's reached into the spotlight and whisked the rabbit into the blackness. Rafe reached into the hat again and pulled out three more rabbits to the delight and multi-toned shrieks of children, accompanied by subdued oohs and ahhs of their parents.

As music from an accordion blossomed, additional lights came on and Rafe cued four monkeys who appeared out of nowhere and performed a gymnastics routine. Then he produced multiple flowers and ribbons from the palm of a single hand before gesturing above, where a male acrobat of inhuman flexibility proceeded to perform a high-wire act that not only defied expectation, but also gravity.

Forty-five minutes of intense, frenzied activity followed, complete with: a black light show; three women performing insane feats on a trapeze; a man who appeared to be eaten whole by a lion before emerging intact from a cannon; toned athletes executing death-defying moves while dangling from translucent ribbons that seemed incapable of supporting even a butterfly; wire-bound women contorting themselves in midair before launching into airborne dances that stretched the limits of the imagination. Between acts, we were entertained by the requisite clowns on unicycles, the sight of which sent shivers down my spine, but their wild antics spurred others to laughter. The spectacles went on and on, and the crowd exhaled a collective sigh of delighted relief when Rafe once again took center stage, bringing the madness to a needed lull. As he spoke, the beautiful music that had become part of the fabric of the atmosphere began to soften, allowing us to be drawn deeply into his hypnotic voice. I felt as if I were alone with him in a softly lit room, and yet I knew he was conveying that sensation of intimacy to every person in the tent.

"As most of you may know, you've just witnessed the return of the world-renowned Forenza and Galasso families, the cherished circus performers who once upon a time visited Beulah with regularity . . . until twelve years ago, of course."

He waited for the sad sighs of the audience to die down.

"Twelve years ago, the Forenza and Galasso families came into receipt of a little boy. Not so little, actually. He was fifteen, but slight, not yet endowed with muscles or a single hair on his fair face. His hands were atremble, his voice shaky, and his very soul battered to within an inch of existence." He stepped to the front edge of the stage. "For he'd witnessed the unspeakable."

He conveyed the intensity of the message through his eyes and voice, letting the audience absorb the significance with a long and heavy pause. Then he spun on his heel and began to pace as he spoke.

"Unspeakable but true. Always true. And that boy, with a small voice and a great passion, convinced the powerful families to forego their plans to travel to Beulah. In fact, he persuaded them never to return again."

The audience gasped.

"Until he asked them to, of course." Rafe paused and seemed to make eye contact with every member of the audience. "'*Why?*' you might ask. And that, my friends, is the story you will experience, body and soul, in this very tent tonight, for tonight marks the first time this story will ever be told. A story starring Beulah—Beulah the wonderful and Beulah the terrible. Your ears will feast upon the tale, but ears are only one way to receive a story. Thanks to that slight but clever boy, through the magic of lights and mirrors and lasers—and even a principle known as destructive interference—you shall feast all of your senses—your entire being—upon the story of how the Forenza-Galasso Circus came—no more!—to Beulah, South Carolina.

"Ladies and gentlemen, boys and girls, I present to you a tale I like to call . . . Ouroboros!"

In a single instant, Rafe disappeared from the stage as if vaporized, and an entirely new scene took his place. The stage was no longer a stage, the limits of the tent completely gone. The setting became Beulah, the audience its citizens. The stage had seemingly transformed into a road, a swamp, tall grasses, trees, and animals, all in full-color 3-D, and the audience was no longer watching. We were there. Almost before the story had begun to unfold, I—and everyone in the theater—heard Mrs. LeGrange gasp and cry out, "Macy!" as if the girl herself had appeared on stage because, of course, she had.

#

Macy rode her bike along Old Pleasant Road, her face lit with hope, wonder, and a sense of disbelief. She looked like she wanted to burst out laughing, but instead, kept shaking her head. Something too good to be believed had grabbed hold of my old friend. Her right foot, adorned with a holed sneaker, pressed her bike pedal to a stop. The well-worn tires made a slight skidding noise as she stopped near the edge of Black Swamp.

"Hey, Hoop, you hunting again?" Macy's voice was spot-on, sending icy chills through my core. I couldn't imagine what the experience was doing to Mrs. LeGrange.

Suddenly, a bright-haired boy of slight but promising build came into view. It was Hoop. He strode up the small hill from the bank of Black Swamp to meet Macy. His bare feet and calves were wet, and he held a fishing pole in his hand. Behind him, his three-speed Schwinn bike lay carelessly on the ground. Like a loyal horse, it seemed to wait eagerly for its master to return so it could perform its duties.

"Hey there, Macy," said Hoop's childhood voice, sending my heart into spasms. "Now correct me if I'm wrong, but today is birthday eve."

Macy smiled, and the entirety of the scene lit up with her.

"It sure is."

"And you've set the whole night aside for me, right?"

"From eight o'clock on, until 1 a.m. anyway. Got special permission from Momma."

A whimper from the front row.

Hoop smiled, not lecherously, but gratefully, like the young gentleman he'd always been. Then he bowed, swirling a hand from chest to hip. "I'll pick you up promptly at eight, m'lady, at your front door."

Macy imitated the hand-swirling gesture. "I look forward to your arrival, m'lord." And then she giggled in such a way that it was difficult to keep from giggling with her.

"If I may be so bold as to inquire," Hoop said, keeping up the pretentious voice, "where are you off to on this fine morning? You have a certain degree of delight upon your countenance."

"Well, of that, you can be sure," Macy said, returning to her regular voice. "I'm on my way to Boyd's. I turned on the radio this morning and caught the second half of the Power Pot numbers." She grinned hard and fast, lifting brows slightly darker than her hair. "You won't believe it, Hoop, but three of my numbers matched."

Hoop nodded and smiled as he patted her arm. "All right, that's awesome."

"That's all you've got to say? It's sixteen million dollars, Hoop! Sixteen *million*. And I'm getting a piece of it!"

"Yep, I know."

Macy frowned. "It's just that, well, you don't seem real excited."

"Sixteen million's nice and all, Macy, but it ain't nothing compared to what I plan to acquire."

"*Acquire*? Does that mean something other than earn?"

"Earn, acquire, finagle. All the same to me. And sure, it'd be nice if you *acquire* your own sixteen million, or even a few thousand, but my goal is to make your millions look like chump change."

"Well, good luck with that, and I'll be sure not to forget about you while I roll around in my paltry millions, or thousands, or whatever."

"Kind of hard to forget someone you're stuck with."

"That how you think of it now?" Macy said with a grin. "That you'll be *stuck* with me when I turn fifteen?"

"Nah, more like stuck together, in a good way, like icing and cake."

She chuckled. "That sounds better."

Hoop pointed a thumb at the swamp. "I'd better get back to it." And with that, he spun around to return to the water while Macy pressed on her pedal to continue toward Boyd's.

"See you tonight!" she shouted.

We the audience were suddenly plunged into darkness again, even more deeply than before. If someone in the tent had torn off their clothes and danced right in front of me, I wouldn't have been able to see it. The blackness felt treacherous, and remained so until the next scene came alive with a single sound: the soft swish of a bike tire with minimal tread skidding to a stop on loose gravel.

The scene brightened to reveal the sun cresting over the ugly, rectangular shape of Boyd's General Store before most of the additions had been added. Macy hopped off her bike and leaned it against the store window, too excited to bring it all the way to the bike rack. She hesitated only a second as she glanced at the sheriff's car in the lot. Finally, she shrugged to herself, pressed her lips together, and entered the store.

As the scene faded, it offered just enough light for me to glimpse Quail in the front row, his shoulders at full mast and his mouth tense as he swallowed with dread expectation. Meanwhile, Adeline DeVore, two seats down, appeared all but frozen as we entered the next scene.

Inside Boyd's General, Macy bounded to the register, giving a quick wave to a younger but stressed-out version of Sheriff Strike Ryker. He was searching for something in the pharmaceutical aisle, looking confused. On the far side of the store, Grace Elbee squeezed loaves of bread and assessed their freshness with a cynical eye, as if convinced that Boyd planned to cheat her no matter which loaf she selected. Her face wore its permanently pinched expression while her free hand clutched her purse to her chest.

"Mornin', Mrs. Elbee," Macy called out.

Mrs. Elbee turned and replied with a cross between a smile and a grimace.

Macy approached the register where Boyd was tapping his foot and applying price stickers to small pieces of candy. "Hey there, Boyd," Macy said, "you're not gonna believe this, but I need to check those lottery numbers. I think that ticket my momma bought might be a winner." She winked at him ever so subtly.

Boyd showed as much interest in Macy's good fortune as a cow would in a passing car.

Through the magic of Rafe's custom-created special effects, I felt like an invisible but paralyzed customer inside the store, and I had to assume that everyone else in the audience felt the same way. It was frustrating, at least to me, because I wasn't free to march over and shake Macy, to tell her that no matter what happened in the next minute, she must keep quiet about it.

Boyd opened the register and pulled out a sheet of paper just as the bell above the door rang out. In walked Quail the Whale. He shouted out a greeting to the sheriff, but he either didn't notice or didn't want to acknowledge Mrs. Elbee because they did not exchange hellos. Quail stood in place, surveying the store, presumably deciding which he wanted to tackle first: the donut bin or the coffee machine. Before he'd made up his mind, the door almost bumped him in the butt. He took a surprisingly light step out of the way and turned to ogle a pair of big breasts in a tight, red sweater.

"Well, if it isn't Beulah's own Adeline DeVore," he said, licking his lips.

Adeline looked less than thrilled to see him. "Good morning, Richie."

"You looking for work, Adeline? Because I've got an opening at my office. Sure could use a fine-looking secretary with a brain between her ears, and I hear you do some *fine* work with your brain."

"I *am* looking for a new job," she said, "but I aim to be something much more than a secretary."

"Well, excuse me all to pieces." Quail laughed and glanced around for someone to join him in his revelry; he came up empty. "Tell you what," he continued to Adeline who was headed for the coffee station, "if your high and mighty expectations don't work out, you come knock on my door." He winked in a lecherous way. "Richie Quail is always open for business."

Adeline shot him a repugnant glare, turned away, and filled her cup.

Richie took a good long look at her backside and could be heard saying, "Mmm, mmm, mmm."

Over by the register, Boyd handed Macy the card containing the list of winning numbers.

"Oh my God!" Macy shouted. "I won! I won! Holy Moly, I won!" She jumped up and down with excitement, clutching her ticket in one hand and the slip of paper in the other. Every few seconds, she'd jump and spin, and then she'd compare the numbers again before yelping out and starting the cycle all over again.

"What in the world?" Richie Quail said as he noticed Macy for the first time and made his way over to the register.

Mrs. Elbee approached, too, from the other side, one stilted step at a time, as if the whole scenario might be a trick to get her to buy the wrong loaf of bread.

"Here, Boyd, you check," Macy said, thrusting the ticket and slip of paper toward him. "I think it's a match for all six but I'm so excited, I can hardly see." Boyd took the items. "I won, didn't I, Boyd? Didn't I? No, it can't be. It must be a mistake. You sure you gave me the right numbers?"

Boyd struggled to concentrate.

"Let me see that," Quail grumbled. He reached across the counter and grabbed the ticket and card right from Boyd's hand. "I'll tell you what's going on." He glared down at Macy. "Hey, ain't you the little girl who was supposed to bring me my money? I been waiting on that rent, you know." He leaned down and got right in her face. "Thought we had us a talk about payroll. And let me tell you what"—he shook the lottery ticket at her—"if you did win anything with this here ticket, it's going right in my pocket. Overdue rent plus interest." He stood all the way up and pulled his head back, holding the ticket a fair distance from his face. "Now let's have a look-see what's happening here."

Boyd squirmed behind the counter, trying to work up some gumption. "Mr. Quail, I—"

But Quail thrust a hand out to shush Boyd. "Hold on there, Boyd. Just hold on." Then he stuffed his ham hock of a hand into his pocket and pulled out reading glasses. They looked minuscule on his face as he compared the numbers. "Well, I'll be a goat-stuffed snake," he said, leaning forward on the counter and holding up the card. "Boyd, this here for the Power Pot?"

"Yes, sir."

"You telling me these are the winning numbers and this little girl has matched all six?"

"Not sure," Boyd said. "You grabbed it 'fore I had a

chance to check."

"I won, didn't I, Mr. Quail?" Macy shouted. "God is smiling on me today! Hot diggity dog! This is going to change everything. Everything!"

A crashing noise rang out from the front row. Lights came on inside the tent but only where they were precisely needed. I couldn't see everything, but I instinctively knew that Melanie LeGrange had dead-on fainted to the floor and kicked her chair on the way down. Before anyone in the audience could react, three medics hovered over her, followed by two armed men in suits. Within thirty seconds, the medics whisked Mrs. LeGrange away on a stretcher and out of sight, seeming to know their way in the darkness. Richie Quail then stood up and faced the audience. He'd no sooner opened his yapper to protest than the two suited men forced him back into his seat. One of them took Melanie LeGrange's vacant seat while the other took Sheriff Ryker's. It happened in a swift and intimidating manner, but so quickly that most of the audience couldn't possibly know what had just transpired. I imagined that the men flanking Quail were each pressing a gun barrel into his side to elicit his continued cooperation.

The darkness blanketed the audience again, so completely that I'd swear I could feel its unyielding pressure against my body. I thrust my hand in front of my face but couldn't make out a single finger. Even in the swamp, I'd never experienced such visual deprivation. It persisted longer than expected, and I heard people take out their cell phones for illumination.

Still no light.

I pulled out my own phone. It didn't work. People's murmurs began morphing into fear as they realized it wasn't just their phone, but everyone's. A panic swept through the audience, yet nobody moved. Rafe must somehow have blocked all cellular signals, but what about the units themselves? Why wouldn't they even turn on? Then I recalled that we'd all passed through a steel barrier on the way in. It had been decorated to the hilt, but had it also deactivated everyone's batteries? Or maybe the cell waves were overloaded with hitchhiking evil spirits unafraid of amulets. I grew panicked. Were we safe? Who were the men guarding Quail? Had Rafe gone mad? Suddenly, I felt a reassuring hand on my shoulder. I turned to see who it was but my eyes were met with pure shadow.

Moments later, lights rose up. There was no one around to have touched my shoulder. Fighting a chill, I faced forward and was immediately lurched back into the scene at Boyd's. We the audience, in the form of our collective, impotent presence, were now seeing things from the perspective of a customer at the coffee station. Macy stood near the register, the sheriff behind her, Quail clutching the ticket at her side, while Boyd fidgeted behind the counter. Mrs. Elbee and Adeline DeVore completed the intimidating circle around my old friend.

"May I have my ticket back, Mr. Quail?" Macy spoke as if there were no doubt that Mr. Quail would hand back the ticket and wish her joyful congratulations. But instead, Quail's fingers tightened and a contorted smile formed on his face.

"Give her the ticket, Richie," Sheriff Ryker said, his voice and eyes weary but certain.

"Of course, of course." But even as Quail said the words, he didn't hand back the ticket. "Now, I'm just noticing that your ticket isn't signed, little lady."

"Momma hasn't had a chance yet," Macy said.

"Ah, yes," Quail said. "My old friend, Melanie. Funny, but when I stopped by that tattoo parlor the other day, the owner told me he'd never even met your momma."

Macy bit down on her lower lip, smiling all the while. "That opportunity didn't quite work out the way Momma and

I had hoped. But don't worry, Mr. Quail, we got the money now. We can pay our rent and the rent of every person in Beulah!"

"That so? Well, you must know it's downright dangerous for you to be carrying this ticket around willy-nilly. Without a signature and all."

"She can handle it, Richie," the sheriff said, stepping up close to Quail. "Give her back her ticket."

"Calm down now, Strike. I'm just looking out for the girl's welfare."

Macy, suddenly and without warning, reached up and snatched the ticket from Quail's hand. "Thanks, Mr. Quail, but something tells me I'm gonna be able to look after my own welfare from here on out."

Both Adeline DeVore and Mrs. Elbee were ogling Macy and the ticket with undisguised envy. Adeline looked pissed, with a stiffened jaw and narrowed eyes, while Mrs. Elbee kept licking her dry lips and blinking compulsively.

"Congratulations, Macy," the sheriff said, leaning down and smiling. "You want a ride home?"

"No thanks, Sheriff. I got my bike."

"Now, Macy," Quail said, "I'm not kidding. You gotta be careful. Who have you told about your winning ticket so far?"

Macy hesitated only a second. "Nobody, Mr. Quail. Just found out myself."

"You sure now?"

"Positive."

Quail then tilted his head and let his shoulders drop. "Surely your Momma must know, though. She bought the ticket, didn't she?"

Macy and Boyd exchanged a quick glance and that was all Quail needed. His nasty smile transfigured into something vile.

"She just doesn't know it's a winner, yet," Macy said. "I'd

best get home and tell her." She then swiftly extricated herself from the tightening ring of envious neighbors surrounding her. "She's waiting on me at the kitchen table this very moment," she yelled back to them. "And thanks, Boyd! I'm pretty sure you'll make some money off this, too."

Macy dashed from the store, her blond hair drifting behind her, the bell ringing out in the still-stunned silence of the disbelievers. Through Boyd's front window, Macy could be seen shoving the ticket into her front pocket and hopping on her bike. As she pedaled away, fading to a vaporous cloud, the scene remained inside Boyd's.

Richie Quail reached across the counter and grabbed Boyd by the front of his wrinkled shirt. He yanked the smaller man forward and nearly pulled him off the ground. "You sold that ticket to a minor, didn't you, Boyd?"

"No, sir." Boyd's eyes found the floor. "Her and her Momma came in the other day. Yesterday, matter of fact."

"You're lying!" He cast Boyd away like a bait fish too small to be useful, then he walked over and locked the front door before lowering the blind on the main window.

"Richie," the sheriff said with no attempt to disguise his weariness, "what do you think you're doing?"

Quail bucked up to full size and skewered each of them with his intense gaze. "We've been thrown together—the five of us—for a reason," he said.

"What are you going on about?" Adeline said. "Let me out of here." She stepped to the register to pay, but Quail drew all the attention in the room yet again.

"Listen up! All of you. Strike, you and Jacqueline, you got what, a hundred thousand in medical bills? Two hundred? Jacqueline's going to live and that's great, but for what? To work three jobs so you can claw your way out of debt the rest of your lives? You're never going to be able to afford those kids she wants to adopt."

Quail spun to Adeline next. "And what about you? I saw you drooling over that ticket. You told me not five minutes ago that you aim to make something of yourself. With a bit of seed money, you could finally do it."

"I know I could," Adeline said. "I got good instincts about business. I just need a leg up."

"So why *her*?" Quail said, pointing in the direction Macy had gone. "Why some little waif of a girl who didn't even buy the ticket legally? Believe me, her mother doesn't know what's up half the time—depressed and crying over that two-bit bounty hunter she was dumb enough to marry."

"Yeah," Adeline said, "I never did like him."

Quail dug in. "He'll get his hands on half that lottery money, you know"—he snapped his fingers—"just like that. While you, Adeline, you work as a lowly secretary for years. And you, sheriff, you count pennies for the rest of your life. Where's *your* breaks?"

"What about me?" Mrs. Elbee said, pinching the plastic covering of her bread. "I deserve a break."

"You sure do, Grace," Richie said. "You ain't had it easy with George drinking away half your earnings." He took the group's measure in one sweeping glance. "Who's looking out for all of you? I'll tell you who: Richie Quail. But none of us gets a break unless we're all in it together. You heard the girl. We're the only people in the world who know she won."

"Stop it right now, Richie," the sheriff said. "I'd best not hear of anything happening to that girl or her ticket."

"What are you proposing, Richie?" It was Mrs. Elbee, squeezing her bread into dough. "'Cause you'd best spit out your idea fast, before that girl gets home and tells the world she's won."

The real Richie Quail—the one in the front row—who, due to the strange phenomenon inside the tent, appeared less real than the one at Boyd's, tried again to rise from his seat, but he was immediately and roughly restrained by Rafe's henchmen, squeaking out nothing but, "Now hold on a gosh-darned—"

Meanwhile, the Quail inside the store got down to business. "Here's what's gonna happen. Either I get a share of that money or nobody does, including the girl."

"Hold on a cotton-pickin' minute," said the sheriff.

"You're crazy," Adeline added. "We can't steal her ticket. She won fair and square."

"That's just it!" said Quail. "There was nothing fair about it. She's a minor, not allowed to buy a lottery ticket. And if I report that technicality, nobody wins."

"But like I said," Boyd stammered, "she was here with her mother." He sounded so sheepish that not even a toddler would have believed him.

"For God's sake, Boyd," Quail shouted, "give me ten minutes and I'll produce a dozen witnesses who claim you sold that girl a ticket while her mother was nowhere in the vicinity, and they'll all be a damn sight better at lying than you."

"I'll be one of them," Grace Elbee said, her voice as reedy as her expression was menacing.

"But, Richie—" the sheriff began.

"It's true, Strike, and you know it. Once I put a bug in their ear, those lottery bigwigs will pounce like starved leopards. They'll force the truth from that girl, and then nobody gets the money."

"Then don't put a bug in their ear," the sheriff said.

"Can't do that," Quail said.

"Why not?" said the sheriff.

Quail smiled, and his malevolence had never been more palpable. "Because I'm Richie Quail and it would go against my principles to stay quiet about such a situation. Now we're gonna track that girl down right now and offer her fifty thousand bucks on the spot. Cold, hard cash—"

"Nobody's got that kind of money," Adeline said.

"I can come up with it if I need to," Quail said. "We tell the girl she needs to give us that ticket or else we report her, in which case nobody gets nothing. Believe me, I'll put the fear of God in that child."

"It'll work," Mrs. Elbee said, breathing hard. "It will definitely work." She bit at the loose skin on her lip, the bread in her hand now the size of a large roll. "But we've got to hurry!"

"I'm still not clear on—" the sheriff began.

"Listen, Strike," Richie said, barreling up to the much shorter man. "This here's your one chance. Pay off your bills and keep that lottery money from going back to the state. The girl wins. We all win."

Adeline approached the sheriff and stood close, laying a hand on his shoulder. "All we're doing, Sheriff, is making a business proposal." Her breathy voice had to be tickling his ear. "Not our fault that she and Boyd broke the rules, and she still comes out ahead, way ahead."

Quail puffed up. "A winning ticket in Beulah, South Carolina—imagine! We could improve this town like nobody's business. Heck, this'll put us on the map."

"We've got to decide now!" Mrs. Elbee yelled, working herself into a fit.

"What about me?" Boyd said in his boldest voice yet.

"We'll cut you in," Richie said, barely affording the wispy clerk a glance. "Not a full share—that wouldn't look right—but more than enough for you to keep your trap shut."

Boyd waggled his head to and fro, weighing the offer.

"Let's go!" Adeline said, grabbing the sheriff by the arm and dragging him along. "Now!"

"She'll be home any second!" Mrs. Elbee shouted, throwing the bread on the counter and declaring she would never pay for such a deformed loaf.

"We're gonna get us some money!" Quail yelled, his hands clapping together and his fat face beaming.

As the sheriff reached the door, he mumbled, "Guess it can't hurt to ask."

In Rafe's world, where we the audience were now willing prisoners, there was no *fade to black*. A new round of darkness slammed down, harshly depositing us back in the present, but only for a split second as the whizzing of tires on a bumpy road, punctuated by snippets of excited conversation, filled our ears.

Chapter 51

A Minute Before the Thump

"You're putting me on!" Hoop said, shoving his fishing kit into his pocket.

"I swear on every home run The Babe ever hit," Macy said, beaming. "You're the first one I'm telling! What a birthday present for Momma, huh?"

Hoop and Macy were on Hoop's favorite stretch of Old Pleasant Road. Not only did cars avoid the road due its array of ruts, bumps, and blind curves, but it had faithfully delivered him scores of times to his favorite snake-hunting hideaway. It was on Old Pleasant Road that he'd spotted his very first hoop snake at age five—or so he claimed. He'd been riding on the back of his mom's motorcycle when she'd paused on the side of the road to adjust her helmet, and a hoop snake had rolled right past her front wheel. While she'd tried to convince him it was nothing but a red bicycle tire, she'd still allowed him to traipse to the swamp in search of it. When he came up empty, he claimed it was only more proof of a hoop snake.

See, Ma? That hoop snake rolled into the swamp, unlooped itself, and swam away.

He'd gone home that day and told his father that the mystery object had been too shiny for a bicycle tire and that nobody in Beulah owned a bicycle with a red tire anyway—certainly not one with black eyes and a mouthful of tail. He declared then and there, at age five, that he'd have himself a hoop snake for a pet one day, shrugging off all arguments to the contrary. His mother had wasted lots of breath trying to talk him out of his fancy notions, but she tended to live in a murky reality, where dreams didn't quite pan out and plans never got much past the planning stage. It'd be years later that Hoop realized the only place his mother felt hopeful was on her bike—a Harley more suited for a man than a woman, but one that had become a natural extension of her body. Hoop liked to believe that when his mom had those two wheels purring beneath her, she, too, might believe in hoop snakes.

Hoop looked at Macy now, discouraged. It was an expression so foreign to him that it felt strange on his face. He kicked a pebble.

"What's wrong, Hoop?"

"This is gonna change things, isn't it?"

"I'll say," Macy said with a wide grin. "I'm gonna be richer than rich."

"No, I mean between you and me."

"Things between you and me ain't even started. Not really."

Hoop gasped. "What are you—"

"Well, you don't think I'm staying in this peapod of a town, do you? I mean, girls with money don't date boys from the likes of Beulah. And as for tonight's plans, well—"

"I can't believe this!" Hoop said. "This is not what I—"

Macy burst out laughing and slugged his arm. "Hoop, I'm kidding. Come on, you know better than that." She looked away bashfully for a moment, but then returned her eyes to his. "Nothing's gonna change, least as far as I can help it. I'll see you tonight, just like we planned."

Hoop smiled and slugged her arm in return. "You do know, don't you, Macy?"

"Know what?"

"That all the money in the world can't bring you happiness."

"Course I know, but it can make being sad a lot more fun."

Hoop laughed, unguarded and big. "Now that's what I

call a fine outlook, Macy, a fine outlook."

"Gotta go," she said. "Gotta get Momma to sign this ticket. Richie Quail just told me so."

Hoop's eyes turned to slits. "You be careful who you trust, now. Keep everything quiet for a while, least till you've got it all figured out. Like, I wouldn't go telling your dad."

Macy looked aghast. "Hoop, are you saying my dad's a no-good, dirty, lying cheater who'd do anything to get his hands on my millions?"

Hoop kicked another pebble and squirmed in place. "Kinda, yeah."

"Well, you about nailed it, then." She winked but then turned somber. "Hey, promise me something."

"Whatever you want."

"If anything comes between me and this ticket, you gotta take care of Momma. I need her to be okay."

Hoop scrunched up his mouth. "Don't even talk like that, but yeah, of course. As long as you promise we'll be together forever."

"You never give up, do you?"

"A giving-up person is *not* a snake-catching kind of person, and I, Macy LeGrange, am a snake-catching kind of person." He shrugged his slim shoulders. "Ain't never gonna change my mind about you. And if you decide not to have me in this life, you'll have me in the next—'cause we're all hoop snakes in the end."

He gazed at the girl he adored, a sudden sense of foreboding pulling him closer. He reached out a sure hand and touched hers, linking them together without pretense for the first time. Then he leaned over her handlebars and planted a soft kiss on her cheek. It was the first time he'd ever touched his lips to her skin, and the warmth of it nearly knocked him off his feet. When he pulled back, she was scrutinizing him, searching, yet awed, as if finally believing that it was indeed possible to find a soul mate in the boy next door.

Hoop smiled in a special way. The boy was known to have a hundred different smiles, but he'd rarely found a chance to use this one. She smiled back before lifting herself onto her pedal and pressing down, but she did glance back one more time as her bike coasted away. "What a day, huh, Hoop? What. A. Day."

Hoop couldn't agree more.

Macy had just gotten going when Hoop headed down to the swamp's edge and stepped knee-deep into the water, silent as a heron, still as a rock. He'd always been able to camouflage himself with minimal effort, almost as if he were born to it. His dad had told him he was more in tune with nature than a stick bug sitting on a twig. *Hiding in plain sight*, his mother used to call it. But when an unnerving sensation grabbed hold of his gut, he whipped around to check on Macy. She tended to wobble when distracted and he suddenly needed to make sure she was okay; a turtle had once landed her in a ditch, and last year, a butterfly had sent her head-first into a patch of poison ivy. She looked fine, though. No wobbling.

He'd just returned his attention to the water when he heard a familiar engine roaring down the road.

Chapter 52

Light—sudden and absolute—coated the audience, but of a different sort this time. Sunlight. Streaming in from the window just over the sheriff's shoulder as he drove his black-and-white down the road. It was still early morning.

We, the audience, were made to feel that we were in the car with the loathsome foursome.

The sheriff sped down the road as if in pursuit of a criminal. Quail, crammed in next to him, hogged more than his fair share of the front seat while Mrs. Elbee was squeezed tight against the passenger door. In the back, Adeline DeVore sat by herself, squished up against eight large boxes.

My perspective—everyone's perspective—was from that of the boxes. Rafe had somehow given us the perspective of the empty seat, yet we were still able to see the contents of that seat.

"What's in these boxes, anyway?" Adeline whined from the back.

"Old clothes and kitchen supplies," said the sheriff. "I was headed to Goodwill this morning after Boyd's."

"Wish you'd done it first," she said.

The sheriff frowned. "Wasn't exactly planning on passengers today."

He rounded the bend where the road veered toward the swamp. Richie Quail, meanwhile, was behaving like a kid unleashed in a toy store for the first time. He reached out and pressed a button near the center of the console, causing splashes of red and blue lights to cascade around the edges of the car.

The sheriff hit his hand away and shut off the exterior lights. "Cut it out, Richie! Don't be touching everything!"

"I never been in a police car before," Richie said,

laughing and pointing. "What's this do?"

"Siren," the sheriff grumbled. "Now sit tight. We'll be coming up on her soon enough. Who's gonna do the talking?"

"I should do it," Adeline said. "I'm real good with kids."

"Please," Richie said dismissively. "If anyone's going to do the talking, it'll be me. That girl owes me two months of—"

"Absolutely not!" Mrs. Elbee shouted. "You're a bear, Richie. I know her. I'll—"

"Maybe we oughta let the sheriff do it," Adeline yelled from the back.

"Yeah," Richie said. "Make it real official-like."

With a rascally grin on his face and a quick side-eye to the sheriff, Quail slammed his pudgy finger down on the thin metal lever to switch on the siren.

The blaring sound stabbed mercilessly in my eardrums. Surely, everyone in the audience was experiencing the same thing. Just as my hands were about to shoot up and cover my ears, I spotted the back of Macy's head . . . Macy's perfect head . . . her honey-blond locks swishing freely back and forth. She pedaled hard, riding on the extreme edge of the road, and she even seemed to be trembling a bit, probably because of the horrible siren bearing down on her.

"Dammit, Richie!" the sheriff screamed. "Draw a little more attention to us, why don't you?"

Richie smacked at the lever and switched off the siren but ended up knocking the lever clean off. It clattered to the floor of the car near the sheriff's feet.

The sheriff glanced down to where the lever should have been. "For God's sake, what'd you do now? You knocked—"

Quail leaned left, jarring the sheriff while reaching down and around his own girth to find a half-inch lever no wider than the spoke of a bike.

"Let it go," the sheriff said.

"No, I'll get it," Quail said. The whole of his weight

pinned the sheriff's body while the upper folds of his massive arm pressed against the wheel, rotating it fifteen degrees to the right.

As time slowed down and my heart became paralyzed with the imminence of the next moment, I tried to scream, to grab the wheel, to steer anywhere else. But I was nothing but a mute, immobile passenger, forced into futility. Forced to bear witness.

Macy's head came closer. Her bike loomed just ahead.

"Look out!" Mrs. Elbee screeched, throwing her arms up in front of her.

"Oh my God! Turn! You're gonna hit—" Adeline DeVore squealed as her white-knuckled fingers grabbed the back of the seat, her nails nearly ripping the vinyl.

The sheriff tried to yank the wheel left, but Quail—

Thump.

That was it.

Such a small, anticlimactic sound.

The sheriff's car, which he'd managed to swerve the slightest bit left out of sheer determination, had gently tapped the left pedal of Macy's bike as he whizzed by.

I, along with everyone else in the audience, careened down the road, trapped inside the vehicle, unable to see the outcome of the actions I now felt responsible for. The sickness, regret, and sorrow encompassing me were so beyond anything I'd ever experienced that I couldn't begin to process them. And I surely couldn't imagine the effect they'd had on young Hoop Whitaker.

I squirmed and wriggled and twisted, trying desperately to glance out the back window of the car to see what had happened to Macy, but when I finally succeeded, I was met with utter darkness. The scene had ended. As horribly and irrevocably as it possibly could have.

"No!" I screamed, and it was only then that I realized I

couldn't even hear my own voice. Because the entire audience was shrieking in horror.

Chapter 53

The Thump

Hoop heard no skid. No screams. Only the terrible thump. He whipped his head around just in time to see Macy floating through the air in a perfect arc, graceful as a ballerina performing the finale of a lifetime.

That was when Hoop became a believer in miracles. Midair, Macy's back bowed itself as if clearing a high bar, her head leading the way, her body following with gazelle-like fluidity. Her hair swept toward the ground, the ends of the strands at the same altitude as the toes of her sneakers. In that upside-down pose, her golden locks resembled extended angel wings taking their passenger for a gleeful ride. Macy's face shimmered, and for a frozen instant, her eyes found Hoop's.

Hoop's eyes exuded a lifetime of love as time stood still. He wrapped Macy in that love, protectively, knowing it had to last for eternity, knowing it was his final chance to convey the depth of his commitment. Part of him left his own earthly body to cradle his true love, body and soul, to soften the blow of her landing. The two became one before her body touched the ground, a feather drifting downward, settling gently. And in that moment, when a spiritual bond managed to exceed the limits of human dimension, Hoop and Macy exchanged vows. He knew she felt it, and she knew he would never let her down.

Back in his body, the moment having passed, Hoop let his mind absorb the horror of Macy's corpse staring blankly at the swamp. An icy darkness incapacitated him. He remained immobile except for the tremors overtaking his core, silent except for the rattling of his teeth. His eyes shaded over, his vision nothing but pinholes. And as his mind became the fullest emptiness imaginable, he didn't fight it. He let Hoop Whitaker die.

Chapter 54

Rafe spared the audience the moment of impact, the crushing defeat of a small girl against a four-thousand pound automobile. Something told me that Rafe knew exactly what had happened at that moment, but that he'd refused to compromise its purity. He would keep it to himself, hidden away, as it always had been.

The scene changed so abruptly, I felt punched in the heart. No soft orchestra strings to ease us out, no moment to mourn in silence. With unforgiving brutality, we were whiplashed to a new visual: the greedy four standing over Macy's contorted body—vultures over road kill—and we were the fifth party, compelled to bear witness once again.

The casual stance of the Lucky Four meant we were entering the scene after they'd overcome their initial shock. Rafe would allow no sympathy to be generated for them in this abysmal scenario, no moment where we felt their pain as they shed their tears or pounded the pavement with revulsion. He'd also chosen to skip their assured desecration of Macy's body when they touched it to confirm her death. All of that was stripped from our experience. We would see only the cold, calculating aftermath.

"No, Richie!" the sheriff shouted. "Absolutely not!"

"You don't have a choice in this, Strike. You just killed a girl."

The blunt assessment seemed to jar the sheriff more than any opponent's clout to the head ever had. "But it was an accident," he said.

The words sounded weak, pathetic.

"Besides," Quail said with a barren voice, "it wouldn't have happened if you weren't chasing her down to steal her lottery ticket."

The sheriff wheeled on the bigger man with a raised but hesitant fist. "You conniving, greedy son of a bitch. This was all your idea! Your ultimatum! I never—"

The twisted evil of Quail's expression knew no bounds. "Do you think any of us are going to stay quiet when the judge asks us why we were in your car? Why you were pursuing this girl—with your siren on?"

Mrs. Elbee crossed her arms and sighed, kneading her own skin in place of the bread. "You *were* after her ticket, Sheriff," she said. "And you *were* driving."

"She's already dead," Adeline DeVore said. "And if we tell the truth now, we might go to jail—and that is *not* in my plan." She'd adapted quickly to the harsh groupthink, but at least she stared down at Macy with a forlorn expression when she spoke.

I glanced at the real Adeline DeVore in front of me. I couldn't see her but could hear her erratic breathing and somehow knew that she was lost to this world for now.

"No one here is going to tell the truth," Quail said. "Let's get that straight right now. From this moment on, we're in this together. For the rest of our lives. Way I see it, we're either complicit in a murder—or we're complicit in winning a lottery. Your choice, folks."

The sheriff looked like he'd taken a left hook to the face and was still trying to unscramble his brains. His words came slowly. "You people disgust me." Nobody paid him much attention.

"How do you propose we explain the body, Richie?" Mrs. Elbee said, gesturing offhandedly to Macy.

"By telling the truth!" the sheriff yelled. "This idea was crazy and wrong from the start. We can't layer lies on top of it."

Quail shook his head and rolled his eyes at the sheriff before squatting down and reaching his fat fingers into Macy's front pocket. Only two of them fit as he fished around in the small space. A collective gasp filled the tent as Quail's intimate violation of Macy repulsed the audience.

"Y'all do what you want," he said, yanking the ticket from Macy's pocket and holding it up triumphantly. "But I'm signing the back of this ticket. You can join me or not. But if a single one of you calls me out on it, I'll turn on all y'all—and you ain't felt nothing till you've felt the wrath of Richie Quail."

"But how can we possibly get away with it?" Mrs. Elbee said.

Her voice faded as the scene's point of view shifted, rotating toward Macy's bike. It had landed in the middle of the road, presumably having flown up and over the car while her body had drifted in the other direction.

The sound of whirring tires filled the tent, and the scene, still rotating, now showed another car coming down the road: an old, mint-green Cadillac, big and lumbering, fronted by a rusty, dented fender.

Mrs. Elbee had just gotten her answer.

The scene closed in on the Caddy's windshield and Avis Whitaker's face became visible behind the wheel. A few faint bars of rock 'n roll rang out, followed by static and then sad country music. It filled the air, playing through the car's speakers. Too late, Avis's merry face looked up from the radio dial. He spotted the bike in the middle of the road, his expression shifting to panic. He veered and slammed on the brakes but still managed to catch a good chunk of the bike. He tried to correct, but to no avail. The car had been traveling too fast and was now compromised by the hunk of metal entwined in its undercarriage.

Avis's eyes suddenly alighted upon four folks he knew well, all standing over the collapsed body of the beautiful girl his son loved. The look of horror and utter sorrow on his face would remain his final expression for eternity as his car thudded with sickening impact into the big oak tree. We all felt the jolt, our heads practically smashing into the wheel, the effect multiplied by the knowledge of Avis's fate.

What took longer to sink in were the implications, as an established reality of twelve years was ripped from our minds. A complete erasure of the blue circle whose hue we had always accepted. This new truth shattered the ease with which we'd blamed the town drunk, and the carelessness with which we'd written checks to charitable causes.

"No," I whispered. "No." I gripped the arms of my chair, nearly pulling them from their screws. What was I supposed to do with this cyclone of emotions? I was melting and shrinking one second, enraged and erupting the next. I wanted to pass out—no—more—I wanted to grab the world by the scruff of its miserable neck and shake it until it behaved. I felt the dire need to exit by force any world that would let such events transpire.

And then, I was yanked back. Along with everyone else.

I felt exhaustion, frustration, and astonishment, as if someone were smearing their emotions directly on my soul. We the audience became one again as the power of our grief superseded all. Our communal horror and sadness could have taken on the force of flying bullets. We had become a lynch mob.

Another time shift on stage. The sheriff was driving *away* from the dual tragedies, no doubt planning to drop off the others and circle back as the hero. Suddenly, there was Hoop—young and vibrant—rushing up from the banks of the swamp. He'd been there all along, a witness to the basest of human behaviors, including the framing of his father. No one could ever have been more alone than Hoop Whitaker at that moment. The people in charge—the adults—had abandoned the scene, leaving a crumpled girl on the ground and a hissing car projecting from a tree like a stubborn root.

Hoop ran to Macy. He leaned down, touched her face, and stroked her hair. Then, very gently, he lowered his face to hers and kissed her lips. "I love you, Macy."

No one wanted to intrude on the moment, but it marched on, relentlessly battering all of us.

The scene closed in on Hoop. His eyes, his carriage, and the set of his features showed a hardened expression, bereft of all innocence and optimism. In its place: resolve. Cold. Calculating. Unwavering.

He gritted his teeth, assumed a defiant, frightening air, and reached into Macy's back left pocket. He pulled out a receipt.

Chapter 55

We transformed into a simple audience gathered in a tent, but life would never be simple again. Rafe stood on stage, his hair its natural color, his eyes their astonishing blue, and his brows real. He must have dyed his hair back this afternoon and been sporting a wig for the first half of the show. Despite the passage of time and an elephant kick to the nose, there was no way to miss that the man on the stage was the boy we'd just seen on the edge of the swamp.

In his hand, he held the receipt for Macy's lottery ticket purchase.

Murmurs of, *Oh my God*, *it's him*, and, *I thought he was dead*, filled the air.

"The winning lottery numbers," Rafe said, reading from the receipt. "Four, one." He tapped the receipt and then flicked a finger skyward. It caused a three-foot-tall, vaporous, red image of the digits to appear in the air above his head. "Macy's birthday," he said simply, by way of explanation.

"Three, thirty-one," he continued. Tap and flick. The numbers materialized above him and I felt as sick as I ever had. "Melanie LeGrange's birthday." He repeated the performance for Darrell LeGrange's birthday. "And eight," he said as the number 8 appeared overhead. "Macy's favorite number." The digit rotated itself ninety degrees. "And the symbol for infinity."

He stepped to the side and waved his hand triumphantly at the smoky numbers, their meaning penetrating the crowd.

"Boyd wrote each person's lottery numbers on their receipts. Hire handwriting experts, as I did. They will confirm the writing on this receipt as Boyd Sexton's. Still"—he waved the receipt dismissively in the air—"circumstantial evidence only—a mere coincidence—with nothing but my word to back it up." He gestured to Richie Quail in the front row. "Could have been Mr. Quail's receipt. Could have been the sheriff's." He glanced at the receipt again and spoke his next words with tremendous skepticism. "Especially if they were also buying aspirin and a birthday card that day." His tone made obvious how ridiculous the odds were.

Rafe made the receipt disappear by tossing it in the air. It transformed into an origami bird and flew away over the audience's head, chirping. I suspected it was a hologram. Then he gestured with a flourish to his right. "What you're about to see, however, is not circumstantial at all."

A car engine rumbled to life. The tent filled with the smell of exhaust, and the sheriff's old black-and-white roared onto the stage, driven by a small, elderly man with oil-slicked hair, and huge, reptilian eyes. He jammed the car to a stop and exited both car and stage with a showman's flair. One of the original Galasso or Forenza brothers, no doubt.

A beam of light zeroed in on the corner of the car's front bumper, next to which a 3-D image of Macy's bike suddenly appeared, the pedal in direct contact with the car.

"Cars have been hitting cyclists since 1896," Rafe said with pizazz, "when a motor vehicle collided with and killed a cyclist in New York City. Today, experts specialize in accident reconstruction. There are even forensic bike savants who become one with the damaged bike. They use it as a snapshot in time and analyze each scrape, dent, and ding to reconstruct the truth." He pointed to the car's bumper and feigned a shocked expression. "But Sheriff Ryker's car was never analyzed. Why would it have been when my father's car screamed, 'Over here! I did it!'?" Rafe crossed the stage, his hand to his chin as if pondering. "Sadly, my dad's Cadillac was telling the truth. It did indeed strike Macy's bicycle, as you saw, dragging it untold yards along Old Pleasant Road to an abrupt and untimely end." He spun to the audience and scanned the many awed faces, lights sweeping out in such a way that they seemed to emanate from his eyes, until he found Sherilyn in the fifth row.

"When you analyze this car, Ms. Lewis," he said, "which I'll be donating to your forensics lab, you will find all the evidence you need. This car has not been touched since Sheriff Ryker inexplicably put it up for auction a month after the accident. My uncles made the winning bid, because they, like I, did not appreciate my father taking the burden of Macy's death to his grave."

A loud but muffled sound erupted from the back of the tent. The lights went up and the audience turned around to see Chad standing behind a wheelchair that held the weakened form of Strike Ryker. I couldn't believe it; the man had been near death a few hours ago. His pallor was no longer that of a dying man but of a person flushed with shame.

"He insisted we come," Chad said quietly, detesting this moment in the spotlight. "Said he'd rather die than hide from the truth any longer."

If Strike could have stood and taken his licks on the chin, I believe he would have. But it was all he could do to keep his head raised. His tears fell slowly, one by one, as if he'd only been allotted a few dozen to last a lifetime. "Hoop?" he said in a scratchy voice. "Is it really you?"

Rafe narrowed his eyes, his anger fresh and raw. "Spare me what follows, Sheriff. I don't care how much good you did with your winnings. I don't care about the medical bills. I don't even care that it was all an accident. What I do care about is that you lied and stole and betrayed everything you stood for, everything this town believed about you. You sold your soul—and nearly destroyed mine."

The sheriff gestured to Chad to push him farther forward.

"If Avis had regained consciousness," the sheriff said

when halfway down the aisle, "I never would have let him take the blame." His feeble voice floated along the tent's perfectly engineered acoustic channels and travelled to each person's ears, as if he were whispering just to them, begging for mercy.

"But he didn't regain consciousness," Rafe said. "As the hospital files now being sent to Deputy Ryker will show, he died—stone cold sober, by the way—because he hit a bike that never should have been there in the first place."

The sheriff's head sunk low and everyone could hear that he was losing his battle for composure.

"I didn't—"

"End the farce, Sheriff! You're only sorry you got caught." Rafe leaped off the stage and approached the cowering man. It seemed unduly cruel. "Would you like to share with the good people of Beulah what else you've done over the years to cover your crime? How you allowed Boyd's drug operation to go undetected so he wouldn't turn you in? How you looked the other way every time Richie Quail and Adeline DeVore bent the rules or received a complaint against them? How you poured compromise into every decision you've made since Macy's death, until you became nothing but a shell of the person you once were? I must ask, Sheriff, was it worth it? Or would it have been better to fight a clean fight?"

"None of it was worth it!" Strike said in what surely passed for a shout in his mind. "None of it!"

"And shall we put the final nail in the coffin?" Rafe spun away from the sheriff and spoke in a quiet voice as he walked back to the stage. "Shall we tell the good citizens of Beulah your true intention when you went to retrieve Boyd Sexton from his tree hideaway? When you were presumably there to return him to federal authorities?"

The sheriff sucked in a gulp of air and looked genuinely frightened. He trembled enough to make the wheelchair judder, as if the hand of justice had reached out and shaken his stained soul. "No, no, it's not true. I changed my mind."

I recalled what I'd witnessed in the minutes before Old Bastard took Boyd for that final swim. The sheriff had already drawn his gun—his personal gun. Boyd had run like his life depended on it. And what was it Boyd had yelled out? *I ain't saying nothing. There's nothing to worry about.* He'd been reassuring the sheriff because the sheriff didn't want Boyd to talk to the authorities any more than Quail did. *You made a deal with those government men, Boyd. You promised them a conversation.*

The sheriff hadn't been looking to bring Boyd back into custody. He'd wanted to make sure the conversation with the feds never took place. *You think those government men are just gonna let you walk away, Boyd? Come on. You're smarter than that. They're expecting something big.*

And Boyd's final accusation toward the sheriff: *Mr. Quail, he checked with everyone. Told me everything was square . . . You're just trying to get me where—"*

Were Boyd's ultimate words going to be: *where no one will see you shoot me?*

I wrenched up from my seat, cutting short the sheriff's denials. "He was there to kill Boyd."

"No, Chloe," the sheriff said.

"I have it on tape!" I yelled, not really in control of my own actions anymore. "Boyd was going to turn all of them in. Quail posted bail and then sent the sheriff to kill him, but Old Bastard did the dirty work for them."

"But I changed my mind." The sheriff's voice couldn't have been frailer. "I changed my mind."

I turned and locked eyes with Rafe. He was grinning at me, proud and amused. "The truth is freeing, isn't it, Clover?" He swiped the inside of his forearm with his right hand, a swift, elegant gesture that would mean little to anyone else. "I do hope it breaks your chains."

I sat, weak-kneed and faint, not daring to witness Chad's reaction to my outburst, and not ever wanting to see the sheriff again. I was teetering somewhere between denial and liberation. Liberation from what, I wasn't sure, but if the percolating feeling within me reached a steady boil, I felt I could take on the world.

Rafe returned to the stage while our much-feared but beloved sheriff had been knocked down for the count. Finally, the Lucky Four had been revealed for the deplorable lowlifes they were.

Thank God Melanie LeGrange had fainted early on. The man who'd paid for her daughter's funeral had only been assuaging his own guilt. The woman whose memorial she'd attended last night had been the first to drool over Macy's winnings—and she'd then squandered those winnings on a shoddy house and a drunkard of a husband. The corporate bigwig who'd donated company profits in Macy's name had only been making up for stolen seed money. Worst of all, the man who had surprised Melanie with his generosity had acted as the catalyst for her daughter's death. He'd even convinced her to leave town in case her suspicions ever got the better of her.

"It's been a long night," Rafe said, "and I don't want to keep you much longer, but I'd like you all to meet the man behind the blog known as *Abhor DeVore*." A huge, foggy image of his own face filled the stage. "On today's final post, you'll find all the evidence needed to topple DeVore Cosmetics. Simple math, really. If anyone had ever bothered to calculate the amount of rare plant serum in Ms. DeVore's products and multiplied it by her sales volume, they'd have realized that DeVore Cosmetics would need to clear half a million acres' worth of specific wildflowers and rare plants in Africa—or, put another way, more than exist in the world. Her company is as corrupt as she. So here's an insider tip for you stockholders out there: sell now." He squared off with Adeline in the audience. "On a positive note, Ms. DeVore, you pull off autumn colors very well, and with orange being the new black, you won't look nearly as washed out as you do now."

The prison guard yanked Adeline DeVore to standing position and led her from the tent by way of the center aisle. Her handcuffed march of shame in front of the entire town promised to be but the first of many humiliations coming her way.

I called out to her. "Miss DeVore?"

She glanced over, her face showing the slightest hope for a reprieve from this hell.

"I think I know who took that Botox picture now."

She sneered and jerked her head away.

With Adeline gone, Richie Quail was finally allowed to burst to life. He shook off the men surrounding him, rose up, and looked downright threatening. "Listen to me, you swamp rat," he shouted at Rafe, "I been around a lawsuit or two. You think you're real clever with this 3-D bullcrap, forcing me to sit here in silence while you disparage my good name, but guess what? You done laid out all your cards now, and you got diddly-squat. You can't prove a dang thing. Grace Elbee's dead; Boyd's in pieces; Adeline DeVore's a convict; and the sheriff's about to get his sorry ass arrested." He smiled eerily and clapped slowly, three times. "Well done! Bravo! But I'll see you in court—when I sue you for slander and take every penny you've got!"

Rafe gazed calmly at Quail. "What follows," he said to the audience, "I saw too late, but I do think you'll enjoy it." He bowed, his right hand trickling down in front of him from head to hip, his fingers dancing all the while, as he backed away from center stage with tiny steps before disappearing from view.

The lights dimmed and the clickety buzzing of a

traditional film projector filled the room. A movie screen lowered, and a new show began. The opening credits read: *Starring Richard Quail; Shot on Location by Grace Elbee*; and, *Produced by R. O. Borose*. The screen showed a grainy image of Richie Quail in the office where I'd interviewed him. He was leaning forward over his desk, his eyes glowering at whoever was holding the low-quality camera.

"Now listen here, Grace, you been getting loonier by day. It's got to stop before you get us all into trouble."

"I don't care anymore," Grace Elbee said.

I suddenly realized we were watching footage filmed by Mrs. Elbee's amulet—footage that Rafe must have uploaded at an earlier date.

"Macy's haunting me," Mrs. Elbee continued, "and it's time we told the truth. Today." Her hand came into view as she slammed her palm on Quail's desk.

"And lose everything we've worked for?" Quail said. "You'd have nothing left. You'd have no way to help your son."

"I'll just sell that cheap-ass house you built for me, Richie. That ought to bring in a couple hundred dollars." Then her voice lost its acidity. "But don't you see? I've been cursed from the moment I took that money. My husband became a different person, and my son started acting out. It's not easy becoming the richest kid in town overnight, you know. And nothing has ever made *me* happy. We killed that little girl, Richie, and—"

Quail flew out of his seat like an ejected pilot, his panicked face aquiver. "Don't you *ever* say those words out loud, Grace! You want to go to prison? Besides, wasn't us who killed her. Strike was at the wheel. Not our fault the man can't drive."

Mrs. Elbee must have stood up, too, because the picture grew unsteady and the angle of the shot changed. "The devil was at the wheel, Richie! He wants us. He wants us *bad*.

That's why I have *this*."

Mrs. Elbee must have removed her amulet at that point and thrust it at him because we saw only a blob of darkness.

"What the hell are you shaking at me?" Quail said.

Muffled noise followed. The point of view changed to an angle below Quail's face. He had grabbed the amulet from her and was examining it. Then he sneered at her. "Look at yourself, Grace! You think some stupid necklace is gonna save you from the devil?"

"It's been working. I'm here, aren't I?"

"You're god-dang certifiable, you know that?"

"Watch your mouth, Richie. He's always listening."

"Who?"

"The devil. And Macy listens, too. She's been calling my house."

The audience saw nothing but the dirty ceiling of Quail's office as he tossed the amulet onto his desk and let out a sigh. In the silence that followed, a faint bell rang out and the low murmur of voices could be heard. A lower-pitched voice exchanged pleasantries with a higher one. Had to be Chad, returning from his lunch date with Sarah in the outer part of the office. The amulet microphone was picking up their conversation.

Back in the office, Quail's voice grew softer and unexpectedly kinder. "Now listen here, Grace, I know things have been hard on you, and I apologize for my gruffness. Truth is, I think you're right."

"You do?" Mrs. Elbee said.

"Sure. It's time to come clean, but you've got to do me a favor. I need a couple days to get my affairs in order. I got a wife and employees to think about. As I'm sure you can imagine, when we tell the truth, all holy hell is going to break loose and I need to be ready."

"Language, Richie. Please!"

"You know what, Grace? I feel better already."

"You see? The devil's loosening his grip. We'll all feel better after clearing our consciences. Strike and Adeline will surely agree, don't you think?"

"I'll talk to them first thing."

Richie then shooed her out. He could be heard saying a quick hello to Chad before closing his office door. But Mrs. Elbee must have left the amulet behind because we were still getting audio and visual from inside his office.

"Goddamn whack job," Richie mumbled as a phone was lifted from its receiver and dialed. He cleared his throat.

"Zeke? Richie Quail here. We got a problem that I need silenced . . . Yeah, permanently . . . Well, take a break from that. I own the damn property, don't I? . . . No, just you. Don't need your brother for this loon . . . It's Grace Elbee, but I need it to look like sui—"

"Richie," said Grace Elbee's voice as the office door opened. "Silly me, I left my amulet on your desk."

The amulet's point of view shifted. "Here you go, Grace. Wouldn't want you to be without that, would we? Not with the threat of evil so nearby."

"Call me as soon as you take care of things," she said.

Quail came back into view as Grace must have clasped the amulet around her neck. He was holding the phone to his ear, smiling at her like a realtor about to close a deal.

"I'm on the phone right now taking care of things, Grace." And then he winked at the woman whose murder he'd just ordered.

Chapter 56

"This is crazy!" Quail shouted from the audience. "You think some half-assed, illegally recorded phone call is gonna hold up in court? I got the best lawyers in the country and they're going to make mincemeat out of you, Hoop Whitaker or Clive Haverhill, or whatever you call yourself these days."

"It would behoove you to know," Rafe said, "that Clive Haverhill makes Bernie Madoff look like a two-bit pickpocket. And you, Richie Quail, can no longer afford the best lawyers in the country."

Quail smirked. "You're bluffing."

"Check your financial statements as of three hours ago. You can't even afford the cheapest lawyer in a third world country."

"You think I put all my eggs in one basket?" Richie shouted, his face turning crimson. "I'm not stupid. At most, you managed one-third of my money."

"Then check with F. G. Investments and Firehoop Management. I'm sure they've done wonders with the other two-thirds." Rafe smiled. "Oh, wait. All me." Then his lightheartedness disappeared and he singed hatred upon Quail with his eyes. "It's all gone, Richie. Every penny. Even the petty cash in that cigar box in the right-hand drawer of your desk, and the six dollars and eighty-two cents in your pocket when you entered here tonight."

Quail patted his pocket as the audience laughed. Empty. "What about—"

"That ten million you invested two days ago?" Rafe threw his hands up in false despair. "All gone. And you'll find that your coveted investment trusts grant you leases to nothing but contaminated, quarantined buildings. As for those hidden accounts you have around the world—not so hidden. They've all been legally transferred to a private account in the name of Melanie LeGrange." Rafe almost glowed with joy. "As I once promised a friend, *I own you, Richie Quail.*"

A gigantic, old-fashioned clock appeared as a hologram or projection behind Rafe. It struck midnight, and twelve beautiful chimes rang out.

"Happy April Fools' Day, everyone!" Rafe said. "Macy would have turned twenty-seven today."

I gasped. Of course, the timing made sense now.

"Today would have been our wedding day," he said.

He swirled his hands above his head and the top of the tent opened, peeling outward from the center until a gaping black hole appeared. As the clock on the stage ticked to 12:03 a.m.—the precise moment of Macy's birth—a boom roared out, followed by another, and another, as the inky sky lit up with a plume of pinks, yellows, oranges, and greens.

Fireworks! Phenomenal, powerful, beautiful, and hopeful. After the grand finale, as the sky faded to black, a star-filled constellation came into view. It was in the shape of two circles—wait, no—two hoop snakes, each biting their own tail to represent the beginning and the end as one. They inched toward each other until they intertwined, linked in mutual eternity. Ouroboros.

Rafe took center stage. A single, lustrous spotlight made him sparkle. As it widened, it showed a red ring encircling him—an actual ring made of translucent metallic tubes, like six giant hula hoops stacked together. Inside each tube were strands of light—red, gold, and violet. Rafe extended his arms and legs fully inside the hoop, resembling da Vinci's Vitruvian man, until he became the spokes inside the stunning multicolored wheel. The entire apparatus rose to the tent's opening above. Deus ex machina, indeed.

The wheel exited the tent and seemed to hover in the sky, though wires were surely involved. But then Rafe, using the power of his body, rocked it into motion. It began to spin, slowly at first, until it got rolling. It fell to the portion of the tent that had not been peeled back. From the indentations in the cloth above, we could see it rolling along the sloped roof.

Hoop had finally become the snake he'd always dreamed of.

The audience rose and rushed out into the night just in time to see Hoop plunging down Dirt Hill in silent illumination, directly toward Black Swamp. I panicked until I remembered that Black Swamp never messed with its own. When the wheel reached the darkened edge of the swamp, a dozen or more searchlights flicked on simultaneously, turning night into day. The wheel—and Hoop—disappeared beneath the water. The lights shimmered across the surface and played against the widening rings where the wheel had submerged.

The audience raced down to get a closer look—to search—but I couldn't do it. It had all become too much. I remained rooted high on the hill, lost in thought and mourning, until I became aware of a looming presence next to me: none other than Richie Quail. He wore a mask of evil so untainted that I knew it wasn't a mask at all. His face burned a purplish hue and his lips bubbled and spit as he growled to himself.

My stomach constricted with worry. Quail was going to jail—he surely knew that much. He had nothing to lose by going after his accuser. Without thinking, I reached over and performed what I hoped was a slick, last-minute favor for Rafe. No sooner had I enacted my plan than Quail took off screaming, remarkably light on those feet again. He barreled down Dirt Hill with one hand on his hat, as if the important thing was to look fashionable while exacting his revenge.

The crowd instinctively cleared a path as Quail rushed forth and stepped into the water, showing no fear—and no respect. The lights on the airboats remained motionless, as did their captains. Ten feet beyond, Rafe stepped out from behind a tree, casual as ever, looking more like teenage Hoop than ever. He'd shedded his jacket, and a shabby, green flannel now hung around his waist. The left sleeve, dangling in front of him, was missing a ragged strip of material—the very strip that Sherilyn had found days ago. Looking at the real Hoop now, down by the swamp, I knew that the man we'd watched on stage tonight had been the true illusion. This Hoop here, amused and elated, taunting and scheming, was the real deal if ever there was one. He grinned at Quail. "What a day, eh, Mr. Quail?"

"It's night, you idiot," Quail said, whipping his hand to his pocket to retrieve his gun.

He came up empty, though, and what a shame, because it was an awfully cute semi-automatic Boberg XR9-S, if I wasn't mistaken. Nice platinum model that felt good in my hand. I shoved it in my purse.

"What the hell?" Quail shouted.

"Gonna have to fight fair?" Hoop said. "How dreadful."

"I had my own money before the lottery, boy, and I'll make ten times that again! You're nothing but a thief."

Quail quick-stepped in Hoop's direction, his fist raised. He lurched a thick, swift arm at Hoop and nearly got hold of him, but Hoop swerved his lithe body back just in time to avoid the swipe.

"You wanna go quietly with my men here, Mr. Quail?" He gestured to the boats. "Or do you wanna tussle?"

"I'm taking you down, kid."

Hoop smiled and darted into the belly of the swamp. Quail shot after him.

Bad move, Mr. Quail, because nobody but nobody knew that swamp better than Hoop Whitaker.

Chapter 57

The lights on half the boats followed Quail's pursuit. Every minute or so, Hoop would yell out, "Yoo hoo! Over here, Mr. Quail!" Sounds of thrashing and splashing would follow.

As Hoop's voice grew farther away, he finally emerged near a swath of high grass two hundred yards away. All at once, with no verbal cue, every single light rotated and shined upon the light-haired, sure-footed swamp lover. Hoop was balancing precariously on a tree root. Nearby, at the edge of one light's cone of illumination, three sets of alligator eyes floated just above the dark, liquid plane.

"Mr. Quail," Hoop shouted, "I recommend you don't come any closer."

"Gotten this far in life without your recommendations, boy."

Quail appeared in the rays of light, a knife in his hand. Where had he gotten that? He walked toward Hoop, only a three-foot-wide patch of grass between them. Quail could cover that with one step and a single extension of his long arm.

"Hoop!" I yelled, my anxiety overtaking me.

But Hoop put up a hand to silence the crowd. "You must know," he said to Quail, "that I have a dozen men with guns trained on you. I had hoped our long-awaited encounter wouldn't end violently."

"If I'm going down, you're going with me." And with that, Quail launched himself forward into grass that rose higher than his head. It nearly camouflaged him, and I feared that Hoop's men would lose sight of their target.

But all the lights zeroed in on Quail simultaneously, as if they'd known precisely where to aim all along. Their combined power made the enormous man shimmer. Oddly, he began to look shorter and didn't seem to be going anywhere at all.

Hoop stood in place with a delighted grin on his face, not the least bit threatened. I hadn't seen him look that content since he'd fallen asleep on Mr. Swanson's canoe one late August evening.

Quail slashed at the air with his knife and finally looked down. He was sinking. By the time he peeked up again, the unforgiving pluff mud had sucked him down to his ample waist.

Hoop tilted his head like a curious dog and pursed his lips. "Surely you know you've got to float, Mr. Quail. You can't possibly—"

"I can't swim!" Quail shouted. "And I sure as hell can't float! Get me out of here! Get me out!"

Quail had now descended to his neck and approximately his third chin. No one ventured forth to help, but really, who could tug a four-hundred pound man from the pluff? As the nutrient-rich mud filled Quail's mouth, he flexed his head back, his face skyward, his expression frantic. The back of his hat rim touched the surface as the swamp slowly digested him, and he cried out a final, "Help me!" before melting entirely into the goo, leaving only his hat.

Hoop turned to the men in the air boats and rolled his eyes playfully. Then he peered behind him, thrust a single finger into the air and made a quick circular motion. A helicopter roared to life, rising up from Mrs. Elbee's back yard. Within seconds, it hovered over Hoop, blowing his beautiful hair wildly. The pilot was the woman whose tent entrance I'd used. She lowered a thick cable with a hook on its end. Hoop leaped up, grabbed it with one arm and let his body dangle. With his free hand, he indicated *down*. The pilot let out more line, and Hoop gave himself willingly to the pluff.

An interminable fifteen seconds passed until the swamp,

as if disgusted with the bitterness of its earlier meal, burped up a mud-coated, blubbering Richie Quail. The chopper's hook was latched into the rear of his belt, giving him what must have been a seriously painful wedgie. As the craft rose up, Quail's feet finally emerged, and when it rose even higher, it revealed a muck-covered, slimy boy-turned-man hanging onto Quail's left ankle for dear life. A flash of white sparkled amidst the brown when Hoop broke out into a huge smile and waved to the cheering crowd.

Chapter 58

The stunned and exhausted residents of Beulah took their time recovering after the helicopter whisked Hoop and Quail away at high velocity, but they gradually took their leave and went home to rehash the evening. Chad passed me at a distance and wheeled his father away, a glance between us not saying nearly enough.

My phone rang and its ordinariness startled me. "Hey, Larry," I said.

"I know all hell is breaking loose over there, and I'm sorry I couldn't make it, but I have another scoop you might be interested in."

"I can't imagine."

"State troopers just found Zeke Carver's truck overturned off the 22 Bypass. Upside down in a watery ditch, and guess who was inside?"

"Zeke?"

"Yep. But here's the thing. The accident happened yesterday. He's been stuck in that truck for twenty-four hours."

"That's impossible. He shot the sheriff *today*. At Quail's abandoned house. I . . ."

I watched the helicopter grow tiny in the distance, its chopping rotors barely audible anymore. Then I glanced at the parked cars still below. Quail's blue Ford F-150 sat by itself in the far corner. Something told me that the fresh mud splattered on its undercarriage would hold traces of tobacco.

"Thanks, Larry. That actually makes sense. Zeke didn't shoot the sheriff, after all." Rafe was proven right once again: Betrayers betrayed.

Boyd Sexton had been prepared to betray everyone. The sheriff, with a bullet from his personal gun, had planned to betray Boyd. Quail had betrayed Grace Elbee in the worst way—by instigating her murder—and then had turned around and tried to do the same to the sheriff. Adeline DeVore—well, surely at this point in her interrogation, she was betraying anyone and everyone to save herself. And poor Mrs. Elbee had betrayed herself from the beginning, believing that she could steal the happiness that had eluded her all her life.

Rafe had taken from each what they had gained from their original betrayal. From Boyd, his drug operation. From Mrs. Elbee, the life she'd so desperately craved. From Quail, his riches. From Adeline, respect and success, and from the sheriff, his dignity and reputation. I shook my head. Tenuous bonds formed on the basis of deception required but a single wobble to destroy them. Rafe had lit a single match—and sparked a final act of a tragedy.

I plopped myself down in the middle of Dirt Hill, the tent behind me dark, the swamp in front of me still and silent. I remained long enough for the crickets and frogs to resume their nightly chorus, until I finally lay back to gaze up at the sky, barely able to fathom the depths to which humanity had sunk here in Beulah.

"What a night, eh, Clover?"

The familiar voice didn't faze me. I swiveled my head as Hoop plunked himself down, parallel to my body. He let out a relaxed sigh, looked upwards, and it felt oh-so comfortable.

"Your flyer didn't lie, Hoop. That show will leave Beulah on tenterhooks for quite some time." I nudged him. "You gonna stop taking my calls now?"

"Absolutely," he said, his voice grinning for him. "Might as well delete my number."

I laughed but then turned more somber. "In the tent . . . That rendition . . . Is that how it really went down? The roles each of the Lucky Four played inside the store and in the car?"

"Some of it was conjecture. But you'll recall that Mrs.

Elbee answered her final call from M. LeGrange. We chatted for a while and she told me her version of events. Not so different from what I'd imagined."

His hand crept over and rested on mine. I was momentarily back on a dock, baiting my hook with a fat worm. I was crouched on dusty turf, waiting for one of Ronnie Fields's grounders. I was sneaking into a tree fort, spotting faces in roots, and flying free on my bike. But most of all, I was back in a lazy canoe, bobbing gently with a friend, immersed in the fantasy that life couldn't get any better.

"Don't let it do to you what it's done to me, Clover. Don't let it disenchant you."

"How could it not?"

"There's goodness in people. More than evil. It's in the Forenzas and Galassos. It's in your buddy, Chad, who still loves you, by the way." He slowly rotated his head to me. "And it's in you. As tough as you try to be, you're still that girl on second base, a bit insecure, a bit awkward, but who was a treasured friend trying to make the best play for the team."

"We're so far from being those kids on second base, aren't we, Hoop?"

He sighed. "Too true. But the essence is within us. Did you know, Clover, that if you cut out a small piece of a hologram—just the tiniest piece—that it still contains the whole image?"

"I did not."

"Well, we're kind of like that. No matter which version of each other we see, no matter what names we're calling each other, there's still a complete Hoop Whitaker in here"—he tapped his chest—"and a sweet Clever Clover in you. The same kids we were, just with a few more layers, a few more scars."

My tattoo felt cool and I smiled. "If you don't mind me wearing a reporter hat for a moment, how did your bike end up in the swamp if you rode it to Boyd's store that day?"

"Boyd must have thrown it in there sometime after. I suspect he never told anyone that he'd seen me that day, because then he would have been forced to confess that I knew everything—and that he'd let me get away." With our hands still touching, I could feel him shrug. "It ended up being a favor because it made everyone think I was dead."

"In that case, don't do me any more favors. So tell me, what was it like being raised by circus folk? I can't even imagine."

"Pretty phenomenal. I traveled the world, learned the ins and outs of a gritty life and got a ridiculously cool education. It's been a remarkable adventure so far."

"What now? A life on the run? I'm guessing you committed fraud and a few other crimes along the way."

He grunted with laughter. "I'm no saint, that's for sure. But aside from that bit of arson, everything I did here was aboveboard. And because of my work for the government, I have highly disreputable friends in very high places. I'm more valuable to them outside of prison than in."

"Good. I prefer you that way."

He pointed to the sky, swiping the constellations with his hand. "It was all real, you know. At least the part about Macy and me, intertwined for eternity."

"What will you do until you join her?"

"Lots of living left to do, Clover. Eternity's a long time, and I don't think Macy will mind if I have a little more fun here before meeting her on the other side."

"Where will you go?"

"Everywhere. I'm breaking out of the snow globe." He turned his head and faced me. "Can you?"

I sighed. "I'm not sure. Beulah's home now. A place I don't have to stay in anymore, but one I might choose to."

"What a week, eh, Clover? What. A. Week."

Chapter 59

Chad and I met for drinks. We hadn't quite reached the stage where we were talking about dating again, but he wasn't seeing Sarah anymore, and I was far from thinking about anyone else. He'd forgiven me for my role in his dad's arrest, and I'd have forgiven him, too, if he'd done anything at all wrong. Which he hadn't.

As for Strike, it would be a tedious process through the courts, sorting through the charges and weighing them against the good he'd done for forty years before the accident and the twelve years after. Chad and Jacqueline had committed to staying by his side through the whole ordeal, and I'd agreed to help however I could.

On this particular occasion, Chad and I toasted to me winning a few rounds of *Dammit, Be Nice, Chloe* during the last few weeks, and to the assignment of a public defender to Richie Quail. The formerly richest man in town had indeed proven unable to afford even the cheapest of private lawyers.

My tattoo rarely burned anymore, and when it did, I cooled it with a silent hush. Without grief hogging so much real estate in my heart, I'd begun to find room for other emotions. Spring cleaning had worked wonders on my psyche. I'd tossed out a rusty, blood-stained knife that had been lurking in my life for far too long, along with a pile of dust that used to be an alligator skin. There was even an old essay I got rid of by mailing it to a P.O. Box belonging to one Rafe Borose, current resident of Mali. Of course, I'd read the essay one more time before kissing it good-bye. The final paragraph would stay with me always:

"In the future, I may not carry a fancy title. I may not have kids, dogs, a beach house, or a three-car garage, but I will have love, family, knowledge, and most of all, adventure.

Nothing will keep me down—not discouragement, disappointment, rejection, or betrayal. For I am Hoop Whitaker, and one way or the other, I plan to live forever."

The End

Acknowledgments

Many wonderful people help me throughout the course of each book. I do, however, take plenty of liberties with the information provided, and my sources can only answer the questions I think to ask; any and all errors are mine. With apologies to true swampers out there, I did take minor poetic liberties with some swamp details in creating the specific features that Beulah needed, but I tried to be true to the nature of these phenomenal wetlands that bring so much richness to the earth. I also took license with current hologram technology, although my hope is that the hologram scenes in this book will be considered passé in the not-too-distant future. Sincere thanks go to:

- o Cracker Larry Teuton for answering my swamp questions and for granting me permission to use some of his colorful, online pluff mud posts as dialogue for Hoop.
- o MJM and JQ for their swamp research, editing, and other invaluable services, not the least of which is encouragement.
- o Buff Ross for writing an incredible article called *Odes to the Lowcountry: Pluff Mud.*
- o Tyler Anderson for his beautiful, original cover art and technical know-how.
- o Steve Councill for legal terms and clever advice.
- o My two brothers for sharing corporate lingo and firearms descriptions.
- o *The Bird* for legal feedback and source-sharing.
- o Lezlie and Darby Anderson for their art research.
- o The Galasso Family for enthusiastic support and the use of their name.
- o My friend, Jack Matosian, for his assistance throughout, from title to synopsis and everything in between.

- My wonderful husband and children who never fail to support me and who tolerate many tasteless, last-minute dinners when I am writing (and when I'm not).
- Most importantly, I thank you, the readers, for making this story more than just vaporous words dispersed into the digital realm.

Note

~**Word-of-mouth is crucial for any author to succeed**. If you enjoyed this book, please consider leaving a review on Amazon, even if it's only a word or two. Reviews are hard to come by and very much appreciated.

Stay tuned after **About the Author** for a sample of RAVELED from the *Crime After Time* Collection.

About the Author

Anne McAneny honed her writing skills as a screenwriter for many years before turning to novels. She lives in Virginia with her family, a spoiled puggle, and an overfed cat. When she's not writing, she enjoys biking and hiking balanced by ample chocolate and cake, a scale that often tips toward the latter. You can find her on her Facebook Fan Page, *Books by Anne McAneny* or on Twitter *@AnneMcAneny*. She relishes hearing from readers so feel free to say hello or leave a comment. Be warned . . . she usually responds.

Circled is part of the *Crime After Time* Collection, stories that revolve around everyday people who feel compelled to investigate past crimes against their loved ones. Their discoveries rewrite the past and reshape the future in exciting, twist-filled plots. Additional *Crime After Time* books include:

Skewed: A tantalizing thriller that opens with a bang. When a crime scene photographer receives two photos in the mail, they upend the narrative of her life and invoke the ire of a long-dormant serial killer.

Raveled: A fast-paced mystery thriller that sends a jaded daughter back to the town and the deadly night that ripped her young life apart.

Foreteller: A pulse-pounding mystery with a touch of the psychic that forces an archaeologist to dig through her own past in order to ensure a future.

Vicarious: *(NEW!)* A nail-biting suspense tale that ensnares a missing girl, a mad artist, and an unreliable witness. Detective Jeremy Upton must rely on conniving neighbors and questionable accounts to find the girl before the clues turn to dust.

Additional books by this author include:

<u>Chunneling Through Forty</u>: The humorous and heartening story of a woman's tumultuous journey through forty.

<u>Our Eyes Met Over Cantaloupe</u>: The uproarious tale of a cupcake shop and a female reporter's exit from her half-baked state of existence.

Sample of RAVELED

Chapter 1

Allison... present

Sixteen years since my last trip to this park and not a tree had changed. Even the sidewalk jutted up in the same angry crevices that had worn out my childhood bicycle tires. Maybe the concrete walkway had reached its breaking point decades ago and decided to fight back, forcing the persistent roots down into the darkness to tangle amongst themselves. Determined to hold its own, the sidewalk put on a daily show for the humans above, pretending that everything below was peachy keen, thank you very much. Nothing to see here, folks. No seedy underbelly thrashing beneath. The citizens of Lavitte, North Carolina, kindly returned the favor. They traveled over the façade every day, smiling and waving and warning kids on training wheels to watch out for the bumps. They jogged over the fractured surface to the beat of their music, pretending that life offered up wishes and dreams, rainbows and sprinkles. No need to stick fingers into the cracks or peel back the surface to examine the source of the sour rumblings beneath. But everybody knew they were there.

If the old physics truism held, that every action was met with an equal and opposite reaction, then what kind of forces jumped back and forth between the man and the sidewalk on Maple Street sixteen years ago? Did the sidewalk absorb his depravity when he grabbed a young girl off her bike on that sweltering August evening, projecting it to the gnarled roots below, or did the evildoer absorb the pretense from the sly footpath that life was nothing but a grand cabaret?

Probably the latter. Seemed to be the choice of most everyone in Lavitte.

"Ding, ding!" A little girl, so Gerber perfect that she looked like a hologram, rang her bicycle bell at me. "Excuse me, Lady."

"Mattie," her mom said, "it's 'excuse me, *ma'am*'."

Thanks, but I'll take *lady* over *ma'am* any day. Christ, I was only a few years older than the mom. Still, I couldn't fault the teaching of proper manners in good ol' Lavitte. Manners were our foundation, our sidewalk. Until they were discarded altogether and replaced with rage.

"Sorry about that," the mom said, her mineral powder make-up and bright denim jeans mirrored by every other mother at the park. "She's still wobbly. Just got her training wheels off. I didn't think she was ready, but you know how dads are, always ready to push 'em out of the nest a little earlier than we are."

I looked around, desperate for her to be talking to anyone other than me, but her reflective lenses aimed squarely at mine whenever she wasn't scanning the area for her daughter.

"Which one is yours?" she said.

It took me longer than it should have to realize she thought I was a card-carrying mom. "I don't have one. Or any, for that matter. I'm not a mom."

"Oh, I'm sorry." Her eyes strayed to the ground before she lifted her slim face back up, a plastered smile concealing her grief. For what? The possibility that my ovaries lacked viable eggs? The presumed melancholy thump of my heart over not having a vulnerable child to screw up for the next eighteen years? If anything, she should be sorry if I did have a kid. But I couldn't afford to alienate anyone on my first day back, so I played nice. Besides, odds were I knew this chick in some capacity or other. It's not that Lavitte wasn't big enough for two big guns; it's that Lavitte wasn't big enough for any two people to remain strangers. If you didn't know a person directly, you *sho'ly knew their cousin*.

"I grew up here and used to play in this park," I said with more saccharine sweetness than my mother's Sweet Sunday Sugar Fudge. "I'm back to, uh,"—uh oh, hadn't worked out an excuse for being back in town yet, but as it turned out, I hardly needed one.

"You're visiting family, of course." She proffered a hand, all bird bones and stickiness from the freeze-pops she'd served the kids earlier. "I'm Abby. Abby Westerling. You probably know the name."

She meant the Westerling part, no doubt. The original Mr. and Mrs. Westerling had owned the big general store in town, then sold some land to a developer and used that money to buy up half of Lavitte. They had a penchant for naming things after themselves, so we were saddled with Westerling Medical Center, Westerling Children's Museum, and Westerling Theater. For all I knew, a raunchy truck would pass by boasting Westerling Trash and Disposal. Why not? Plenty of garbage here in Lavitte.

"Yes, I'm familiar," I said. "You married a Westerling?"

"Unfortunately, not a direct one." She giggled. "Well, that sounds plain wrong. What I mean is, I married a Westerling cousin. We're the poor relations."

The three-carat diamond on her left hand screamed otherwise, but might also suggest a desperate cousin, scrambling to keep up with his surname.

"I was a Murphy before that," she said.

I knew a huge Murphy family in middle school. Nine kids, with several delinquents among the academic standouts. The boys were mostly ugly, the girls auburn-haired and cute. More than a few hated my family. She might be one of them. I didn't pursue it as she seemed the type to volunteer plenty.

"So, who are you visiting?" she asked.

"My mom still lives here but she might put her house on the market. My dad passed away a while back, so I try to come and see her a little more often."

Hey, it was almost the truth. More than the local sidewalks offered.

"Sorry about your dad. Your mom must appreciate the visits. What's your name, by the way?"

I realized I hadn't introduced myself. Guess it was time to watch the dark shadow crawl over pretty Abby Murphy Westerling's face as she tried to recall the outcome of the trial. She'd have to sort the truth from distorted childhood memories. Surely, her recollection of events had grown sinister and inconceivable, like a cancer, until it was something best not spoken of, best not acknowledged, treated as folklore. But here it was in the flesh. Or at least its descendant. I could lie. No skin off my back. But I had come here to do exactly the opposite. Might as well start the ball rolling through the dirt, muck, gossip, and disgust, dredging up all the denials until it snowballed into a big pile of rottenness, untenable and best disposed of at the Westerling Dump. The very ball I'd come here to stick a big fork in. Dig in, everybody!

"I'm Allison."

The first name alone gave her a small start as she searched my face for clues. The nose, definitely the same perfect nose as the mother, so elegantly sloped and dimpled at the tip that even mannequins envied it because theirs looked so plastic. But I was never envied by other humans. At least not in Lavitte. Not after that night.

Abby repeated my name, possibly without realizing it. "Allison." Quietly, it slipped from her lips, like a secret, a whisper of a memory. I took off my sunglasses and wiped them with the thin blue tee-shirt I'd thrown on this morning, giving her a glimpse of my eyes. That usually did it for people. The eyes. Because my father's eyes had been nothing less than mesmerizing, right up until the day he died, when they bulged a bit more than usual. Regular pieces of onyx, his eyes were, shined to brilliance. And they were big. Big as puddles. Disproportionately large for his face. *Doe eyes*, the ladies used to say. *Unexpected,* one of the Charlotte newspapers had reported. And I'd inherited them as if they'd been transplanted. At least they fit on my face somehow. *Balanced by my full lips,* my mother would retort in the old days when I complained I looked like an alien. Nowadays, peering into the endless pools of chocolate liquid swirling deliciously on my face, my mother probably felt sick to her stomach. She never made her Sweet Sunday Sugar Fudge anymore. Who would eat it if she did?

"Allison Fennimore," I said, my plump lips framing a smile. "You probably know the name."

Abby Westerling found a quick, urgent excuse to leave my company. She gathered her Gerber Peas baby, murmured an apology to the other mothers, maybe with a cautioning nod in my direction, and skedaddled. Whatever. Nothing could hurt me now. I was Lavitte's favorite Teflon Daughter.

Chapter 2

Allison... present

I pulled into the two-car, detached garage of my childhood home, wondering why I'd driven to the park in the first place. It was only a mile away and the exercise would have done me good. Being out of the city was already costing me a good thirty blocks a day of serious hoofing.

The brakes on my mother's Buick squealed as I pressed them, so I added *Fix Brakes* to the mental list of things I needed to accomplish before returning home. Ironic that my mother had to pay to get her car serviced.

"Car brakes," I repeated to myself in an effort to remember the task long enough to write it down in the kitchen. Hopefully my mom hadn't thrown out the list I'd started this morning, which included *Leak in Basement*, *Stuck Shower Door*, *60-Watt Bulbs for Back Porch*, and *Call Realtor*. The types of things the man of the house might do, especially if he was good with his hands. Like a mechanic.

As I walked toward the house, I tried to envision the structure the way a buyer would: two-story colonial with a basement; lots of windows for sunlight; fresh marigold paint; flowered patio; stone walkway; cute and homey; cursed. I sighed. Maybe it had been long enough that it would finally sell.

Couldn't believe my mother had stayed here all these years, like a wound begging for salt. Even if she'd been forced to take a loss, she could have started over again in a town where the Fennimore name was less notorious, where images of little Shelby Anderson didn't crop up like a fated internet search the moment people heard Artie Fennimore's name. Or pictures of Bobby Kettrick's golden mug, with the too-white teeth and the square jaw that looked like it came from anywhere but Lavitte. Heck, there might be dozens of Arthur Fennimores out and about in the country whose name conjured joy in people's minds. Imagine that. An old children's game of word association popped into my head. *You say horsey, I say ride. You say Fennimore, I say joy.* Ha! Too far-fetched even for me.

I entered through the back door into the kitchen, staring at the list I'd made. What was it I wanted to put on there? Something to do with the house? With transportation? Oh yes, the brakes. I wrote it down. This was how my mind worked lately. In circles. Between my brother going to mandatory rehab, my mother dabbling in dementia, and the recent airing of *Big Crimes, Small Towns* on cable, I felt trapped on a mental merry-go-round, the gears grinding against the bones of my inner ear, the music stuck in a dissonant minor chord. In the old days, Lavitte residents would have jotted down *Artie's Autos*, but nowadays they simply wrote *Fix Brakes*.

"You're home already, honey?" my mother said. "Did school get out early?" She shuffled into the kitchen as if her legs didn't have the energy to lift her feet. Odd the way the dementia came escorted by physical weakness. As if the mind told the body to match the message. Other times, she was her old self and walked with a smooth gait that looked youthful compared to her sixty years, as if her hips contained springs and her feet could negotiate clouds.

"Hey, Mom, it's me, Allison. I'm here visiting from New York, where I live. I'm all grown up."

If only. I guided her to one of the wooden chairs I'd always found too heavy for the kitchen, more suitable for a dining room. But the dining room had been forever cluttered with my mother's projects—ranging from a collection of wreaths for the Christmas Bazaar to the infamous scrapbooking attempt during which she'd hot-glued half a dozen photos to her fingers before giving up. Oh well, it was never boring and a few of her projects had turned out okay, like the pressed flowers, the knitted hats we never wore or needed, and the intricate jewelry she'd beaded for years after my father's death. It had kept her busy and, most of all, alone—away from the judgment of so-called friends.

"You didn't get in trouble with the principal, did you, Allison? You're usually so good."

Yes, that was Allison Fennimore. Sweet girl. Teacher's pet. Good listener. Hell, any 15-year-old who could sit quietly though a day of testimony in which her father was called *a sociopathic slaughterer out for revenge over the theft of a few screwdrivers* had no choice but to be a good listener. But good and a quarter'll get you a cup of coffee. Lousy coffee at that.

I'd lost the reputation overnight, of course. Because a good girl couldn't possibly come from a man who shot people in cold blood or yanked young girls off their bicycles. The same man who couldn't even get up the nerve to do whatever it was he wanted to do to the girl in the first place, who killed without rhyme, reason or remorse. Of course, who could show remorse for something they denied doing? To show remorse was to show guilt. And my father never felt guilty about anything, at least not that I knew of. Arthur "Artie" Fennimore was famous for putting it all in God's hands and believing that if God was at the wheel, then He knew what He was doing and there must be a gold-plated and indisputable reason for it. If Artie Fennimore took his fist to his wife on the occasional, drunken Saturday night, that was God's fist. God must have been trying to teach Justine Fennimore a thing or two about pleasing her man. If God every so often felt the need to withhold affection from a socially awkward young girl, He might as well use Artie Fennimore to do His bidding.

Always seemed like an excuse to me.

"Everything's okay, Mom," I said. "No call from the principal coming your way. Can I make you some tea?"

"No thanks, honey, I think I'll just rest. I'm so tired. Must be that time of the month."

My mother hadn't had a time of the month for eight years, but if she wanted an excuse for a good nap, let her enjoy it. If anyone deserved an altered state of consciousness, it was Justine Fennimore. She shuffled toward the spare room I'd converted to a bedroom so she wouldn't have to manage the stairs as often. Then she turned back to me and tilted her beautiful face, framed by dark hair worn in the same, short coif since her twenties. Her lips parted to say something, but then a slow shock crescendoed on her face as she rejoined reality. Not a fun place to be.

"Kevin," she said, the two syllables of my brother's name carrying enough weight that it made her shoulders slump.

"Yes, Mom, Kevin should call today. Around three." Precisely at three, actually, because that was Kevin's allotted time for his five-minute call.

I waited for my mother to lapse into concerns about Kevin getting off the school bus at three, hoping for her sake that she was still in Dementiaville, but no such reprieve today. Clarity had come and she knew full well why he would call at three. It must break her heart, at least what was left of it.

"I've got to go out again, Mom, but Selena's in the sunroom if you need anything."

Selena, a tall, muscular, Guatemalan woman I had hired as my mom's caretaker, made out like a bandit. Twenty bucks an hour to make sure her charge didn't wander off or do anything dangerous. Not sure how Selena accomplished these responsibilities while napping on the couch most afternoons, but so far so good. Whenever I walked in on her, she swore she wasn't asleep, but rather, she suffered from a bad case of dry eye syndrome and needed to minimize her corneal exposure to air. After explaining this the first time, she'd tried to sell me the Brooklyn Bridge.

"I'll be back in time for Kevin's call," I said.

I could have told my mom where I was headed, but it would have ripped out another piece of her soul and forced it through the shredder. That's how it had been for me when I got the call from Kevin a few weeks ago. My landline phone, silent for months at a time, had rung early in the morning, throwing me for a dreaded loop. My friends knew I worked until 3:00 a.m. and they were forbidden to call before noon...

*** *Twenty Days Earlier* ***

"Hello?"

"Allison, it's Kevin."

I breathed a sigh of relief. At least it wasn't someone calling to report a death or an arrest for murder—distinct and precedented possibilities in the Fennimore family. "Kevin? Thought you could only use the phone—"

"Look, I don't have a lot of time," he said. "Cashing in a favor to call this early."

"Cash *me* in a favor and don't tell me what you had to do for your favor."

"Can you get in here tomorrow? I need you to do something for me. It's big."

I sat upright, not an easy accomplishment on my cheap mattress. "Is it legal?" I asked, realizing too late that eager ears were probably monitoring his call and would perk up at the mention of skirting the law.

"I want to reopen the case," Kevin said. "You know, against Dad."

I laughed and slumped back. "Kevin, please. You get a few sober months under your belt and you suddenly have time for deep reflection? Oh, I know what's going on here. What's the title?"

"Of what?" he said, his patience with me often a surprise.

"The book you're writing about Dad. Going with <u>Lavitte Lasher</u>? <u>The Fennimore Fiend</u>? No, too reticent. I've always been partial to <u>Maniac Mechanic</u> myself."

"Stop screwing around," Kevin said. "Although those titles aren't bad."

"What's this about then? Seeking closure?" My tone mocked him for even considering the concept. Children of convicted murderers, guilty or innocent, had no relationship with such psychological malarkey.

"This is the longest I've been sober, Allie. Give me a chance."

"A chance to what? Open old wounds? Make Mom miserable? Step into the insanity of claustrophobic Lavitte? No thanks."

"Something's rolling around in my head," he said.

"Teachers used to call that your brain."

"You're going to Lavitte, anyway, right?"

"To put Mom's house on the market. Not to reminisce about Bobby Kettrick."

Kevin sighed. I could picture him now. Callused hands, dark, shiny hair, and a scruffy growth on his face that the women loved. At least women who also enjoyed leather jackets, flea-bitten mattresses, and cheap, imported beer. But above the stubble, the same full, crooked lips as mine, the scar on his left cheekbone from the playground seesaw, and the vibrant olive eyes—when his brain wasn't swimming in alcohol.

"I need you to talk to some people," he said. "I got it all coordinated. You wouldn't believe how the stars are aligned."

"Please don't go all *stars-aligned* on me, Kev. Besides, Dad is dead. What does it matter?"

The confluence of discussing my dad's case while staring at the bland piece of art on my wall called *Possibilities* actually made me tremble. I forced myself to close my eyes and fight the impulse to slam the phone as loudly as I could in my brother's ear. He was supposed to be the mellow one, the cool, distant guy who didn't talk about the case, the one who let me know it was okay to gloss over it.

"I gotta go," Kevin said. "Favor's up. Come by tomorrow. It's your day off anyway."

"I've played this record too many times," I said, tugging at a piece of hair with my hand. "Only scratches left. Sorry you wasted your favor."

I reached the heavy phone receiver out toward its cradle. Slowly. Part of me didn't want to disconnect from the bizarre fantasy that I could storm into Lavitte, rip through its healed skin, and reveal the infection still lingering there. But most of me wanted to move forward, away from a past with tentacles so tangled in my soul that to completely disconnect might be to die.

"Tomorrow at nine!" Kevin shouted just before I let the phone drop into its nest. A brother who knew me too well, as if he sensed the phone was distant from my ear. I hung up. Now I'd never get back to sleep. I lurched from the comfort of my mattress and yanked the blinds up. Dust flew out from between the neglected slats and made me cough. I brushed it away but it hung in the air like tear gas. I staggered back to bed and curled into myself, knotted up on the inside, my eyes wide and wondering.

Reopen my dad's case? What the hell was he thinking? Where was he when the case was still fresh, when the people and places weren't covered in denial and grime, the events untainted by their infamy? I knew where. Drunk in some godforsaken rented room, or sobbing it out with some tattooed hooker, always trying to forget. Maybe if Kevin could avoid prison after rehab, he could put his off-the-charts I.Q. to better use than trying to steer around a Subaru driven by a blotto, 17-year-old, lacrosse star. The young athlete had entered the New Jersey Turnpike going the wrong way on the same night that Kevin had decided to pay me a visit in New York City. Kevin had tried his damnedest to avoid the kid, but Kevin was a Fennimore; we never landed on the lucky side of the rainbow. According to the skid marks, Kevin had managed a masterful swerve followed by a NASCAR-worthy spinout, but he who doesn't die in that pathetic scenario loses. Kevin's blood alcohol level tested on the edge of New Jersey's stringent legal limit. At least they'd gone easy on him and put him in mandatory rehab first. With good behavior and positive counselor reports, he might get a lighter sentence, but he still needed to pay the price for killing a teenager while under the influence. Hardly a first in our family.

Chapter 3

Allison... nineteen days earlier

Of course I went to see my brother. The medium-security rehabilitation facility couldn't have been more contradictory. Rusted, barbed wire fencing around a wildflower-dappled field. Armed guards stationed at posts festooned with climbing vines of trumpet honeysuckle. An architecturally impressive medieval building with the latest in bulletproof, wired windows. Confined freedom. Open space with restricted boundaries. Pretty yet ugly. Even the name fought against itself: Drywaters. A clever play on drying out and getting sober? Probably didn't sit well with the guys who abstained from the liquid poison and opted for the straight-to-the-vein high. The whole place made me itch inside where no fingernail could scratch. As an inmate, I wouldn't know whether to explore my inner feelings or hunker down in a paranoid corner and babble sweet nothings.

I checked my face in the rear view mirror. Still me. I'd given up on make-up six years ago. No matter what I tried, people noticed my eyes. Enhancing them was like putting a banana split on top of a hot fudge sundae, and minimizing them meant overdoing everything else. With no desire to make any part of my existence conspicuous, I settled for a thin layer of moisturizer and a pinch of the cheeks. Besides, it was my brother in there. No matter what I did, I'd still remind him of Dad.

A male guard with dirty fingernails and the odor to match searched my purse. A female guard with stubby fingernails and a butch haircut patted me down. I mused as to why a metal detector couldn't replace them. Perhaps because it couldn't grunt and give directions with dismissive head nods. After another dozen layers of security, including sign-in sheets, an *actual* metal detector, a relinquishment of the package I'd brought, and a verbal confirmation that I wouldn't pass Kevin any illegal substances, the visiting room proved underwhelming. For all that trouble, I should have been wheeled in on a throne and offered a platter of hand-peeled grapes while Kevin sat on a velvet cushion at my feet. The fold-out tables and metal chairs would have to suffice.

"Hey," I said to my fatigued-looking brother, the only guy in the room aside from the bored guard. Kevin's eyelids looked heavy enough to sink a ship, and the usually erect posture that added power to his six-foot frame seemed defeated. I performed jazz-fingers to show off my empty hands. "Brought you some brownies, and those gross hard candies you like, but some dude with a wonky eye is giving them a CAT-Scan. Making sure I didn't slip an alternate life in there for you."

He gave his usual half-grin, the one where the right side of his mouth curled up to meet the far end of his right eye. When we were younger, I made it a challenge to make Kevin laugh. I mean really laugh. It was the only way to see his teeth. And he was handsome as anything when he flashed those choppers and let loose with an unguarded reaction to life. These days, those teeth had to be in deep hibernation, hidden behind pale lips on a face that desperately needed some sun.

We'd never been the hugging type, at least not as adults, but Kevin did stand up and lift his chin as I approached. "Hey, Allison. Thanks for coming."

"Didn't have much of a choice. You kinda played the *I'm In Rehab* card."

We sat down across from each other, the chairs scraping loudly in the cold, high-ceilinged room. No noise-reduction optimization from the architect here as the only soft thing around was the guard's gut. The cavernous quality of the place made me feel like one of those mountain climbers who appeared as a mere dot in a panoramic shot of sheer rock. I should have packed some spare oxygen for this meeting.

"Mom doing okay?" he said.

"Sometimes. On my last visit, her caretaker hinted that my presence brings on more of her spells."

That made Kevin chuckle. "You and me. We bring out the best in people."

We discussed the assisted living community Mom was considering as her next residence. It would be quite a leap to go from a homey, inviting, four-bedroom house to a pre-furnished, pastel-colored community where walkers outnumbered strollers and her current acre of grass would morph into a professionally maintained spit of sod. Kevin expressed his disgust with her desire to stay in Lavitte. I expressed my disgust with the housing market. With the family business out of the way, I gave him the floor. He was the one who'd called for this meeting, after all. I let him ramble on for ten minutes about everything in our dad's case that bothered him, like the lack of a clear motive for my father to shoot Bobby Kettrick in the middle of the night in his own auto body shop. Or why Dad claimed to have screwed on a silencer to shoot a gopher at six a.m., but not to shoot Bobby through the heart hours earlier. Kevin rolled his eyes multiple times over the utter lack of motive for our father to kidnap and kill young Shelby Anderson. With no history of violence against anyone except his own wife, our dad had become a notorious double-murderer of two teenagers in a town where people didn't even break the 18 MPH limit. Now, finally, with the whiplash speed of a sloth, things seemed to bother Kevin.

I offered as much to the conversation as the fly on the edge of the table. Kevin didn't seem to care. He needed me because I could walk out of here. My hands could dig and scrape with abandon, and my mouth wasn't confined to five-minute segments of freedom. I could be his eyes and ears, a tool in his hands.

"Please, Allison. Just talk to a few folks. They're all gonna be there."

"Who's going to be where?" I said, wrenching my eyes from the fly's frantic maneuvers to my brother's fixed, intensive plea.

"Enzo Rodriguez is going home for his cousin's wedding. Smitty'll be in town for the 15-year reunion, and to visit his mom and dad. They still live on Marshall. And Jasper Shifflett is nearby, I think. He might attend the reunion. If not, I hired a private investigator to dig him up."

"Tell your P.I. to try Mars."

Kevin laughed. "I know, right? Anyway, you have to talk to them. It's the perfect combo. Enzo, Smitty and Jasper. They'll be right there in Lavitte and that'll make them more vulnerable. They won't be expecting it."

"Expecting what?"

"A confrontation about that night. Especially from you."

If I were the hitting type, I'd have slapped some sense into my brother. As it was, I settled for abject nausea and said one of the few words that still held power in my life. "No, Kevin. Just no." I emphasized my point with a horizontal slice of my hand through the air, like an ump calling a play safe, which this one surely wasn't. "That's the last group of people I want to see. Have you forgotten what our dad did to the town hero?"

"I know. I know." Kevin sounded more energetic than he had in the sixteen years since he'd left Lavitte. "Listen, you found a better way to deal with all of this than me. Maybe because you were younger."

"Yes, dealing with your dad's murder trial at age fifteen is a walk in the park."

"Either way, you took the high road. I never rose above sewer level."

"Don't beat yourself up," I said with an uncharacteristic sensitivity that only Kevin seemed able to root out in me. "You send Mom money and you've always looked out for me."

"Not like I should have. But hey, nothing like involuntary rehab to sober you up. And now that I'm finally ready to confront some issues, I'm stuck in this shithole." He lowered his head to utter his next statement, and I could see his mouth curling in embarrassment. "I, uh, I did some hypnosis in here, believe it or not."

"Not."

"Seriously," he said, animated by my pessimism. "It's amazing what they'll spend your tax dollars on. I'm hoping for a total breakthrough. I gotta believe there's something from that night that'll piece it all together, maybe smooth out this rocky road I've been on."

The guy across from me sounded nothing like my brother and my scowl let him know it.

"Look," he said, "even though you think I've squandered all my potential—"

"*Squandered*. Break out the SAT guide."

"Shut up." Curvy grin. "I've learned a lot about human nature over the years, and there's too much that's not right about that night. One thing's for sure: They lied."

"Who?"

"Everybody."

"Conspiracy theory? Taking a page out of Jasper Shifflett's book, are we?"

Jasper Shifflett. Two years ahead of me in high school. Probably considered his own birth a conspiracy between his parents. He might have been right, too, because he sure hadn't won the lottery with those two: Frail and Frailer. Jasper had been too smart for his own good. He'd hung around with Bobby Kettrick and Smitty in high school as part of a havoc-causing trio, playing the part of the smart, calm one or the evil genius, depending on the level of cannabis coursing through his veins. I never did understand his attraction to Bobby and Smitty; maybe their presence helped numb his overactive brain.

"Here's a universal truth," Kevin said. "Everybody lies to save their own ass, or the ass of someone they love. As soon as

Dad became the scapegoat, the whole town piled on to save themselves."

"Going all negative Zen on me now?" I said.

"Live the life I've lived and you'll learn: never put anything past anybody. I mean anybody."

I slanted forward far enough to stir the interest of the nearby guard, but he had too good a slouch going to follow through with anything. "That's real breaking news, Kev. What else you got? That people suck?"

"You're gonna do this, right, Allie? I got a detective in Lavitte putting the files together from Dad's case. Nice guy. Blake Barkley."

"Sounds like a cartoon dog." An image of a bloated, burping detective in an ill-fitting suit filled my mind. With a hound dog face, of course. I pictured him standing over my diminutive father, beating a confession out of him while checking his watch repeatedly to see if it was time to go home and crack open a beer. He'd already have humiliated my dad by flashing pictures of the young victims—the cobalt-eyed, fast-footed Bobby Kettrick, and little, freckle-faced Shelby Anderson.

"Here's the thing, Kevin, Mom's not gonna know otherwise even if you do discover some breakthrough."

"*I'll* know otherwise."

My patience began a slow collapse. Discussing the past was not a muscle I flexed. Ever. The entirety of my remaining muscles tensed up with the sudden overuse of this atrophied one. I tried to shake it off with a measured glance around the room, taking in the dust dancing in the morning sun, and the crack in the wall behind Kevin's head that resembled the east coast of the United States, but my eyes returned to the pleading, desperate expression of my formerly robust sibling. "Again," I said, "why does it matter?"

Kevin inhaled slowly, looked down at his fingers. I followed his gaze, shocked to see my father's hands at the ends of his arms. The sight softened my snide expression. So that was it. Kevin was turning into my dad and he wanted a new ending.

"There's this empty space in my head," he said. "It hurts like hell. All the time. And it rattles." He shook his head so I could hear it, then smirked. "Whacko, right? How can empty space rattle? But that's just it. It's not empty. There's something there and I can't get to it. You know when you can't think of a word?"

"I know it too well lately."

"It's *that* feeling, multiplied by a thousand, multiplied by sixteen years. Not knowing the details of that night is eating at me. It's like the space has teeth, and it's hungry—and it's growing. I even feel it in my stomach. Sometimes at night, my whole body shakes." He put up a hand to stop me from the predictable retort. "And no, it's not the DT's."

"Too easy," I said. "Give me some credit."

"Anyway," he said, "if I could wrap my mind around it— even if the truth is worse than anything we think—at least it would end this torture."

I guffawed. A worse truth? Like my dad left victims buried in shallow graves from Maine to Florida? That he fathered a secret family who all grew up to be killers themselves? Well, you never knew.

Kevin bit his lower lip and looked me straight in the eyes. "I managed it all these years by drinking and drugging."

"Alert the presses," I said, my sympathy meter in need of a serious jolt.

"There's a reason they call it serving time," he said. "Too much time to think and nothing to numb that spot except dealing with it." He drove the knuckle of his index finger into his head like he wanted to bore a hole and pull out the diseased emptiness. I could picture him yanking out a contaminated, throbbing blob with a grotesque mouth, and big, wet lips. It would scream at him: *You wanna know what happened that night? You really wanna know? 'Cause I'll tell you. And once I tell you, you can't put me back. I'll be out in the world to stay and I'm not easily dealt with. Still wanna know, sucker?*

I wasn't sure how I'd answer the disgusting thing. I'd grown accustomed to life in denial and ignorance.

"It's like trying to do a Rubik's Cube blind," Kevin said. "You gotta be my eyes, Alley Cat. Can't you at least try? I have money stashed away. I can cover you for—"

"It's not the money, Kevin!"

"What is it, then?"

"I got my own issues, you know. And when I do something, I really do it. I dive into this cesspool, I might drown."

"I'll resuscitate you."

I sighed. "You know me. Writing ten-page essays when the teacher asked for three. Working five hours overtime when the boss asked for two. Besides, it'd be me against Lavitte."

"When'd you ever let that stop you?"

He knew exactly what to say. We were cut from the same frayed cloth, after all.

His face hardened, making his eyes glaze over. For a moment, he looked like my mother in one of her less aware states. "I don't want to end up like Dad, you know?"

I knew.

***We hope you enjoyed this sample of RAVELED
RAVELED is available for purchase m Amazon.***

Made in the USA
Columbia, SC
02 November 2017